LIAR, LIAR

LIAR, LIAR

A novel by

LATRESE N. CARTER

Q-Boro Books
WWW.QBOROBOOKS.COM

An Urban Entertainment Company

Published by Q-Boro Books

Copyright © 2007 by Latrese N. Carter

ISBN-13: 978-1-933967-11-0
ISBN-10: 1-933967-11-0
LCCN: 2006936053

First Printing June 2007
Printed in the United States of America

10 9 8 7 6 5 4 3 2 1

This is a work of fiction. It is not meant to depict, portray or represent any particular real persons. All the characters, incidents and dialogues are the products of the author's imagination and are not to be construed as real. Any references or similarities to actual events, entities, real people, living or dead, or to real locales are intended to give the novel a sense of reality. Any similarity in other names, characters, entities, places and incidents is entirely coincidental.

Cover Copyright © 2006 by Q-BORO BOOKS all rights reserved
Cover layout/design by Candace K. Cottrell
Editors: Alisha Yvonne, Melissa Forbes, Leah Whitney

Q-BORO BOOKS
Jamaica, Queens NY 11434
WWW.QBOROBOOKS.COM

Prologue

Stormy

For five months I secretly struggled with my decision to marry my fiancé, Camden. Not because I didn't love him or didn't want to be married, but because of the stunning revelation that he was previously involved in a clandestine homosexual relationship with a member of our church.

When the big day came, I was a nervous wreck. I should have been admiring my dress, adjusting my veil, and practicing my smile in the mirror because I was about to be a princess for a day. But instead of having joy in my heart, I was on edge, wondering if my fiancé was still gay. It wasn't fair that I had to be concerned about my soon-to-be husband's ex-lover showing up at our wedding. I imagined if he did, my handsome groom wouldn't be gazing into my eyes as I recited my vows to him, but instead he would be looking over my shoulder and into the eyes of his former paramour—too much for any bride to worry about on her wedding day.

I paced the floor, wearing a hole in the plush carpet. I

clenched my hands and released them over and over again. I started sweating profusely as nervousness engulfed me. The butterflies that vigorously swam in my stomach made me want to vomit. I clutched my abdomen in an attempt to ease the nauseous feelings. It didn't work.

Tears gushed from my eyes and my body was trembling as I reflected upon the words in an anonymous letter sent to me just days before.

Please don't marry Camden, the letter stated. *He's lying to you when he says he has changed. Don't marry him or you will regret it.*

I was flooded with an array of emotions and the pressure was way too much to endure. I flopped down on my bed and massaged my temples. I closed my eyes in an attempt to erase all negative thoughts. No such luck. The memories of Camden's past cluttered my mind.

"Stormy, what's wrong?" my friend Leigh asked, rushing into my bedroom. She clutched my trembling shoulders. "What's wrong with you? You're shaking all over. You look like you're on the verge of a nervous breakdown."

Not realizing Leigh had entered the room, I quickly attempted to regain my composure. I couldn't let on that I was nervous as hell about marrying Camden. My friends and family already doubted the marriage, and to find out I doubted the marriage, too, would gleefully give them a reason to call off the wedding. I couldn't let that happen. I had to put on my game face. I had to make everybody believe that I was secure with my decision.

"I'm fine, Leigh. I'm just suffering from wedding day jitters and need some time to clear my head before all the festivities start."

"From the looks of things, I would say it's more than just wedding day jitters." I chuckled.

"No, really . . . I'm good."

"It's still not too late to change your mind, you know?" Leigh said, obviously not believing me.

"For the last time, Leigh, I'm fine!" I was getting a tad bit irritated. I was already edgy and didn't need anybody adding to my stress.

"Well then, it's time for you to get dressed. Your mother said the makeup artist, photographer, and limousine will be here shortly. So come on. We're all waiting for you to put on your gown."

"I'll be there in a minute."

When Leigh disappeared on the other side of the door, I attempted to get myself together mentally. I prayed and asked God for strength. I asked him to stop allowing Satan to consume my thoughts.

"Camden has changed," I spoke aloud. "He's no longer the same man who snatched my heart from my chest a year ago." He promised me that he'd changed. Reverend Brooks, Camden's father and our pastor, had also given me his word that Camden was no longer struggling with his desires for men. And if a man of God said it, then I had to believe it.

I took a deep, intoxicating breath and then looked down at my diamond engagement ring. The sun shone through the window so brightly that it seemed to make the diamonds on the ring glisten. I actually thought I saw the diamonds smiling at me. Surprisingly, this gave me the boost I needed to get up and get moving.

As I headed down the hallway to my parents' bedroom to get dressed, I began to feel my confidence level rise–just a bit. *I'm making the right decision to marry Camden*, I thought as I entered my mother's room.

"Girl, what took you so long? We've been waiting forever," my feisty friend Nicole joked. She had never liked Camden from day one—said it was something in his shifty eyes. But being a true friend, she promised to support me in my decision to make him my lifelong partner.

"Sorry, y'all," I responded. "Just needed some time alone."

"No problem, Dominique," another good friend said. "But now that you're here, let's get you into your wedding gown."

I eyed my beautiful wedding dress hanging from the closet door. My heart thumped anxiously. *There's no turning back now*, I thought as I walked over to the door and took the dress off the hanger. My mother and bridesmaids assisted me as I slowly stepped into the gown. As I pulled the dress up over my breasts, I began to feel as if I owned the day. I looked in the mirror and admired how stunning I looked in my white, strapless, satin gown with side draping and beaded champagne lace appliqués. *Cinderella ain't got nothin' on me!* My confidence steadily ascended, although butterflies continued to do the backstroke in my stomach.

As my teary-eyed mother cautiously placed the tiara on my head, making certain not to mess up my long, flowing, Shirley Temple curls, I convinced myself that I was making the right decision. *Camden loves me*, I repeated over and over again in my head. *He wouldn't have asked me to marry him if his heart truly wasn't in it.*

After having my makeup applied and photographs taken, I was finally ready to become Mrs. Camden Brooks. But before I stepped one foot out of the house, I made a pre-marriage vow to myself: *If I find out that Camden is not true to me and has reverted to his homosexual behaviors, he will live to regret it!*

Chapter 1

Stormy

Two years prior to dating Camden, I was head over heals with Marcus Davis. Marcus was my world. He really knew how to treat a woman—so I thought. My opinion of him quickly changed once I discovered Marcus had a secret.

One breezy, spring night, Marcus and I were out cruising. He really knew how to spoil me, and I had no problems letting him. We were on our way to Red Lobster for dinner when he began to say all the things I loved to hear.

"Stormy, have I ever told you that you're the best thing that's ever happened to me?" he asked as he drove down Interstate 695.

"No, Marcus." I blushed. "What makes me the best thing that's ever happened to you?"

"You have the total package—everything a man could ever want. You're goal-oriented, smart, and educated. Not to mention, you're stunningly beautiful. I can't keep my eyes off you."

"Oh, Marcus. You're so sweet. That's why I love you."

"I'm just getting started. I'm not even finished telling you how I know I've found a gem in you. I've never met a woman who's so giving of herself. You're not self-centered and materialistic like some women I've encountered. You truly look at a person's heart and not what's in his wallet. So if I've never told you before, I'm telling you how much I love you, and I'm glad God placed you in my life."

"You may want to quit now before I tell you to skip the restaurant and go back to your house instead." Marcus chuckled.

"Hey, you know I have no problems skipping dinner so I can gaze into your beautiful hazel eyes and caress your caramel-colored skin. I'd like nothing better than to run my fingers through your long, flowing, brown hair, and to get a glimpse of that bangin' body of yours. You may only be five feet tall, but your assets are in all the perfect spots. I'm talking voluptuous—a lot to hold on to when making love." He laughed.

"So, you just want me for my body, huh?" I playfully hit him on the arm.

"Come on, now. You know me better than that. Our physical connection is just a tiny part of this relationship." I leaned over and gently kissed his cheek.

"I love you, too, Marcus. You're the best thing that's happened to me. I've told you about all the ups and downs I've had in past relationships, so you know that dating you has been a breath of fresh air for me."

I loved Marcus dearly. I had envisioned myself being his wife since the first day I laid eyes on him—a fine specimen resembling Boris Kodjoe. We had so much in common, especially our love for teaching. We both majored in English in college and were middle- school English teachers. We met at a countywide English teacher's convention one summer, and then it was on.

Being twenty-six years old—only four years away from thirty—I'd been looking to settle down and marry Mr. Right. Initially, I didn't think Mr. Right existed after enduring nothing but heartache in my relationships with men. Most of my anguish started during my college days at the University of Maryland Eastern Shore.

Instead of going away to school and focusing on my education, I wanted to break out of my shell and explore life. I wanted to find out what the buzz was about this thing called sex. All the girls in high school had been braggin' about it. Being the youngest and only daughter of Drake and Victoria Knight, I was on lock and key most of my childhood. My older brothers, Trey and Jordan, were allowed to run wild, but my parents' plan for me was totally different. They made certain to keep me close to home so they'd raise a young lady—not a fast-tail girl as they called it. Their philosophy was that sexual intercourse was only to be had by married couples. But I couldn't wait that long.

Once I stepped foot out of Baltimore and landed on UMES soil, I was on a mission to find a man, start a relationship, and get my freak on. Unfortunately, being sheltered all my life, I allowed myself to become involved with a canine named Chad. Eventually he totally broke my heart. All he wanted was sex—not a relationship. He had no problems with whispering sweet nothings in my ear, trying to get me to drop my panties, and sadly, it worked.

To my dismay, I found that giving up the "goodies" was not totally worth it. Chad gave me two sexually transmitted diseases at once. I was crushed. After that devastating experience and realizing sex was overrated, I began to focus on what I was at UMES for—my education. If only I had listened to my parents when they told me to keep my legs closed.

After graduation I threw myself into my teaching career. Didn't date much. Not that I didn't want to, but I couldn't seem to find a genuine man. I was often lonely and became more and more depressed as the clock ticked by and the years passed. I still wasn't in a serious relationship. Hell, I wanted to be married. It was my heart's desire, but I just couldn't find the right one. That is, until I met Marcus.

The idea of marriage only seemed to be a huge dream, but once I became involved with Marcus, I felt my vision may just one day become a reality. Marcus was the type of man every woman wanted—romantic, affectionate, secure in his career, and financially stable. And best of all, there were no ex-wives and baby mama drama to deal with. I couldn't for the life of me understand why some woman hadn't snatched him up before me.

I sat gazing at Marcus as he continued to drive. He'd just paid me several compliments at once, making me even more proud to have a man like him.

"Hey, babe, I've got to go to the ATM real quick," Marcus announced, pulling into Wachovia Bank's parking lot. "I'll be right back."

"Hurry up. I'm starving," I teased.

I watched Marcus slide his bank card in a slot so he could enter the enclosed area where the ATM machine was located, as I sat in the passenger seat patiently waiting for him to return. We must have been surrounded by pollen because I became aggravated by my hay fever. I began sneezing repeatedly, so I searched my purse for some tissue. After having no luck, I reached into Marcus's glove compartment, rummaging for a napkin or something. I was happy to see a small packet of Kleenex. I grabbed it, took out a few, and then began wiping my nose. As I leaned in to replace the remaining Kleenex, my heart fell when I spied something round and hard. I slowly removed the object to examine it. It was a gold ring, very obviously a wedding band. I eyed it suspiciously.

This can't be what I think it is. Could it?

When Marcus finally returned to the car, I confronted him.

"What's this?" I asked, holding the ring in his face. He didn't answer. He just stared at me blankly. "Marcus! What is this?" I yelled.

"I . . . I . . . I can explain," he responded, stuttering.

"I'm listening."

"Stormy, believe me, I was going to tell you—"

"Tell me what? Stop beatin' around the bush. Are you married?"

"Y-y-yes, I am."

"What? Please tell me you're lying. Please tell me this is some sick joke!"

"Hear me out. I am married, but not happily . . . haven't been in a long time."

I felt sick to my stomach, and I couldn't believe my ears.

"How long have you been married?"

"Three years," he practically whispered.

"Three years!" I screamed in his face. "Three years, Marcus! I can't believe you're telling me this shit now. We've been dating for a year and only after I find your goddamn wedding band you tell me you're married. How could you?"

"I was going to tell you tonight, after dinner. My wife finally agreed to sign the divorce papers, and you and I will be able to get married," he boasted like he had just told me I'd won a new car.

I didn't know if I wanted to hear any more, but I continued to question him anyway.

"Do you still live with her?" He nodded. "You bastard! I've been in your house. I've slept in your bed. I've fucked you on your kitchen counter all while you were married to and living with another woman!"

"Calm down, Stormy. You've got to believe me when I tell you that it's over between my wife and me. That's why I don't wear the ring anymore. Yes, we still live in the same house, but we sleep in separate bedrooms. She's making plans to move out soon. I don't love her. I love you."

"Fuck you, Marcus! You don't love me! If you did, you wouldn't have lied to me all this time. Is that why you spent the entire car ride telling me how much I mean to you? How much you love me? Bullshit! You were just tryin' to butter me up."

"That's not true, dammit! I do love you, and that's no lie."

I shook my head in disbelief. I had spent twelve months of my life thinking I'd found the man for me—the man I wanted to grow old with—only to learn he had been lying to me the entire time.

"How dare you play with my heart, Marcus? How dare you make a fool out of me? Just . . . just take me home! Take me home!" I was fuming.

I wanted to cry, but the rage brewing inside me wouldn't allow tears to fall. I couldn't believe that I'd been having an affair with a married man and had no idea. How he hid his marriage so well, I'd never know. We'd spent damn near every waking hour together. We took lavish trips, I'd met his family, and he'd met my parents, who absolutely adored him. My brothers embraced him, and that was huge considering they didn't think any man was worthy of me. Marcus had the nerve to attend church with me, and he even expressed his love for me, dropping hints of marriage to my pastor, Reverend Brooks, when he met him one Sunday after church. Then suddenly I had to find out the man who meant so much to me was married.

During the drive home, Marcus kept trying to plead his case. He tried to convince me that he didn't tell me because he had anticipated a speedy divorce, but his wife had been protesting it. He begged me not to throw away what we shared. He professed his love over and over. All the while, I pinned myself against the passenger side door and stared out the window as if he wasn't talking at all.

I kept kicking myself for not knowing. How could I have not noticed a woman's presence in his home? Where was she all the nights I was lying in their bed? How could I have been so stupid? I could only surmise that that naïve little girl still lived inside me.

When we arrived at my house, Marcus was still begging for my forgiveness.

"Stormy, we can work this out. I know we can. I was wrong for not telling you. I apologize. I was afraid of losing you. But I promise to be open and honest with you from here on out. Just don't give up on us. I love you, and I know you love me."

Without responding to his pleas, I slowly turned to him and looked him dead in his eyes. With all the saliva I could gather, I spat in his face. Hurriedly, I got out of the car and slammed the door behind me. Marcus sped off without saying another word.

When I entered my empty apartment, the first thing I noticed was a framed picture of Marcus and me from our trip to Negril, Jamaica. I walked over and snatched it from my bookcase, then threw it against the wall, causing the glass to shatter into tiny little pieces. It was then that tears fell from my eyes.

"Why me, Lord?" I cried out. "Why is this happenin' to me? Why can't I ever be happy? Why can't I find someone to love me without all the lies and deceit? Why . . . why . . . why? All I want, Lord, is for you to send me a God-fearing man who will love, respect, and be loyal to me. Am I asking for too much?"

I cried myself to sleep because my Mr. Right turned out to be Mr. Wrong. I wondered where my future husband was. I desperately wanted him. No, I needed him. I just couldn't be alone again—not again.

Chapter 2

Camden

*B*AM!
I sat straight up in the bed after I heard what appeared to be glass breaking. I hopped out of bed and peeped through the blinds of my apartment window.

"Shit!" I exclaimed as I rushed to throw on some clothes. I ran out my front door at the speed of lightning. I bolted down the stairs, skipping every other step. "Goddamnit! That bitch Terry struck again," I said, looking at the ghastly sight.

My windshield was cracked with a huge brick planted firmly in the middle of it. My car windows were smashed, and all of my tires were flattened. To put the icing on the cake, YOU WILL BE WITH ME OR DIE! was written across the hood in bright red letters. I was irate. I didn't know what my next step was going to be, but I had to do whatever I could to get as far away from Terry as possible.

I never thought I'd come about a relationship by happenstance, but that's exactly the way it went down. I hadn't planned on making a commitment because I didn't want to be tied to anyone. Then one day I must have slipped and hit my head because I fell in love—or maybe it was just strong like—with Terry. We met while I was in college at St. John's University in New York City. I can honestly say my initial attraction was to the sexy voice, lively spirit, almond complexion, and long, swingy dreadlocks with gold tips. And those mean pair of legs in walking shorts didn't go unnoticed either. As much as I wanted it to be just sex between us, it turned into something more.

Terry didn't work. That was the luxury of having a great-grandfather who was the founder of Smith and Sons Funeral Homes, the largest African American owned funeral service in the United States. When Mr. Smith died, the inheritance was passed down to Terry, and the business continued to flourish. No one in the Smith family was hurting for money.

Fortunately, for me, I was able to reap the benefits of being involved with someone who came from wealth—expensive clothes, shoes, and jewelry. Terry soon became known to me as *Pooh*. We spent time in Cancun, Miami, Las Vegas, and Toronto, and I never spent a dime of my own money.

After our last trip, I got the surprise of my life when we returned to New York. Pooh bought me a new car and had it delivered to my door while we were out of town. It was a silver-colored Acura TL. I almost peed on myself. The car was bangin'.

I was "living the life," all at someone else's expense. All I had to do was continuously profess my love and perform well in bed, and I'd get anything I wanted. Life was great! I was one spoiled mofo. I left parents who coddled me, only to find a lover who was willing to continue where they left off.

Our relationship went great for a year and then things began to go downhill. Terry was in love with me and wanted more than I could give. I started to feel smothered. I couldn't eat, sleep, or shit without being hovered over. I felt like I was back at my parents' house. We also started arguing a lot over stupid, petty stuff, and I was tired of all the drama.

After twelve months of being in love, or so I thought, I was miserable and wanted out. I didn't care about the money anymore. I realized I just needed to take what I'd acquired during the relationship and get out. After asking for some space, the shit hit the fan. Terry was bitter about me ending our relationship, but that was to be expected, considering how much I had gained without giving much in return.

In an attempt to sever all ties, I stopped calling, refused to return any phone calls, and halted all contact. That obviously struck a nerve because I saw a new, ugly side of my former lover. To my surprise, the person I once knew as Pooh suddenly became my stalker. Messages were left on my answering machine, but I simply erased them. Bad idea. The unanswered calls resulted in unannounced appearances at my job, stirring up a big scene in front of the customers each time. Then to top it off, Terry would sit outside my house and wait for me to get home. I couldn't seem to get a moment's peace.

As I sat on the side of my bed, heartsick about my Acura being vandalized, I contemplated calling the police. But before I could pick up the receiver to do so, my phone rang. I looked at the caller ID and immediately recognized the number. More anger came over me, so I answered the phone.

"What the fuck do you want?" All I heard was Terry's laughter. "This shit ain't funny. Stop harassin' me!"

"I told you I loved you, but you just used me," that psycho accused.

"How the fuck did I use you? Never mind. That doesn't even matter. I just want you to stay the fuck away from me. If you don't, the next time I'm calling the police."

"Well be prepared to call them! I'm not going to stop fuckin' up your life until you come back to me."

"What makes you think I want to be with you after this shit? You must be crazy if you think I'd ever be with you again."

"OK, well this time it was your car. Next time it will be your apartment, your job, or maybe your life, you bastard!" the bitch hissed, and then hung up the phone.

I was heated! I didn't know what to do. There I was all alone in New York City. Originally I decided the Big Apple was the best place to attend college and to get away from my overbearing, Bible-toting father. During my last year of high school, my friends Jared and Hassan set a plan in motion for all of us to attend St. John's because we were big fans of the basketball team. Besides, we had a strong desire to be a part of the New York scene. So, with the hopes of getting away from Baltimore and from under the microscope of being Reverend Brooks and First Lady Brooks's son, I ran as far away as I could.

Of course, my parents hated my decision to go to New York to major in Business/Hospitality Management instead of going to some divinity school. My father, being the pastor of True Gospel Christian Center, one of the largest mega churches in Baltimore, wanted me to follow in his footsteps. I guess he thought I'd carry on his legacy. But that wasn't my dream. Besides, the skeletons in my closet outnumbered my clothes and shoes combined, so me attempting to lead others in the right direction wasn't ever going to happen. I didn't even know what direction I wanted to go. But what I did know was that I was tired of being a preacher's son, having to continuously walk the straight and narrow. I just wanted to be me.

So, once I stepped foot in New York, I knew it was the place for me. I loved the university and all the new people. And because my childhood friends, Hassan and Jared, attended the same university, this made the setup perfect. We spent most of our time exploring the city. It was awesome.

There was always something to do, no matter the time of day or night. It was true that New York never slept. We went to clubs, got drunk, and indulged in sex, sex, and more sex. Sometimes after a night of partying, I would wake up in bed with a strange person I didn't even remember meeting. The sad thing was it didn't bother me one bit. I was just happy to be living my life in freedom.

On graduation day, I had the pleasure of telling my parents that I had decided to stay in New York.

"Are you serious?" my mother asked with a look of disappointment. I was still her baby—her only baby—and she didn't want to let me go. But I couldn't go back home. I'd grown to love being away and didn't have plans to return—ever.

Two weeks after graduation, I landed a job as the manager of Sean "Diddy" Combs's restaurant, Justin's Bar and Grill. From that point on, I worked and partied and partied and worked. Life was good. That is, until all the shit started with my ex.

"Well, well, well. Fancy meeting you here," a voice behind me said. I was startled when I turned to see none other than Terry.

"Look! I'm working, and I don't have time for your tantrums tonight." I turned around to complete a purchase order for supplies.

"Don't turn your back on me, motherfucker! Look at me when I'm talking to you."

I looked around to see if any of the customers had heard the outburst. They had.

"Shhh. Just leave. It's over between us. Why can't you see that?" I whispered.

"You used me, Camden!" Terry screamed for everyone to hear. "And I'm not gonna let you get away with it. You think you can fuck me, take my money, and then walk out on me. Never! I'll kill you first! I will!"

"Excuse me, Camden. Is everything OK?" one of the security guys asked, rushing over toward me.

"No! I think someone needs an escort out of here," I said, staring at Terry unblinkingly.

"No need for me to be escorted because I'm leaving. But you betta watch your back!"

I didn't respond. I was too embarrassed. I just wanted the foolishness to end and for things at the restaurant to return to normal. I disappeared to my office to hide for a few minutes.

For the next week, the harassment continued. Horrendous scenes became the norm when the restaurant was crowded. The profanity and the vulgar outbursts grew worse. The comments went from me being a user to me being a pencil-dick bastard who couldn't fuck.

After several complaints from customers, word finally reached the higher ups. I was called in to work on my day off and listened as a higher level manager explained that whatever was going on in my personal life was affecting business. I was fired. I tried to explain and plead my case, but it was too late. I had to clean out my office within the hour.

Once I cleaned out my office, I headed home. I was feeling kind of down. I really liked my job at Justin's and if it weren't for that asshole, Terry, I'd still have it.

When I walked into my apartment, it was ransacked. My furniture was in shreds and there was a dead rat lying on my kitchen table. Everything in my refrigerator was poured onto the floor, and the table and chairs were turned upside down. I slowly walked toward my bedroom and the smell of bleach instantly crawled up my nostrils. My clothes were thrown around the room, covered with bleach. My television screen had a big hole in it. My shoes looked like they'd been eaten by an angry pit bull.

The scene was horrific. Nothing appeared to be missing,

but the place looked like it was hit by a whirlwind and it was one hell of a mess. I called the police, but since there was no incriminating evidence left behind, they took a report, snapped pictures, and handed me a business card. The officers instructed me to call them if anything else happened or if I could find some proof against the perpetrator. *But if there's a next time, I could be dead,* I thought. *How could I call the police if I were dead?* The cops were good for nothing.

Being stalked and terrorized was not how I'd planned to live. New York was supposed to be my outlet—my happy place—my freedom spot. But there was no longer freedom or happiness as long as Terry was on the loose. As much as I hated to admit it, I knew I couldn't continue to live in the Big Apple. What reason did I have to stay? I was jobless, soon to be homeless, and my sense of security had been shot to hell. There was no other choice but for me to return home to Baltimore.

Chapter 3

Malik

Pow! Pow! Pow! Pow! Pow! Gun shots rang out.

I heard my grandmother downstairs screaming for all the children to come in the house. As always in rough, inner city neighborhoods, wannabe street gangsters had gone on a shooting spree with no regard for innocent lives.

Pow! Pow! Pow! More shots.

"Malik! Is Sonny up there with you?" my grandmother called out frantically.

Sonny was my grown-ass uncle who lived with us in our subsidized townhouse in Cherry Hill. He was an alcoholic who bore resemblance to Ned the Wino from *Good Times*. I teased him often by calling him a shriveled up prune. Shooting craps on the corner outside the Korean convenience store was one of Sonny's favorite pastimes, although he caught a few ass whippings from cheating people out of their money. I was never surprised when neighbors came knocking at the door to inform us that he was laid up in an alley, bleeding from a beat down. That's one reason why my grandmother was so worried when she heard the firecracker shots outside.

"No, Grandma. He's not up here."

"Oh, Lord!" she cried out. "Please make sure my baby is all right."

I started hearing sirens as they grew closer to my block. I heard a lot of commotion outside from all my nosey neighbors. Just like most black people in the hood, there was always a crowd of people who flocked to the scene of a crime.

"Malik, can you go across the street to see what the fuss is about? Find out what happened for me," my grandmother said nervously.

My grandmother, Delores Blackwell, was a healthy sixty-three-year-old woman who didn't look a day over forty. She reminded me a lot of Shirley Caesar. She was no more than five feet tall and brown-skinned with a wide nose and high cheekbones. Her shoulder length hair was full of gray streaks. She tried to cover up the fact that she was graying by dying her hair black and wearing hats, especially on Sundays when she wore those big church hats.

I knew she was sending me to inspect the scene because she was scared that it was Uncle Sonny who'd been shot. I also knew she couldn't bear seeing her son lying on the ground across the street had it been him. It would most likely kill her.

As I proceeded to survey the scene, Ms. Rose, a neighbor who was the same age as my grandmother, came running out the house wearing a flowered housecoat, pink slippers, and pink sponge rollers in her hair.

"No! Not my baby! Not my baby!" she screamed.

Damn! I know she's not screaming 'cause somethin' happened to my boy. Not Li'l Marvin. It couldn't have been Li'l Marvin, Ms. Rose's grandson, who got shot. But as I approached, my worst fears were confirmed. Li'l Marvin had blood seeping from his skull. He'd been shot in the head.

I quickly turned away, saddened, because Li'l Marv and I were like family. We'd known each other since we were babies. We had a special connection because he was raised by his grandmother, too. Just like me, Marv's parents didn't want him either.

Life was rough for me. I never had it easy, not even on the day my poor excuse for a mother gave birth to me. Actually, hell started breaking loose for me while I was still in the womb. My father left my mother when she told him she was pregnant. He told her that he wasn't ready to be a father and was out of the picture soon after that.

My mother loved my father and the day he left her was the beginning of her demise. After two months of trying to be a mother to me, she just gave up. To ease her depression she chose drugs over me, soon leaving me in the care of my grandparents, Richard and Delores Blackwell. In hindsight, that might have been the best thing she could have done for me because living in the gutter or the crack house where she currently resided would've been no life for me. As for my father, I never met him and didn't care to.

I thank God for my grandparents. If it had not been for them, I might have ended up in foster care. Although their children were grown, they opened their hearts and home in the public housing projects. My grandparents didn't have much money, but they made the most of what they had. They took damn good care of me, too. I was never hungry or dirty. They made sure I attended school every day and helped me with my homework nightly. Once when I was eight years old my grandfather told me that he wanted me to overcome my circumstances and not become a product of my environment. He encouraged me to achieve more than he had, and he promised to do everything possible to ensure that.

Unfortunately, soon after that speech, my grandfather died of a heart attack. I felt as if my world had literally come to an end. He was the only father figure I had ever known. *Who would be my father now?* I wondered on many nights as I cried myself to sleep. I took his death hard and didn't think that I would ever bounce back from it.

After his passing, my grandmother had to find a job outside the house to help make ends meet. She began working at a ritzy hotel in the Inner Harbor as a maid. I hated that she had to work because I was left at home with Uncle Sonny's drunken ass. Although he was the eldest child of my grandparents, he was far from being a father figure. Besides, there was no way I'd be receptive to his advice or guidance, since he was a washed up Vietnam veteran who had no job, not a pot to piss in, nor a window to throw it out of. Drinking, watching game shows, and telling war stories—half of which I think he fabricated—was all he knew how to do.

Although my grandmother was struggling to take care of the household, she always remained faithful to God. She had attended True Gospel Christian Center all of her life, and I was a member there also. I can remember days of only paying attention to the choir, and then ducking out to the corner store to buy chips and soda once Reverend Brooks started his sermon.

Toward the end of my sophomore year in high school, I began to lose focus and my grades started to drop. This, of course, upset my grandmother, so she did what she felt she had to do—took me to Pastor Brooks's office for a meeting. She began to tell him about my performance in school. Reverend Brooks, being the *savior* that he was, simply told her not to worry.

"My son, Camden, will be home this summer from New York. He's almost done his junior year at St. John's University. I'm sure he'll be happy to mentor Malik."

"Oh, thank you, pastor," Grandma said with tears in her eyes. "I think this is a wonderful idea. Maybe Camden can not only keep Malik on the right track, but get him interested in going to college as well."

Grandma and Reverend Brooks acted as if they'd come up with the best plan since the invention of the Internet. I, on the other hand, wasn't too happy. I just wasn't interested in school anymore, and neither Reverend Brooks nor his son was going to change that. Besides, he was five and a half years older, so I felt we'd have absolutely nothing in common.

"Hello, Malik, this is Camden. Pastor Brooks's son."

"Hello," I responded dryly. I wasn't impressed by his call.

"My father tells me you're having some problems in school. Is that true?"

"Yeah, but it doesn't matter now anyway. The school year is almost over."

"Well, I'll be home before the school year ends. Maybe we can get together and find out what's going on. I've fallen off track a couple times myself during my teenage years, so I know what it's like. I may be the pastor's son, but I'm nothing like him. I want to help you through your struggles, but don't expect a whole lot of scriptures from me. I'm not the preacher type."

Camden made me laugh. My feelings about him began to change about midway through our conversation. He and I talked for about thirty minutes before hanging up. *This might not be a bad idea after all.*

My initial ill feelings were wrong about Camden. He was a lot of fun to hang out with. He not only helped me get through the final weeks of school, but he also became like a big brother to me during the summer. Camden would take me shopping, to the movies, nice restaurants, museums, plays, concerts, amusement parks, and other fun places. I was happy to have a big brother to look out for me and to take me away from life in the hood.

Just weeks before I entered eleventh grade, Camden left for New York to complete his last year of college. I was devastated. I was losing yet another male figure in my life. But Camden promised he'd stay in touch, which turned out to be a lie. Not only did he not keep in contact with me after he left, but he didn't return home after he graduated. He decided to make New York his home.

I was determined to stay strong, though. I continued to remain focused in school because I didn't want to disappoint my grandmother and Reverend Brooks, and even though he had forgotten about me, I didn't want to let Camden down. After graduating from high school, I enrolled in Baltimore City Community College, majoring in Computer Information System, but my lack of focus toward education reared its ugly head again. It didn't take long for my grades to plummet, and I began to seriously question whether I belonged in school. I loved computers, but a higher education was my grandmother's vision for me. How could I fulfill a dream I never owned?

Several of my family members suggested I give up on college to pursue modeling.

"With your looks, I bet you could pose for Sean John or Tommy Hilfiger," they said. They boasted about how six-foot, light-skinned, curly-haired guys were blowing up the modeling scene. I had no clue if what they said was true, but I wasn't into modeling—kind of always thought it was for girls. But I couldn't deny believing that light-skinned, curly-haired brothers were back in style.

Now at the tender age of twenty-one, I still didn't know what I wanted to do with my life, but I wasn't going to give up on school. I couldn't—not after all the love and support my grandmother, Reverend Brooks, and the church members who helped pay for my tuition and books. I just couldn't let him down.

As much as I wanted to forget Camden, I couldn't. When he was in the picture, he helped me too. Because of him, I was exposed to a whole new world. He was my big brother, my partner, my dawg, and then some. I longed for the day he'd come back so we could kick it again.

Chapter 4

Stormy

"Stormy, why are you still in the house?" Nicole shouted into the phone. "Church starts in twenty minutes and you're gonna be late, as usual."

"Yeah, Stormy, you should've been gone by now. You and Dominique always sashay up in church when the sermon's about to start. I find it odd the way you two always seem to get to church after everybody's given their tithes and offerings," Leigh yelled into the mouthpiece of Nicole's cell phone.

"Shut up, Leigh. And you, too, Nicole," I joked. "I'm leaving out now. Save me a seat." I hung up and grabbed my purse to head to church.

Leigh McNair and Nicole Jenkins had been my friends for twelve years. We all met during freshman orientation at Western High School. Each of us, scared and intimidated about being the new kids on the block, bonded quickly. We were inseparable from that point on.

The saying about how opposites attract is very true when

it came to my friends. Leigh was the brown-skinned, confident, plus-sized one with a big heart. She did accounting for a prestigious firm and was quite good at it.

Nicole, who was originally from Philadelphia, relocated with her parents to Baltimore just before she entered high school. She was what the fellas referred to as the sexy, chocolate girl with the hourglass figure. Men were most attracted to the two cantaloupes she called breasts that stuck out of her chest, and she was also often complimented on her big, brown eyes. Nicole was my lively, aggressive friend. She too had a heart of gold, but she had no problems speaking her mind and cursing you out if you crossed her. I often wondered how her bedside manner was as a licensed practical nurse.

And then there was Dominique—my friend the kindergarten teacher. She was the shy, meek friend who we all met in college. She happened to be one of our roommates who shared an on-campus apartment with us. She had been more sheltered than me, growing up in a predominantly white suburb of Baltimore. Attending a historically black college exposed her to a world she had never experienced. Dominique quickly learned that she could not be introverted while living with us. We vowed to bring her out of her shell, and that we did.

Dominique had a flawless, cinnamon-brown complexion and always wore her hair in micro-mini braids. But Dominique was self-conscious about her body. She was extremely petite with no accented curves. A push-up bra didn't even help to accentuate her breasts. But she was extremely beautiful inside and out.

It had been two weeks since the fiasco with Marcus and I wasn't up to going to church. I was too distraught to even get out of bed. But Leigh, Dominique, and Nicole kept scolding me about not giving the Lord some of my time. I found this extremely odd since none of them were regular

28 *Latrese N. Carter*

churchgoers until I begged them to go to church with me. It took me months of convincing them to visit True Gospel, but once they did, they really enjoyed it. It seemed strange that they had called and made me feel guilty about missing a Sunday. In hindsight, I realized that my friends' forcing me to attend church on that Sunday was the best thing they could have ever done.

I sat in the red-cushioned pew of True Gospel, attempting to listen to Reverend Brooks's sermon—*Too Blessed to Be Stressed*. During a brief scan over the congregation, a familiar face caught my eye—a handsome creature. It was Camden Brooks, the pastor's son. I hadn't seen him since the day he left to go away to college. I had heard through the grapevine that he didn't come home after he graduated because he wanted to stay in New York. My parents alluded to the fact that Camden didn't return home because he wanted to be free from his parents, which wouldn't be too farfetched.

Growing up, I remember Camden hated being the pastor's son. He felt he had to be a "good boy" in church, but at heart he was bad to the bone. I also remember we had a teenage crush once, but it amounted to nothing because my father wasn't having it. He was not impressed that Camden was Reverend Brooks's son.

After service ended, I told my friends I'd hook up with them later, after having dinner with my parents. That was a lie. I purposely lingered around talking to other church members, hoping that Camden would notice me. It seemed that all the parishioners must have been glad to see him because it took him forever to finally make his way over to me. I tried to act like I didn't see him heading toward me. I slowly gathered my purse and Bible, acting as if I was preparing to leave.

"My, my, my. If it isn't Stormy Knight," Camden said with a huge grin.

"Hi, Camden!" I said as I greeted him with a hug and took a whiff of his cologne. "It's good to see you."

"It's good to see you, too, girl. You lookin' good as ever."

I tried to be cool, but truth be told, my panties were getting wet. I couldn't take my eyes off his luscious lips and his pearly white teeth. I wanted to kiss him, but I knew it would be as inappropriate as kissing one of my students.

Camden and I were engrossed in conversation for almost an hour. We were only interrupted one time by Malik, a male youth in the church that Camden once mentored. Malik seemed a bit perturbed that Camden didn't end his conversation with me to hang out with him, but to me it was a good sign. During our talk, Camden explained that things hadn't worked out for him in New York and he was back in Baltimore for good, working as a manager at the Marriott Hotel.

Neither of us wanted to end our reunion, but realized that time had gotten away from us. Camden asked me for my telephone number and promised to call me later that evening to talk more—to catch up. I searched through my purse for a pen and paper to write down his telephone number. I wasn't about to let this man get away. Maybe he was the man I'd been praying for. I quickly wrote down my home and cellular numbers, as did he. As we exchanged papers, I felt Camden's fingers gently and seductively slide across mine. At that moment there was a gush in my underwear like a pregnant woman whose water had broken. Embarrassed, I told Camden I'd talk to him later and subtly ran out of the church. Camden called me later that night, and the night after that, and the night after that.

Camden and I had only been dating for a few weeks when I knew without a doubt that I was in love. Not only was he a fine, dark brown hunk with a shiny bald head resembling a milk dud, but he was the most charming man I'd ever met. When I was out with Camden, he was the perfect gentleman. He catered to me as if his life depended on it, opening car doors and doors to buildings for me. I never carried an umbrella if it rained, and I never spent a dime of my own money.

Camden was also an excellent cook. The first time he invited me over to his apartment, he cooked a seafood dinner that included golden fried jumbo shrimp, grilled crab cakes, steamed broccoli, and rice pilaf. The meal was delicious—a real treat. He explained that while he was the manager at Justin's he picked up some culinary skills. I was impressed. This man seemed to be the perfect mate—a God-fearing, sexy gentleman who could burn in the kitchen. What more could I ask for?

A year into our relationship, Camden took me to Morton's Steakhouse. We were seated in a small, intimate dining room for couples only. After we stuffed ourselves, we held hands and reflected on our relationship—how it had blossomed. I reminded him how I didn't even want to go to church the day I ran into him, and if it hadn't been for my friends, we probably wouldn't have ever hooked up. Then out of nowhere, Camden did the unthinkable, bringing me to tears.

Chapter 5

Camden

"I love you, Stormy. You're the light of my life. You're the best thing that's ever happened to me. I can't see me living a day without you. Will you marry me?" I asked in the middle of the restaurant, getting down on one knee.

I pulled out a black velvet box, which contained a princess cut, one-carat diamond. Stormy's face lit up, but she also seemed shocked. I waited for what seemed to be an eternity before she gave me an answer.

"Yes, Camden! Yes, I will marry you!" Stormy finally said as the other patrons in the restaurant looked at us.

I placed the ring on her finger, and we kissed as if we were the only two in the restaurant. The customers gave us a round of applause and then our waiter brought us a free bottle of champagne to toast our engagement.

"Did you plan this?" Stormy asked.

"Sure did. I've known for a while now that I wanted to marry you, but I wanted to wait for the right time to propose. Tonight felt right, so I did it."

"Camden, I love you. And I'd be honored to be your wife." Stormy smiled as her eyes glistened with tears. It felt good to see her face glowing as well as her left ring finger. I was lucky to have a woman like Stormy by my side. She'd help my transition back home to be a smooth one.

After all the turmoil in New York, it was painful for me to call my parents and ask them if I could come home. Of course, without giving it a second thought, they welcomed me with open arms. I, on the other hand, dreaded it.

I loved my parents. I truly did. All in all, they were very good to me—they spoiled me rotten. As their only child, they gave me the best of everything. I attended the best private schools, and they kept me in expensive clothes. I couldn't ever remember wanting for anything.

I wasn't the best student in high school, but my parents always went to battle for me when my teachers had a complaint. They bailed me out of trouble often, even when I should have suffered major consequences. I remember an incident when I was seventeen years old and went to a party. Being young and dumb, I got drunk that night and attempted to drive home. I never made it. Because I was drunk, I misjudged the lanes and sideswiped another car while trying to switch lanes. I called my parents, and they rushed to the scene. My father used his influence as a pastor to keep the driver from calling the police. It worked. Dad wrote him a check and sent him on his way. Of course, my punishment lasted for weeks, but it could have been far worse. I must say, being the only child of a wealthy, well-known preacher had its rewards.

My purpose for staying in New York was to get away from my parents—more so my father. He was too overbearing. He enjoyed spitting scriptures at me all day long and preaching to me how I should have been living my life. I just wasn't living up to his standards and that disappointed him. So, having to move back home to my childhood bedroom was not ideal for me. I set a plan in motion to only live with my parents until I found another managerial position and an apartment.

It took two weeks to find a job and I found an apartment shortly thereafter. Stormy was by my side the entire time. She encouraged me and supported me until I could get on my feet. She was a special gift. There wasn't a day that she didn't remind me that she loved me or showed she appreciated me. It was nothing for me to find Post-it notes hidden in my coat pocket that read *I love you* or *Have a blessed day at work*. I was amazed by her affection and compassion, and I enjoyed our closeness and intimacy. Whenever Stormy was in my presence, tranquility filled my heart. She made me feel safe. She made me feel loved. That was why I couldn't let her get away. I had to make her my wife.

Stormy and I made a beeline to my apartment from the restaurant. We wanted to seal our engagement by making love. When we entered the living room, I immediately began to disrobe.

"Take off your clothes," I seductively whispered as I gazed into Stormy's eyes. "I want to make love to my future wife."

She seemingly happily agreed. We never made it to my bedroom. Our clothes were spread across the living room floor. Stormy aggressively pushed me down on the couch, then straddled me. She leaned down and gently kissed my lips. She pulled back, looked at me, and leaned in to kiss me again. I had never felt so much passion from her as our tongues locked. With my member throbbing, I knew I'd be unable to handle lengthy foreplay. I slowly inserted myself into her wetness. Slowly we grooved to the soft tunes of Barry White's "Secret Garden."

Our bodies totally entwined for an hour before I heard Stormy moan my name in ecstasy. I could tell she was about to climax.

"Oh, Camden." She spoke softly and then fell limp. I was no longer able to control myself. I exploded.

"I can't wait for you to be my wife so we can do this all day, every day." Stormy laughed.

"Me too. Let's talk about setting a date."

"Sure. After round two. I've got to clear my *head* before I can look at the calendar," I teased.

A few days later, I met up with my boys—Hassan, Jared, and Malik—to give them my news. They were all surprised, but I truly felt each of them was happy for me. We sat at our usual bar spot, having a few drinks as they each gave me well wishes.

"Here's to Camden and Stormy. Wishing you much happiness in the future," Hassan toasted.

"So, when's the big day?" Jared asked.

"Next year in April. Stormy wants a spring wedding. It's pretty much out of my control. I'm just gonna get my tuxedo and show up."

"I admire you, man. I really do. I'm hoping to be in your shoes soon, my brotha," Hassan said.

Hassan Garrison was one of the nicest guys in Baltimore City. He was always the perfect gentleman—just the total opposite of Jared and me. He had that mocha-colored skin, a smooth mustache, and the low, wavy hair cut which always seemed to attract the ladies, but still, he was single. He was looking for that special someone to spend the rest of his life with—someone with intelligence and a drive to succeed—his perfect match.

Jared Moore, on the other hand, was a bad boy like me. He liked to play the field, but wasn't against settling down. He was just waiting for the right woman to give him that special feeling, letting him know it was time to be serious and possibly get married. Until then, he was going to do his thing with whomever he wanted and as much as he wanted.

Women often told Jared he reminded them of Taye Diggs. He'd tell them he hated their comments and that he wanted to be recognized for his own sex appeal, for just being Jared. But secretly, Jared loved the compliment.

We continued to sip our drinks, then Jared made a comment that scared me.

"I don't admire you, Cam," he said. "That means only one coochie for the rest of your life. Are you crazy?" I couldn't believe my ears.

"Get out of here, man. Marriage is gonna be great. I can feel it," I asserted.

Jared couldn't hold his face straight for long. He chuckled.

"I'm just jivin', Cam. I'm proud of you, son. Let me know how this marriage thing is. If you tell me it's a'ight, then maybe I'll think about it in ten or twenty years." We all laughed.

I looked over at Malik, who didn't seem to be having a good time. I wondered what was going through his mind. He seemed withdrawn, somewhat depressed. It was unlike him not to have a good time when he hung out with the guys, especially at the bar. I needed to know what was wrong.

"Yo, Malik. Can I talk to you outside for a minute, man?" I asked.

Malik didn't say anything. He just followed me. Once outside, I turned to him.

"What's up with you, man? You look like you lost your best friend."

"I feel like I did," he responded in a low tone.

I knew what he was getting at, so I took a deep breath before asking him to elaborate.

"What do you mean?"

"I guess now that you're marrying Stormy, we're not gonna be friends anymore, huh?"

"Why do you say that? Nothing's gonna change. You,

Jared, and Hassan will always be my dawgs. Marriage can't change that. Never." Malik gave a sideways chuckle.

"Don't be offended when I tell you I don't believe you. Camden, you know I've only had one male figure in my life—my grandfather, who died when I was eight years old. Then you and Reverend Brooks come along and embrace me like family. I grew fond of you and your family, and then you abruptly left to go to college. You promised to call. You didn't. You promised to write. You didn't. You promised to come home to visit. You didn't. You were supposed to be my big brother, and you left me high and dry. Then when you do return home, you're all up in Stormy's face. You think including me in on your dates is the same as hangin' out with the fellas. It's not. Ever since you started dating her, you've changed. So forgive me if I'm not jumpin' for joy about the news of your engagement, but your past behavior proves that you don't know how to be in love without cutting your friends off, too."

"I'm sorry, Malik. You've got a point. I'm not going anywhere this time. I'm just getting married."

Malik looked at me with an I'll-believe-it-when-I-see-it expression. I couldn't be mad at him, though. He was right. He'd had such a rough life. No mother, no father—only his grandparents, and I knew he looked up to me.

"Malik, I don't know what else to tell you, man," I said, placing my hand on his shoulder. "I can only reiterate that things will not change between us. My boys will be my boys, including you, little bro. I won't let Stormy or anyone else come between us."

We started back into the bar, but before we did, Malik looked at me with a raised eyebrow and a coldness in his eyes that said he didn't trust me.

Chapter 6

Stormy

"Hey, Leigh. I'm sorry to call you at the last minute, but I'm not gonna be able to pick the flowers today. We'll have to do it another day."

"Why?" Leigh asked in a disappointed tone. She was excited about doing the floral arrangements for the wedding—to put her amateur florist skills to work.

"My cousin Dante just called. He said he needs to talk to me about something urgent."

"What about?"

"Don't know. I'm hoping it ain't nothin' bad."

"Well, call me when he leaves to let me know what's going on."

"I will. And please call Nicole and Dominique for me. Tell them I'll reschedule picking out flowers soon, and be sure to tell them I'm sorry."

"Will do. Talk to you later."

I wondered all day what Dante had to talk to me about. I hoped he wasn't coming over to dampen my spirits because

I'd been flying high since Camden's proposal. This was the happiest I'd been in a long time.

With my wedding only ten months away, I began to experience premarital bliss. I never realized I could be so happy—so at peace. My mother and I were knee-deep in planning, and things were going smoothly. My parents were paying for everything, so financing the wedding wasn't an issue. Mother was a tremendous help. Secretly, I knew she would make sure her only daughter had the kind of ceremony people would talk about for years to come. I didn't experience all the crazy, stressful drama and horror stories I'd heard other brides share.

My wedding dress was breathtaking—simply gorgeous. When I slipped it on for the first fitting, I felt like a princess. Camden also became a bit more involved in the wedding planning. Initially he just wanted to show up and leave the planning to me. But I wasn't having it. It was *our* day, and he needed to be a part of everything. So eventually, he came around.

The doorbell rang. *Finally, Dante's here.*

"Hey, big cousin, Dante!" I said just after opening the door. He leaned in and gave me a bear hug. "Stop it! You're squeezing the life out of me!" I laughed.

It was true. Dante was six feet two inches tall and on the thick side—not fat, but big and solid. Dante was older, but he only had me by six months. He had always been extremely protective of me. He often felt like more of a brother than a first cousin. On the streets he was known as *Rock*. I never understood why people called him that, but his street life was something I distanced myself from. I never wanted to be caught up in his mess. He swore he was trying to work toward getting his CDL license so he could drive delivery trucks for Coca-Cola. But that was yet to be seen.

"What up witcha, Storm?" Dante asked.

"Nothing. I was having my bridesmaids over to help me

pick out flowers, but I cancelled when you told me there was something you wanted to discuss."

"Sorry to interfere with your plans. I just really needed to talk to you," he said with a look of despair on his face. The last time I saw him look like that was when his father passed away only three years before. I immediately knew something was wrong.

"What's going on, Dante? You're makin' me nervous."

I perched on the love seat in my living room as Dante sat on the couch directly across from me.

"I heard something yesterday that I think you should know." Dante spoke softly and slowly as if he really didn't want to tell me his news. I was starting to get worried.

"What?" Dante sighed before he spoke again.

"First, let me start by tellin' you, I ain't the one to believe everything I hear in the street. But what I've got to tell you, I believe because the source is credible."

"What is it, Dante? What'd you hear?" My heart rate picked up. Dante was scaring me.

"OK, Stormy. Brace yourself." Dante paused before continuing. "I heard Camden is messin' around with somebody else."

"What?" I frowned. I wasn't sure if I really comprehended what he had said. "Who told you that?"

"I can't tell you. Just know my source is trustworthy. If it wasn't, I wouldn't have come to you with this."

"Come on, Dante. Who told you Camden was cheatin' on me? I need to know. Is it an ex-girlfriend of Camden's? Tell me," I pleaded.

"Stormy, I promised I wouldn't bring up any names."

"Dante, we're blood!" I spoke angrily. I wanted to know where those rumors about Camden came from and Dante was going to tell me. "Our mothers are sisters. The last I heard, family comes first before street folk all day long. So spill it! Was it an ex-girlfriend or what?"

I must have made him feel guilty with my little speech because he reluctantly gave in.

"Naw. It wasn't no ex-girl. It wasn't even a girl."

"Then who?"

"I heard it from Omar," he said hesitantly.

"Omar? You mean Omar that used to go to True Gospel? Deacon Singleton's son?"

Omar used to be an active member at the church but he "dropped out" of church and chose the street life. I hadn't seen him in years, but he and Dante were extremely close— both being previously involved in selling drugs. I'd recently heard that along with Dante, Omar had left the street life behind and gotten a job.

"Yeah, that's him. He works with Camden and recently caught him in a compromising position."

"You've got to be kiddin' me." I sat in disbelief with my mouth hanging wide open.

"I wish I was. I really do."

Not really wanting to know the answer, I had to ask anyway.

"Did Omar tell you who Camden was cheating on me with?"

Dante didn't answer. He just stared at me with a you-really-don't-want-to-know look.

"Yep, he told me and that was the shocking part."

"Why?" My eyes widened.

" 'Cause he said he caught him messin' around with that young boy, Malik, from the church."

"Malik? Malik? Get the fuck out of here! Malik is like a brother to Camden. They're really good friends. Besides, if he was messin' around with Malik, then that would mean he is gay, and Camden is not gay!"

"Look, Stormy. Calm down. I know you don't want to believe that Camden's gay, especially with him being your boo and all, but I wouldn't make this up. And you know

Omar. Have you ever known him to make up something this deep? You might just have to face reality that Camden is gay, bisexual, or whatever you want to call it. Not to mention, word on the street is that he's been sleeping with men for years."

My heart was racing. I felt myself wanting to explode. *There's no way in hell Camden is gay. He couldn't be.*

"Dante, if Omar told you Camden is gay, then he told you a bold-faced lie. Camden's engaged to me. Why would he propose to me if he was gay?"

"I don't know why he proposed to you, girl, but I believe you need to check this guy out, because if he's gay, then you need to reconsider marrying him."

"Camden is not gay, Dante! And he sure as hell ain't sleeping with Malik. Maybe you misunderstood Omar. Maybe he was in a drunken stupor when he told you. Maybe his speech was slurred from being high off weed and you misunderstood him. Whatever the case, Camden and I will talk about this. But I'm sure it's all a lie or a misunderstanding."

Dante stood to leave. He looked like he was disappointed in me for not believing him, but I wasn't going to take his word on this.

"I'll talk to you later," I said as I hurriedly ushered him out my apartment door. I needed to call Camden ASAP.

I can't believe this shit. Camden . . . gay? Pu-lease!

When Dante left, I immediately ran to the phone to call Camden. I got his voice mail. *Damn.*

"Camden, this is Stormy. Call me when you get this message. It's important."

As soon as I hung up, he called right back.

"Hello?"

"Hey, love," Camden said.

"Camden, I really need to talk to you about something important. When can you come over?"

"I'm with Hassan and Jared shootin' some hoops right

now, but I can be over there in about an hour. Why? Is somethin' wrong?"

"I'm a little bothered by something, but I'll talk to you when you get here."

"Are you sure you don't want to talk now?" Camden asked.

"No, I'll wait till you get here. Just hurry up."

"OK, I'll see you in a few. I love you," Camden said.

I hung up.

I spent the next hour pacing and watching the clock. I was worried about how I was going to approach the situation. It weighed heavily on my mind as the clock ticked slowly. My feelings fluctuated between confusion, anger, and fear.

Why would Omar fabricate lies about Camden? Or are they lies? Is Malik gay? Have he and Camden really been messing around? It can't be true. If Camden was gay, why would he ask me to marry him? None of this makes a bit of sense.

As thoughts continued to flutter through my mind, the doorbell rang. It was the moment of truth. I walked to the door and opened it without a smile. I rolled my eyes at Camden, turned around, and walked away, leaving him standing at the door.

"Damn, Stormy. I can't get a kiss?"

"Camden, we need to have a serious talk, and I don't have time to beat around the bush. Sit down." I spoke firmly. Camden looked at me incredulously.

"What's wrong? You look upset."

"I am upset. More upset than you can begin to imagine."

"Well, come sit next to me and tell me what's going on." Concern flooded Camden's face.

"I'm not sittin' down!" I snapped. "I'm too upset to sit."

"Well then, tell me what's going on," he snapped back.

I took a deep breath and slowly exhaled. As much as I'd

practiced what I was going to say, the words still didn't come out easily.

"E-e-earlier today I had a talk with my cousin, Dante. And he had some not-so-good news for me."

"What'd he say?"

"Camden, he told me you were cheating on me."

"Whhhaaaat? Cheatin'on you? Why the hell would he tell you something like that?" he frowned.

"Well, he knows we are in the middle of planning a wedding, you know that big day when we promise to spend the rest of our lives being faithful to one another. He might've figured it would be a good idea for me to know that you weren't being faithful to me before I married you. Ever consider that?" I asked sarcastically.

"Dante's a motherfuckin' liar!" Camden shouted. "He hates me, Stormy, and you know it! He'll make up just about anything to keep you from marrying me. Who did he say told him this shit anyway?"

"I can't tell you that," I said as I looked down at the floor. "But the person is a reliable source."

"What the hell you mean, you can't tell me? I wanna know."

I ignored him. I wasn't telling him a damn thing until I finished dropping my bombshell.

"Camden." I paused and covered my face with my hands. "There's more."

"Oh, God. What other lies did he tell you?"

"He told me you're cheatin' on me with your little brother, Malik," I said as I looked directly in his eyes. I was dying to see his facial expression, looking for signs of guilt or a hint of being busted. There was neither. Instead he laughed.

"I'm cheating on you with Malik?" Camden asked, amused. "I'm cheating on you with Malik? Stormy, I know you don't believe that shit. If I was cheatin' on you with Malik, then that would mean I'm gay, and you know damn well I loves me some coochie, girl! Wasn't I just up in yours last night?" Camden reached out to touch me, but I stepped out of the way. I wasn't in the mood for jokes, and I didn't think there was anything to be laughing about.

"What's wrong with you, girl? I know you don't believe these lies. You of all people know Dante hates me. He's hated me since we were kids running around the church. You know how he's always accused me of thinking I was better than everybody since my parents have money. And things haven't changed now that we're grown. It only makes sense that he'll try his best to break us up. It's a damn shame people have to go to this extreme to come between us. But you can't believe any of this. You can't. It will tear me up inside if you deem these rumors true."

"Camden, I don't know what to believe at this point."

I wanted to believe Camden, but I needed more information. I needed to get to the bottom of the rumor. Then it hit me. Leigh. She was extremely close with Malik. I realized I could ask her to investigate the whole mess for me. If anything was going on between Camden and Malik, Leigh would find out for me. Camden interrupted my thoughts.

"What the fuck do you mean, you don't know what to believe? Are you gonna believe your cousin, the cousin that's been hatin' on me for years, over me?"

"Camden, stop yellin' and cursin' at me! That's right! You heard me loud and clear. I don't know what to believe! But I have someone doing some investigating," I lied. "I'm waiting to hear back from someone very soon."

"Fuck this!" Camden threw his hands up in the air and got in my face.

"I'm truly disappointed that you think I'm cheatin' on you—topping it off with a goddamn man. That's some bullshit! I'm leavin' before I say some things I might regret.

Once you and your little PI friends finish playing Sherlock Holmes, call me. I'll be waiting for your apology."

Without saying another word, he was gone. He slammed the door in my face. I just fell against it and cried. This was supposed to be the happiest time in my life, not a time to be faced with the accusations that my fiancé was gay. *Could this really be true?* I really didn't have the answer, but one thing was for sure, I wasn't letting it fly. I was on a mission for the truth, and for Camden's sake, he needed to be the one speaking it. I was not the one to be played with. I planned to make sure he had hell to pay.

Minutes after Camden's departure, I called Leigh and begged her to come over right away. She was out with Dominique and Nicole at the mall. She must have heard how upset I was because she asked me what was wrong. I told her I'd tell her when they arrived. She told me they were on the way. I didn't call them to pick out floral arrangements for the wedding, but instead because I needed my friends desperately after the information I had gotten from Dante. I needed other opinions. I needed shoulders to cry on and most of all I needed to ask Leigh to do some probing for me.

"Stormy, what's going on?" Leigh asked, rushing in my front door with Nicole and Dominique trailing behind. "You sounded upset on the phone."

"I am upset. And pissed off. And confused. And scared. And a whole lot of other shit. I'm just fucked up in the head right now."

"Tell us what's going on," Dominique said.

"All right. Sit down, 'cause you won't believe what my cousin Dante came over here to tell me."

"What?" Nicole asked.

I lowered my head. It was so hard to bring myself to even say the words Camden and gay in the same sentence.

"OK. He came over to warn me about marrying Camden. He said that he heard from his boy, Omar, that Camden is cheatin' on me."

"What?" Nicole asked, looking dumbfounded. "He's doing what?"

"Dante said Camden's cheating on me. And that's not the worst part." I shook my head from side to side in disbelief. "You won't believe who he's supposedly cheating with . . ."

"Who?" they shouted in unison.

"His so-called little brother, Malik."

"Malik! Malik who?" Leigh questioned, obviously shocked.

"Your Malik. Malik Blackwell, Sister Blackwell's grandson."

"Well, if he's supposedly cheating on you with Malik, does that mean he's gay?" Dominique inquired.

"That's what Dante says. But I don't believe Camden's gay. He can't be. He and Malik are like brothers. I guess being close friends with another male these days makes you gay, huh?" I asked, trying to convince myself.

"This is some crazy shit," Nicole said. "Have you talked to Camden about this?"

"Yeah. He just left. He denies everything and is pissed off with me for not believing him."

"Why don't you believe him?" Dominique asked.

"Honestly, I hope all of this is a bunch of lies. I want Camden to be telling the truth. But why would Dante lie to me? Why would he and Omar make up something so horrible?"

"I feel you on that, Storm. I don't think they'd manufacture such a horrific story just to keep you from marrying Camden. I'm sorry to say this, but it might be true. You know I've always told you I thought Camden was shady. I wasn't thinkin' gay, but there's just something about him. Something in his eyes makes me think he's not always on the up and up," Nicole said. I cut my eyes at her.

"This is not a Camden bashing session, Nicole," I barked. "I'm lookin' for advice. I want to know what y'all think I should do. Camden says it's not true. Dante and Omar say it is. I just don't know who's telling the truth."

"You need to find out if your man is a fruit!" Nicole asserted. I didn't respond. I rolled my eyes at her, letting her know I didn't appreciate her calling Camden a fruit.

I looked over at Leigh, who hadn't said much since I told them the news.

"Leigh, why haven't you said anything? Don't you think this is messed up?"

"Yeah, it's messed up," Leigh said with a sigh.

"What's up with you? Why you looking like that? Do you know something we don't?" Nicole asked, looking at her strangely.

"No, I don't know anything about Camden being gay, nor have I heard he was messing around with Malik, but I have heard some other things."

"What have you heard?" I asked, looking surprised.

"Well, I don't know how true it is, but I recently heard that Malik was gay. There are rumors that he had sex with some guy from his school. I really don't know if it's true, though, but I've always kind of thought Malik was gay."

"Hell, he might be. That boy is always hangin' out with a bunch of women at the church, including you, Leigh. So either he's gay or a playa, and we all know Malik Blackwell ain't no playa," Nicole joked.

"Leigh," I said, looking at her sincerely. "You and Malik have a close relationship. Would you call him and ask him about all of this? He may open up to you and tell you the truth."

"I don't think I really want to get involved," she responded.

"Get involved? What the hell do you mean you don't want to get involved? If that punk is gay and has been bumping butts with Stormy's man, she has a right to know!" Nicole hissed.

"Yeah, Leigh, I want you to call him and find out what you can, do something investigating for me. I would have never in a million years suspected that Malik was out there like that, but if it is true, then the friendship between him and Camden has to cease immediately. That's probably the reason this rumor got started. Malik is probably a homo, and because he hangs out with Camden, people assume both of them are."

"That's a good point, Stormy," Dominique agreed. Nicole smirked. I guess she realized I was grasping at straws, not wanting to believe Camden's sexuality might be in question.

"All right. I'll find out what I can. I'm gonna call Malik when I get home," Leigh finally agreed.

"You better hope Camden hasn't gotten to him first," Dominique chimed in. "He could've threatened him into not talking."

"You may be right, but I may be able to get him to open up to me. We'll see. I'll call him as soon as I walk in the door."

"Oh hell no you won't, Leigh. Don't call him. Just show up," Nicole ordered. "Don't ask him nothin' over the phone. You need to be lookin' him dead in the face to see if he's lyin' or not."

"Yeah, Leigh, just go over there. Don't give him any warnings or time to get his story straight. Catch him off guard," I suggested.

"All right, y'all. Stop telling me how to handle this. I've got it under control."

"Well look, I've just got one piece of advice," Nicole said. When you ask Malik about this shit, look at his eyes when he responds. If his eyes roll up and shift to the right, he's lyin! Then immediately call Stormy and yell 'code ten' into the phone. Stormy, that's your cue to get a knife from the kitchen, hop in your car, drive over to Camden's apartment, and do a Lorena Bobbitt on his ass." We all laughed at Nicole.

"Girl, you're one crazy broad!" I said.

Nicole sucked her teeth and gave us a y'all-think-I'm-joking look.

"I ain't crazy, but I'd make sure he wouldn't be sticking his thang up in nobody else. Shit, you don't play with people's emotions or lives like that. If you're gay, then be gay. But don't fake the funk. I can't stand fakers and if Camden's being dishonest about his sexuality, then he ought to have his sex organ tossed on the side of the road like a bubble-gum wrapper."

Nicole had a point. If Camden had been lying to me about his sexuality, then he was due his just desserts, but I couldn't plan the consequences just yet. I needed to find out more information. I had to wait to hear back from Leigh.

Leigh set out to go talk to Malik. She told me she would call me as soon as she talked to him. I had no idea if Leigh would be successful in resolving this matter for me, but I knew I'd be on pins and needles until I heard back from her.

Chapter 7

Malik

The phone rang. I was lounging on the couch, watching my favorite movie, *Antoine Fisher*. I didn't really want to be disturbed until I eyed the caller ID and saw Camden's number.

"Hello?"

"Who the hell have you been talkin' to?" It was Camden. He sounded irate. And since he'd called coming off at me wrong, I decided to mess with him.

"Who the fuck is this?" I asked, playing dumb.

"Don't play with me, Malik! You know who the fuck this is! Who have you been running your mouth to?" Camden shouted in my ear.

"First of all, you need to calm down! When you call me, you betta come correct. Second of all, you need to explain whatcha talkin' about?"

"You know damn well what I'm talking about! Who did you tell that you and I were messing around?" Camden demanded to know.

"Man, Camden, get the fuck outta here! I ain't told nobody jack and I don't appreciate you callin' me asking me some bullshit like this!" I was livid that he was blaming me about our relationship getting out. I really hadn't said anything to anyone.

"Well, when we fuck, we're the only two in the room, so who the hell else told, Malik?" Camden questioned. "I sure as hell didn't tell anybody. So, it must have been you!"

"You need to calm down with that shit! Why the hell would I tell anybody? Why would I put myself out there? That's just plain stupid! Think about that shit and call me back when it sinks in!" I was about to hang up when I heard Camden yelling.

"Wait! Wait! Don't hang up!" Camden yelled. "If it wasn't you, then how did Stormy's cousin, Dante, find out?"

"What does he know or think he knows?" I was curious as hell now.

"He told Stormy that someone told him that I was cheatin' on her—with you!"

"What? Who told Dante that?"

"I don't know. That's why I'm calling you."

"Look, Camden, man, like I said, I ain't told nobody nothin' and I definitely wouldn't say anything to Dante. So, we need to figure out how this got out."

"Yeah, we do, but until then, we need to take a break from each other," Camden said sternly.

"Why?" I yelled into the phone.

"What you mean, why? Shouldn't the reasons be evident? Somebody knows somethin' about you and me, and that somebody told Dante, who in turn told Stormy, and Lord only knows who Stormy is going to tell. Besides, Stormy is pissed at me, the wedding may be in jeopardy, and I don't need this mess getting out any more than it already has." Camden sighed. I could hear fear in his voice. "Do I also have to remind you that my father is a minister and pastor of a major congregation and it would kill him and my mother if they heard about this, not to mention their reputations in the community?"

"So, when did you start caring about your parents' feelings, or Stormy's feelings for that matter? We've been messing around since you were in college. I put my life on hold and waited for you while you were away at school. After you graduated, you decided not to come back home and I still waited for you. Now I have you back in my life and you want to cut me off again? Oh hell no! I love you, Camden. You were my first and only love, and I don't think I can make it without you. I've experienced things with you that I never have with anyone else, and now all of a sudden it's over? I don't think so! Not this time. I'm tired of being the one who loses out. Maybe you need to stop trippin' and face reality. You are gay!" I was pissed and I wasn't finished.

"And let me tell you something else, Mr. Camden Xavier Brooks, I put up with your lyin' ass when you told me that Stormy meant nothing to you. Then all of a sudden, a chick who meant nothing to you was hanging out with us during our quality time together. Then out of the blue, you propose to her. Once again, I sat back and watched the man I love plan a fuckin' wedding without sayin' a word. But today, I am gonna say something 'cause I'm tired of your shit. You make me sick!"

"Malik, listen," Camden said in a mellow tone, "you know I love you with all my heart, but I love Stormy, too. You know I can't ever be with you because of what my family will think. Hell, does your grandmother know about you?"

I didn't respond because the answer was no.

"Yeah, that's what I thought. I'm going to marry Stormy no matter what. She's good for me and to me."

"If she's so good then why are you still fuckin' wit me while you are engaged to her?"

"That's my point exactly. This is all too much for me, and

with someone out here yapping their gums about us, I have no idea what's bound to happen next. So, Malik, we've got to end this now. Please know that I love you, but I have to marry Stormy."

I couldn't believe he had the nerve to sound sincere as he said that ridiculous crap to me.

"Camden, is that your final answer?" I asked sarcastically.

"Yes, Malik, that is my final answer. I love you, but we can't be together anymore. Please make sure you don't tell a soul about us. Take this shit to the grave."

"Have a nice life!" I scoffed and hung up the phone. I was crushed, but Camden was sadly mistaken if he thought he could get rid of me that easily.

Camden pissed me off. I didn't know why he thought he could keep playing me like his yo-yo.

I was too wired to sit around the house, so I got dressed to head out to the bar. I needed something to help me get my thoughts together. *I have to find a way to get Camden back in my life*, I thought as I snatched a pair of jeans and a T-shirt out of my closet.

As I was getting dressed, there was a knock at the door. I didn't go downstairs to answer it because I figured it wasn't for me. I hoped it would be Camden coming to say he was sorry for breaking things off with me, but I didn't think so. Then I heard my grandmother call my name.

"Yes, Grandma?"

"Leigh is here to see you. Do you want her to come up to your room?"

"Yeah, Grandma, she can come up," I said, not too pleased about her unannounced visit.

Why is Leigh over here? I really wasn't in the mood for company. I wanted to get to the bar, have a drink, and sort some things out. Leigh appeared at my door, not acting her usual bubbly self.

"Hey, Malik," she said in a sullen tone. "It looks like you're on your way out. Do you have a few minutes to talk?"

"What's up, Leigh? I was on my way to the bar, but I have a few minutes for you."

I had met Leigh a few years ago, right after Camden returned to New York and dropped me like a hot potato. For some reason, she reached out to me and asked if she could adopt me as her younger brother. Seeing as how I didn't have a mentor in Camden any longer, I latched on to Leigh and the rest was history.

"Thanks," Leigh said, sounding as if she had a lot on her mind. "Do you mind if I close the door?"

"Naw. Go 'head."

"I apologize for coming over unexpectedly, but I really need to talk to you face to face," Leigh said solemnly.

"About what? Sounds serious."

"It is, Malik. It's very serious." She looked like she had the weight of the world on her shoulders, and she seemed a bit hesitant to say whatever it was that she had come to say.

"Tell me what's going on," I said, anxious to know the nature of her visit.

"I'm not sure if you've heard, but Stormy and Camden are having some problems—problems involving you," she said as she looked at me.

"What the hell do I have to do with Stormy and Camden's problems?" I asked, knowing the answer to my own question.

Leigh walked over and sat on the edge of my bed. She softly patted the space beside her, signaling me to sit. I did. She reached for my hand and grabbed it gently. She looked into my eyes and spoke.

"Malik, Stormy was told recently that Camden was being unfaithful to her." She paused. I nodded my head for her to continue. I wanted to know more, although I suspected where this conversation was headed.

"She was told he was cheating on her with you." I widened my eyes and raised my eyebrows in shock.

"Me? Me? Where'd she get that bogus info from?"

"Her cousin, Dante. He knows somebody who supposedly saw you and Camden in a compromising position at Camden's job."

I dropped my head and stared at the floor. I didn't know someone had actually seen us. I thought someone had started this 'rumor' based on hearsay or suspicions, not anything remotely close to the truth.

Leigh placed her hand under my chin and raised my head. She looked into my eyes.

"Malik, you're my fam, so I need you tell me the truth. Have you been involved with Camden in any way other than as friends?"

"No, Leigh," I responded defensively. I got up and walked over to my dresser. I wasn't looking for anything in particular, just trying to avoid eye contact with Leigh. I was fearful my face would reveal my lies. Leigh walked up behind me and gently turned me around to face her.

"Look at me," she said sternly. "Tell me the truth! Are you or have you ever been involved with Camden?"

"Why would you ask me something like that? You know you and Camden are the closest people I've ever had to siblings. He's my brother just like you're my sister. Does that mean I've been involved with you, too?" I laid it on thick, but wasn't really sure if I sounded believable.

"Don't give me that bull, Malik! I've heard the rumors about you being gay before. I never wanted to believe them, but now these accusations about you and Camden have surfaced. I need to know the real deal. So, look at me in my eyes and tell me the truth."

I looked intently into Leigh's eyes, prepared to mouth the words that Camden and I have not been involved, but I couldn't. I couldn't say it if I had to look her in her eyes.

She'd surely know I was lying. So, I decided to do the un-thinkable—I told her the truth.

"It's true," I whispered.

"What did you say?" she asked.

"It's true—about Camden and me." I spoke with more volume this time.

Leigh's jaw dropped. Her eyes were the size of golf balls.

"It's true? It's . . . it's really true?" Her voice trembled.

"Yeah, it's true. The stories you've heard aren't rumors." I walked over to the other side of the room. I couldn't stand looking at the surprised expression Leigh wore on her face.

"How long? How long has this been going on between you and Camden?"

"Leigh, I really don't think you want to know all of the details. It's too involved and if I tell you everything, a lot of people will be affected. I've never told anybody but Cam-den that I was gay. If I open up to you, then I might be sub-jecting myself to being ostracized by my family, friends, and people at church."

"Malik, I will not look at you any differently. I promise. You can open up to me," she said sincerely.

After thinking for a brief moment, I decided to spill my guts. I trusted Leigh and I needed to get this off my chest. Leigh sat down on my bed again and I sat in the chaise lounge chair on the other side of my bedroom.

With great difficulty, I opened up to Leigh. I explained that the relationship between Camden and me started when I was in high school—after Camden became my mentor. I soon realized that some of my problems in school stemmed from me struggling with my sexuality. I had never told any-body until I got close with Camden. He was just so easy to talk to. So, one day, I told him that I thought I was attracted to men. He didn't seem surprised at all. In fact, he said he knew all along. Then he shocked me and told me that he was bisexual—he was attracted to both women and men. I was floored.

It was after my confession that our relationship changed. We continued to do our usual hanging out, but when he dropped me off at home, our nights ended differently. He started giving me kisses before I got out of the car. I had never had an experience with a man or a woman, but those kisses made me feel good. I wanted more. We then took it to the next level. We no longer went shopping or to the movies. Instead, we would go to a hotel.

During our first hotel rendezvous, I had my first sexual experience—ever. When we settled into the room, we ordered pizza and watched a little television. I couldn't really concentrate because I was anxious about what was going to happen next. Out of nowhere, Camden turned to me and asked if I wanted him to please me. I eagerly said yes. He unbuckled my belt and pulled my pants down. He then lay me on the bed and climbed on top of me. We kissed affectionately until he moved his way down toward my manhood and started to please me orally. I had never felt such ecstasy in my life. I then returned the favor. I had no idea what I was doing, but Camden was a good teacher. He made sure to educate me on how to please him. Before long, he came all over the bed.

After regaining his composure, he lay on top of me again and asked if I was ready for him to enter me. I told him yeah, although I was a little apprehensive. When he tried initially, it hurt like hell, but Camden had a remedy for the pain. He pulled a bottle of lotion from his bag and massaged me. Before I knew it, Camden was inside me and we were going at it. The sex was so good that I really didn't want it to end, but Camden erupted and we were done. From that moment on, I was hooked.

We snuggled and talked for a while after we were done.

Camden started asking questions like: How did it feel? Was it good? Did I regret it? I told him I enjoyed every bit of it and that I hoped it would continue. Before we left the hotel he made me promise not to tell anyone. Camden explained to me that if his mother and father ever found out they would disown him. He also explained how crushed my grandmother would be if she found out because she had a lot of respect for Camden because of all he did to help me improve in school. I agreed never to tell anyone. We kissed and then left the hotel room. It's ironic that when Camden came home from New York, he became the manager of that same hotel.

Leigh sat in silence with her hand cupped over her mouth after I finished telling her everything. I wasn't sure if she was in shock or if she was going to throw up.

"Are you OK?" After a few seconds, she spoke.

"I'm at a loss for words. I just don't believe this. You and Camden? I would have never thought that Camden would take advantage of you like that. He's the one who turned you out!"

"Shhh, Leigh. I don't want my grandmother to hear you. Camden didn't turn me out. I always knew I was gay. It was Camden that made me finally face the truth," I said matter-of-factly.

"So what happened when he went back to school? Did you two continue to have sex?"

"No, not really. He basically dumped me. When he decided to stay in New York I was mad as hell, but I decided to go on with my life."

"Have you dated any other men?"

"Nope. I've only been with Camden. So those rumors you said you heard before aren't true. Those must be suspicions."

"I'm so sorry that you've been going through this. It's ob-

vious that bitch Camden only thinks about himself and nobody else. Have the two of you been seeing each other since
he's come back from New York?"

"Yup. We've been meeting at least two or three times a
week at the same hotel where he works. The whole time
he's been plannin' to marry Stormy, he's been fuckin' me."

"This motherfucker has to be stopped. He can't continue
to play you and Stormy! We can't let him get away with
this," Leigh said, pissed.

"Yes we can, Leigh. It's over between Camden and me." I
explained my earlier conversation with Camden. I told her
how he cut me off and begged me not to tell a soul about
our relationship.

"So why did you tell me?" she questioned.

"Yo, I didn't want to. But you kept asking me to look you
in the eyes and I knew you'd see right through me. Besides,
I trust that you can keep this between us. Right?"

"Malik, you know I've got to tell Stormy. She's my friend
and I can't let her marry Camden after what I just learned
from you."

"No! You can't tell Stormy," I said excitedly.

"Why not? She needs to know, Malik. She's engaged to a
gay man. I can't let her make the huge mistake of marrying
him. What kind of friend would I be if I didn't tell her?" I
took a deep breath.

"Leigh, if you tell Stormy, then she may tell someone
else, and I don't want this to get out. I don't want my grandmother or anybody at church finding out. Please promise
me you won't tell Stormy."

"I don't know if I can make you that promise, Malik.
What if the shoe was on the other foot? Wouldn't you want
to know? It's only fair that she knows. But I'll be very careful how I present things to her. I'll let her know it's not your
fault."

"All right, Leigh. I'm not comfortable with this, but please warn me before you tell her. I need to prepare myself for the backlash once she finds out."

"OK, I promise to keep you informed."

"Good. Well, I'm on my way out to get that drink I so desperately need. Camden really fucked with me tonight and I need to try to clear my head."

"You really love him, don't you?"

"Yeah, I do."

"Well, don't drink too much if you're gonna drive."

"I won't." I kissed Leigh on the cheek and she left. I heard her downstairs talking to my grandmother while I put on my tennis shoes. I wondered when she was going to tell Stormy the truth about Camden and me. Even though I acted as if I didn't want Stormy to know, deep down I really did. There was no way Stormy would ever marry Camden if she knew he was bisexual. She would surely break things off with him, and then I could finally have him all to myself.

Although I secretly hoped Leigh would divulge everything to Stormy, I wondered about the ramifications when this secret got out.

Chapter 8

Stormy

Camden called all day, every day, but I couldn't conceive speaking to him at the moment. There was really nothing he could say to me. Until I could find out if Leigh got any information out of Malik, Camden and I had nothing to talk about.

My parents called to ask if I'd stop by to visit them, but I couldn't face them. I was too down in the dumps, and I didn't want them to see me that way. Besides, if they found out about the rumors of Camden being gay, they'd try to hurt him or have my brothers do something to him. I just didn't need to heighten the situation with more drama, so until I had more facts, my family had to remain in the dark

I arrived at Leigh's house around six o'clock in the evening. She invited me over because she wanted to talk about what she had discussed with Malik. She opened the door before I could ring the doorbell.

"Hi, Stormy! Come on in, girl."

"Hi, Leigh," I said dryly.

"Do you want something to drink?" she offered.

"No, thanks. I'm here to find out what Malik had to say. I've been terrified of having this conversation with you because my gut tells me your news isn't good. So let's cut out the idle conversation and get to the point. What did Malik have to say?" I asked nervously. I held out hope that she had good news to share.

Leigh joined me on the couch and looked into my eyes sympathetically. I could tell she was burdened—her face said it all. My hope faded. My heart pounded. My palms were sweaty. I knew she was about to drop the bomb on me.

"Stormy, I did speak with Malik last night about this Camden situation. I also just left a message for him on his voicemail letting him know that you and I would be talking today."

"Why'd you call him? Why does he need to know that you're talking to me?"

"Because, I didn't want to betray him. You know we're just as close as you and I are. So this isn't easy for me because I love both of y'all."

Tears welled up in Leigh's eyes. Her tears confirmed my worst fears. I felt my eyes stinging as I, too, was about to cry.

"Stormy, you're the sister I've never had and I would have had a heavy burden withholding this information from you." Leigh wiped her tears.

"Camden's been fucking with Malik, hasn't he?" I asked, already knowing the answer to my question.

"Yes, Stormy," Leigh whispered softly. "They've been having sex since Malik was in high school, around the time Camden became his mentor."

"What?" I screamed in shock.

"It's true. Camden took advantage of Malik when he was younger and now he's been stringing him along all these years. Since Camden's return to Baltimore, they've been meeting at the hotel where Camden now works. He's also been having sex with Camden since Camden proposed to you."

"You got to be kiddin' me. Even now? They're messin' around now?"

"Supposedly Camden just broke it off with him. They are no longer together.

Malik says he's hurt because he really loves Camden."

"Love? Love? They love each other?"

"Well, I'm not sure how Camden feels about Malik, but Malik is caught up."

"This is sick! My freakin' fiancé is having sex with another man." I felt like I was going to throw up all over Leigh's white couch. "Why would he do this to me, Leigh?" I wailed. "What have I ever done to him for him to treat me like this? I can't believe this shit. I hate him! I hate him! We're planning to get married and he's out here fucking a man!"

"Stormy, look at me!" Leigh said, grabbing my shoulders. "You need to get yourself together and go talk to Camden. He needs to tell you the truth. Go and see him. Demand that he tell you the truth." Leigh's voice was firm. I snatched my purse from the couch.

"This shit is unacceptable and I am on my way to tell him just how unacceptable it is. He better hope and pray that my Club isn't in the car, because I just might bust his head with it."

"Do you need me to go with you? I don't want you to wind up in jail," Leigh said.

"No, I'll be fine. I'll call you later." I stormed out of Leigh's townhouse and ran to my car.

I felt like I was on an emotional rollercoaster. This shit just kept getting worse and worse. I would have never suspected all of this would have been happening after getting my visit from Dante.

As I drove to Camden's apartment, I thought about all the ways I could physically hurt him. I thought about cutting his throat, slicing off one of his testicles, or sticking a knife in his asshole. Then I realized that I might go to jail, as Leigh suggested, and I didn't want that.

I hadn't called Camden to tell him I was on my way. I was just going to pop up and if he had his ass in the air when I arrived, he better hope I wasn't armed with a weapon.

When I drove up, I saw his car parked outside his building. *Good, he's home.* I walked up to his door and knocked like I was a police officer busting into a crack house. He answered the door and looked at me as if I were an alien.

"Stormy, why are you knocking on my door like you're crazy?" he asked with an attitude.

I didn't even answer. I brushed past him and entered his apartment. He slammed the door.

"What are you doing here? I've been calling you for two days and you haven't returned any of my calls. Now you just show up at my apartment busting in like a madwoman. So, I ask again, what are you doing here?" Camden looked furious. I didn't give a damn. He had some explaining to do.

"I'm the one asking the questions here, you lying son of a bitch! I have a few questions of my own, and if I were you, I'd tell the truth."

"What are you—"

"Shut the hell up! I told you I'm asking the questions, dammit." I got right up in his face. "Have you ever had sex with Malik?"

"Hell, no!" he said as he backed away from me. "Stormy, I told you that shit your cousin said ain't true."

"This has nothing to do with Dante, but everything to do with what Malik told Leigh." I studied his face, but there were no changes in his expression. "That's right, Camden, Malik told Leigh everything. He told her how you have been fuckin' him since high school, the fact that you've been fuckin' him since you proposed to me, and that the hotel where you work is the place where all this fuckin' takes place. So, what do you have to say, Camden? Why don't you just admit that you're a faggot?" Camden was silent for a minute, then spoke calmly.

"Once again, you have succeeded in allowing someone else to poison your mind with garbage. I'll tell you this one last time and then I'm not saying it again: I am not gay! I don't know what the hell Malik told Leigh, and what Leigh told you, but it's all lies. I'm sick and tired of all these people getting involved in our relationship. None of our friends are married, so don't you think they might just be a little jealous of our happiness? That includes Leigh and Malik. I think you should be smart enough to notice when someone is tryin' to sabotage our relationship. Now, you're here with me, all upset and shit, and where are your friends? Where's Malik? Where's Dante? They're probably sittin' at home having a good laugh on you. You're allowing them to fuck up this relationship and I'm extremely disappointed in you. I thought you were better than that."

"So, are you saying it's all a lie?" I asked, giving him an evil stare.

"Yes, Stormy, it's all a lie. If I wanted to be with someone else, I wouldn't be marrying you, baby. You've got to believe that. I'm not cheating and I'm surely not gay."

I hoped Camden didn't think he was getting off that easily. His little speech would not do. I needed to know more.

"Camden, I'm not comfortable with all of this. You say one thing and Malik is saying another. The only way to get to the bottom of this is for the three of us to talk."

"For what?" Camden asked defensively. "So he can tell more lies?"

"Well, if he is telling lies, then I want you to tell him that to his face," I said as I pulled out my cell phone. As I dialed a telephone number, Camden asked me who I was calling. I ignored him.

"Hi, Sister Jones." Sister Jones was the church's secretary. "It's me, Stormy. I'm doing fine. I'm calling because I would like to make an appointment to see Reverend Brooks as soon as possible. It's urgent."

Camden was waving his hands in my face and I just turned my back on him. "Tomorrow evening? At seven o'clock? OK, I'll be there. Oh, and can you please let him know that Camden and Malik will be with me? Thanks, Sister Jones. I really appreciate it. You have a good evening, too. Bye." I flipped my cell phone closed and I turned to face Camden with a sinister grin. He looked as if he had seen a ghost.

"Why did you make an appointment with my father for tomorrow night?"

"Because one of you low down dirty bastards is lying, and I am gonna get to the bottom of it. Since Reverend Brooks knows us all well, I figured he could probably determine which one of you is lying," I said with a smirk.

"Stormy, you know I don't like my parents in my business. I'm not meeting with my father tomorrow night at the church! You can go, but I'm not!" Camden was emphatic.

"Oh, yes you will, or I am cancelling the wedding. Now try me!"

"Stormy, I—" I cut him off.

"Have your ass at True Gospel tomorrow night at seven o'clock or else!" I walked out the door and didn't look back.

I also planned to contact Malik as soon as I got home to inform him of the meeting as well. I wanted him to refuse to attend because I had a little ultimatum for him, too. I was not worried, though. They'd both show up and hopefully we'd get to the truth!

Chapter 9

Malik

What in the world have I gotten myself into? I thought after hanging up with Stormy. She called irate and hysterical after she learned about my relationship with Camden. Thankfully, Leigh called to leave a message letting me know she planned to talk to Stormy, so I wasn't totally caught off guard when Stormy rang my phone. However, I was surprised by the tongue lashing she gave me as if I were the only one at fault. Had she called Camden and laid into him as well?

I listened to her rant and rave about how I ruined her relationship. I didn't appreciate her audacity to call my house and I definitely wasn't in the mood for her tantrum, so I interrupted her.

"Listen, Stormy, I realize you're upset, but I'm not the one you need to be talking to. Camden is your fiancé, not me, so please take all this drama to him. I don't wanna hear it." She ignored me.

"I've talked to Camden and he denies everything. He said you were lying."

All I could do was laugh. Leave it to Camden to make me out to be the bad guy.

"Is what you told Leigh true?" Stormy asked.

"Whatever I told Leigh is between us and I'd prefer not to discuss that with you."

"Then maybe you'd prefer to discuss it with Reverend Brooks."

"Reverend Brooks? What does he have to do with this?"

"Either one or both you and Camden are liars. So to get to the bottom of this, I've scheduled a meeting with Reverend Brooks to bring all this mess to a head."

"I'm not meetin' with Reverend Brooks or you. There ain't nothing I gotta say. Camden is your fiancé. You deal with it. Keep me outta this mess."

"Be at True Gospel tomorrow evening at seven o'clock sharp or I'll be sure Sister Blackwell hears all about this. Now try me!" She banged the phone down in my ear.

I was fucked. I wanted Leigh to tell Stormy about Camden and me, hoping they would break up. The last thing I ever expected was for this to be taken to Reverend Brooks or my grandmother. If she ever found out that I was gay, she'd be heartbroken, and I didn't want that. Reluctantly I succumbed to attending the meeting, but I wasn't happy about it. Actually I was on the verge of shitting bricks.

I called Leigh to tell her about Stormy's phone call. I wondered if she'd known all along that Stormy was going to take this to our pastor.

"Leigh, your girl Stormy called me bitching about me messing around with Camden. She was livid. And she's scheduled a meeting with Reverend Brooks tomorrow. Had I known she was gonna take it to this extreme, I would've never told you. I regret ever telling you now, 'cause I got a funny feeling this is about to get ugly."

"I'm so sorry, Malik. I had no idea she was going to contact Reverend Brooks either. But you've got to understand her position. She's engaged to a man who she's been told is a homosexual. He says it's a lie. You say it's true. She doesn't know what to believe, but in her heart she wants to believe you're the one lying. She's trying to seek the truth and I guess she figured Reverend Brooks, someone we all know, love, and respect, will resolve this matter by getting to the truth."

"There's got to be a better way. I don't want to meet with the pastor. What the hell am I supposed to say? Um, Reverend Brooks, I want you to know that I've been having sex with your son," I said sarcastically.

"No, Malik, don't say that. Just go in there and tell the truth. Reverend Brooks is a man of God. He will love you regardless. He may not like this situation, but he won't turn his back on you."

"I'm a little nervous about all of this, but there is nothing I can do but tell the truth. Just keep me in your prayers, Leigh, because I have a feeling that Camden is gonna lie about everything, making me look like a fool. And if he does, I'm gonna punch him in his motherfuckin' mouth." Leigh started laughing.

"Malik, don't hit him. Just call him on all his lies."

Just then my phone beeped. Someone was calling on my other line. I spied the caller ID. It was Camden's cell phone number.

"Leigh, I'll call you back later." I clicked over. "What the fuck do you want?"

"Malik, listen. I didn't call you to argue. I just want to know if Stormy called you."

"Yeah, she called. Why?" I was being short with him.

"Did she ask you to go meet with my father?"

"Yup. Why?" I was short again.

"Are you gonna go?"

"I have no choice. Your witch of a fiancé threatened to tell my grandmother about us if I didn't show up."

"Malik, I'm begging you, please don't confess anything in that meeting. I don't want my father to know about any of this, so please don't reveal anything about our relationship. OK?" Camden was really begging hard and I was getting a kick out of it.

"How am I supposed to sit in the house of the Lord and lie to a man of God?"

"Don't worry about all of that. I lie to him all the time. It's easy," Camden said, sounding real slick. *Who brags about lying to their parents?*

"That's why you are so fucked up now. Maybe if you stopped lyin' all the time, shit would go right in your life."

"Whatever, Malik. Just don't tell my father anything about us. We'll just act like we have no idea where these rumors are coming from. We'll deny, deny, and deny. OK? Promise me that, please."

"All right, Camden, whatever you say." I slammed the phone down in his ear.

The nerve of him to ask me to promise him something when all he had ever done was make and break promises to me. Please! I had no idea what I was going to say when I got in Reverend Brooks's office tomorrow. My mind was telling me to lie about everything—to keep my lifestyle tucked away in the closet. But my heart was telling me to tell the truth, hoping that this would cause Stormy and Camden's relationship to end, leaving him open for me. Either way, there would be a lot at stake.

The meeting tomorrow weighed heavily on me. I was drained. I was burdened. I decided to do something I hadn't done in a while. I prayed. I asked God to lead me in the right direction, to give me the right words to say. And before I got up off my knees, I had my answer. I knew exactly what I was going to say.

Chapter 10

Stormy

I was sick—mentally and physically. I couldn't go to work, so I called my school and left a message on the secretary's voicemail, letting her know I wouldn't be in. Then I called the substitute teacher hotline to put in a request to cover my classes due to my absence.

I couldn't sleep a wink the previous night, tossing and turning because I was worried about the meeting with Reverend Brooks later that day. When I finally did close my eyes to sleep, I was awakened at four o'clock in the morning with severe stomach cramps, followed by a bad case of diarrhea. I must've gone back and forth to the bathroom ten times before the bubbling in my stomach subsided.

"Damn you, Camden." I cursed him under my breath. I hated that he had put me in this situation of uncertainty. My heart wanted desperately to believe that the rumors weren't true, but the statistics said otherwise. I had Omar, Dante, and Malik, through a supposed confession, saying that my fiancé was indeed a gay man. Then there was only one person who said the opposite, and that was Camden, the person who stood to lose out more than anyone in this situation, thus his reason for being untruthful. At this point, I didn't know what or who to believe, but I was certain it would all come out by seven o'clock.

After I finally got over my bout with diarrhea, Nicole called and asked if she could take me to lunch. She sensed that I would be uneasy about tonight and wanted to help get my mind off the upcoming conference. We met for lunch at Pizzeria Uno restaurant in the Pratt Street Pavilion at the Inner Harbor.

"So, how's it going?" Nicole asked. "Is your stomach feeling any better?"

"A little. I've stopped running to the bathroom, but now my butt is raw from wiping all morning."

"TMI, Stormy. Too much information." She laughed.

We sat in silence for a few seconds before she spoke.

"Do you want to talk about it? If you do, I'm here to listen. If you don't, we don't have to."

I rested my elbows on the table and covered my face with my hands. I wasn't crying, but I was weary, worried, and stressed.

"I'm scared, Nicole. I'm scared it's all going to be true."

"I know you are, but look on the bright side, if you find out Camden's been lying about his sexual orientation, you can get out now. Some women don't find out that their husband's been living a down low lifestyle until after they've been married for years and have a couple of kids. So consider yourself blessed if you find out Camden's been frontin'. Then you can move on and find someone else who's *straight* and will appreciate you enough not to lie to you."

Nicole and I talked for hours. We had long since finished our pizza and salads, but I needed the distraction and the pep talk. She even made me burst into laughter when she discovered a thong that she had been searching for was in her pants pocket. It seemed that she had put it there after a tryst with her ex-boyfriend and forgot where it was. So when she washed her jeans, the thongs were still in the pocket. Needless to say, the embarrassment on her face when she reached in her pocket looking for her lip gloss, only to pull out the thongs instead, made me laugh so hard that blood vessels popped out of my forehead.

Just moments before we departed, she informed me that she had a secret, something she had wanted to tell me for a while, but never had the nerve to verbalize. Surprisingly, she told me she had a crush on Camden's friend, Jared.

"You what?" I asked. "You can't stand Camden, so I'm shocked that you'd be interested in anybody connected to him."

"Girl, that man is fine! I'd like to ride his pony morning, noon, and night."

I suggested trying to hook them up, but she quickly shot me down.

"In light of what's going on with Camden right now, I'll pass. This situation makes his entire crew suspect."

"I understand," I said and dropped my head. Nicole's statement brought my thoughts right back to what was about to happen in just a few hours.

Before Nicole and I parted, she prayed with me, hugged me, and instructed me to call as soon as I got home.

I arrived at the church at six-fifty PM. I didn't see Camden's or Malik's car in the church parking lot. I wondered if my threats had gotten to them or if they had decided to blow me off. I walked into the church office and informed Sister Jones that I was there for the meeting. She told me that Reverend Brooks was on a conference call and he would be finished in a few minutes.

As I nervously waited for Camden and Malik to show, I prayed.

Lord, I come to you with a humble heart. I have no idea what is about to be revealed in this meeting, Lord, but I'm asking that you please allow me to know the truth, no matter what it is. If it's not meant for me to marry Camden, then please let this meeting reveal that. I love Camden, Lord, and I want to be his wife, but I can't keep enduring this pain. I've been through a lot during these past few days and I don't know how much more I can take. If this meeting produces a negative outcome, then I ask for your strength to handle that and to walk away from Camden. Please direct my path. I thank you, Lord, for loving me although I fall short. I ask all these blessings in your precious name. Amen.

I lifted my head and Camden entered the church office. I briefly looked at him and then put my head back down. I wasn't praying any longer; I just couldn't stand looking at his face. The sight of him made me sick! Obviously not getting the message, Camden walked over to where I was sitting and parked his behind in the empty chair next to me.

"Stormy, are you OK?"

"What do you think?" I asked coldly.

"Is there any way we can talk about this without getting my father involved? I'd really rather handle this between us." Camden spoke softly.

"Why? Surely you don't have anything to hide." I was being sarcastic, but I really wanted to know.

"No. I don't have anything to hide, but I just don't want my father in my business," Camden whispered, not wanting Sister Jones to hear.

"Well, it's too late. We're here now and we are gonna get to the bottom of this whether you want to or not."

"Please, Storm—"

His speech was interrupted as Malik walked into the office. Before he could sit down, Sister Jones announced that Reverend Brooks was ready to see us. My heart sank. I started to feel queasy. I took a deep breath before I walked into Reverend Brooks's office. It was the moment of truth.

Reverend Theodore Brooks often boasted from the pulpit that becoming pastor of True Gospel Christian Center at age thirty-five was one of his proudest moments. He was the assistant pastor for three years under the leadership of the late Pastor William Winn, the founder of the church. When Pastor Winn died, the church board unanimously elected Reverend Brooks to become the new pastor. He was honored.

After two years with Reverend Brooks as pastor, True Gospel's membership grew from six hundred members to two thousand, coming from as far as Washington, DC, Virginia, Delaware, and Pennsylvania. The word spread quickly throughout the city and beyond that good things were going on at our church—especially amongst the women. Women flocked to the church in droves, not only to hear the word of God from a man who had been anointed to preach the gospel since he was fourteen years old, but to gaze at this man of God who stood tall, dark, and handsome in the pulpit. He was an older version of Camden, minus the bald head. And his demeanor screamed strength, power, and dominance—qualities that kept the women flirting. But it didn't work. He loved his wife, First Lady Sheryl Brooks, and was undoubtedly faithful to her.

Reverend Brooks was known to be an honorable man, committed to God and to rebuilding communities. He was instrumental in spearheading several ministries in his church, which reached thousands outside the church, including the Prison Ministry, Addictions Ministry, Family/Domestic Violence Ministry, and Adopt a Soldier Ministry for those military men and women serving in Iraq and Afghanistan. Reverend Brooks also walked the streets of some of Baltimore's most crime ridden neighborhoods, trying to save souls. Because of his dedication to save lives, he generated a faithful following, all of whom loved and respected him, and sought his advice. This was my reason for dragging him into the middle of this situation. I didn't want to put Camden on blast with his father, but I needed my pastor, our pastor to intervene and get to the bottom of this mess.

Reverend Brooks opened his office door wearing a huge grin.

"Well, if it isn't my three favorite members—my son, my soon-to-be daughter-in-law, and my adopted son. Come on in."

His study was almost like a one-bedroom apartment without a kitchen. There was a living room/dining room combination at the entrance of his office. Then toward the back of his office was where his maple wood, U-shaped desk sat. I noticed the plants surrounding the office gave it a feminine touch, probably the work of the first lady. There were also framed diplomas from Morehouse College where he received a bachelor's degree in political science, and Howard University School of Religion. Then to the rear of his study was a bedroom with a king-sized bed and a full bathroom. Camden used to tease his father by calling his study a preacher's pad.

I tried to return Reverend Brooks's enthusiasm, but I couldn't, and apparently neither could Camden and Malik.

"Why the long faces? Y'all look like somebody died." Reverend Brooks's smile faded as he sat in the burgundy, executive chair behind his desk.

The three of us sat in the three chairs directly in front of his desk, with me in the middle, Camden to my right, and Malik on my left side. No one answered his question.

"My Lord. Is it that bad? The cat's got all three of your tongues. Will somebody please tell me what's going on?"

"Reverend Brooks, Camden and I have a problem that we need to resolve.

"Oh? What seems to be the problem?" he inquired.

I looked at both Camden, who wore an irritated expression on his face, and Malik, who had a blank expression. I could tell both of them were upset about being there, so I took the lead. "I'll tell you what's going on since neither of them can open their mouths," I said, annoyed.

"Go ahead, Stormy." Reverend Brooks looked a little on edge. He sat back in his chair, appearing to brace himself for what I was about to say.

"Reverend Brooks, as you know, Camden and I are engaged to be married," I said.

"Right, right. I'm so happy for the two of you. I'm glad he finally found someone to calm him down and make him an honest man," he said with a nervous chuckle.

"Well, that's just the problem, pastor. I don't think Camden has been honest with me."

"What do you mean?" Reverend Brooks looked puzzled.

"Reverend Brooks," I paused as I thought back on the recent visit from Dante, "I had a visit recently from my cousin, Dante. During his visit, he informed me that Camden was being unfaithful to me.

"Really?" the pastor asked, cutting his eyes at Camden.

"Yes, really. I was devastated, but that wasn't it. I found out more."

"Stormy, please—" Camden pleaded.

Camden's obvious signs of fear started to show, which caused his father to want to know more.

"Go on, Stormy," Reverend Brooks insisted.

"He told me that not only was Camden not being true to me, but that he was cheating on me with Malik," I said, pointing at Malik. He appeared unfazed by my comment, looking like I had just said that Malik's favorite snack was potato chips. Camden, on the other hand, lost his cool.

"I'm not cheatin' on her with Malik! We've been through this five hundred times within the last few days, and I'm sick of defending myself. I'm not sure what you plan to gain by having this meeting, but the rumors are a lie. They're a lie, Dad! If I were cheating with Malik, then I'd be gay, and I'm not gay!" Camden shouted.

"Well, Malik told Leigh something different, Reverend Brooks!" I retorted. "He told her that he and Camden have been having sex since he was in high school. They've even been having sex while Camden and I have been planning our wedding. Didn't you, Malik? Didn't you tell Leigh that?"

Malik didn't answer. He just sat in the chair and stared at the floor.

"Well, Malik, what do you have to say about all of this?" Reverend Brooks sternly asked. "Are you having sex with my son?"

"Dad?" Camden said.

"Be quiet, Camden! I am not talking to you! Now, Malik," Reverend Brooks said with his attention turned back to Malik, "let me ask you again. Are you having sex with my son?"

"No, sir! I'm not having sex with your son," he whispered.

I almost stood from my chair.

"You liar! Why did you tell Leigh that then? Stop lying, Malik, and tell the truth! Camden must have talked to him before the meeting and told him to lie about their relationship."

"Stormy! I wish you'd shut your lips for a second and let me finish," Malik said testily.

"Go on, Malik," Reverend Brooks encouraged.

"Reverend Brooks, I am not currently having sex with your son, but I have in the past," Malik said boldly.

"Stop lying, Malik! I've never had sex with you!" Camden yelled as he jumped up out of his chair, knocking it over on the floor.

"I'm sorry, Camden, but I can't lie to your father. He's been good to me and my family, and I will not sit and lie to his face." After Malik spoke, Camden picked up his chair, sat back down, and put his face in his hands. He was being exposed and couldn't handle it. Malik continued. "It's true, Reverend Brooks. Camden and I have had sex on many occasions. It started when I was in high school, a little after Camden started mentoring me. I admitted to Camden that I thought I was attracted to men, and he admitted to me that he was bisexual."

"I can't believe you're lyin' like this," Camden muttered under his breath.

"Camden, I'll let you know when I want to hear from you. Right now, I just want you to keep your mouth closed," Reverend Brooks bellowed as he pointed his finger at Camden.

"But, Dad! Am I supposed to sit here and listen to these lies?"

"I'm not going to tell you again to shut up. Please continue, Malik."

"Anyway, after that discussion, when we went out, it was a different type of interaction. Each outing would end with a kiss. A couple of weeks later we met at a hotel, and that's when I had my first sexual experience with Camden." Malik then turned to Camden. "Camden, you can deny it all you want, but you know you and I have had sex on numerous occasions."

At this point, I was crying uncontrollably. My chest had gotten tight and I felt short of breath. *This is much more than I bargained for,* I thought. *I can't believe Malik just confirmed that my fiancé is gay.* Deep down I hoped he was lying, but I knew he wasn't.

I tried to catch my breath before speaking. I looked over at Camden, who was crying. I wasn't moved by his tears and neither was his father.

"Camden, what do you have to say for yourself?" Reverend Brooks questioned, but Camden didn't respond.

"Camden, I'm waiting for an answer!"

"Dad," he sad, sobbing, "Malik is lying to you. You've known me all my life. You know I'm not gay."

"What does Malik have to gain by lying on you, Camden? Why would he come here and make up such a story about you? Why would he tell me that you and he are having a homosexual relationship, knowing that I preach against homosexuality all the time? Camden, I think you're the one lying. As a matter of fact, I *know* you're lying and Malik is telling me the truth. You're trying to cover your tail and I can see right through it." Reverend Brooks was angry, but he tried to remain calm.

"Dad, I'm not—"

"Camden, be quiet. I really don't want to hear anything that comes out of your mouth at this moment. You have lied so much to your mother and me that we don't believe a word you say anymore. You've been so dishonest over the past few years that if you told me your name was Camden Xavier Brooks, I'd ask you to produce a birth certificate. You disappoint me, son. You have hurt Stormy, the woman who loves you dearly and wanted to be your wife. And on top of all of that, you've exposed Malik to this homosexual mess when you were supposed to be his mentor. Some mentor you were! You were supposed to be guiding the boy in the right direction, not guiding your penis into his butt."

I listened intently to Reverend Brooks rip into Camden. I knew he wanted to say more, but he composed himself in front of Malik and me.

"What am I going to do now?" I cried when Reverend Brooks came over and put his arms around me. "I love Camden with all of my heart, but I can't marry a man who's gay!"

"Stormy, with God's help, you'll heal from this. I know this seems like a nightmare now, but the Bible says, 'Weeping may endure for a night, but joy comes in the morning.' You are a blessed child of God and this too shall pass. I'm sorry that this had to happen to you, but it's good that this revelation was made before you walked down the aisle. Even in the bad times, God is always faithful."

He then turned to Camden and looked at him in disgust.

"You owe Stormy an apology for causing her this pain. She doesn't deserve this heartache," Reverend Brooks said.

Camden didn't say a word. He didn't even look at me.

"Malik, I want to thank you for being honest with me. I'm sorry for what my son did to you. He was supposed to be a role model and he failed miserably. I'm going to pray that you are delivered from homosexuality and can live a life that God wants you to live." Malik was quiet—didn't even look up at Reverend Brooks.

"Stormy, I guess you know the wedding is off. Not that you'd want to marry Camden in light of these new revelations. But I cannot, in good conscience, marry the two of you knowing that Camden is unfit for marriage. However, I do believe God is able and can do all things but fail, so maybe after much prayer and a bath in holy water, Camden may be fit to be your husband. Until then, this wedding is not going to happen."

Sadly, I agreed with Reverend Brooks.

"Camden's not ready and I can't marry a man I don't trust, let alone one who's attracted to another man. But thank you for taking the time to speak with us." I gave Reverend Brooks a good-bye hug. I wondered if he could feel my anguish and my broken heart as we embraced. I slowly slid the engagement ring off my finger and hurled it at Camden's head. Unfortunately, I missed.

As I proceeded to leave the pastor's study, Camden attempted to creep out behind me, wanting to talk to me. But Reverend Brooks stepped in his face, so close their noses touched, and ordered him to sit down. The last thing I heard before I closed the door was Reverend Brooks yelling, "Boy, you better be praying that I don't lose my religion, because I am about to lay you to rest."

Chapter 11

Camden

Two months had passed, and I still hadn't spoken to my father. The moment Stormy and Malik left his office after that dreadful meeting, he laid into me like never before.

"How could you?" he exclaimed, staring at me as if I were Lucifer. I sat there looking at the floor because I had no explanation for my actions. "How could you stoop so low? I'm shocked and disappointed in your behavior, and before you part your lips to deny it, don't bother. I ain't buying nothing you selling, 'cause I know you slept with that boy. But what I'm baffled about is why. I know you to be a lot of things, Camden, but a faggot isn't one of them."

I quickly cut my eye at him for his use of such a derogatory word.

"That's right. I said it and I meant it. I'm sick of you, Camden—just sick. I've always known you hated being a preacher's son. I knew you used to get into stupid trouble just to prove to everybody that you weren't a goody-goody.

I know you tried to distance yourself from your mother and me to gain your own identity, but I never would have thought that my son, my only child, would turn out to be a gay man who preys upon little boys."

"I didn't prey—"

"I'm not finished! I thought I saw a positive change in you once you started dating Stormy. I thought you'd finally gotten yourself together. But I see I was wrong." He paused to take a sip of water. I hoped it went down the wrong pipe, causing him to choke so he'd shut up.

"Do you know who I am, Camden?"

I didn't answer. I knew that as soon as I opened my mouth to speak, he would tell me to shut up. So I just looked up at him.

"I'm a well respected man in this city and I will not allow you or your despicable behavior to disgrace my name. At this point, I'm disappointed that you're even my son."

I gasped. I knew he was angry, but not that angry. I couldn't believe my father had just said those words to me. He cut me so deeply that I felt like I was bleeding internally.

"It's time for you to get your life in order. You better start fasting and praying to rid yourself of those demon spirits, or else I'll be forced to ban your from the church and ultimately the family."

When I walked out of his office, I was distraught and seething at the same time. I hadn't talked to him since.

I didn't know if I was angrier at Stormy for involving my father, Malik for telling my father the truth about our relationship, or at myself for living such a fucked up life. After a few days of soul searching, I realized it was the latter. I was disappointed in myself and embarrassed. I was most upset that my business was made public and that I'd hurt the three most important people to me—Stormy, my mother, and my father.

My father had basically disowned me, but my mother remained supportive. Of course she was disappointed when she learned the news about Malik and me, but she wasn't about to turn her back on her only child. She came over often to visit, brought food, and prayed with me. She also encouraged me to come back to church, but I refused. I didn't want to run the risk of seeing Malik or my dad.

After about a month of begging me to come back to church, I gave in to my mother. But the soul purpose for my visit was to see Stormy. I didn't. However, I did bump into my father after service. He gave me a quick hello and went about business as usual. I was appalled at how the good reverend, Mr. Holy and Righteous was judging me. Did the Bible not say, "Judge not lest ye be judged"? Shouldn't he had been forgiving me rather than condemning me? So much for being a man of the cloth.

Malik had tried to contact me once during these past two months, but I ignored his call. It was definitely for the best because I was so pissed at him that if our paths crossed, I would shove my fist down his throat. What the hell did he have to gain by revealing our personal relationship to my father and Stormy? Did he think that would make me want to be with him? I hoped not because that couldn't have been further from the truth. If anything, I despised him from the minute he opened his mouth to my father. I totally regretted ever being involved with his tender, jive ass. I loathed Malik, and if I never saw him again, it would be too soon.

As the weeks and months progressed, doom and gloom surrounded me. I knew I was wrong for what I'd done and I felt so guilty about hurting Stormy. But the guilt only mounted after having a confrontation with Jared and Hassan. I was hanging out with them at our usual spot for happy hour when Jared's statement hit me like a ton of bricks.

"So, Cam, I hear you up to your old tricks again."

"Huh?" I said as I took a sip from my Corona bottle.

"Man, don't huh me. I heard what really went down with

you and Stormy. You tried to kick it to us like you called off the wedding because you wasn't ready to be tied down, when in reality, she found out you were fuckin' with that young boy, Malik."

"Look! I'm here to hang out with my boys, not talk about Stormy and me."

Hassan must have noticed the tension between Jared and me, so he interjected before Jared could say another word.

"Cam, we can respect that, but all we want to know is why. Why would you mess up a good thing with Stormy to be with a man—a young buck at that? The shit is baffling to me, Cam."

"I don't expect y'all to understand. Hell, I don't even understand. It just seems like they're forces within me beyond my control."

"Bullshit!" Jared shouted.

"Believe what you want," I retorted defensively, "but I didn't choose to be attracted to both sexes. It's something I've been battling for years."

"Well, you know how I feel about that gay shit, Cam. You my boy and all, but I don't want to be exposed to it. You know if you were any other dude, I wouldn't be caught dead with you. But because I've known you since we were in diapers, I'm still your boy," Jared said.

I knew Hassan and especially Jared hated finding out about my lifestyle. I hid it for years, but slipped up one day and got caught at St. John's in my dorm room. A female coed came to visit my roommate and walked in on me and another male student doing the do. Unfortunately, this particular female was friends with Hassan. I knew immediately that she would tell, so I beat her to it. Without getting into great detail, I told Hassan and Jared that I was confused about my sexuality and that I was attracted to men. Hassan was shocked and dismayed, and Jared was horrified. He asked tons of questions. But after reassuring them that there was no attraction toward them and that I wouldn't be wearing dresses and makeup, they accepted the situation—somewhat. They made me promise to keep this hidden lifestyle to myself and we all kind of acted like it didn't exist. So around them, I only talked about girls. When they learned I was dating Stormy, they were elated. I guess they figured my phase with the same sex had dissipated.

"Calm down, Jared," Hassan said. "No matter what, Camden's always gonna be our dawg. He's already lost his future wife. That's got to be painful enough. He doesn't need us beatin' up on him too."

"I ain't beatin' up on him. I'm just disappointed. I don't like this shit, Cam. You need to get yourself together. This going back and forth is for the birds. So, who or what do you want?"

"I want Stormy. I really want her to be my wife."

"Why?"

"Because I love her."

"Good answer," Jared approved. "As long as you're rolling with the ladies, then I'm rolling with you." He gave me a pound and ordered another round of drinks.

I knew most black men were extremely homophobic and weren't fond of being around bisexual or gay men, but being friends since childhood made it a tad bit difficult for the three of us to end a true friendship. As long as we continued to act like I'd never had relations with men, and I didn't involve them in any way, which I never did, our friendship would remain intact.

After some time passed, Jared and Hassan tried to lift my spirits about my failed relationship with Stormy. They tried to give me tips and pointers on how I could win her back, all of which might have worked had I been unfaithful to her with a woman. No matter how hard they tried, nothing helped me to get my mind off of Stormy and how I had truly messed up the best thing that had ever happened to me.

My biggest dilemma throughout these last two months was trying to find some way to get Stormy back into my life. I missed her dearly and I quickly found out that the old saying, "You don't realize a good thing until it's gone," was so true in my case. I tried calling Stormy on numerous occasions after the meeting and she didn't accept any of my telephone calls. I constantly left messages for her to return my calls, but she never did.

I vowed never to give up on Stormy and me because I knew deep down she still loved me. If only I could get through to her and convince her that all I wanted was her, and that was the God's honest truth. My total desire was for Stormy—not Malik or any other man. I had been fighting the demons for weeks now with prayer and I believed I'd changed. But how could I ever sway Stormy to trust me again?

After watching the movie *Love and Basketball*, I got the courage to give Stormy a call. It had been a while since I dialed her number, but after I saw Omar Epps and Sanaa Lathan eventually get married and have a child at the end of the movie, I somehow thought there was hope for Stormy and me. So I called.

I fully expected Stormy not to answer, but surprisingly she did.

"Hello," she answered in an unenthused tone.

"Hello, Stormy. How are you?" I was nervous. I really hadn't prepared myself for a conversation with her because I didn't think she'd actually pick up. Now I didn't have a clue as to what to say.

"What do you want, Camden?"

"I want to talk to you—to hear your voice."

"Why?" She sounded irritated.

"Because I need to tell you some things."

"Tell me what?" she asked, giving me major attitude.

"Just hear me out. Don't hang up."

I poured out my heart to Stormy like never before. I must have apologized for my actions fifty times for deceiving her about my sexuality, but I confirmed that my love for her was never a deception. I informed her of how I'd changed my life and that my only desire was for her to be my wife. I asked her to please give us another try and I promised I would be true to her. I didn't want her to answer at that moment, but I asked her if she would allow my words to sink in before giving me an answer.

"No, Camden," she said flatly. "You hurt me and embarrassed me like no other man has ever done. I do still love you, Camden, but my love for you won't allow me to give you another chance. Besides, I don't trust anything you say. You say you've changed, but I have no proof, and your word alone doesn't mean a whole lot to me. In fact, it means nothing."

"All I can tell you is what's in my heart. I'm a changed man, Stormy, and that's no lie. Come on, you know our God, and you know he has all power in his hands. Our God can do all things but fail. So if you believe he can turn water into wine, and that he made the blind man see, and that he made the lame man walk, then you ought to know that our Lord and Savior has the power to remove anything within me that's not approving in his sight. You've got to believe that."

"I've heard all you said, Camden. Sorry, but I'm not putting my heart at risk again. Now I've gotta go."

"Love you." I spoke quickly, but not fast enough. She hung up.

I didn't know if my mind or ears were playing tricks on

me, but I thought I heard something in Stormy's voice. I felt she still wanted me, but was scared to trust me again. I wasn't going to give up until I made her my wife.

The phone rang, getting my hopes up that it may be Stormy calling me back. It wasn't.

"Yes?" I answered.

"Camden, this is your father. I'm on my way to see you. We need to talk. I'll be there in ten minutes." He disconnected the call.

The nerve of this man to call me and invite himself over to my apartment. He hadn't made an effort to talk to me in a month of Sundays, so what could he possibly want now?

Chapter 12

Stormy

Depression, anger, embarrassment, and grief all consumed me during the two months following that God awful meeting in Reverend Brooks's office. During the first month, I felt as if someone had died. When I wasn't working, I stayed locked up in my apartment and cried as I mourned the loss of my relationship and how Camden had destroyed my life. I kicked myself for believing he was the one—my so-called Mr. Right. I came to the conclusion that my ideal mate didn't exist. I thought I'd found him in Camden, but I was dead wrong.

I attempted to grieve in private, so I played hooky from church and denied all invitations from my friends. However, they called and visited me.

A few days after the meeting, I had the humiliating task of explaining what happened to my parents and brothers. I called a family meeting at my parents' house, and included Leigh, Nicole, and Dominique.

As I pulled up in the driveway of my parents' colonial

style, single family home, I began to dread breaking the bad news to them, especially my father and brothers. My mother, Victoria Knight, a woman who possessed the qualities of poise, grace, and beauty, would be the only one who would remain calm. I think her strong belief in God allowed her to be mild mannered. I also think her career as a second grade teacher for thirty years contributed to her mellow, patient demeanor. She was the exact same way when we were children. But people shouldn't be fooled, because her sweet nature didn't make her a pushover.

My father, Drake Knight, was of average height and slender with a light brown complexion matching mine. He was the hell raiser in the family. I guess my parents complemented each other. It also gave a good balance in our home—kind of like good parent, bad parent. My father wasn't actually the bad parent, but he was tough as nails. Education was a priority for him since he was a college professor, and he couldn't stress it enough. Daddy was a man who put God at the center of his life and he made sure we did the same. It wasn't until a few years ago when my father's strong, dominant personality changed. He was told he might have colon cancer. After months of testing, all the results were negative. Of course there was relief amongst the family, especially with my father, but after that scare, he didn't appear to be as hard anymore. He was still stern and set in his ways, but that tough exterior had diminished substantially.

When I entered the family room of my parents' home, everyone was seated comfortably, waiting for me. I grew more nervous about my news once I laid eyes upon my brothers, Trey and Jordan. Trey was the eldest child, and he felt it was his duty to protect his younger siblings. He also thought he was the cutest thing walking the earth. As one of the athletic trainers for the Baltimore Ravens, Trey had a tight body with a chiseled chest. He had beautiful brown eyes with long, girly eyelashes that matched his light brown skin. His hair was cut into a short, mini Afro, and sometimes he wore a goatee. I knew he would be the toughest one in the room. He was a younger version of my father with a little more aggression added to the mix. I was most afraid of his reaction when I told everyone about Camden and me.

Jordan, on the other hand, would probably be upset, but he wouldn't be ready to draw blood as fast as Trey. Jordan possessed a lot of the same qualities as our mother. He was extremely low key until a situation warranted him being off the hook. Jordan used to be a firefighter, but now he worked as a fire investigator. In his line of work, he ran into lots of women, which had earned him the title of playboy. Being proud of his title caused him to keep his short hair cut every week and his five-o'clock-shadow-like beard neatly trimmed. He also lived at the gym, trying to build a muscular frame like Trey.

"Hi, everybody. Thanks for coming over," I said as I joined them in the family room. I sat on the couch next to my mother, the person I knew wouldn't blow a gasket after she heard what I was about to say.

"Nice of you to get us all together," Mommy said. "We need to do this more often. Y'all know I love to cook."

"I plan to get me a piece of peach cobbler before I leave, Mrs. Vickie, so don't you worry. You're cooking will not be in vain," Nicole said.

I sat there while they continued to engage in small talk. I allowed any topic to divert the attention off of me. If I could have, I would have never divulged what had happened between Camden and me, but since my parents were shelling out money for a wedding that wasn't going to take place, it was only right that they knew.

"Stormy, why are you so quiet?" Daddy asked.

"I just have a lot on my mind right now. That's why I

called everybody over here. I need to tell you all something." When the time came to tell my family what had gone down with Camden, I became visibly distressed, causing my mother to hug me.

"What's wrong, baby? You don't look good."

"The wedding is off," I said while fighting to hold back my tears.

"What you say?" Trey asked.

"I said the wedding has been cancelled."

Gasps and sighs filled the room.

"Why, Stormy? What happened?" my father inquired.

"Dad, it's so hard to talk about. Every time I think about it, pain envelops me."

"Now I understand why you stopped wanting to discuss wedding plans," Mommy said. "Because there is no wedding. What could have possibly caused you and Camden to cancel your wedding plans?"

" 'Cause Camden's not the man I thought he was." I wailed as I fell into my mother's arms.

"Mr. and Mrs. Knight, Trey and Jordan," Leigh interjected, "if you don't mind, I'd like to explain what happened. I think it's much too hard for Stormy to talk about without getting chest pains and shortness of breath like she's been experiencing since all of this happened. So I'll give you the quick version of what happened, and Stormy can give you more details later, when she feels up to it."

"Fine by me," Trey said. "I just wanna know what went down and why my sister is in tears right now."

I lay in my mother's arms as I listened to Leigh explain how in such a short period of time, the happiest days of my life became the worst.

"There's no easy way for me to say this," Leigh said. She paused, obviously uneasy about having to tell my parents the truth about Camden. "Um . . . well, Stormy found out that Camden wasn't who he said he was."

"What does that mean?" Jordan asked, confused by Leigh's vagueness.

"I'm trying to be delicate with my words, considering Stormy's emotional state. But in a nutshell, Stormy found out that Camden was being unfaithful."

"Oh, yeah?" Trey said angrily. "That dude was cheatin' on my sister?"

"Yes, he was, but that wasn't it. He was involved with Malik Blackwell, Sister Blackwell's grandson."

I sat and waited for Leigh's last statement to sink in. My mother and father didn't say a word. They just comforted me as I painfully listened to Leigh fill them in on how I obtained the information about Camden's infidelity, the confrontation with both Camden and Malik, and finally the meeting with Reverend Brooks. Mom and Dad remained calm. They embraced me, told me I'd be OK, and promised to help me get through this.

But Trey was seeing red.

"You mean to tell me Camden's gay? Tell me you're lying," he said as he rubbed his knuckles.

I just looked at him. I didn't answer his question. I wish I could have told him all of this was one huge lie, but I couldn't.

"Where is Camden now?"

"I don't know. Why?" I could see the wheels turning in Trey's head. He wanted to track down Camden.

"Because we need to pay him a little visit," Jordan said, looking at Trey. They were both now on the same page and somehow drew Nicole into wanting to find Camden as well.

"I'm comin' with y'all. I know where he lives. We can go over there and *talk* to him," Nicole said.

The three of them were on a mission to kick Camden's ass, but my father quickly intervened.

"Look, you all, now is not the time to go lookin' for Camden. Your sister needs you more right now than Camden needs his butt kicked."

"I agree with you, Dad," Trey said. "But he hurt Stormy in the worst way. He's gay and he lied about it. Then he cheats on her with another man. That's unforgivable and he needs to be dealt with."

"Camden will have his day," Daddy said. "Believe me, I want to put my hands on Camden just as much as you do, but that's not the answer. And that's not God's way. Stormy is our focus right now, not Camden. So you, Jordan, and Nicole need to calm down. What we need to do right now is pray."

Reluctantly they agreed not to do anything to Camden, but I heard Trey whisper to Jordan and Nicole that Camden would get what was coming to him when he least expected it. We held hands and stood in a circle. I listened intently as my father prayed for peace of mind, healing, and relief from depression and anger. He asked God to dry my tears and replace them with laughter. And most of all, he prayed for my strength, something I needed an abundance of as I dealt with these tough times.

Daddy's powerful prayer made me feel better. I started to realize that being surrounded by my family and friends would help me to get through this terrible situation a lot better than being cooped up in my apartment all alone.

Since the meeting with my parents several weeks ago, I had started to feel a little better each day. I had begun the healing process. The anger and resentment I felt toward Camden had subsided just a little bit. I could only assume that was one of the reasons I answered the phone when he called. The fact that I still loved him and missed him also played a part in my decision to pick up the phone.

When I heard his voice, I acted as if I couldn't stand him—that I didn't want to be bothered, but for some odd reason, it was refreshing to hear his voice. Why? This man had made me feel worthless and took me to the lowest level of depression that I had ever known, but deep down I still loved him. It was crazy, but I couldn't deny it.

I've changed, Stormy . . . I love you, Stormy . . . I only have desires for you were the words I heard in my mind as I reflected on our conversation. I wanted to believe Camden, but I couldn't. He'd told the biggest lie I'd ever been told. I couldn't possibly see how I could ever give him my heart again. I still loved Camden, but the only way I would marry him was if Jesus himself stood in my apartment and gave me his blessing. And since Jesus probably wouldn't be making any appearances, there wouldn't be a union between Camden and me—ever!

It was a beautiful fall day. I walked out onto my balcony to take in the sunshine. I was slowly but surely coming out of my funk, partly because I had finally allowed myself to forgive Camden. I found that the anger and resentment I had been carrying around for months hurt me more than it helped me. It was kind of equivalent to the saying: it takes less muscles in your face to smile than to frown. It took way too much of my energy to hate Camden and I spent a lot of time doing exclusively that. So with much prayer, I gave my burdens to the Lord and asked him to replace my hurt with forgiveness. And now I could peacefully say that a burden had been lifted.

Camden had called a few times. He continued to beg for my forgiveness, professed his love for me, reiterated his 180-degree life change, and asked if we could get back together.

"Nope, can't do it," I told him. "You're lucky I'm even talking to you after what you did to me." But Camden wasn't giving up, and I wasn't giving in.

I finally decided to attend church. I'd always been taught

that you were supposed to praise God when you were in a storm, when times were at their worst. I hadn't done that, so I owed God my praise.

While I was getting dressed for church, my telephone rang. I picked up the phone and it was Trey.

"Hey, Trey."

"Hey, Storm. How you doing?"

"I'm feeling great. Right now I'm getting dressed for church," I said cheerfully.

"Word? You're going back to True Gospel? You must be feeling better."

"I told you I was. No more doom and gloom for me."

"Well, I was just calling to check on you. You know Mommy, Daddy, Jordan, and I have been worried about you. We haven't heard from you lately and I needed to check on you to make sure you were all right."

"Good looking out, big brother. I appreciate your support through all of this. Thanks for being such a good brother," I said sincerely.

"No need for thanks. I'm doing what I'm supposed to do. Oh, and I want you to know, I'm on the hunt for that faggot, Camden. When I see him, I'm going to drop kick his ass like a football."

"Trey, don't! I'm over it and I want you to be as well," I pleaded.

"Sorry, Storm, I'm never gonna get over what he did to you. Just know that when I see him, I'm going to fuck him up!"

I didn't feel like listening to Trey going on about Camden, so I cut our conversation short.

"All right, Trey. I gotta go finish getting dressed. I'll talk to you later."

"Peace, Stormy. I'll holla at you later." The phone rang again. *Damn, I'm going to be late for church if the phone doesn't stop ringing.* I figured it was Trey calling back, so I answered with a bit of an attitude.

"Helllllllo."

"Hi, Stormy, it's Sister Jones," the voice sang.

Sister Jones was one of the nicest members at True Gospel. She was a heavyset, light-skinned woman with fat cheeks. Every time she smiled, her faced glowed, kind of like her glowing personality. Sister Jones loved working at True Gospel. She had been the secretary ever since I was a child. After she became widowed five years ago, she ate, drank, and slept the church to take her mind off of being alone.

"Oh, hi, Sister Jones. How are you?" I asked, wondering why she was calling me.

"I'm blessed and highly favored by the Lord."

"That's great."

"Stormy, I'm calling you on behalf of Reverend Brooks. He wants to know if you'll be in church this morning."

"Yes, I will. I am getting dressed now. I'll be at the eleven o'clock service."

"Great! Will you be able to meet with him after service? He'd like to talk to you."

"Sure, Sister Jones. I can meet with him. Do you know why he wants to see me?"

"No. He just told me to call you to see if you were available."

"Well, thanks for calling. I'll be there."

"OK, I'll let him know. God bless you."

"God bless you, too."

During the entire service, I wondered why Reverend Brooks wanted to see me. My mind raced back and forth so much as I searched for a reason, that I couldn't fully concentrate on the service. But I did find time to focus as soon as the reverend stood up to preach.

"Today's topic is *Overcoming Sins*," Reverend Brooks

stated after he read the Bible scripture relating to his topic. He wiped his forehead with a handkerchief and continued. "We're all sinners and we all sin daily, including me. But what you've got to realize is that sin is often connected to some type of pleasure. You've got to learn to open your eyes as Satan entices you, lures you, and baits you into sin. You've got to learn to flee from the devil and seek God when these temptations arise."

Reverend Brooks preached his heart out as if he was try- ing to reach deep within the depths of someone's soul. He closed his sermon by telling the congregation to pray and repent for the sins we have committed. He told us to avoid temptation and to turn to our fellow brothers and sisters for support. Finally he quoted scripture from James, chapter four, verses seven through ten.

"Therefore submit to God. Resist the devil and he will flee from you. Draw near to God and He will draw near to you. Cleanse *your* hands, *you* sinners; and purify *your* hearts, *you* double-minded. Lament and mourn and weep! Let your laughter be turned to mourning and *your* joy to gloom. Humble yourselves in the sight of the Lord, and He will lift you up."

Reverend Brooks opened the doors of the church as the choir softly sang "I Surrender All."

"It's not too late to repent," he said as he held out his open arms. "God loves you no matter what sins you've com- mitted. All he's asking is for you to confess your sins and ask for forgiveness. I'm a living witness that he will forgive you."

As the church quietly mediated and prayed during altar call, a loud scream came from the back of the church.

"Come on, son," I heard Reverend Brooks say, which caused me to lift my head. "It's not too late, son. God loves you and so do I."

I knew our pastor had a habit of calling a lot of the

younger male members "son," but the word son as he said it now sounded a tab bit different. When I looked up, I was surprised to see Camden meandering down the center aisle with his hands raised, tears streaming down his cheeks as he shouted, "Forgive me! Forgive me!" I hadn't even known he was in church. He was the last person I expected to see converted by the pastor's sermon.

When Camden reached the altar, he fell to his knees and I heard him repeatedly scream, "Forgive me, Lord, for I'm a sinner!" The sound of his voice was heart wrenching. Tears welled in my eyes and goose bumps popped out on my skin. The hair on the back of my neck stood up and a feeling of worship came over me. The congregation was moved as well as they witnessed Camden fall to his knees and plead for God's forgiveness. Some of the members cried with Camden, others fell to their knees and began to worship, some broke into a shout giving God praise, and I heard one parishioner yell, "Bless him, Lord!" over and over again. As for me, I was overcome with the Holy Ghost. All I could remember was my face being buried in my lap as I cried and praised God. The spirit was high and the entire church worshipped as Reverend Brooks ministered to Camden, who lay prostrate.

After the benediction, I ran over and spoke to my parents before my meeting with Reverend Brooks. I waited for them to comment on Camden's repentance, but they didn't.

When I entered the church office, Sister Jones told me Reverend Brooks was waiting to see me. I knocked before I entered and he yelled, "Come in," from the other side of the door. When I entered, he immediately came over and hugged me.

"How are you doing, Stormy?"

"I'm doing fine, Reverend Brooks," I said as I sat down.

"Are you sure, Stormy? It's been a while since I've seen you. I've been worried about you, you know? I've been asking your parents how you are doing and they said you are taking things one day at a time."

"That's true. I recently realized that with time, God heals all wounds. So I've been healing."

"Well, just remember in the midst of it all, continue to come to church and give God praise."

"I know, Reverend," I said as I lowered my head. "I didn't want to come to church and subject myself to seeing Camden after all that happened. It would have been too hard for me to face him and the congregation for that matter. I've heard we've been the talk of the church."

"That is true. We all know how church folk can be when it comes to gossip, especially in the black church."

We both laughed.

"Stormy, I'm sure you've been wondering why I asked to meet with you."

"Yes, sir, I have."

"I wanted to talk to you about Camden. I know my son hurt you in unimaginable ways. It hurt me terribly to find out my son could be so cruel to another human being, especially to one he says he loves. I was so angry with Camden for a long time that I, too, didn't want to see his face. I stayed on bended knee many nights praying to God and asking him to help me forgive my son. It took weeks, but finally after some time, I did. I forgave him and I vowed to help him. I've prayed consistently for his deliverance from homosexuality."

As I sat listening to Reverend Brooks, I was still confused as to why I was there, but I soon got my answer.

"Stormy, I've got some good news for you." He smiled.

"Really?"

"God is a deliverer!" he said proudly.

"What do you mean, pastor?"

"My son, Stormy, my son. He's been delivered from those demons that had him attracted to men. I spent about three hours with him recently. When I walked into his apartment, I just grabbed him and held him in my arms. I asked him if he wanted to be free and he told me he already was. He explained that God had delivered him. With me not believing anything that Camden says, I decided to take matters into my own hands. I had to touch and agree with Camden as I sought the Lord on his behalf. Stormy, as Camden sat on the side of his bed, I poured holy oil over his entire body. Then I placed both my hands on his head and began to pray. We prayed and cried and cried and prayed for at least an hour. And during that prayer, I could see the demons fleeing from his body. I could see his cleansing, his transformation happening before my very eyes. It was then that I believed Camden had been delivered and no longer had desires for men."

I sat in amazement with widened eyes as Reverend Brooks told me this remarkable story about Camden.

"You don't know how happy I was when I left his apartment that night. I praised God all the way home, because I knew God had worked a miracle on my behalf, on our behalf. Then it was only confirmed during service today that Camden is truly serious about his transformation. When he lay prostrate today and confessed his sins, I knew God had truly cleansed his spirit and made him whole again. I don't know about you, Stormy, but I'm overjoyed."

"I'm happy that things are going well with Camden," I said, not really knowing what to say. I think I was still floored by the demons fleeing from Camden's body. I had heard stories of spirits leaving a person's body, but had never truly observed it myself.

"Stormy, Camden still loves you. When we talked, he expressed to me how sorry he was for hurting you. He knows you're the best thing that's ever happened to him and he doesn't want to lose you."

I sat staring at Reverend Brooks, still at a loss for words.

"Now, I have one question for you: Do you still love Camden?"

"Um, y-y-yes, I do, Reverend Brooks."

"Well, Stormy, since you still love Camden and he clearly loves you, I was wondering if you'd give him another chance, consider being his wife again. But before you answer, please know that I love you like a daughter. I wouldn't ask you to rekindle a relationship with Camden if I thought for one minute he wouldn't be true to you. I honestly believe in my heart that Camden is through with that other lifestyle. Prayer changes things, and I know without a shadow of a doubt that prayer changed my son. I think it would be beneficial for him to be around a beautiful, Christian woman like you consistently. If you recall, when I preached today, I mentioned supporting your brethren and helping those who are struggling with sin. Since you're mature in your faith, I think you can do this. I think you're the boost that Camden needs. Just an ounce of love from you will be the strength he needs to stay the course."

"I don't know, Reverend Brooks. I told you during our last meeting that I don't trust Camden anymore. I would hate to marry him only to find out that he's still, um . . . um . . . gay."

"I understand your feelings, Stormy, but I'm telling you, Camden is a totally different person now. I've seen the transformation with my own eyes. I told you at our last meeting that as a man of God, I couldn't in good conscience marry the two of you, knowing my son was dealing with demons. I no longer feel he is. I'm confident that if you marry him, you'll be happy. You're a good woman and I want you to be my daughter-in-law. You don't have to answer me right away, but I really want you to think and pray about what I am saying. You saw Camden with your own eyes today. I think you know in your heart he's changed. But don't go on my word alone. Call him, go out with him, and see for yourself. Then get back to me once you've made up your mind."

"OK, pastor. I will take some time to think about all of this and I'll let you know." Reverend Brooks and I embraced, and then I left his office.

As I walked to my car, my head was spinning like a Ferris wheel.

Could Camden really be a changed man? But how? I've always thought once you were gay, you were always gay. But is anything too hard for God? Could God have changed Camden's heart and desires? What would my family and friends say if I decided to marry Camden? I was going crazy with what to do.

Should I marry Camden? Is he really the one for me? I wondered. I had a great deal of respect for Reverend Brooks, so I knew he wouldn't ask me to consider marrying Camden if he didn't think his son had changed. He was a man of God, and I knew he, of all people, wouldn't put me in a position to have my heart broken again.

When I walked through the doors of my apartment, my heart was heavy. I prayed to God all the way home, hoping for an immediate sign as to what I should do about Camden. I decided to lie across my bed and sleep on it. No such luck. I couldn't sleep. I tossed and turned as I struggled with what to do.

Finally after I fought with myself for hours, I picked up the telephone and dialed Camden's number.

"Hello, Camden, this is Stormy. Can you come over?"

Chapter 13

Camden

"Hi, Ma, how are you?" I asked as I walked into my parents' bedroom. My mother was lying across the bed reading the Bible. My father was out with the deacons from the church doing their monthly hospital and nursing home visits to the members on the sick and shut-in list.

"Camden, what a wonderful surprise," she said, sitting up and placing her Bible on the nightstand. She held out her arms, gave me a hug, and kissed me on my cheek. I smiled because I loved my mother, First Lady Sheryl Brooks, dearly.

My mother was the dictionary definition of dignity and class. She was one of the most beautiful women I'd ever seen. She and Stormy shared the same caramel complexion and long, flowing hair, which is why I thought Stormy was the most attractive woman I'd ever crossed paths with. She reminded me a lot of my own mother. At fifty-five years old, my mother finally retired as a rehabilitation counselor. She never really had to work once my father became the pastor of True Gospel, but she had wanted to remain active outside the church.

After I was born, my mother and father tried for a second child, but they were met with great challenges. After several medical tests, my mother learned that she had an abnormality with her fallopian tubes, causing her to be unable to have any more children. Therefore, she gave me all the love and affection she had. She loved me no matter what, and would always stand firm in her defense of me, which caused her and my father to clash. My father wanted to treat me like a man, but my mother said I was her baby. That's why my past and present behaviors had bothered me so, knowing that I'd disappointed the one person who had been in my corner from day one.

"I just wanted to come by to see you before I went on my date with Stormy," I boasted.

"Date with Stormy?"

"Yes, Ma. Date with Stormy. That's why I'm here. I wanted to fill you in on what's been going on with us."

She smiled a huge grin. She propped her pillow up against the headboard and leaned back.

"I'm all ears."

"Do you remember the Sunday that the Lord moved in me like never before? The Sunday Daddy preached about overcoming sins and I went to the altar?"

"Sure do. Just like yesterday."

"Well, later that night, Stormy called me."

"Really?"

"Yeah. She was in church that day and she saw me. I didn't even know she was there."

"So, what did she say?"

I explained to my mother that Stormy and I had been talking off and on for a while before that particular Sunday. I told her how I had been apologizing and professing my love to her and proclaiming how I was a changed man, but inwardly I felt that my pleas had fallen on deaf ears. It wasn't until Stormy saw me for herself in church that she believed that I had, in fact, changed. So we gradually began talking and trying to light the flame that had been blown out once my involvement with Malik became public knowledge. We decided to take things slowly since she still had major trust issues with me, but I was on a mission to win back her heart, as well as her trust. We'd gone out to dinner on several occasions, I'd taken lunch to her school during her break, I had flowers delivered to her apartment, and I'd left love notes under the windshield of her car.

"Wow, Camden, it seems like you've been working overtime to win Stormy back. Do you think it's working?"

"I think so, Ma. We've been working on it, secretly, for a while now. We kind of kept it to ourselves, because we really didn't know where this was headed."

"Are you planning to still marry her?"

"I am. In fact, I'm going to ask her again tonight."

"That's great, Camden! But before you do, let's have a serious mother to son talk."

Oh God, I thought. I had no idea where my mother was headed with this mother to son talk, but I hoped she wasn't going to take a page from my father's book by lecturing me.

"OK, Ma, let's talk."

"First, I want to congratulate you on reuniting with Stormy and hopefully making her your wife, but there are a few things I want to know before I can give you my blessing to pursue a marriage with Stormy or any woman for that matter. Can you tell me how this whole . . . um . . . attraction to men started?"

"That's a good question, Ma. I've wondered the same thing for years. I can only tell you that I've felt an attraction since I was in high school, but I never acted on it until I was away at college. It may have been before then, but I don't think I fully understood until my teenage years. I was afraid to act on my feelings, though, knowing who my father is and what the Bible says. But after a party one night during my freshman year in college, I hooked up with a guy who threw himself at me, and I didn't resist." I looked at my mother, who appeared to be becoming a little uncomfortable with the details, so I tried to back off a bit.

"Ma, what I've surmised is that it was something I was born with."

"Born with?" my mother asked in a defensive manner. "I don't know, Camden. I don't think God, who created us in his own image, allows people to be born gay. That's not his image."

"Then can you explain why children are born with both male and female genitalia? Or why children are born with Down Syndrome, mentally retarded, or with missing limbs? If we are created in God's own image, then explain why babies are born every day with some type of ailment or condition that God never had."

"Camden, I think those things are genetic issues."

"Exactly. Then maybe what I went through is genetic. I don't know if I'll ever have an answer, Ma, without help from a psychiatrist or somebody. Like I said, I think it's something within me that I had to pray long and hard to ask God to remove."

"So, you no longer have feelings for men?"

"Nope. Not at all.."

My mother then inquired about Malik. She asked why I had chosen him. I explained that had Malik never opened up to me about his sexuality, I never would have gotten involved with him. But, Malik all but invited me to be with him sexually. He played the innocent one who was turned out by me, but it couldn't be further from the truth.

"Have you heard from him in the past few months?" Mommy asked.

"He actually called me last week and left a voice message

apologizing for how things went down with Dad. I wasn't moved by his apology. It came too late and the damage had been done. I'm in the process of working on my relationship with Stormy, and Malik is the last person I want to hear from, so I deleted his message."

"Now, Camden, I have one more question and I want you to look me in my eyes when you answer." Her tone was firm and her facial expression was serious. "You know, I believe the words in the Bible from cover to cover. And I know my God can do all things, including deliver you, but are you 100 percent sure that you're done with Malik and men, period?"

As I looked her directly in her almond-shaped, dark brown eyes, I responded.

"Yes, Ma, I am 110 percent sure. Malik and all my other deeds in New York are in my past. I'm now looking forward to my future with Stormy." She wrapped her arms around me.

"I believe you, son. Now go and make Stormy your wife."

"All right, I'm off. Wish me well."

"Godspeed, baby. And oh, tell Stormy I want her legs under my table for Thanksgiving dinner. I'm cooking a big feast this year to celebrate the two of you getting back together, and possibly a marriage."

"Stormy will most likely be with her parents on Thanksgiving, but I'll give her your invitation."

I kissed and hugged my mother before I left. She wished me luck as I left to meet Stormy. We had planned a nice, quiet dinner at her apartment. The open talk I had with my mother was like therapy. Nobody had ever taken the time to ask me why I felt the way I did, or how it came about. Instead, people judged and criticized me. They didn't even take the time to assist me in my struggle because condemnation was the bandwagon everybody quickly jumped on, including the church folk. But I planned to make all those

people who talked bad about me eat their words. I was
going to show them that people do change, and once I got
my girl back, they'd all be wearing egg on their faces.

During dinner I told Stormy about my entire conversation with my mother. She was impressed with my frankness
to open up to her about it. Although I knew that the conversation was a bit uncomfortable for her to hear, she
needed to. It was important for her to know my entire past
in order for her to feel comfortable about our future.

As we lay on a mink blanket on the living room floor cud-
dling in front of the television, I felt that the timing was
right. It was time for me to pop the question to Stormy, but
this time with a more sincere heart.

"Stormy, I know I hurt you in indescribable ways, and for
that I am sorry. If given the opportunity, I'd apologize to
you for the rest of my life. You're the most wonderful person I've ever met. You're beautiful, smart, and I love you
more than life itself. Being with you completes me and I
want to know if you'd accept this ring again, to make me
whole once more. Stormy, will you marry me?"

Stormy's eyes glistened with water. "Camden, when you
hurt me, I vowed that I'd never, ever take you back. And for
a while, I was true to my word. But after seeing how you've
changed, coupled with the abundance of love I have for you
in my heart, I'm...I'm...I'm willing to try again. So, Yes,
Camden, for the second time, I will marry you."

"Are you sure now?" I asked as I placed the engagement
ring on her finger for a second time.

"I'm...I'm sure," she stuttered.

I could sense her hesitation, but I reassured her that I
would never hurt her again.

We sealed our renewed relationship with a kiss, and we
cuddled and eventually fell asleep.

Chapter 14

Stormy

Thanksgiving Day was truly a day to be thankful. I was the happiest I had been in months. Unbeknownst to my friends and family, Camden was my fiancé again and we'd planned to get married on our original wedding date in April.

It wasn't an easy decision to accept Camden back into my life. I loved him and my love for him didn't dissolve when we were apart. But there was a tiny piece of me that still had doubts, although it was not something I dwelled on consistently. At this point, I just put all my trust in the Lord that what both Camden and Reverend Brooks had said about the transformation was true.

The conversation with Reverend Brooks was enlightening. He was right. Camden was a new creature. He actually catered to me in ways that he had never done before. His romantic, caring, passionate nature reminded me of why I fell in love with him. I was such a sucker for his charming ways and it didn't hurt that he was so damn fine.

Keeping the secret that Camden and I were back to-gether was killing me. I was scared to tell anybody because I knew there would be objections to our union. I went back and forth for weeks trying to determine the best time to re-veal my secret to my family and friends.

Eventually I decided to break the news on Thanksgiving Day, after dinner. No day was more befitting of such won-derful news than Thanksgiving. Of course, I invited Do-minique, Nicole, and Leigh to come over after dinner with their families, but not for support this time. I needed to in-form them of the news as well. They'd truly been kept in the dark about my rekindled relationship with Camden.

In the midst of getting ready for dinner, I heard a knock at my door. I looked out the peephole and saw Camden's smiling face. I opened the door.

"Hi, baby. What are you doing here?"

"I wanted to check on you to see how you were holding up. I know you've got to be anxious about telling your par-ents that the wedding is back on. Are you sure you want to do this alone? I can go with you if you'd like."

"No, baby," I said as I kissed him on his cheek. "I'm a big girl. I can handle my parents. They may be a little shocked when I tell them, but they will support me because they love me."

"Well, I'm going to my parents' house for dinner. If yours happen to kick you out for being back in a relation-ship with me, then you know the invitation stands at my parents' house."

"It's not gonna be that bad. They may not be jumping up and down for joy when I tell them, but they won't kick me out."

"You'll be in my thoughts. Please call me once you tell them. I am dying to know how they take the news."

"OK, sweetie. I'll call you as soon as I leave their house. Tell your parents Happy Thanksgiving for me."

"I will deliver your message," he said as he walked toward the door. "Stormy, just think, this time next year we'll be spending Thanksgiving Day as a married couple. No more going to eat dinner with our parents separately."

"I know! I can't wait!"

"Don't forget to call me after you talk to your parents."

"I won't, Camden. I promise to call you from my cell phone as soon as I get in the car."

"I love you, Stormy!"

"I love you, too."

I left my apartment thirty minutes after Camden left. As I drove to my parents' house, I prayed. I needed every ounce of confidence I could muster to tell my family I was marrying Camden. It wasn't that long ago that I sat in their living room crying my eyes out and telling them the wedding was off. Now I was doing just the opposite. I wondered what their reaction would be when I told them. What would Trey and Jordan say? How would Dominique, Leigh, and Nicole react to the news? Would they support me? I didn't know the answer to any of these questions, but time would soon tell.

When I pulled into my parents' driveway, I knew there was no turning back. When I got to the door, I let myself in with my key. I never returned it after I moved into my own apartment. I was greeted at the door by Jordan. He hugged me and then introduced me to his new girlfriend, Lynette, a short, petite, midnight black woman with a very outgoing personality. Jordan was such a skirt chaser! Last Thanksgiving he was with Denise, and the Thanksgiving before that he brought Imani. I just couldn't keep up with him and all his women. That's why I never called them by name.

I went into the kitchen where my mother was taking the rolls out of the oven and my father was carving the turkey.

"Hi, Mom and Dad! Do you need any help with anything?" I asked as I embraced them.

"Nope. We're just about finished with everything," my father said.

"Go in the living room with your brother and his new girlfriend until dinner, honey. We're fine," my mother said.

I walked into the living room only to catch Jordan kissing Lynette on her neck. What a pair of balls he had to be kissing all on this girl in our parents' house. I felt like I was ten years old again because I wanted to tattle on him, but I decided against it. Instead, I cleared my throat to get their attention.

"Jordan, where is Trey?" I asked.

"He's on his way. He went to pick up Daneen," he answered, never taking his eyes off Lynette.

Daneen was Trey's Tyra Banks look-alike, long-time girlfriend. She really could have been considered Trey's common-law wife. They had been together for years, but for some reason Trey wouldn't officially commit to her. His philosophy was: why buy the cow when I can get the milk for free? I thought she was crazy to stay with him all these years without getting a ring, but that was their business. I had a much bigger issue to deal with, coming up right after dinner.

Trey arrived a few minutes later with Daneen in tow. Shortly after, my father set the food on the table and was ready to say the Thanksgiving blessing.

"Let us all stand and hold hands and give thanks. Dear Lord, we come to you with our hearts filled with thanks. Lord, we thank you for allowing us to see another Thanksgiving. We thank you for all the blessings you bestowed upon us throughout this year. We thank you for allowing our family to come together once more to break bread. Dear God, you're an awesome God and on this Thanksgiving Day, we give you all the glory, all the honor, and praise. In Jesus' name. Amen."

"Amen," we said in unison.

Usually I'd complain that it took my father too long to say the Thanksgiving blessing, but this year I thought he was too quick. I was thinking that the faster he prayed, the faster everyone would eat, and then I'd have to break my news.

Once Daddy finished praying, everyone dug in. Trey wasted no time, diving into the baked macaroni and cheese, ham, collard greens, and mashed potatoes.

"Jordan, pass them rolls, my brotha," he said while stuffing his face with a piece of turkey.

"Dag, Trey, slow down," I teased. "What's the rush? There's enough food for everybody."

"Girl, you know that football game is on. I'm tryin' to see the Cowboys."

"Why are you so pressed to see the Cowboys and you work for the Ravens? You're such a traitor."

"The Ravens ain't playin' today, and I've always been a Cowboys fan. They're America's team."

"No offense to the women in the room, but I've got to agree with my son. Thanksgiving is about family, but we've got to get our football in, too."

"Oh, Drake, give it a rest. How often do we have our three children for dinner? Y'all grown now and act like your parents don't exist anymore," Mommy joked.

"Come on, Ma. I'm here all the time," Jordan said.

"Yeah, you come when we're not here so you can raid our refrigerator and steal our detergent to wash your clothes," Mommy teased. "Lynette, I've got some stories to tell you about my youngest son."

"Ma, don't start." Jordan laughed. "Let's just enjoy our dinner," he said with gravy dripping from his lip.

"So, Trey, Jordan, when y'all coming back to church? I ain't seen y'all in a while. Makes me wonder if we raised our boys in church," my father said.

Jordan smirked.

"Dad, you know I work on Sundays. Fires aren't just started Monday through Saturday. Besides, I've got issues with a certain church member and I ain't trying to take nobody's head off in the house of the Lord." He cut his eye at me, letting me know he was referring to Camden. This wasn't a good sign at all.

"I'll be back, Dad. As soon as the football season is over and I'm not working on Sundays," Trey said. "I'm actually eager to show my face in True Gospel because I've got some business to take care of." Trey, too, was making a backhanded comment about Camden. I could see now that they were not going to take the news of my marrying Camden well at all. Their comments only made me more nervous about talking to them after dinner.

"Enough, you two," Mommy interjected. "We didn't raise y'all to be no gangsters, so stop acting like it. Can't you see your sister has healed from what happened? She's smiling and glowing again, and that's all that matters. So leave that boy alone."

The rest of our meal was spent talking about the upcoming Christmas holiday and how we planned to do the gift exchange this year. As always, cheap Jordan wanted to draw names, but it was only four of us, excluding him. He was too cheap to buy us one gift apiece. Of course, he was overruled. Lynette and Daneen talked about taking advantage of the black Friday sales, but I wasn't stepping foot in one mall or department store. Black Friday, the day after Thanksgiving, and Christmas Eve were the worst two days to go shopping. Those were the days customers appeared on the news fighting over the last Transformer, PlayStation, or Barbie doll.

After the delicious Thanksgiving feast, Mommy brought out sweet potato pie and vanilla ice cream. Just then, Leigh arrived.

"Happy Thanksgiving, everybody!"

"Happy Thanksgiving, Leigh," Mommy said. "I was

wondering when my girls were coming over to eat dessert. I was hoping you didn't forget me this year."

My friends came over to my parents' house every year to have dessert with us after having dinner with their families. This was one reason why I decided that today would be a good day to tell everyone about Camden and me. There was no better time when everybody was together, so I didn't have to tell the story over and over again.

"Dominique and Nicole are outside trying to find a parking space. They'll be in shortly," Leigh said.

Oh hell! It's almost time to reveal my secret.

When Nicole and Dominique came in, they joined us in the family room where everyone had assembled to watch the football game on the big screen television. *It's almost time,* I thought as I waited for Mommy to finish in the kitchen so she could join us. I didn't like the fact that Lynette and Daneen would be all up in my business, but I didn't want to be rude and ask them to leave while I talked to my family.

Finally the moment arrived. Mommy came into the family room to put her feet up. She said she was tired and couldn't wait to get to bed. My father sat down beside her on the couch and rubbed her feet.

Awwww. That's the kind of husband I hope Camden will be. As we all sat around talking, I decided it was time.

"Everybody, I have an announcement to make." They looked at me with surprised expressions on their faces. I continued. "The last time we were all here, I was extremely distraught."

"Yeah, because of that punk, Camden," Trey said.

I cut my eyes at him and then resumed speaking.

"Yes, Trey is right. I was distraught because of Camden. I was an emotional mess, but I'm a witness that prayer changes things."

"Yes, it does!" my father chimed in.

"God turned everything around for me. I haven't told any of you this, but Reverend Brooks and I talked. He told me that Camden was a changed man and that he'd made a complete transformation. Reverend Brooks made Camden his personal project and prayed over him until he was delivered from his demons." As I looked around, everyone stared at me like I had three eyes and horns coming out of my ears. But I wasn't going to allow their stares to discourage me. "After Reverend Brooks told me about Camden's transformation, I had to see it for myself. So, we began dating again."

"What the—" Jordan said. I cut him off.

"Let me finish, please! We started dating again and I noticed the substantial change in Camden up close and personal. So we decided to renew our relationship. The wedding is back on and we're getting married in April."

"Stormy, I'm totally against this," my father spat. "That boy hurt you, baby, and I don't think you should move backward. It's never good to return to past relationships. I would advise you to move forward and leave Camden in the past."

"Yeah, honey, I agree with your father. I believe in the power of God, but I'm not so sure Camden has made a complete turnaround in such a short period of time."

"Mom and Dad, I didn't believe it either when Reverend Brooks called me into his office and informed me of the change. But I've been around him for the three months. I just explained to you that I've seen it for myself. He even treats me better now than he did before."

"Stormy, I think you need psychological treatment," Trey said.

"Why?" I frowned, displeased with his statement.

"Because, why do you want to marry a man whose had sex with men? Does that make sense to you?" he asked sarcastically.

"You could say that about anyone who has had relationships with other people before they got married. If Daneen marries you, she has no idea how many other women you've been with, right?"

"This is not about Daneen and me. This is about you wanting to marry a faggot."

Trey was starting to piss me off. I was on the verge of cursing him out, but I had to remember that I was in my parents' house.

After the exchange between me and Trey, Leigh walked over to me.

"Stormy, are you sure you want to do this? He hurt you so badly before, and I don't want to see you go through that ever again."

"I'm sure, Leigh. Even when I was hurting, I still loved Camden. I think hate overpowered me initially, but as time went on I realized that I never stopped loving him."

"I don't see nothing wrong with you marrying Camden," Lynette interjected. "I think people can change. I know a dude who used to be gay and now he's married with children." I looked at her, wondering what the hell she had to do with this. But then I smiled because she was on my side.

"Lynette, this has absolutely nothing to do with you. Please stay out of this," Jordan said sternly. "And just because he's married with children doesn't mean he isn't still gay!" Lynette rolled her eyes behind his back.

I looked over at Dominique and Nicole and I could read their faces clearly. They silently agreed with my parents and brothers. Damn, the only support I had was from Lynette, a woman I didn't even know. At that moment I began to wail.

"I don't care what you all think. I love him and he's going to be my husband in April whether y'all like it or not!"

"Well, look here, young lady. I'll be damned if I will walk you down the aisle and give my only daughter away to a homosexual. So if you're marrying him, then you better find someone to take my place or walk down the aisle by yourself," my father proclaimed, and then stomped out of the room.

I cried even harder and my mother rushed over to comfort me. She apologized for my father and told me she would talk to him. She also explained that she didn't agree with me marrying Camden, but would support my decision. I hugged her tightly as I sobbed.

When my mother left the room, Jordan continued to voice his disapproval.

"Stormy, you are much smarter than this. You are a beautiful young woman with a good head on your shoulders. Why are you settling?"

"I'm not settling. I know you don't believe this, but I love Camden with all my heart. I want to be his wife!"

"Stormy, you know I love you like a sister, but I can't believe you. I think you *are* settling," Nicole said. "Why are you marrying a man who hurt you the way Camden did? I don't give a fuck how 'delivered' his father said he is; once you get it in the butt, you're always gay. Camden will always be gay, and deep down I think you know it."

"I can't take any more of this! Y'all are supposed to love and support me no matter what!" I yelled. "I can't believe y'all are treatin' me like this. I refuse to stay here any longer and listen to this mess. If you all can't accept my future husband, then that's the same as not accepting me." I started gathering my things to leave. Once I had my coat and purse, I turned around and screamed, "All of y'all can kiss my ass!"

I stormed out of the house without even saying good-bye to my parents.

Chapter 15

Malik

I couldn't believe the words that had just come out of Leigh's mouth. I was sitting on the side of my bed, dazed, trying to digest the words she'd just shoved down my throat only ten minutes ago. Could it be true? Was Camden really going to marry Stormy? The better question was: was Stormy going to marry Camden after finding out about his secret lifestyle?

"Get the fuck out of here," I said in disbelief. I refused to accept that this marriage was actually going to happen.

Ever since the meeting with Reverend Brooks, I had not heard from or seen Camden. I tried to contact him once, but he didn't answer his cell phone. I left a message, but there was no response. So I gathered that he was still pissed at me for exposing him in front of his father and Stormy. In hindsight, I regretted my decision, because I'd lost my friend and my lover. But I felt my back was up against the wall and I had no other choice.

I hadn't been to church since the confrontation because I

was afraid of the reception I'd get from the congregation. I was fully aware of all the church ladies' gossip. I almost dropped dead one Sunday afternoon, about a month after the meeting, when my grandmother came home and confronted me.

"Malik, is there something you need to tell me?" I honestly had no idea what she was talking about.

"No, Grandma," I said as I looked at her strangely.

"Are you sure? 'Cause I've been hearing some things at church that I'm not too happy about."

It was then that I knew exactly what she was talking about. I had to come up with a lie quickly.

"Oh, Grandma, are you talking about those rumors about Camden and me?"

"Yes, I am," she said sternly.

"That's old news. We've already talked about that with Reverend Brooks. The rumors had come to the attention of me and Camden a long time ago. We were so upset that we went to Reverend Brooks about it, and now everything is cool. He just told us that the devil was always busy and not to let what people say bother us."

"Why didn't you tell me about it then? Why did I have to hear it through the grapevine?" She was obviously upset.

"I didn't want to talk about it. It was too embarrassing. I wasn't proud about the rumors being spread about me being involved with our pastor's son. But it's over now. The buzz around the church ain't true and I wish everyone would stop talking about something that's already been squashed. Besides, Stormy and Camden are getting married. Maybe after they marry, the gossip will stop." I actually didn't know Camden and Stormy were getting married at that time. The last I heard the wedding was off. So now I was wondering if I spoke the marriage into existence when I lied to my grandmother about it.

"If you say so, Malik. But in the future, I want to hear

these things from you, not from Sister so and so, who heard it from Sister so and so."

I laughed slightly and gave her a hug.

"OK, Grandma. I promise not to keep anything like that from you again."

After finding out my grandmother had heard about Camden and me, I laid low, trying not to run into anyone. But obviously I was lying too low because I didn't even know Camden and Stormy were dating again, let alone planning to get married. *Damn! I can't let this happen.*

I marinated on the news of Camden and Stormy's upcoming nuptials for a couple hours. It was then that I realized I had to come up with a plan to stop them from getting married.

I'm in love with Camden and I can't allow him to marry that witch. She doesn't love him like I do, and she never will.

I paced around in my bedroom, whispering to myself.

"What to do? What to do?" Then it finally hit me. I was going to call Stormy and mess with her head. I had devised a plan to call her and reveal things to her about her fiancé that no woman would ever want to hear. Maybe after she learned what I knew about her man, she'd call the wedding off.

I dialed her home number and waited for her to pick up. On the fourth ring, she did.

"Hello!"

"Stormy, this is Malik," I said bluntly.

"What do you want?" she asked with an attitude.

"I just want to know somethin': Is it true that you and Camden are gettin' married?"

"You have some nerve calling me. I don't owe you an explanation about anything concerning Camden and me. But, since you all up in our business, I'll let you know. Yes, we're getting married. Why? How does that concern you?"

"Why are you marrying a man who's gay? I mean, we

aren't friends or nothing, but I wouldn't want that for my worst enemy." I was being sarcastic.

"Well, Malik, my and Camden's relationship is none of your concern. You need to get a life and stop worryin' about what Camden is doing. Get it through your thick head that he doesn't want you!"

Oh no this bitch didn't. Was she trying to get tough with me? It was time for me to put her in her place.

"You don't have to get smart! I really don't give a fuck what y'all do. I just wanted to know why you're entering into a marriage with a man who's obviously leading a double life."

"What did you just say?" she asked incredulously.

"You heard what the fuck I said, but just in case you didn't, let me make it plain: Your man likes dick! He likes suckin' long, black poles. He enjoys lickin' assholes. He excitedly bends over and anticipates the entrance of the one-eyed snake in between his butt cheeks. Do you understand now, or do I need to break it down to you further?"

"Fuck you, Malik!" Stormy screamed into the phone.

"No, fuck you, you stupid bitch! You're one crazy broad to marry a man that you know has sex with men. I didn't know a person could be so stupid."

"What you don't know, little boy, is that people change. Camden's a changed man and he doesn't want you, or any other man for that matter. I understand that you're bitter because Camden chose me over you, but you need to get over it. Get over your hissy fit. Go pick your shattered, little heart up off the floor, piece it back together, and move on! Camden and I are getting married and that's that!"

"Oh, yeah?" I laughed. "Well, I hope you don't think it's going to be happily ever after. You are in for a lifetime of misery and heartache. Your man is G-A-Y and there ain't nothing you can do to change that." She laughed back.

"Malik, you are pathetic and desperate. I'm in the process

of making the final preparations for my W-E-D-D-I-N-G to my future husband, C-A-M-D-E-N." She spelled out the words to mock me.

"Camden is never going to be true to you. If you think that, then you must be on crack!"

"Yeah, yeah, yeah! I think you said something to that effect earlier. If there's nothing else, I have to go. You're boring me."

"Well, let me leave you with this: Whatever Camden dishes out to you in this fake-ass marriage, you deserve because you have shit for brains to be marrying a man who you know is a homo! So on your so-called wedding day when Reverend Brooks tells Camden to kiss the bride, I hope that you taste my dick in your mouth. Peace out, dumb bitch!" I slammed the phone on the cradle.

I was heated. I lay across my bed to calm down. I didn't know if I had said enough to Stormy to make her rethink marrying Camden. But if I hadn't succeeded in getting her to change her mind, I'd be crushed. All I kept thinking was that this wedding couldn't happen. It just couldn't.

An hour later my phone rang, interrupting my thoughts. I contemplated not answering it because I was in no mood to talk to anybody. But when I spied the caller ID, I saw it was Leigh, so I answered.

"What's up, Leigh?" I asked dryly.

"What the hell did you say to Stormy?" she asked angrily. No hello, no how are you, no nothing. She was just a ball of fury calling to question me about my conversation with Stormy.

"Look, Leigh, I'm not in the mood right now. I'm sure Stormy gave you all the details of our conversation. I don't feel like rehashing it."

"Don't try to blow me off. I want to know why you called, upsetting her."

"I don't give a fuck if she's upset. Her feelings are the last thing on my mind right now. I just broke some shit down to her and then told her that she was stupid if she goes through with this wedding."

"Malik!" Leigh snapped.

"What?" I snapped back.

"You didn't have to be so mean to her. She's never done anything to you."

"I wasn't being mean to that witch. I was just telling her the truth. If her feelings are hurt it's only because it's hard to hear the truth sometimes. She's a big girl. She'll get over it."

"She thinks you are going to stop the wedding. Is that true?"

"I don't know."

"What do you mean, you don't know? Malik, please don't do that. Just let Stormy and Camden be happy," Leigh pleaded with me.

"I don't give a fuck about their happiness. What about me? What about my happiness?"

"I know it hurts, Malik, but you've got to let Camden go. He's moved on and you have to do the same. Besides, since Stormy thinks you may be stopping the wedding, she's going to have extra security at the door to stop you from entering the church."

"What?" I laughed. "Security? What security?"

"She said that she's going to have four of her male cousins acting as security to ensure that you don't do anything crazy."

"True Gospel is a public place. No one can keep me out!"

"What you say is true, but is it really worth it? Do you think stopping their wedding will make Camden come back to you? It will only infuriate him and make him hate you. I beg you not to do anything stupid. Just let them be. OK?"

"Whatever!"

"Promise me, Malik!" she said sternly.

"I'm sorry, Leigh, I can't promise you anything."

"Malik, you need Jesus! I'm going to pray for you."

"Yeah, you do that. In the meantime, I'm on my way out. I'll holla at you later."

"Think about what I said, Malik. I mean it. You better not bring your behind to that wedding. If you do, I'm going to whip you myself."

"Well, be ready to put me across your knee." I laughed. "I'm out!"

I must've been a serious threat if this chick had called out the dogs to keep me from attending the wedding. I laughed at the idea of having security keep me out. *She must not know who I am.* It didn't matter if she requested the presence of the entire Baltimore City Police Department to keep me out. I was still going to be at that wedding.

Chapter 16

Stormy

The Wedding Day

It was finally here—my wedding day. This was the day I had struggled with for the past five months. It had been extremely stressful trying to convince my parents and brothers to support my marriage to Camden. My mother had her reservations about my upcoming nuptials, but she wanted me to be happy, so it wasn't hard to convince her. My father, on the other hand, was another story. He still wasn't open to the idea at all. My mother tried day and night to get him to change his mind, but he wouldn't budge. Finally, she suggested he speak with Camden and Reverend Brooks to help him see things more clearly. Surprisingly, he agreed.

My later father explained that he met with Camden at his apartment. He called to ask if they could have a man-to-man talk. Camden eagerly agreed because he desperately wanted my father's approval. During that meeting, Camden explained to my father that he indeed had made a complete turnaround. He explained that he was battling some evil spirits, but the Lord intervened and removed them. Camden apologized repeatedly for hurting me months ago and promised with his hand on the Holy Bible that he would never do it again. My father said he felt somewhat better after leaving Camden's apartment, but he wasn't fully convinced about Camden's transformation. He did admit, though, that after talking to Camden and looking in his eyes, he felt he was sincere.

An hour after meeting with Camden, my father went to see Reverend Brooks at the church.

"Reverend," he said, "I'm coming to you because I don't feel good about giving my daughter away to your son, in light of everything that's happened. But because I love you and respect you as my pastor, and I've never known you to steer me wrong, I'd like to get your honest opinion about Camden. Has he really been delivered?"

Without hesitation, Reverend Brooks responded.

"My God, yes! I saw it with my own eyes, Brother Knight. He's not that same demon possessed man he was before. He's truly living his life as one of God's children should. I don't have a daughter, but Stormy is the closest I've ever had to one, and I wouldn't allow my son to marry your daughter if I thought he hadn't changed. I wouldn't put her heart in jeopardy."

"All right, pastor. I'm gonna have confidence in your judgment on this one. I hope what you say is true." Then my father walked right up to him, and said, *"If in your heart you marry the two of them, knowing your son hasn't changed, their blood will be on your hands. You better hope and pray that he doesn't hurt my daughter again or there will be hell to pay."*

Daddy said Reverend Brooks was shocked by his words, but fully understood his position. He assured my father that everything would be fine.

Once my father left Reverend Brooks's office, he called me and asked me to come over. When I arrived, my mother,

Trey, and Jordan were all assembled in the dining room. I greeted everyone and joined them at the table. My father began to speak.

"I asked you all over here tonight because I wanted to let you know that I've decided to give Stormy and Camden my blessing to get married."

"Really? Daddy—" I said excitedly.

"Let me finish, please." He held up his hand for me to be quiet. "I had a meeting with both Camden and Reverend Brooks and they assured me that Camden is, in fact, a changed man. I have to admit that I'm still not 100 percent convinced that Camden has changed, but you can only take a man at his word. And after looking into Camden's eyes and hearing the sincerity in his voice, I believe that he in fact does love Stormy. The boy even pulled out a Bible and swore on it that he'd changed. What sealed the deal for me was talking to Reverend Brooks. He told me he saw the spirits fleeing from Camden's body as he prayed for him. I've never known the man to lie, and he knows his son better than we do. So as a respected man of God, I'm holding him to his word. But I did tell him that I hoped what he said was true because if Camden hurts you again, Stormy, both of them will pay."

"Drake!" my mother snapped. "Did you threaten our pastor?"

"Sure did. If he knows that Camden hasn't changed and he marries them anyway, then their blood is on his hands."

"That's right, Dad! I totally agree," Trey chimed in. My father continued.

"We are a family. The Knight family has always supported one another and today will not be any different. Although we may not be elated with your sister's choice of a husband, we have to support her. We love you, Stormy, and want you to be happy. So if you really want Camden to be your husband, then tonight your mother, brothers, and I give you our blessing to marry."

I couldn't believe it. I was overjoyed. I jumped up and ran over to my father and hugged him.

"Thank you, Daddy, thank you. I love you." My mother and brothers joined us and our family shared a group hug. That night a tremendous burden was lifted from me. The wedding plans continued and the date of the ceremony quickly approached.

In the final days before the wedding, I received another hard blow. As I was checking my mailbox, I noticed a letter addressed to me with no return address. I went into my apartment and opened the letter.

Dear Stormy,

As your wedding day draws near, I feel the need to give you some words of wisdom. Please don't marry Camden. He will not be true to you. You are fooling yourself if you think that he is no longer gay. Camden is the biggest undercover faggot that you will ever meet. He's lying to you when he says he has changed. For your sake, I suggest you cancel this wedding and run as far away from him as you can. Being with him will bring you nothing but heartache. I know it's hard for you to believe the words of a person who is to remain anonymous, but trust and believe that what I say is true. Camden is today and will forever be an undercover homosexual and you deserve better. I know this for a fact. DON'T MARRY HIM OR YOU WILL REGRET IT!

Sincerely,
God's Messenger

As I read the letter, little beads of sweat formed on my forehead. I grabbed my chest and starting panting. With all the stress of planning a wedding, the fact that Camden had put me through so much during the prior months, and now to receive this letter was too much for me to bear. I fell to the floor, curled into a fetal position, and cried.

Who would send such a letter? I pondered. My first thought was Malik, but he would have never cared about my feelings, and the sender seemed to have considered my best interests. I just wished I knew the identity of God's Messenger.

I called Camden and asked him to come over immediately. When he arrived, I shoved the letter in his hand.

"Read this," I said.

I studied Camden's face as he read the letter. He seemed to be unmoved by its contents. After he read it, he balled it up and walked toward the trashcan in my kitchen.

"Why are you throwing it away?" I questioned.

"Because it's garbage, Stormy. Plain garbage. You can't allow yourself to get all worked up over somebody who sent you something anonymously. It shows they didn't have the balls to confront you face to face, so I refuse to get upset about a letter from someone so cowardly."

"Do you think it was Malik?"

"Don't know, don't care," he said firmly. He walked over and pulled me into his arms. "Baby, we're getting married no matter what," he whispered as we embraced. "We've come too far to let anyone, and I mean anyone, come between us. You know the man I am today and you know the words in that letter don't reflect who I am right now. So, baby, please, I beg you, please, do not let this get you all worked up."

I was puzzled and disturbed by Camden's reaction. He actually handled the whole thing well, a little too well. The only reason why I agreed to let it go was because the person who sent the letter remained anonymous. It wasn't like the letter was from Dante or Leigh. I had no way of proving its validity, so I couldn't put much effort into being upset about someone who didn't care enough about me to reveal his or her identify.

As I reflected upon the negative, I also had positive moments as well, so I decided to take strength from those moments to help me move on. I now had the support of my family and I was thrilled to know that they would all be at the church to share in my special day. Most of all, I was ecstatic to have my Daddy walk me down the aisle.

OK, Stormy girl, it's time. You've made a vow to yourself, so now it's time to go and marry your man. I looked in the mirror and smiled. *Go get married, girl.*

On the ride to the church in the white, Mercedes limousine, my nervousness hadn't subsided and it didn't help that Nicole had jokes.

"Stormy, you better hope Camden shows up at the church."

"Why? Why would you say that?" Her comment had me shaking.

"Your mother told us when you were in the bathroom that Trey and Jordan went to see Camden this morning. It seems they threatened him." Nicole laughed. She obviously thought this was humorous, but it wasn't to me.

"Oh, my God. What did they say?" I cupped my mouth with my hands.

"We don't know. She didn't tell us," Leigh said. "All we know is that the both of them paid him a courtesy visit."

"Yeah, Stormy, they may have Camden running for the hills by now," Dominique teased. I couldn't understand why they thought this was so funny. And why would somebody tell me all of this right before my wedding? Maybe I could have called Camden to see if he was OK if they told me earlier.

"Sike!" My three *so-called* friends yelled in unison.

"We're just messing with you, girl. Your mother didn't tell us that," Nicole said.

"Y'all! Don't play like that," I pouted, but was really relived. "Y'all supposed to be my friends. Why would you play such a cruel joke on me? I was about to have a damn fit up in this limo." Finally I laughed as well.

"Just a little jokey joke before you jump the broom. You's gon' be marr'd afta while," Nicole said in a southern drawl.

We spent the remaining moments talking about the upcoming honeymoon in Barbados. I was eager to go, having never been to the Caribbean before. But I couldn't really get excited about my honeymoon until I got through the wedding ceremony first.

When we arrived, I was greeted at the limo by my wedding coordinator, DeVona, a tall, vivacious, beautiful woman who knew the art of planning a wedding. She instructed me to stay in the limousine until it was my turn to enter the church. Everyone else in the wedding party went to their respective places. Sitting there alone, I noticed that my stomach was still full of butterflies. *Why won't they disappear?* I wondered as I stared at my engagement ring. I was hoping it would smile back at me, but it didn't. This wasn't a good sign.

My father walked up to the limo. He opened the door to help me out.

"Hi, beautiful," he said, kissing my cheek. "Are you ready?" I gave a nervous grin.

"As ready as I'll ever be."

With the help of my father and DeVona carrying the long train of my dress, I entered True Gospel church. My father and I were standing arm and arm as the doors of the church sanctuary opened. Everyone in the congregation stood. My father and I proceeded down the aisle while the organist played "Here Comes the Bride." My vision blurred from the tears forming in my eyes as my father guided me to the altar to give me away to Camden, my future husband.

Chapter 17

Malik

When Leigh informed me that the wedding was on again, I broke down and called Camden, but my calls went unanswered. I left messages for him to call me, but he never did. Finally I got desperate. I went to a payphone and called him. I figured if he didn't recognize the telephone number on the caller ID, then he'd answer. I was right! He answered immediately.

"Hello," he answered. The sound of his voice made me melt. I missed Camden and all we shared. I wanted him back. I finally got the nerve to speak.

"Hi, Camden. It's me."

"Malik?"

"Yeah, it's me," I said softly, fully expecting him to slam down the phone in my ear.

Surprisingly, he did not hang up.

"What number are you calling me from?"

"I'm at a payphone." He laughed.

"So, you wanted to talk to me that badly, huh?"

I didn't answer his question. I just jumped right in to what my heart was telling me to say.

"Camden, I'm sorry. I'm so sorry for how things went down. I want things back the way they were. I want you back in my life. Please, whatever you do, please don't marry Stormy." I felt like I was fighting for my life. It didn't matter that I was sounding like a girl, begging on the phone.

"I love Stormy, Malik. I'm gonna marry her," he stated frankly.

"What about me? Does your love for me turn on and off like a water hose, or were you lyin' to me every time you said you loved me?"

"I do still love you, Malik," he whispered. "But we could never be together. My family wouldn't approve."

"Forget your family," I bellowed.

"Malik, just know that I love you today, tomorrow, and forever, but we can't ever be together. I'm gonna marry Stormy because she's good to me and for me. You've got to understand that and let go of us."

"I can't."

"Well, you've got to try. And I've heard rumors of you stopping the wedding. Is that true?"

I didn't respond.

"Malik, I know you heard me. Are you planning to stop the wedding?"

Still I didn't answer. I just breathed heavily into the phone.

"Please don't! It will be a huge embarrassment to me, Stormy, and especially you. If you come and make a scene, it will only keep the rumors going and none of us need that. Besides, if you interrupt our ceremony, it wouldn't stop us from getting married. We'd just do it in private. So think long and hard before you think about making such a bold move. Hopefully, you love me enough not to humiliate me."

I listened to his words, but all his banter went in one ear and out the other.

"All right, Malik, I've got to go. I wish you the best in all your future endeavors. I'm sorry if I've hurt you in any way, but I've got to do what's best for me. But no matter what, know that I'll always have mad love for you and you'll always have a place in my heart. Take care, Malik. Love you. Bye."

"Love you," I said sadly. Then I heard a dial tone.

That was two weeks ago and I had not heard from him since. I guess he was really going through with this bogus wedding.

We'll just have to see about that. He told me he loves me. . . .

I parked my car two blocks away from the church because I didn't want anyone to spot it. I walked up to the church on the opposite side of the street in order to survey the situation before I entered. Just as Leigh informed me, there were four dudes that I recognized as Stormy's cousins, who stood at the door of the church. Big-mouthed Dante was one of them. I laughed. *Didn't they know there was more than one entrance to the church?* I wondered as I crossed the street and walked around to the church parking lot to a door that led to the banquet hall. I walked up the back steps, entered the rear of the sanctuary, slid into the very last pew, and slouched to avoid being seen. I saw my grandmother near the front of the church. I damn sure didn't want her to see me here because she would surely be alarmed, considering all the talk that had gone around the church about Camden and me.

I looked at my watch and it was five minutes to four. The wedding was scheduled for four o'clock. I was hoping that it would start on time. *The sooner it starts, the sooner the whole farce will be over.*

As I waited for the ceremony to start, I looked around the

sanctuary. It was beautifully decorated. I surmised the wedding colors were red and silver because all of the wedding décor was in those colors. There were flowers on every other pew and an arch at the altar. Although I couldn't stand Stormy, I had to admit she had taste.

My thoughts were interrupted when Camden entered the sanctuary with Reverend Brooks, and his best man and cousin, Tyler, who bore a strong resemblance to Shamar Moore. Camden talked about Tyler often during our time together. Tyler was a year older than Camden. It seemed that they had a really close relationship, growing up almost like brothers. Camden explained that Tyler always dreamed of being a star in Hollywood. After college, he landed in a movie production in California. I hadn't seen him much because he rarely visited. I wondered if he knew all the dirty little secrets that were hidden in Camden's closet.

Damn, both of them look good, I thought as I gazed at Camden and Tyler, who both looked pleasing to the eye in their black tuxedos with red vests and ties. I continued to look at Camden, wondering why he was doing this. Why was he marrying this girl, knowing he was gay? Then my thoughts were interrupted by the start of music.

The song "Mama" by Boyz II Men played as Camden's mother, First Lady Sheryl, entered the sanctuary escorted by Trey. She was followed by Stormy's mother, Mrs. Victoria, who was escorted by Jordan. Once they were all seated, an instrumental song played. The bridesmaids, Nicole and Dominique, were escorted down the aisle by Hassan and Jared, followed by Leigh. *That's my girl.* She looked beautiful in a red, strapless, A-line dress with a beaded bodice, pleated waist with a front cascade, and her silver shoes. I made a mental note to sing, "The Woman in Red" by Stevie Wonder when I talked to her later. After the bridesmaids were positioned at the altar, two ushers came to roll the aisle runner. The flower girl, who was Tyler's three-year-old daughter, entered, throwing red rose petals. Everyone was awed, and they cooed at her as she walked down the aisle. Then we were asked to stand. I hesitantly stood to await the entrance of the woman who was about to marry my man.

As I stood, some of the church members noticed me. Some were staring, others pointed and whispered. Many seemed shocked to see me.

"I wonder what he's doing here," I heard one young woman say.

"He's coming to get his man, girl," another joked. They laughed and gave each other a high five. I tried to ignore them. None of them had seen me since the gossip started about Camden and me. But I was just as shocked to see so many of them show up for this sham of a wedding. *They are only here to see if it's actually going to take place. They all know that Camden is gay, so they want to see if he'll actually go through with marrying Stormy.*

As Stormy and her father proceeded down the aisle, I watched her attentively. She was weeping as if someone had died. I rolled my eyes at her.

This bitch, I said in my mind. The sight of her made me angry. She was about to marry my man, and the thought made me want to puke. Once she made it to the altar, her father and mother stood.

"Who gives this woman to this man?" Reverend Brooks asked.

"We do," Stormy's parents gleefully answered. *Wrong move.*

Reverend Brooks began the ceremony with a prayer and the scripture reading—first Corinthians, chapter thirteen, verses four through seven. I was humored as I sat and listened to Reverend Brooks read the words of the scripture.

"Love is patient, love is kind. It does not envy, it does not boast, it is not proud. It is not rude, it is not self-seeking, it is not easily angered, it keeps no record of wrongs. Love does not delight in evil but rejoices with the truth. It always protects, always trusts, always hopes, and always perseveres."

Ha. Ha. I chuckled inwardly. *Kind . . . not rude . . . not self-seeking . . . rejoices with truth . . . always protects . . . always trusts.* This was a joke. Please. Camden wasn't going to abide by any of the words in that scripture. I sat in awe as I witnessed this atrocity. I couldn't for the life of me understand why these two idiots were getting married. They knew neither of them was ready. Neither of them was going into this marriage whole-heartedly, and both of them knew damned well that this wasn't how God intended for marriage to be.

After the scripture reading, Reverend Brooks asked Camden and Stormy to face each other.

"Is there any reason why the two of you should not enter into marriage?" he asked. They both shook their heads.

"Liars," I mumbled under my breath, then quickly scanned the people around me to make sure they hadn't heard me. Then Reverend Brooks addressed the congregation. "Do any of you have just cause as to why these two should not join in holy matrimony?"

This was just the part I had been waiting for. It was my cue to show my tail. I waited for a couple of seconds, and when no one else displayed the gall to speak up, I realized it was my duty to do so. I stood up and cleared my throat. Heads immediately turned in my direction. People looked at me as if I was a fire-breathing devil wearing a red patent leather thong with a pitchfork in hand and horns coming out of my head. I didn't care, though. I was there on a mission to take back what Stormy had stolen from me—Camden.

As I opened my mouth to speak, I made eye contact with Leigh. Her eyes were pleading with me and she mouthed, "Please, Malik, don't!" I looked away from her and back at

the congregation staring at me. This time, I saw my grandmother looking at me, perplexed. I knew she had to be wondering why I had stood up in the middle of Stormy and
Camden's wedding.

It was then that I decided I couldn't do it.

*I cannot stop the wedding. It will kill my grandmother to be
embarrassed in her church home because of her gay grandson.* Besides, I told her there was nothing between Camden and me
when she confronted me about the rumors. So because of
her, because of the only woman who ever gave a damn about
me, I decided to flee.

I ran out the back of the church without saying a word. I
bolted down the stairs and out the banquet hall doors. I made
a mad dash for my car. When I got there, I felt as if I was
hyperventilating. I couldn't catch my breath. I opened the
car door, sat in the driver's seat, and put my head against the
steering wheel. As I tried to catch my breath, tears began to
roll down my face. The man I loved was marrying another,
and there wasn't a damn thing I could do about it.

Chapter 18

Stormy

When Reverend Brooks asked if anyone knew just cause for Camden and I not to be married, the congregation was silent. Then I heard someone clear his throat. My heart sank. I immediately thought about Malik. *Was he here? He couldn't be. How could he have gotten past my cousins?* I wanted to turn around to see what was going on, but I was too scared.

After what seemed like an eternity, Reverend Brooks continued with the ceremony. I silently let out a sigh of relief.

"Camden and Stormy have written their own vows," Reverend Brooks announced as Camden and I faced each other, holding hands. Camden was first. He looked me directly in my eyes.

"I, Camden Xavier Brooks, take you, Stormy Adair Knight, to be my best friend and my wife. I promise to cherish our union in times of joy and times of sorrow. I vow to faithfully love you, respect you, treasure you, protect you, comfort you, and encourage you as long as we both shall live."

As Camden spoke his vows, his eyes showed nothing but love and sincerity. I think I even saw tears forming as he professed his love to me.

"Now, Stormy, please recite your vows," Reverend Brooks instructed.

"I, Stormy Adair Knight, take you, Camden Xavier Brooks to be my husband, my partner for life, and my true love," I said proudly with a heart filled with joy. "I offer you my solemn vow to be your faithful wife in good times and bad. I promise to love, support, and uplift you throughout our walk together. When our way becomes difficult, I promise to stand by you and strengthen you. With every heartbeat, I will love you. Through our Lord and Savior Jesus Christ, our love will never fail."

We then exchanged matching wedding bands. My wedding band was a fourteen-karat gold, diamond enhancer that fit perfectly with my engagement ring. Camden's wedding band was similar with only the round diamonds. Reverend Brooks held the rings before us.

"These rings are the shape of a circle that should never be broken," he advised. "Once you place the bands on each other's fingers, your bond should never be destroyed."

Our soloist, Veronica, sang "I Believe in You and Me." As she sang, I smiled because I truly believed in Camden and our marriage even if no one else did. I fought to hold back tears as she sang. Once Veronica finished, Reverend Brooks said a prayer of unification. Camden and I held hands tightly during the prayer. I quietly prayed along with Reverend Brooks.

"Dear Father in heaven, I ask that you bless these two young people as they embark upon a new life together as one whole. Keep them during times of triumph and wrap them in your arms during times of trials. God, I'm asking you to bless this union and allow them to go forth as one. In Jesus' name, let the church say amen."

"In the power vested in me and in the eyesight of God, I now pronounce you husband and wife," Reverend Brooks pronounced once the prayer was complete. You may now salute your bride." And Camden did exactly as he was instructed. He raised my veil and kissed me long and passionately. I think Reverend Brooks subtly cleared his throat, reminding us that we were standing in front of the church with the congregation watching.

"Family and friends, I now have the pleasure of being the first to introduce you to my son and my daughter, Mr. and Mrs. Camden Xavier Brooks." The congregation stood, applauded, and cheered as we exited the sanctuary.

The wedding reception was awesome. It was held at Martin's West and the room was beautifully decorated with our wedding colors—silver and red. The atmosphere seemed to be filled with love.

The evening began with Tyler, Camden's cousin and best man, giving a toast.

"I'd like to say congratulations to my cousin, my brother, Camden, and his beautiful bride, Stormy. I wish you much love and happiness today and every day. God bless you both."

"Thank you," Camden and I mouthed from our seats at the head reception table.

Next, Leigh offered her words of wisdom.

"To Stormy and Camden. I think I speak for everyone assembled here this evening when I say that you two make a lovely couple. I pray that your marriage will be blessed and filled with nothing but joy. Throughout your relationship, there have been some good times and some not so good times, but remember that the good times always outweigh the bad. Take strength from all the positive things in your marriage and never, ever let the happiness you feel today subside. Best wishes on a happy and long life together. And remember, what God has put together, let no man put asunder."

After eating our mouthwatering meal, which included prime rib, stuffed chicken breast, fresh string beans, and mashed potatoes and gravy, Camden and I shared our first dance. As a married couple we glided across the floor to the tender and soulful sound of Luther Vandross's "If This World Were Mine."

The entire time we danced, Camden whispered in my ear.

"You have no idea how much I love you," he said. "I'm so happy you're my wife." I responded by telling him that I was proud to be Mrs. Camden Brooks.

My father and I danced to Celine Dion's "Because You Loved Me." I love my father dearly, and it was because of his love that day and throughout my life that I was able to marry the man of my dreams with a joyful heart. That moment with my father was very special to me.

We continued with the reception formalities of cutting the cake, and the bouquet and garter toss. Crazy Nicole caught the bouquet and Jared caught the garter. Tradition said that the person who caught the garter had to place it on the person who caught the bouquet. I burst into laughter. All I could do was reflect on the conversation when Nicole told me she had a crush on sexy Jared. Now she was going to meet him up close and personal in the middle of the dance floor. This moment was priceless, and only I knew why. Jared was instructed that the higher he placed the garter above Nicole's knee, the more years of marriage would be guaranteed for Camden and me. Nicole, not being shy, quickly lifted her bridesmaid dress and gave Jared easy access. Jared, being the smooth gentlemen he was, began slowly pushing the garter up her leg. Once he passed her knee, Nicole's face lit up. Her expression made me wonder if he accidentally brushed up against her thong. Camden and I stood watching them and laughing. I couldn't wait to tease her about this later.

Afterward, the party was on! Once the music started playing, everyone jumped up and started grooving. Camden's and my parents were also busting a move during the reception. I chuckled as I thought about it because the four of them were such conservative, church-going folks. If only the whole congregation could see them now! Trey and Jordan were doing their things with Lynette and Daneen. I was glad to see they were enjoying themselves, despite their feelings toward Camden.

For our last dance, Camden and I requested that the DJ play "Ribbon in the Sky" by Stevie Wonder. As we began to dance, the members of the wedding party, our parents, and the remaining guests formed a loving circle around us. I was overwhelmed with elation. I didn't want this moment to ever end.

The next day Camden and I were flying to Barbados for our honeymoon. We were going to spend seven beautiful days in the Caribbean. But before our flight, we decided to spend our wedding night at the Inner Harbor Marriot Hotel in the honeymoon suite.

"This suite is breathtaking, Camden. I may not ever want to leave."

"Nothing but the best for the best. If you think this suite is nice, wait until you see the suite that awaits us in Barbados," he said as he caressed me from behind. "I love you, Stormy. You've made me the happiest man ever."

"I love you, too, Camden."

After getting out of our wedding attire, we showered. I put on a sheer, candy apple red negligee and Camden wore matching silk boxer shorts. He walked up behind me and started kissing my neck.

"Our honeymoon officially starts tomorrow, but tonight

is our wedding night. Let's make this a wedding night to remember," he suggested smoothly.

"Take me to the bed so I can fulfill your request," I whispered seductively.

I was a little apprehensive about making love to Camden
now that I knew he'd had sex with men. I spent many nights
prior to the wedding wondering if I'd be able to consum-
mate our marriage. Initially, Camden lost his sex appeal and
I questioned his masculinity, but I prayed for weeks to overcome my reservations before our wedding night. And now,
as Camden and I were about to embark upon our first sexual
experience as a married couple, I was not only hesitant
about being with Camden sexually, but I wondered if he
truly desired me.

*Can I satisfy him? What if having sex with me isn't good
enough? What if his gay desires aren't really gone? Oh God, I
pray that I can be woman enough to please him, and keep him
from having homosexual desires. Should I ask him to wear protection?* These were thoughts no woman should ever have on
her wedding night.

Camden picked me up and carried me to the plush, king-
sized bed. He gently placed me on the bed and began kissing me passionately. He abruptly stopped kissing me, gazed
into my eyes, and told me he loved me. At that moment,
tears fell from my eyes and ran down my cheeks. Camden
kissed my tears away. He lowered his body toward my wet,
pulsing love triangle. He raised my negligee and began
tongue kissing my navel as I arched my back and started in-
voluntarily thrusting in anticipation. He then used his hands
to pry my legs apart. After separating my legs, he looked at
what he was about to feast upon. He lowered himself between my legs and skillfully used his lips and tongue to deliver me to a state of ecstasy. It didn't take long for me to
climax, making my whole body convulse.

After I licked my juices from his face, Camden dropped

his silk boxers to the floor. I anxiously awaited his entrance. Camden eased himself inside me. The very first delicious stroke was like being in heaven. I knew we belonged together. As I enjoyed the fullness of his continuous rhythmic motions, I smiled inside because my body craved this pleasure.

My thoughts were interrupted when Camden flipped me over and placed me on top of him. I rode him—long, slow, and deep. The more he moaned, the harder and faster I rode him, like a mechanical bull. Not only was I trying to please him, but I was attempting to completely block out any thoughts of his past sexual experiences.

We basked in the intoxicating moments, completely drenched with our sweat. Finally, we climaxed simultaneously as husband and wife.

"I love you, Mr. Brooks," I said, gasping for air.

"I love you more, Mrs. Brooks," he whispered, gasping for breath himself.

I smiled and laid my head on his chest. He wrapped his arms around me.

Making love to Camden as husband and wife was better than before. It seemed the connection was different. *I love this man with my whole heart.* I closed my eyes to savor the moment. With closed eyes, I silently prayed that every day of our marriage would be as satisfying, joyful, and fulfilling as this very moment.

Chapter 19

Malik

"Malik, boy, are you a queer?" my inebriated Uncle Sonny questioned when he barged into my bedroom a couple of hours after I returned home from Camden and Stormy's wedding. I was in no mood for one of his drunken stupor interrogations, especially the way I was feeling after I left the church. It took me a good twenty minutes to get my breathing under control and another five to dry my tear-drenched face. I usually didn't cry after all the misery I'd experienced in my life, and disappointment was easily accepted, but this was my first heartbreak. The drive home was horrendous, as all I could think about was how Camden was gone forever. I was inundated with emotions of anger, sadness, and abandonment, which caused me to lash out with rage while driving.

"I hate him. I'm gonna fuck their marriage up. I hope their plane crashes on the way to their honeymoon. I hope they both burn in hell," I muttered to myself during the entire drive home. So when I arrived home, I wasn't in the right frame of mind to put up with Uncle Sonny's inquiry.

"What?" I asked testily. Not only was I somewhat offended by his bluntness, I was shocked that those words had spewed from his mouth.

"You heard me, boy. Are you a sissy?"

"Uncle Sonny, you better go 'head wit that, man. I ain't no sissy." And that I wasn't. It's one thing for me to be attracted to the same gender, but I was far from a sissy.

"Don't flip off at me. I heard Mamma downstairs on the phone talking to somebody about you showing up at that wedding causing a big stir at the church."

I didn't even know my grandmother had come home. I was so out of it when I got home that I must not have heard her come in.

"What did you hear Grandma say?" I asked.

"Something about you causin' a ruckus at the church by showing up to dat weddin'. And how you got people talking 'bout you and Reverend Brooks's son being queers," he slurred.

"It's not true, Uncle Sonny. Camden's married—to a woman. Neither one of us is gay."

"All right, boy. You better make sure you ain't. 'Cause Uncle Sonny ain't never seen you wit no girlfriend. You need to go on out and get you some sweet stuff. It'll have your nose open wider than Mo'Nique's hips."

I hurriedly rushed Uncle Sonny out of my room, slamming the door behind him. I attempted to hit him where the sun didn't shine, but missed. Now I was faced with another issue—my grandmother. She was bound to think something was up now that she was aware of my theatrics at the wedding. Grandma couldn't have seen me because it all happened in a few seconds, but with the rumors spreading around the church like wildfire, it probably only took a matter of minutes before she heard about the whole ordeal. Since she hadn't come to say anything to me when she arrived home from the wedding, she was most definitely pissed off.

I walked over to my bedroom door, slowly opened it, and stuck my ear out to find out if my grandmother was still on the phone. She was. I tiptoed to the top of the stairs and listened. I had no clue who she was talking to because I could only hear one side of the conversation.

"I don't know what's wrong with that boy," I heard her say as I eavesdropped. "I don't know if it's true or not. . . . If it is true, it's because his no good daddy was never around to teach him how to be a man. . . . I ain't sayin' nothing to him. He told me it wasn't true. . . . I don't know what to believe. All I can do is keep him in my prayers."

A little saddened by what I overheard, I quietly walked back to my bedroom. I chose to keep my distance from Grandma because she sounded as if she was a bit upset. It was best I stay locked up in my room because I was not ready for a confrontation with Grandma.

"So them bitches got married, huh?" I asked Leigh. It was two days after Camden and Stormy's wedding and we were eating dinner at Old Country Buffet.

"Malik, must your mouth be so foul?" She rolled her eyes.

"Of course. When it comes to Camden and Stormy, I have nothing nice to say. I already can't stand her and I'm on the verge of hating him."

"Why? Because he moved on?"

I frowned. Leigh had no clue what my disdain was all about.

"It's more than him just moving on, Leigh. It's about all the lies, the deceit. I feel used. I feel taken advantage of. It's kind of like he kept me under his spell, so I'd be with him

and only him. He said and did any and everything to keep
me hanging on by a thread, so I'd never move on to anyone
else. He had to be my only focus. Then after a bunch of
empty promises, he came back home from New York only
to hook up with Stormy and marry her. So, yeah, I'm bitter
and I'm hurt."

"I can understand your point, but I think your anger is
misplaced when it comes to Stormy. She, too, was one of
Camden's victims."

"If she was such a victim, then why did she marry him?"

"The same reason why you still want to be with him," she
said with a smirk.

I laughed and threw up my hands.

"You got me. You got me."

"Malik, you've got to let it go. You're young. You've got
so much to live for. Don't let this mess with Camden stop
you from going forward, being the man God destined you
to be. There are plenty other fish in the sea, maybe even a
female fish," she teased.

I was beginning to think being with a woman couldn't be
half bad after all the stress Camden put me through. But she
was right. It was time for me to find other interests, other
friends. It was time I broadened my horizons and stepped
out with some other folks. It was time for me to get out of
this rut and face the reality that my relationship with Camden, as I had known it, was over. He was married now and
there was nothing more I could do to bring him back to
me—nothing.

"You're right, Leigh. I'm going to start going out more.
There's this guy in my computer graphics design class that's
been digging me for a minute. I never gave him the time of
day because I was all up in Camden's ass—literally." I
laughed. Leigh scowled.

"Malik. I don't wanna hear about you being in nobody's
ass. Now go on and tell me about this classmate."

"Well, the dude's name is Beau. He's about five foot seven, petite, with a tight booty," I joked, messing with Leigh again. She didn't respond. She raised her eyebrows and gave me a stop-playing-with-me look. "Since the spring semester will be ending next month, I need to holla at him as soon as possible."

"Don't rush into anything," Leigh advised. "Take your time. Let your wounds heal. Remember you're still recovering from the effects of Camden. That's the mistake women make. They jump from relationship to relationship without healing from the previous hurt. That causes a lot of unnecessary baggage in a new relationship. Take it slow, Malik. Take it slow."

"I promise not to rush into anything. I'm not even looking to date. I just want to hang out with some new people. And speaking of not rushing into anything, what's up with you? Where's your man?"

"There is none. I got sick of the games, so I kicked Kevin's sorry tail to the curb."

"Really?" I asked, shocked. Leigh and Kevin had made such a cute couple. They had been dating for about two years. I always thought they would end up married. Guess not.

"Malik, I'm twenty-seven years old. I'm smart, educated, self-sufficient, and I don't need a man to define me. Yes, it's wonderful to be in a relationship, but I ain't for all the drama, especially your-man-is-cheating-on-you drama."

"You mean like your girl, Stormy?" I eagerly asked.

"That's different," she defended.

"How?"

"Because Stormy loves Camden with every fiber of her being. I don't think I've ever loved a man that deeply before."

"Please. Stormy don't love Camden as deeply as you think. That wench just wanted to get married for bragging rights. She just wanted to be the first of her friends to have a husband. Why else would she marry a man that's gay? Come on, Leigh, would you?"

"Honestly, no, Malik, but I'm a totally different person. Besides, how do you know why Stormy married Camden. That's just your assumption because you're ticked at her, but you really don't know."

"Whatever."

"Believe what you want, Malik, but Stormy loves Camden. Yes, she's taking a big risk marrying him, knowing about his past, but as Christians we know that God in His infinite wisdom can do all things."

"So why didn't you stay with ol' boy you kicked to the curb? Didn't you think God could change him?"

"Like I told you, having a mate is great. I'm all for promoting happy, healthy relationships, but if you don't mean me no good, then I'm not putting up with it. Would I have married my ex knowing he was a cheat? No. Would I have married Camden? Hell no. But Stormy's heart isn't my heart. So she made the best choice for her. I can only pray that God watches over that marriage, 'cause I've got a feeling they gonna need it."

"Oh, yeah, they are gonna need it all right, 'cause Camden hasn't changed. He put on that show for y'all with the hopes of convincing himself and everybody who witnessed that bogus wedding that he's a new creature in Christ. But I know better. He may have fooled y'all, but he ain't foolin' me."

"I don't think you would admit if he did change. You're so caught up in your own feelings that you don't want to see a change in Camden. You only want the worst for him and Stormy. It's time to let it go, Malik. I stood at the altar with him and I saw the love in his eyes as he recited his vows to Stormy. Until I know differently, I believe our Lord worked a miracle in his life and delivered him."

"I'll be sure to contact the Academy Awards, because he sure has earned an Oscar for his performance. I applaud him. He's done good."

Leigh didn't want the rest of our dinner to become a Camden and Stormy bashing session, so we engaged in meaningless conversation. After a while, I saw Leigh's lips moving, but I wasn't totally there. My mind was still heavily on Camden and how I was going to go forward with my life. My mind knew it was time to get over Camden, but my heart was telling me a totally different tale. I fought myself inwardly, trying to make the right decision. Should I attempt to break up their marriage? Or should I find a replacement? Should I listen to my heart or my mind? I had no clue, but I knew only time would tell.

Chapter 20

Stormy

Our Caribbean honeymoon was awesome. We stayed in a junior suite at the Crane Beach Resort, which was just as big as my entire apartment. The entire suite was furnished with antiques. The bedroom had a beautiful canopy bed that I fell in love with.

The first marital decision we made was to participate in activities on our honeymoon that neither of us had ever done before. We wanted to step out and enjoy this experience. As a new couple, we wanted to embark upon some new experiences—together. And that we did. During the days we played tennis, which neither of us had done before, except for in physical education in high school. We went horseback riding, road motor scooters, and relaxed on the sand beside the clear blue waters. It was highly recommended by the locals that we participate in the black culture tours, which gave us an uplifting and educational look into the African heritage of the island. Not wanting to depend on taxi services, we hired our own personal driver to chauffer us around as we toured. The views during the tour were extraordinary.

During the evening hours, we went to dinner shows, party cruises, and stayed up all night in various clubs where reggae and calypso music played all night long. On our last night there, we went to a club that had an open bar. Camden and I didn't waste any time hopping on that deal. Unfortunately, we didn't recognize our limits and were became stumbling drunks on the way back to our hotel room. Damn shame we couldn't recall anything that happened after our blood alcohol levels rose way beyond the legal limits.

In between sightseeing and having fun, Camden and I made love.

"Camden, damn, do you ever think about taking it easy on a sista?" I asked one night after we had just finished making love. We were laid up in the heart-shaped bed on the disheveled, white, satin sheets. Camden had just successfully given me a workout that would take me a least a week to recover from.

"I'm sorry, babe," he said, wiping the sweat from his forehead. "Your stuff is so good, I can't help myself." He leaned down and kissed my cheek. Then he kissed my neck. Before I knew it, we were entwined and at it again. Each sexual experience was more loving, intense, and fulfilling than the time before, and the connection was great. We were continuously humping like rabbits.

On our final day in Barbados, we had a seafood lunch in the relaxed atmosphere of the Crane Seafood Restaurant. As we were being entertained by the live band, my mind rushed forward to arriving home. I didn't want to go. I wanted to stay in Barbados forever.

"Camden, can't we stay here forever?" I asked as he took a bite of his grilled crab cake sandwich.

"I know, baby. This place is so beautiful. I don't wanna

leave either. But maybe we can come back to celebrate our one year anniversary."

"That's a plan," I agreed.

When we returned home from the honeymoon, Reverend Brooks and his first lady gave us a down payment for a home in a newly built community in Randallstown. Camden and I had agreed to purchase a home in this new development, but we didn't think it would be this soon.

Our original plan was to live together in my apartment and within a year or so, we'd look into buying our first house. But Camden's parents gave us the best wedding gift of all when they handed us an envelope with a check made out to Mr. and Mrs. Brooks. The memo line read: down payment on your new home. It took Camden and I only four weeks to seal the deal. It seemed that my father-in-law, having connections all over the country, had a good relationship with the developers, who had also done some work for the church. So it didn't take long for us to sign on the dotted line.

One week before our move-in date, Camden and I drove past the house and watched the builders add finishing touches to our new home.

"Camden," I said, holding his hand while we stood in the street and gazed out at our new home, "I love it."

"Me too, Storm. It's perfect for us. Not too big, not too small."

Camden and I stood in the street with our tongues interlocked in front of our soon-to-be new home.

"OK, Cam." I pulled away from him. "Somebody may call the police," I joked.

"Just wait until we move in and christen the joint. I'm talkin' kitchen counters, stairways, living and dining room floors, bathtubs, the entire house. No place is off limits."

"Is sex all you think about?" I asked.

"Yep. I'm trying to have me some babies."

I ignored his comment because having children was the last thing on my agenda at this point. I wanted to focus on being married and being a good wife before I brought a baby into the mix.

"Stormy, this place is nice," Dominique said a couple of weeks later after completing the tour of our new town-house.

Our new home had two bedrooms and two and a half bathrooms. The eat-in kitchen had a huge pantry as well as stainless steel kitchen appliances. The large bay window in the living room brightened the entire downstairs area. There was a wooden deck on the back of the house that led to the backyard. The finished basement, which served as our family, computer, and entertainment room was Camden's favorite place in the house. The home theater system, complete with a plasma television, contributed to Camden becoming a permanent fixture in that room.

"Thanks, girl. As you can see I'm still in the process of decorating. Camden gave me the bathroom in our master bedroom for my use only, and the hallway bathroom is for him. But he's taking the longest time getting back to me with the colors he wants."

"You can never go wrong with blue."

"I don't know," I said as I flopped onto the sofa.

"What's wrong? You look frustrated."

"I am. There's so much to do in so little time."

"What are you talking about?"

"Girl, not only is this house decorating taking up all my time, so is the whole process of having my last name changed. I didn't realize how tedious this could be. Everything, with the exception of my birth certificate, has to have my maiden name replaced with my married name. Some companies made it easy and allowed me to change my name over the phone, while others want a copy of our marriage license, along with a letter requesting a name change."

"Do you have to change everything over now? I know couples who've been married for years and the wife still receives mail with her maiden name on it."

"No, I really don't have to, but I'd rather get it out the way while it's on my mind."

The cell phone provider was one of the companies that needed to see proof. During the process of changing my name and establishing a household budget, Camden and I decided to get a joint cell phone account. I agreed to pay the cell phone bill if he paid the cable bill. This arrangement worked out perfectly.

When Camden and I attended church for the first time as a married couple, shortly after the honeymoon, Reverend Brooks made it known to the entire congregation.

"Saints, before we go any further in this service, I need to recognize my son and his lovely wife. They've just returned from their honeymoon and have just moved into their brand new home. Let's give God praise for this beautiful, young couple." The congregation stood and applauded.

"Amen!" several members shouted as they clapped.

"Praise God. . . . Hallelujah. . . ." others shouted. The reception was warm and it made us feel special.

After service, the congregation was still congratulating us. I felt like it was our wedding day all over again. We received dozens of gifts from church members who were unable to attend the wedding or who attended but had promised us a gift later. Camden and I couldn't wait to get home to open them.

Camden and I acted like kids on Christmas when we got home, tearing the wrapping paper off the gifts, or ripping cards open, anticipating money inside.

"Look, Camden," I said, holding up a fifty-dollar bill. "This is from Deacon and Deaconess Brown."

"Wow. And look here. This is a check for two hundred dollars from the Usher Board. They must have all put in and gave a collaborative gift."

Card after card, Camden and I hit the jackpot. We could hardly contain ourselves.

"Money, money, money, money . . . moooney!" We sang the old O'Jays tune as we danced around on the bed.

"Camden, we should open a joint bank account and deposit this money," I suggested.

"Cool with me, but I do want at least five hundred more to hook up my family room . . . um, I mean *our* family room."

I playfully jumped on his back.

"Don't think all your time is gonna be spent in the family room." He laughed and wrestled me to the bed.

Finally, after a few days of running around like a chicken with my head cut off, I hooked up with Leigh and Nicole. They both were doing well, but Nicole dropped a bombshell on me that was truly unexpected.

"Brace yourself, girl. I've got something to tell you."

I was sitting on the edge of my chair, dying to hear the news. I glanced over at Leigh, who sat with a smirk on her face. I could tell she already knew.

"What? What? Tell me."

"Guess who I'm dating?" Nicole asked.

"Who?" She was killing me. Why couldn't she just tell me without playing the guessing game?

"Jared."

"Jared who?" I asked.

"Camden's boy, Jared."

"Girl, get out!" I covered my mouth in shock. The last we talked she wasn't trying to give him the time of day. And the last I knew, Jared was a playboy.

"Yep. It's true. Sparks were flying after he put that garter up my thigh at your wedding. We secretly exchanged numbers and have been talking ever since."

I was surprised that Nicole would date Jared, but I was happy for her. I guess something good did come from catching the bouquet at a wedding. I was sure once Camden found out, he was not going to be too happy about it because of how he felt about Nicole. He tolerated Nicole because she was my friend, but he really didn't like her, and the feeling was quite mutual. But I'd tell him to mind his business and let them be happy.

I soon realized that the start of a new life could be hectic with moving, changing my name, returning to work, and trying to return to a normal routine. But all in all, married life had been wonderful thus far. Camden was a great help, keeping me sane through everything. That was why each night, before I fell asleep, I looked up to heaven and mouthed, "Thank you, God, for giving me such a good husband."

Chapter 21

Camden

Two months after our lavish, spring wedding ceremony, I realized I had made a big mistake marrying Stormy. I started to feel uneasy right after the honeymoon, a little after we moved into our new house. I remember sitting at the settlement table, watching the deal be completed. I was beside myself. I wanted to get up and run, but somehow I managed to restrain myself. Once the transaction was complete, I felt as if I had committed myself to a permanent ball and chain. Now I was in a new marriage and a new house, and I found myself holed up in the family room.

Stormy was so excited when we moved into our new home. I wished I shared her enthusiasm, but I didn't. Of course, I was in love with the idea of having a brand new house that I didn't have to kick out the money for, but that was about it.

After some time, I finally had to admit to myself that I had gotten married for all the wrong reasons. Don't get me wrong, I loved Stormy with all my heart, but I was not in love with her. I didn't feel for her the way a husband should feel toward his wife. I'd tried hard to be a good husband, but I started to feel my so-called old ways creep up on me.

I felt awful for feeling this way. Stormy was such a good woman. Any man would be happy to have her, but I was just not that man.

These were the times I wished my cousin, Tyler, was in Baltimore. Although Tyler didn't agree with my hidden lifestyle, I was sure he would be a great resource for me during a time when I felt so conflicted. I had always admired Tyler for being so charismatic and magnetic with people, especially women. He, his wife, and their beautiful daughter made such a beautiful family. If only I could have turned out more like Tyler, then maybe I wouldn't be in the mess I was in right now—a bogus marriage.

Knowing Tyler as I did, I knew exactly what he'd do. He'd stay in his marriage and be the man, the husband that God referred to in the Bible. I had to do the same. I couldn't back out now. There was just too much at stake. Besides, I needed to have a woman on my arm for appearance' sake. I made the decision to get married when I knew I shouldn't have, so now I was going to have to deal with it. Hell, her family had finally accepted me, my parents were off my back, church-folk were no longer gossiping, and we had purchased a new home, opened up a joint account, and done a host of other things married couples do. There was no way I could mess all of that up. There was no turning back. It was going to be hard acting as if I was happy, but it was something I just had to do.

Malik had consistently been in my thoughts. I often wondered how he was doing. I looked for him at church on Sunday mornings, but he never came. I guess he refused to attend church knowing that he'd probably see Stormy and me together.

I had been trying to fight the urge to call him. I knew if

he heard my voice, he'd curse me out, and honestly, he had every right to do so. The least I could do was apologize to him. Although it was probably way too late, better late than never. After going back and forth with the idea, I finally convinced myself that I'd give Malik a call to apologize for the way I had treated him.

You're just gonna say sorry and that's it, I told myself. *You're married to a good woman now and you've got to do right by her.*

One day soon after I made the decision to contact Malik, business was slow at the hotel. I decided to take an early lunch break and make the call. Being a manager had its perks. I walked into my office and grabbed my keys from my desk. I trotted out to my car to ensure my privacy. I looked over my shoulder several times to see if anyone noticed me. That was a telltale sign of guilt. As I dialed Malik's number from my cell phone, my stomach was in knots. To say I was nervous was an understatement. The phone rang three times and just as I was about to hang up, he answered.

"Hello?"

"Hello, Malik, it's Camden." There was silence.

"What do you want?" he asked dryly.

"Hey, man, I know you're pissed at me, but I wanted to call to apologize for everything."

"Fine time to apologize! It's been, what, two months? It took you this long to finally apologize?"

"I've been busy, Malik. This is the first time I've had to really call and express how sorry I am for hurting you."

"Damn right you're sorry. You're truly one sorry ass bastard!" I laughed.

"I deserve that."

"Oh, you deserve that and more. You better be glad my grandmother was at the church the day of your wedding because I would have blown your shit right out of the water."

"Well, I'm glad you didn't."

"So, how is married life?" Malik asked in a sarcastic tone.

"It is what it is."

"What does that mean?"

"I really don't want to go there right now. I'm on my lunch break. You've been on my mind lately and I just thought that today would be a good day to apologize to you."

"Do you miss me?" Malik blurted.

"Yeah, I do. More than you'll ever know." *Shit!* I wasn't supposed to say that. I was just calling to apologize. Right?

"Although I can't stand you, I miss you, too," Malik said, laughing. "Besides, you had me all messed up when I talked to you a couple of weeks before the wedding. Had you told me you hated me, it would have been easier to move on. But you didn't. You told me you still loved me and that stuck with me. I was more pissed that you were marrying Stormy after you professed your love to me. What's up with that? I get the feeling you're telling her the same thing, too."

"Look, I can't talk about this right now. Do you want to hook up after I get off work?" I asked, realizing that those words never should have come out of my mouth.

"Why do you want to see me?"

"I just need to see you. There are some things I need to get off my chest," I answered.

"Where do you want to meet? You're married now, and we need to be careful."

"You're right. How about we meet in Columbia, at the lake?"

"All right, Cam. What time do you want to meet?"

"Well, I get off at nine o'clock tonight. Why don't we meet around ten?"

"That sounds good. What are you going to tell Stormy?"

"Don't worry about Stormy. I got this!" I chuckled.

"Keep thinkin' you Mr. Big Stuff. You better tell her something believable before she has the FBI looking for your ass."

"Like I said, I got this," I said with confidence. I knew my wife, and I was fully aware of how to cover my tracks.

"OK, cool! Well, I'll see you at ten. Don't be late."

"I won't." I hung up the phone smiling.

Malik handled things a lot better than I had expected. Talking to him stirred up a lot of feelings. I didn't know why I couldn't get that young boy out of my system. There was just something about him. I couldn't wait to see him tonight. I had made up my mind that we were only going to talk. I didn't want to be unfaithful to Stormy, especially so soon after we had said 'I do.' However, thinking about the act was just as bad as actually doing it. That's why I devised a plan to only talk to Malik, and not take it any further. My life was already complicated enough, and I didn't need a side relationship with Malik to make it even more difficult. Besides, I owed it to my wife to honor my marriage vows.

At seven o'clock, I called Stormy to tell her that I would be home late.

"Hello?" She answered the phone cheerfully.

"May I speak to Mrs. Brooks?" I asked playfully.

"This is she."

"What are you wearing?" I inquired seductively.

"What?" She was taken aback.

"I said, what are you wearing?"

"I don't think my husband would appreciate me giving that information out over the phone, especially to a strange man."

"Come on, I won't tell if you won't."

"OK, well since you'll keep it a secret, I don't have any panties on," she purred, mocking Eartha Kitt in *Boomerang*.

At that point, I couldn't keep up the charade. I just burst into laughter.

"Girl, you are crazy."

"You called here playing games, so I played along."

"Whatcha doin'?"

"Lying across the bed watching Oprah. I set the DVR to record it because I had to stay late at school to grade some papers."

"Girl, you and Oprah. Don't you get enough?"

"Nope, sure don't. How is work going?"

"It's OK. It's been a slow day. There's been a lot of people checking out, but not a lot checking in. I'm savoring these slow days, because in a few weeks when summer hits, the tourists will be coming in nonstop. But I'm calling because when I get off at nine, I'm gonna swing by Hassan's house."

"OK, baby, be careful. I'll probably be asleep when you get home."

"I promise not to wake you. Love you, Mrs. Brooks."

"Ummmmmm, I love the sound of that. I love you, too."

When I got off the phone with Stormy, I felt kind of bad. She was such a gem. It was a damn shame that I was lying to her. Everybody knew that one lie had to be covered up by another and another. But something inside me wouldn't allow me to break off my meeting with Malik. Now I had to call Hassan to let him know what I had told Stormy.

When I left the hotel, I called Hassan. He answered.

"What's up, Mr. Married Man?"

"Aw, nothing man. Just chilling. What's up with you?"

"Not a thing. I'm just sitting here watching *Hustle & Flow*."

"Do you have any plans for tonight?"

"Nope. I'm just chilling in the house for the rest of the night. Besides, tomorrow is a work day. I don't function too well at work when I hang out late the night before."

"Cool! Um, Hassan, Stormy may call your house looking for me. If you see my home number on your caller ID, don't answer it."

"Why?"

"Well, I told her that I was going to be with you, but I'm going to take care of some business."

"What business?"

"I can't really get into all of that right now. I'll tell you about it later."

"I don't like the sound of this, Camden. I really don't want to be in the middle if something goes down."

"You're not going to be in the middle. I'm not asking you to lie for me. I'm just asking you not to answer your phone if you see my home number pop up on your caller ID."

"I don't like the sound of this. I'll do it this time, but don't keep asking me to do this."

"Thanks, man, I owe you."

"You owe me nothing but an explanation."

"You got that. I'll call you tomorrow. Oh, and if Stormy does call your house, hit me on my cell phone to let me know."

"Yeah, yeah," he retorted.

"Thanks again. I'll talk to you tomorrow."

"Peace," he said before hanging up.

After I covered all my bases, I headed toward Columbia Lake. I was anxiously anticipating seeing Malik. I had to remind myself that I was a married man.

We're only going to talk, I told myself during the drive. *Nothing more.*

Chapter 22

Malik

I glanced at the bright red, illuminated numbers on the clock that sat on my dresser. I only had forty-five minutes to get myself together to meet Camden. I stood in my closet, looking for something to wear. Finally I chose a pair of jeans, a Polo shirt, and Timberland boots. I then splashed on Burberry, Camden's favorite cologne. I knew after one good whiff, he'd be all over me. I knew Camden was married now and I shouldn't be having these thoughts, but I couldn't help what I felt. Although he hurt me, I still loved him.

I missed Camden over these last few months. Being with Camden made me feel good and I hadn't felt the same since he got married. When we were together, he showed me some of the good things life had to offer—education, nice clothes, fine dining, and excellent sex. Being with him allowed me to experience life outside the hood, and that alone kept me wanting him.

A couple of weeks after Camden married that witch,

Stormy, I hooked up with my classmate, Beau. I wasn't really feeling him. I just kicked it with him to help me pass the time, to keep my mind off Camden. One evening, I met up with Beau at a bar. We had a good time. Beau was easy to talk to and didn't mind spending his money buying me drinks. The next thing I knew, I was telling him my life story. Of course, when you're vulnerable, you usually fall for anything, and I did just that.

I was so drunk at the end of the evening that I couldn't drive home, so Beau offered me a ride. Somehow we wound up in dark, deserted, Clifton Park, and the next thing I knew, clothes were coming off and we were going at it. I didn't know I could be so flexible. I'd never had sex in a car before, so this was all new to me, but I handled it like a pro. After sexing each other up and down, he took me home. Before I got out the car, we promised to keep in touch.

Beau and I kicked it a couple more times after that, but I really wasn't into him like he was into me. My heart and mind were still on Camden. One night after having sex at his place, I told Beau I couldn't see him anymore. He seemed disappointed, but said he understood. I thanked him for the fun times and left. Now when I saw him in class, we exchanged pleasantries and kept moving.

No matter how hard I'd tried, I couldn't seem to get over Camden. When he called me to apologize, I wanted to curse him out. I wanted to tell him how much I hated him. I wanted to tell him to go fuck himself, but I couldn't bring myself to do it. Something about his voice made me weak, so weak that now I was on my way to meet him, something I knew I shouldn't be doing.

Just as I was about to leave the house, my grandmother called me from the living room.

"Yes, Grandma?"

"Are you going out for a while, or are you coming right back?" she asked.

"I'm going out for a while. Why? Do you need something?"

"Well, my stomach is upset and I wanted you to get me some Pepto-Bismol."

"OK, Grandma. I'll run to the store and buy you some, and bring it right back."

"Thank you, baby." She smiled.

I wondered if my grandmother knew something was up. I found it extremely coincidental that her stomach was bothering her just as I was on my way out the door to meet Camden.

It was nine-thirty. I was going to be late, but Camden could wait a few minutes. My grandmother didn't ask much of me, and as much as she had done for me, how could I not get her some Pepto-Bismol? I hurried to the store, made the purchase, and returned to the house.

When I finally got on I-95 to make my way to Columbia, it was nine forty-five. I was definitely going to be late, but so what? Camden could wait. As much as he had put me through, he should be glad I was even coming to see him at all. If he really wanted to talk to me, then he'd have to wait for me.

I couldn't shake this feeling that something was weighing heavily on Camden's mind. He sounded as if he were in a funk when we talked earlier. He didn't get into what was bothering him over the phone, but I planned to get it out of him tonight.

I arrived at the Lake at ten-fifteen. I drove around looking for Camden's car. The park was dimly lit, so I had a hard time spotting his car. I called him on his cell phone and he led me to his location. For some reason, I felt a little anxious. I got out of the car and walked over to a bench where Camden was sitting.

"Hey, you," I said, nudging his arm.

He turned around and smiled that brilliant smile with his straight, white teeth.

"Hey, yourself."

"Have you been waiting long?" I asked.

"No. I got here at ten on the nose."

"So what have you been doing while you've been waiting for me?"

"Thinking," he answered and lowered his head.

"About what?"

"Malik, it's just so deep," he answered with a look of distress on his face.

"I have nothing but time, so talk," I said, anxious to know what was going on.

"I shouldn't have ever gotten married," he revealed bluntly.

"Ain't that the truth?" I asked sarcastically. I knew it wasn't time for an I-told-you-so, but I couldn't resist.

Camden smirked and then continued.

"I made a mistake when I married Stormy."

"When did you realize that?"

"Shortly after we closed on our new house. I realized that it was time to settle in and really be a husband. Initially, during all the wedding prep, the wedding, and the honeymoon, I was cool, but now doing that daily husband routine is getting monotonous."

"Are you having sex with her?" *So what if the question is inappropriate. I need to know.*

"Yeah, we are, but it doesn't get me off," Camden responded sadly.

"Why?"

"Because I want you."

My mouth flew open so wide you could see my tonsils.

"What do you mean, you want me?"

"Just like I said, I want you. Stormy doesn't fully satisfy me sexually. She doesn't come close to you."

"Well, you know what that means?"

"What?"

"That you're still gay. If you are so-called 'delivered,' then thoughts of me or any other man shouldn't even be poppin' in your head."

"You're right. I thought I was delivered. When I married Stormy, I really thought I had put all of that behind me. We had sex on a regular basis, and I mean good sex. But it didn't take long for me to become bored with it. Our lovemaking wasn't as exciting as it used to be. That's when it hit me. My feelings for men had never gone anywhere. I had just suppressed them."

"Damn, so what are you going to do?" I questioned, really concerned for him.

"There is nothing I can do now. I made the dumb decision to get married, and now I have to live with it."

"But Stormy doesn't deserve that." *Did I just say something in support of Stormy? Must be crazy.*

"I know she doesn't. She's really a good person. I do love her, but not like a husband should love his wife."

"So, I ask again, what are you gonna do?"

"I'm going to take it one day at a time, but I'm going to . . ." Camden paused.

"What? Finish your sentence."

"I'm going to need your help."

"My help?"

"Yes. Will you stick by me and help me get through this?" His brown eyes connected directly with mine.

"How am I supposed to help you?" I asked, confused.

"Just be there for me when I need you. That's all I ask."

"In what way?"

"In every way possible," he said seductively, just before he leaned in to kiss me.

I couldn't fight it. I wanted to, but I couldn't. His soft, plump lips felt good against mine, so I went with the flow.

The moment felt right and I didn't want to mess it up, but I had to know some things. I pulled away from his luscious lips.

"Camden, you know I love you, but I don't want to get caught up in no mess. If anybody finds out that we are seeing each other again, all hell is gonna break loose. That's the last thing both of us need."

"I agree. We'll be careful this time. And you, Malik, have to keep your mouth shut. You have just as much to lose as I do. You can't say shit to Leigh!"

"I promise you, I won't. So, what's the plan?"

"Since neither one of us knows anyone in Columbia, we can continue to meet here. I'll find us a cheap motel and that will be our meeting place. You can call me on my cell or at work. I won't call your house and you don't ever call mine."

"I don't know your telephone number."

"Whatever, Mr. Slick. You know damn well you can get it if you want it."

I laughed because he was telling the truth.

"Go 'head, finish telling me your plan."

"You can also call me at work. I'll keep you informed of my work schedule so you will know when to call."

"How often will I get to see you?"

"Well, I am going to have to do the husband thing from time to time, but I'll make time for you at least once a week, if not more. It's all going to depend on how things are going at home and with my work schedule."

"You seem to have it all worked out. I don't know how you are going to pull this off."

"Hey, I've got it all covered. I've even thought of starting arguments with Stormy just so I can have an excuse to leave the house."

"You ain't shit." I laughed.

"But you love me anyway."

"Whatever!"

"Don't try to play hard. You know you do," he said, trying to kiss me again.

"You're right, I do love you. I wish I didn't."

Camden looked down at his watch and realized it was getting late. He suggested we leave. I didn't want to leave him, but I knew I couldn't stay any longer or we'd get thrown in jail for indecent exposure and sodomy. We locked tongues, said good-bye, and agreed to talk tomorrow.

During the drive home, I felt good about having Camden back in my life, although I didn't like being second choice. I'd accept it for now because I enjoyed the exposure to the affluent lifestyle Camden represented, and for the banging sex.

Mr. Married Man seemed to have this affair mapped out so well that it appeared he had done this undercover cheating husband thing before. Knowing Camden, he probably had. I hoped things went as smoothly as he described, because if not, heads would roll.

Chapter 23

Stormy

As I turned over in the bed, I noticed Camden's side was empty. I spied the clock and it read 1:18 AM. I began to worry. Camden had called to say he was going to be late, but I didn't expect him to be out *this* late. *Where could he be?* I picked up the telephone to see if he had called while I was sleeping, but there were no new messages. I then called his cell phone and his voicemail immediately picked up. This was unlike Camden. He had never been out this late unless he was working. I thought about calling Hassan, but I didn't want to call his house this late on a weeknight.

I got this feeling in the pit of my stomach that something wasn't right. I couldn't go back to sleep, so I continuously tossed and turned. As I lay in bed in the dark, Satan crept into my thoughts. He had me thinking the worst about my husband. *Has he been hurt? Is he out cheating?* I tried to push out the negative thoughts by praying, but once I said amen, the worried thoughts returned.

Finally I heard the front door open. I looked at the clock

again and it read 1:45 AM. Since he was coming through the door, I figured he was safe, so now my worry became anger. *Why is he coming in the house at almost two o'clock in the morning? He must have lost his mind*, I thought as my blood boiled.

I lay still, acting as if I were asleep. I listened to him move around downstairs. Then I heard him climbing the stairs. When he entered the bedroom, he moved stealthily, like a snake slithering through grass. I guess he was trying not to wake me. Little did he know I was already awake.

Once he took off his clothes, he slid into our bed. It wasn't long before he was snoring. I wanted to kick his ass out of the bed. He had some nerve to be snoring like a baby while I was wide awake. I decided to let him sleep, but tomorrow we would deal with this situation.

The next morning I was groggy due to lack of sleep. Camden, on the other hand, was able to sleep late because he had the day off.

I had no idea how I made it through five periods of teaching English. I had been dragging all day. During my lunch break, I put my head on my desk to get a quick nap. I didn't even bother to eat. I was so consumed with thoughts of where Camden was the previous night that I didn't have much of an appetite. My hope was that we could talk when I got home from work, and that would settle my uneasy feelings.

When I arrived home, Camden greeted me affectionately as he usually did. I gave him a quick peck on the lips and walked upstairs. He asked what was wrong with me and I told him I was tired. He then reminded me that we had Bible study that night, and he asked if I would be up to going. I told him that I would.

We left the house at seven-thirty to make Bible study at eight o'clock. I still was not in a good mood. We rode in the car in silence until Camden spoke.

"What's wrong?" he asked. "Are you still tired?"

"No, I'm not still tired. I took a nap when I got home from work," I said nonchalantly.

"Well, what's wrong? You seem bothered about something."

"I'll talk to you about it later." I guess he was satisfied by my answer because he didn't press me. During Bible study, I didn't hear a word Reverend Brooks said. I could only focus on the conversation that I was going to have with Camden when we got home. I was searching for the right way to bring it up without causing a huge argument.

On the way home, Camden and I rode in silence. When we got into the house, I went straight to the bedroom to put on my nightgown. While I was undressing, Camden came in the room.

"My, don't you look sexy."

"Save it, Camden. I'm not in the mood," I snapped.

"What's wrong with you?" Camden asked sarcastically.

"Where were you until almost two o'clock in the morning?"

"I told you, I went over to Hassan's house."

"So, you were with Hassan all night long?"

"Yes, I was," he asserted.

"And you couldn't call to tell me that you'd be out until two in the morning?"

"I didn't know I had a curfew."

"You don't have a curfew, but I find it strange that you were over Hassan's house all night long, especially on a weeknight. Doesn't Hassan work?"

"Yes, he does work, but he was going through some things and he wanted to talk. Time just got away from us."

"So, if I call Hassan right now, he'll verify that story?"

"Call whomever you want. I don't appreciate being checked up on like some child. I'm your husband, nor your kid!" he shouted.

"Then act like a husband and don't stay your ass out until two o'clock in the damn morning!" I shouted back.

"Well, guess what? I really don't want to continue to hear you bicker about something so petty, so I'm going back out. And this time I might just come back at four in the morning."

"Well, don't be surprised if you can't get in!"

"Whatever!" he yelled as he stormed down the steps. Then he slammed the front door closed. I was livid. I immediately called Leigh.

"Hello," Leigh answered.

"Leigh, it's Stormy. Camden and I just had our first fight!"

"Aw, Stormy, I'm sorry to hear that. What happened?"

"He came home last night at almost two in the morning and then he wanted me to believe the lie that he was with Hassan."

"Why would he be over Hassan's that late?"

"Supposedly Hassan is going through something. Camden claims he was there to help him through his problems."

"And you don't believe that?"

"Hell no!"

"Why?"

"I just don't! My gut tells me he's lying."

"Let me make a suggestion: Before going off on your husband, accusing him of lying, make sure you have proof that he's done something wrong. You can't accuse him if you really have no proof. If you want your marriage to survive, you've got to trust him. I know it's hard considering all you've been through in the past, but until you have evidence, you shouldn't jump all over him."

"I guess you're right. I messed up, huh?"

"Yeah, you did, but everybody makes mistakes. Just apologize to him and this will blow over before you know it."

"OK, I will. Thanks for letting me vent."

"Hey, what are friends for?"

"I'm going to get ready for bed now. I'll talk to you tomorrow. Thanks, Leigh. I love you, girlfriend!"

"I love you, too. Goodnight."

I thought long and hard about what Leigh had said. It was at that moment that I realized I had major trust issues with Camden. I guess in the back of my mind, I was fearful that he was cheating or out creeping with some man. But as Leigh said, I had no proof. So at that point, I had no choice but to trust him.

Before going to bed, I asked God to forgive me and prayed that Camden could forgive me, too.

One week after the big argument, things had not gotten better. I never apologized to Camden because he came home in the morning after our argument at three-fifteen. I was furious that he would have the audacity to come in that late after we had argued about it. He was truly being disrespectful, and when I approached him about it again, he claimed he was out clearing his head. I asked where he was, but he refused to tell me. Leigh's conversation popped into my mind immediately, and that's when I backed off. I concluded that if he was doing something wrong, it would eventually come out.

The next day I sat at the kitchen table balancing my checkbook to prepare to pay the bills. I didn't get very far because the first bill I opened sent chills down my spine. I couldn't believe what I was seeing. I scanned the bill repeatedly, trying to make sense of the information it contained. Then it hit me. *I finally had the proof in my hands that Camden was indeed doing wrong.* My mother always said, "What's done in the dark will come to light," and Camden's indiscretions just had.

Chapter 24

Camden

"Do you think Stormy suspects anything?" Malik asked after I called him to tell him that Stormy had been throwing me mad shade recently. I explained that Stormy's nastiness didn't start until after the first night Malik and I met up in Columbia.

"I'm not sure. I know she's not happy about me coming in the house after hours. That's why we've been beefin' so much lately."

"You're getting sloppy, Camden. You told me you had it all under control, but you don't."

"What do you mean?" I questioned, slightly offended that he doubted my surreptitious cheating methods. I actually thought I was doing a pretty good job, if there was such a thing as being a "good cheater."

"I told you that I didn't want to get caught up in no mess. I don't wanna have to deal with Stormy calling my house, your father having meetings with us in his office, Leigh coming over to question me about you—nothing. So if you are gonna creep, then you need not ruffle Stormy's feathers. I enjoy spending time with you, but if the late hours are going to cause your wife to be suspicious, then maybe we need to meet during the day or something. Come on, Cam. I'm the young one here. Shouldn't you be schooling me, not the other way around?"

Malik had a point. My recent behavior was causing Stormy to be extremely suspicious and curious about my whereabouts. She constantly questioned me each time I stepped foot out the front door and as soon as I returned home. I could tell she knew something was up and I wasn't making the situation any better by giving her reasons to question me. In my haste to show her that I wasn't her child, I had only dug a deeper hole for myself, causing a light to shine upon me and my injudiciousness.

"You're right. I've been messin' up. I'll hold it down a little better than I have been."

"Yeah, you betta. I'm serious when I say I ain't for the games. I love you and all, but I don't want the drama. I finally got my grandmother to stop believing the rumors soaring around the church. I ain't trying to go there again. You dig?"

"I got you. Just calm down. We're cool. I'll step it up more at home. By the way, she called me just before I called you. She sounded a little more upbeat than she had over the past few days."

"What she say?"

"Something about my parents inviting us over for dinner tonight."

"Well, make sure you lay it on thick for your parents. You know God talks to Reverend Brooks—the holy one. You know he has a kindred spirit with the Lord. He may already know about us," Malik joked.

"Not funny, Malik. I'm about to be out. I have an hour before quitting time and then I'm headed to my parents'

house. I'll try to call you later. If I don't, know that I'm trying to smooth things over with Stormy."

"Yeah, step your game up, playa. Peace."

I didn't know how Stormy would be acting at my parents'
house this evening during dinner, but I hoped she would
stifle that nasty attitude that had consumed her these last
few days. I prayed that she wouldn't show any signs of any
problems in our marriage, because my father would be all
up in our business trying to provide marital counseling. I
didn't want that. So I was going to put on my husband mask
and play the role of a loving, committed spouse.

Chapter 25

Stormy

After I finished paying my bills, I sat deep in thought contemplating what I should do with the disturbing information I had discovered. I finally decided to call Reverend Brooks to ask if Camden and I could come over to talk with him. He eagerly agreed, not knowing that I was about to drop a bomb on him about Camden's recent behavior. I then called Camden on his cell phone and asked him to meet me at his parents' house. He questioned why I was going over there, and I lied and told him that they invited us over for dinner. He seemed to be reluctant, but finally agreed. I was relieved because I didn't think he would comply since we hadn't been on good terms lately. I was sure things were bound to get worse after tonight because he'd know I fabricated the dinner invitation just to get him over there to confront him about his lies.

I didn't like running to Camden's father, but there was no other way I could confront Camden and get to the truth.

He was quick on his feet when it came to lying. He would have told me a lie so believable that I would've been convinced that what I saw with my own eyes wasn't really there. I couldn't risk him trying to deny his actions, so I chose to confront him in front of his father. I knew it seemed extremely juvenile, but after what I saw, I didn't know what else to do. If anybody could help me, I knew it would be my spiritual leader, my pastor, my father-in-law.

When I arrived at the Brooks's home, I noticed Camden's car wasn't there yet. When I rang the bell, Mama Sheryl answered.

"Hi, baby girl." She hugged me and invited me in.

"Hi, Mama Sheryl," I said, calling her by the name she asked me to call her after Camden and I got married. She always wanted a daughter and I was the closest she'd ever have to one.

"Theo told me that you and Camden were stopping by. I'm in the kitchen trying to whip up something to eat. Are you hungry?"

"No, not really. I don't want to impose. I came over because I want to talk to you and Reverend Brooks about something," I said, following her into the kitchen.

"You don't look too good, baby. Is everything all right?"

I really didn't want to get into all the details without Camden and Reverend Brooks being present. Besides, since Camden still had a key to his parents' home, I didn't want him to walk in and overhear my conversation with his mom and then sneak back out the door.

"No, things are not all right. I am troubled right now and I don't know what to do."

She must have sensed my hesitancy because she asked me if I wanted to wait for Reverend Brooks and Camden to arrive. I told her yes.

"No problem. Let me get Theo," First Lady Brooks said.

I sat at the kitchen table feeling as if the world was on my shoulders. While deep in thought, I heard Camden enter the house.

"Camden, we're upstairs. We'll be down in a minute," his mother called down the stairs. "Stormy's in the kitchen."

"OK, Ma, I'll see you when you come down."

Camden entered the kitchen and gave me a kiss on the cheek. I didn't even acknowledge him. He hadn't kissed me for the past few days and now that we were sitting in his parents' house, he wanted to pretend to be a happy couple. I wasn't having it.

"What's Ma cooking? It smells good."

"I don't know," I mumbled.

"Stormy, are you going to have that stank attitude the whole time we're here? If so, we can go home. I don't want my parents to know there's been tension between us lately. I'm sure they'll catch on once they see that look on your face."

"Too late!" I announced. "They already know something is up."

"How do they—" His father walked into the kitchen to greet us, interrupting Camden. Mama Sheryl was right behind him. Reverend Brooks joined me at the table and asked Camden to have a seat as well. Mama Sheryl stood at the stove stirring a pot of collard greens.

"So, how are the newlyweds doing?" Reverend Brooks asked with a smile.

"We're doing fine, Dad," Camden quickly answered.

"No, we're not, Reverend Brooks. That's why I called you," I chimed in.

"Now, which one is it? Are you doing fine or aren't you?" Reverend Brooks questioned.

"Nothing is wrong, Dad. Stormy and I had a little spat a few days ago and she's still upset about it."

"What was the spat about?" Reverend Brooks inquired.

"It's not a big deal. I came home a little late the other night and Stormy is upset about it."

"A little late!" I yelled. "A little late! How about two o'clock in the morning and the very next morning it was three!"

"Why are you coming home so late, son? Were you working?"

"No, Dad, I was not at work. The first night I was with Hassan, and the next night I was out clearing my head after our argument."

"I don't believe for a minute he was with Hassan," I retorted.

"Why is that, Stormy?" Reverend Brooks asked.

"This is why," I said as I handed Reverend Brooks our cell phone bill. Camden sat across the table and gave me dirty looks. If his eyes were bullets, my body would have multiple wounds.

"What is this, Stormy?" Reverend Brooks asked, looking confused.

"This is our joint cell phone bill. After we got married, we got new cell phones with a joint account. I agreed to pay the cell bill if Camden paid the cable bill. Yesterday as I was preparing to pay my bills, the cell phone bill was the first bill I opened. Usually I don't look at the detailed billing portion, but due to Camden's recent behavior, I thought I should. As I scanned the bill, I kept seeing the same number. There are incoming and outgoing calls made at all hours of the day and night. This piqued my curiosity, so I called the number. There was no answer, but when the voicemail came on, I nearly fell to the floor. It was Malik's voice!"

Reverend Brooks looked at me incredulously. I leaned forward and pointed out the highlighted calls that were all to or from Malik. Then I glanced over at Camden.

"Can you explain why the night you were with Hassan,

calls were made to Malik?" I asked him. "Can you explain why the night you stayed out until three in the morning, calls were made to Malik?" He stared at me without saying a word, so I continued. "Malik's number appears twenty-seven times on this bill. Can you explain that?" Camden still didn't answer.

"Yeah, son, can you explain that? Are you still communicating with Malik?"

"Yes, I am, but only as friends. There is nothing between us. You've got to believe that," Camden sputtered.

"Oh, son, please don't tell me you're doing this again. Please tell me you're not."

"Dad, I'm not doing anything. Yes, I've been talking to Malik, and yes I saw him the night I told Stormy I was with Hassan, but believe me when I say, nothin' happened. He and I are just friends. That's it."

"Camden, I told you to leave that boy alone," Reverend Brooks bellowed. "There's no need for the two of you to talk about anything. You are a married man now. Can't you get that through your thick skull?"

"Yeah," Camden said sarcastically.

"Then you better act like it. As of today, there is to be no more communication with Malik Blackwell. This so-called friendship is over." Reverend Brooks then looked over at me. "Look at your wife. Can't you see the pain in her face? Why must you continue to hurt her?" Camden lowered his head.

"I'm not trying to hurt her. I didn't think it was a big deal."

"It is a big deal, and the sooner you realize that, the better. Now, I said no more communicating with Malik! Do you understand?"

"Yes, Dad, I understand. I won't talk to Malik anymore," Camden responded in a childlike manner.

I couldn't believe the shit I had just heard. We'd only

been married for a hot minute and Camden was creeping around with Malik already! I wanted to curse him out right here and now, but I was in a Christian home, so I held my peace. Mama Sheryl came over to me and rubbed my back.

"Stormy, are you OK? You haven't said much."

"What can I say? Camden and I haven't been married that long and already he's lying and sneaking around, seeing Malik. How can I ever trust anything that he says?"

"Stormy, you can trust me. I haven't done anything wrong," Camden pleaded.

"No, I can't! All you do is lie and cheat. I should have never married you!"

"Calm down, baby. I know you're upset, but you shouldn't say things you really don't mean. Camden has messed up, but that doesn't mean he still can't be a good husband to you," Mama Sheryl said, defending her son.

I didn't respond to what Mama Sheryl said. My only focus was the realization that Camden was still a liar and possibly a cheater.

"Stormy, I'm sorry," Camden said. "I didn't mean to hurt you. I promise I won't talk to Malik anymore."

I didn't respond to him either. I just rolled my eyes. Then I looked at Reverend Brooks.

"I don't think he's changed. He's still that same Camden that hurt me a year ago. I guess your prayers didn't work."

"Don't ever doubt God—" Reverend Brooks stopped talking because Camden's cell phone started ringing. We all sat and looked at him, wondering if it was Malik.

"If that's Malik, tell him I need to speak with him," Reverend Brooks roared.

"It's not Malik. My caller ID says that the number is unavailable. I have no idea who this is."

"Then answer it," I demanded, not believing him.

"Hello," Camden said, answering his phone. "Hello? Hello?" Camden flipped his phone up and said that whoever it was had hung up. At that point I was done and ready to leave. I didn't want to be in Camden's presence any longer. I stood up, hugged Reverend Brooks and Mama Sheryl, and told them I was leaving. They tried to stop me, but I kept walking. As I approached my car, I heard Camden calling my name. I muttered under my breath, "go to hell," got in my car, and headed home.

Thirty minutes after I got home, Camden came through the door. I hoped he would have stayed at his parents' house because I didn't want to see his face. I was lying across the bed when he entered the bedroom.

"Stormy, can I talk to you for a minute?"

"For what? To tell me more lies?"

"No. I'm not going to lie to you. I want to tell you how sorry I am for talking to Malik behind your back. I know that makes me look guilty, but you've got to believe me, baby, when I say I haven't broken our marriage vows. I married you because I love you. I don't love Malik. I don't want to be with him. I only want you. I've told you before that I'm not the man I used to be. Everybody knows that I love my wife and I'm not going to betray you with anyone!"

He sat down next to me on the bed and lightly caressed my cheek with the back of his hand.

"Before we got married, I gave you my word that I wouldn't hurt you and I'm standing by that. I would not have gone into this marriage knowing that I couldn't be true to you. I promise, baby, I will never hurt you again. Never."

For some strange reason, my heart wasn't as hard anymore. Camden's words did something to me. They seemed to have a ring of truth. Why would he marry me knowing that he was still gay? He wouldn't. I didn't think anybody could be that cruel to another human being.

As I let Camden's words sink in, I realized that I was probably too hard on him earlier at his parents' house. I shouldn't have said those things. Yes, I was angry with him for talking to Malik, but I didn't have to be so harsh toward him. Maybe he and Malik were only talking as friends. Maybe I had jumped the gun by saying he hadn't changed.

"I'm sorry about the things I said to you earlier. I was out of line."

"Apology accepted! I understand that you were hurt when you found out that I had seen Malik. I deserved it."

"Are you sure there's nothing between the two of you?"

"I'm positive," he affirmed.

"I want to believe you, Camden, I really do, but the past continues to haunt me and I'm scared," I admitted.

"I promise to protect your heart. I'm not going to hurt you," Camden assured me as he leaned in to kiss me.

Surprisingly, I returned his kiss with full feelings. I had missed my husband and I hated the tension between us during the last few days. Camden began kissing my neck and my body tingled after each kiss. I wrapped my arms around him as he began to remove my clothes. Within seconds, we were totally naked. I was trying to go with the flow of the lovemaking that was about to happen, but thoughts of the cell phone bill and Malik crept into my mind. All the events from the day were interfering with the sexy feelings I was about to experience. I closed my eyes to allow myself to enjoy the moment, but again, there was a block. As Camden lay on top of me, about to insert himself, a picture of Malik's face entered my mind. I squeezed my eyes tightly shut, hoping the vision would go away. It didn't. I pushed Camden up.

"Stop! I can't do this."

"What do you mean you can't do this? What's wrong now?" he asked angrily.

"Can you put on a condom?" I asked.

"Why? We haven't been using condoms."

"I really think we need to be safe."

"Safe for what?" he yelled. Then he got off me.

"Camden, wait," I yelled as he began picking up his clothes from the floor. "Where are you going?"

"I'm going out! I don't want to stay here and make you feel unsafe!"

"Camden, that's not what I meant. I—" Before I could finish speaking, he was out the bedroom door. I listened as he stomped down the steps, opened the front door, and slammed it shut. As I listened to him speed off, I wondered if asking him to use a condom was wrong. I suppose it was out of the ordinary since he was my husband and we'd never used them before. Maybe I had made a big mistake.

I laid my head on my pillow, saddened as I realized that I had probably just pushed Camden into the arms of Malik.

Chapter 26

Camden

I was in disbelief as I drove to the Explorer's Lounge to meet up with Hassan and Jared. They had asked me to have a drink with them tonight and I declined because I wanted to spend some time with Stormy to make things right. But when she asked me to wear a condom, I felt like shit. I was her husband. And as far as I was concerned, husbands didn't wear condoms with their wives. Not to mention, we had never used them before. Now all of a sudden she wanted to have safe sex? Her actions led me to believe that nothing I said to her earlier had mattered. She really didn't trust me. Yes, I told some lies during my spiel, but I thought she forgave me. Maybe she saw through the lies, hence her reasoning for asking me to wear a condom. But I didn't care. She made me feel dirty, and I was pissed.

When I arrived at the lounge, I headed straight to the bar and hopped on the barstool. Hassan and Jared were there drinking Coronas and shooting the breeze.

"What's up, playas?" I asked, giving them both a pound.

"Hey, Cam!" Jared said, looking surprised to see me. "I didn't think you were meeting up with us tonight."

"I wasn't, but after what went down at home tonight, I decided to take y'all up on the offer to hang out."

"You and Stormy got into it, huh?" Hassan asked.

"Sure did."

"What happened?" Jared questioned

"Man, I'll tell y'all once I get a drink. I need something to calm me down right now." I ordered a rum and Coke. I didn't usually drink hard liquor, but I needed something strong to lessen my anger. "How long have y'all been here?" I asked.

"For about an hour. I got here a little late because I stopped by to see my honey," Hassan bragged.

"How are things going with you and Cymone?" I asked.

"Cymone and I are doing well. She's the type of woman I think I could marry. She doesn't mind catering to her man." Hassan laughed.

"I know what you mean, my brother. Nicole caters to me, too," Jared said, bragging as well.

"What? Nicole caters to you? I can't believe that," I said in disbelief.

"Believe it, man. She's not as hard as she appears to be. I think she's been through a lot with men in the past and that's why she puts up her hard exterior. But she's a good person with a kind heart," Jared said, defending Nicole.

"The only side I've seen is the bitch side. She and I have never gotten along. But hey, I'm glad things are going well with the two of you. I wish I could say the same about her friend."

"What's going on with you and Stormy?" Jared asked.

I began to explain all the sordid details of what happened between Stormy and me. I told them about meeting with Malik, the cell phone bill, the meeting at my parents' house, and then her having the nerve to ask me to wear a condom.

"She asked you to strap up? Damn, she don't trust you at all," Hassan joked.

"Hell no, she doesn't trust his ass. Look what he's put her through. I'm surprised she hasn't asked you to wear a condom before now," Jared added.

I really didn't appreciate Jared's comments, but I let them slide and continued the conversation.

"She made me feel like I was grimy. That shit infuriated me more than y'all can imagine." As I finished up my first drink and ordered a second, I started to get angry all over again.

"So, Cam, when you called me the other night and asked me to cover for you, you were off to see Malik?" Hassan queried.

I lowered my head and hesitantly confessed to my friends.

"I saw Malik a couple of times," I said softly.

Hassan and Jared were my boys, my best friends, but I knew they were going to blast me for seeing Malik, especially since they didn't really approve of my undercover lifestyle.

"Yo, Camden, I thought you left that dude alone. Come on, now. You're married. It's one thing to mess around with Malik when you were single, but to do it while you're married is wrong, man. You're my boy and I love you, but I can't support you on this," Hassan expressed.

"Yeah, man, you know I've tried hard not to judge you, but I *am* judging the fact that you are cheating on your wife. You've only been married for a couple of months and you're cheating already. That's foul, man," Jared said, agreeing with Hassan.

"I'm not cheating. I only met with Malik to talk. I did not have sex with him."

Although I was telling the truth, they looked at me as if they didn't believe me.

"I don't think you should be seeing him at all. Nothing good can come from it. You need to put your marriage first and let Malik go on about his business," Hassan scolded.

"True," I agreed. I know that you're right, but I thought that I was really over the homosexual thing. It wasn't until recently that the feelings began to consume me again."

"Man, I can't stand this," Jared exclaimed. "Tell me this ain't you, man. Tell me this ain't true. I've known you all my life and I'll never be able to accept you . . . you . . . being like this."

"So, what are you sayin', Jared?" I asked.

"I'm saying that it's getting harder and harder for me to deal with. I hate even talking about it. I thought we agreed not to discuss this disgusting mess."

"Well, y'all asked me what happened between Stormy and me. If you didn't want to know, you shouldn't have asked. Look, I don't want to have these feelings, but I do. I'm starting to believe there's nothing I can do about it."

"So, let me ask you a question, and I want an honest answer," Jared said.

"Shoot."

"Why did you marry Stormy if you knew you still had these feelings? Why put her through that? Why put yourself through it? Why not be true to who you are? Why keep putting up a front?"

"I'm going to tell you guys the truth. When my relationship with Malik became public, I was embarrassed. You guys know that I'm a private person and the last thing that I ever wanted to surface was the fact that I liked men. My parents berated me, Stormy hated me, the church folk looked down on me, and y'all gave me the blues, too. I got tired of hearing how I had disgraced the family name. So I tried to do the right thing. I tried to fight the demons. For a while I thought I had conquered them, but now I know that my feelings were just suppressed."

"In other words, you married Stormy to cover up your homo lifestyle," Jared said with disdain.

"I'm ashamed to admit it, but yes. Don't get me wrong, I love her. But if I'm honest with myself, I probably married Stormy so that the rumors would stop. I wanted my parents to stop looking at me as if I was a big disappointment. I didn't like hearing the whispers when I walked into the church. I didn't like the stares that I got from people who felt that what I was doing was going against God's word. I hated all the negativity that surrounded being bisexual, homosexual, gay, whatever. I needed it all to stop. So I got married, hoping that it would."

"Camden! How could you do that to her? She doesn't deserve this. If you're still having feelings for men, then you have to be honest and tell Stormy. You can't keep living a lie," Hassan exclaimed.

"I agree with everything that you've said, but I can't end my marriage. The timing is not right. I need Stormy with me right now."

"Look, I'm not going to tell you what to do, but all I say is watch your back. You know this shit is going to come back to bite your ass one day. I just hope you're ready," Jared exhorted and got up from the bar.

Just as I was about to catch up with Jared, my cell phone rang. I noticed that it was an unavailable number again. *Who keeps calling me from an unavailable telephone number?* When I answered the phone, the caller hung up.

"Shit!" I spat.

"What's the deal?" Hassan asked.

"Somebody keeps calling me from an unavailable number, and every time I answer, the person hangs up. I need to get my cell number changed."

"Do you have any idea who it could be?"

"No, I don't," I said, although I wondered if it was Malik. I decided to excuse myself and walked to the pay phone to call him. I couldn't call him from my cell phone any longer since Stormy discovered our calls to each other on the bill.

When I dialed Malik's number, he answered on the first ring.

"Who's this?"

"What do you mean, who's this?"

"Camden?" Malik asked, sounding unsure.

"Yeah, it's me."

"Where are you?"

"I'm at the Explorer's Lounge with Jared and Hassan. Stormy and I had a fight and I needed to get out for a while."

"What's the issue this time?" Malik snickered.

"I'll tell you when I see you," I said, not wanting to get into the details over the telephone. Besides, he was going to be pissed when he found out Stormy and my parents knew that we'd been talking again.

"And when is that?"

"Can you meet me at our special place in an hour?"

"I'll be there."

"I'll see you then."

I decided to ask Malik about the hang-ups I'd been receiving on my cell phone. "Malik, have you been calling my cell phone and hanging up?"

"No. Why would I do that?"

"I've been receiving hang-up calls from someone calling from an unavailable number, and I wasn't sure if it was you or not."

"Naw, man, it's not me."

"Cool. I'll see you in a few minutes."

"Peace."

The hang-up calls were puzzling and bothered me because they were happening more and more often. I planned to get my cell number changed as soon as possible. This could be my excuse to get my own cell phone plan with a new number. Hopefully this would alleviate the hang-ups and put a stop to Stormy analyzing the bill.

I walked back over to the bar and Jared had returned. I had never seen my friend so angry at me. It bothered me, but I wasn't living my life for him.

"Hey, y'all. I'm about to be out," I said, not wanting to be subjected to any more ridicule. "I'll holla at y'all later."

"I hope you're going home," Hassan said. I didn't respond. I left my money on the bar and proceeded to leave.

"Be careful, Camden. You're playing a dangerous game. And you need to remember that what goes around, comes around," Jared warned as I walked away.

"Yeah, yeah, yeah! I'll deal with it if and when it happens. Until then, I'm going to do my thing."

I left the lounge in a hurry, as I was eager to see Malik. Having a couple of drinks along with being horny was a lethal combination. I had every intention on breaking my marriage vows that night since I was being accused of it anyway. And I was more than positive that Malik wouldn't ask me to wear a condom.

Chapter 27

Malik

I slept in late the morning after renewing my sexual relationship with Camden because I didn't leave the Econo Lodge in Columbia until three o'clock in the morning. After lying in bed, enjoying my memories of the previous night, I finally decided to get up, shower, and get dressed. I turned on the radio while I ironed my clothes. An Atlantic Starr old school jam was playing, so I sang along.

"Secret lovers, yeah, that's what we are. Trying so hard to hide the way we feel. 'Cause we both belong to someone else. . . . Not me," I added, and continued to sing. "But we can't let go, 'cause what we feel, is oh, so real. So real, so real, so real . . ."

"Secret Lovers" by Atlantic Starr perfectly described my relationship with Camden, especially the part that said, "We gotta be careful so that no one will know." Unfortunately, Camden informed me last night that Stormy saw my home and cell numbers listed on their cell phone bill numerous times and she had informed his parents. At first, I was a little shaken by the news.

Then I was pissed at Camden after he admitted he wasn't as good at cheating as he boasted. It never entered his mind that Stormy would be checking the detailed billing portion of the bill. And I went along with the idea of calling his cell, thinking he had covered his tracks. Obviously he hadn't. Camden reassured me that everything was going to be fine. He claimed he successfully handled the situation with both Stormy and his parents. That remained to be seen.

I was almost certain Camden was in the dog house at this very moment for coming home in the wee hours of the morning. I continuously reminded him it was getting late, but he professed to have everything under control. That brotha swore he had written the book on how to be a good cheater. He talked a good game, but I was not letting my guard down. I was going to constantly watch my back because the last thing I needed was drama from the Brookses, or my grandmother finding out that I lied to her about messing around with Camden.

As I was getting dressed, Sister Jones, Pastor Brooks's secretary, called on the phone.

"Hi, Sister Jones. To what do I owe the pleasure of your call?"

"Reverend Brooks wants to speak with you," she said in a serious tone.

My heart damn near fell in my stomach. I knew exactly what Reverend Brooks wanted, but I asked Sister Jones anyway.

"Why does he want to speak with me?"

"Reverend Brooks didn't tell me. He just asked me to call you and to transfer the call to his office if you were home."

"OK, you can transfer me."

"Hold on."

As she put me on hold, I took a deep breath and prepared for the wrath of Reverend Brooks.

"Malik," Reverend Brooks said sternly.

"Hello, Reverend Brooks. How are you?" I asked, trying to be polite.

"I'm not doing too well, Malik."

"Oh? What seems to be the problem, Reverend?"

"You and my son are the problem, Malik! I've been informed that the two of you have been talking and secretly seeing one another. Is that true?"

Had I not been informed that Reverend Brooks saw the cell phone bill with my telephone numbers on it, I would have lied. But I knew he was fully aware what was going on, so I told him the truth.

"Yes . . . yes, sir."

"Why? Why are the two of you talking?"

"We're only talking as friends. There is nothing going on between us."

"Son, you do realize that Camden is married?

"Yes."

"Then you need to act like it!" he scolded. "There's no need for you and Camden to communicate. I thought all of this was settled the day you left my office. Whatever you and Camden have going on should have been over then. I'm disappointed to know that it's not!" His voice was harsh.

I remained silent, not knowing what to say. I just continued to listen to him rebuke me.

"As of today, you will not talk to my son anymore. You need to work on getting yourself right with the Lord and pray for a change in your life. Indulging in homosexuality and adultery goes against the word of God, and I will not have this kind of behavior going on in my church."

"Sir, I'm not committing adultery," I lied. It was only just a few hours ago that I was rolling around the sack with Camden.

"I don't care what you say. I know there is something going on with you and Camden, but it ends today. Do you understand?"

"Yes, sir, I understand."

"Good! Because if it doesn't, you'll have to deal with me. And you don't want that. Not after all the love and support my members, my wife, and I have shown you. College ain't free, you know? Now I hope this is the last time I will have to talk to you about this matter."

"Don't worry, I got your message loud and clear."

"I'm glad to hear that. Have a blessed day," he said before hanging up.

So much for Camden having things under control. I should have known his father would intervene once he saw that cell phone bill. I thought about calling Camden to tell him about my conversation with his father, but determined there was no need. As much as I hated to admit it, being involved with Camden was doing more harm than good. I had to let him go. It was going to be hard, but it was the right thing to do. I just hoped Camden would understand

Chapter 28

Stormy

For nearly a month, I rationalized away the idea that my marriage was in trouble. My marriage to Camden was nothing like the way God described in the Bible. I reflected on familiar scriptures that explained the husband's role in a marriage.

The book of Matthew, chapter nineteen, verse six stated, ". . . they are no longer two, but one flesh. Therefore, what God has joined together, let not man separate." Ephesians, chapter five, verses twenty-two through twenty-nine stated, ". . . the husband is head of the wife . . . Husbands, love your wives, just as Christ also loved the church . . . so husbands ought to love their own wives as their own bodies; he who loves his wife loves himself. For no one ever hated his own flesh, but nourishes and cherishes it . . ."

I was fully aware that the Bible also addressed a woman's role in marriage as well, but I wasn't reflecting on those because I was doing the best I could as a wife. Maybe I should be more submissive or maybe I could keep my tongue free of insults and evil, but Camden's recent behavior warranted a full barrage of the evilest and most insulting words I could muster up.

However, I did feel some guilt after the condom incident. So in hopes of redeeming myself, Camden and I made love twice since then without a condom. I didn't feel the previous connection we once had. It was a far cry from our wedding night. I kind of felt like he just wanted to climb on top of me, do his business, roll over, and fall asleep. It was empty sex and I didn't like it, so I stopped initiating, and he didn't approach me either. At that point our sex life became pretty much nonexistent. Besides, he was rarely home anymore. And when he was, it seemed as if we were worlds apart. If I was in the bedroom, he was in the family room. If he was in the bedroom, I stayed in the kitchen. He even sometimes slept in the spare bedroom.

I'd tried to remain humble throughout this trial and sought the Lord daily for his guidance. During my prayers, I heard the Lord tell me to forgive Camden for his actions and each time I got off my knees, I had every intention to abide by God's words. Unfortunately, many of those nights Camden didn't come home.

One day I woke up and decided to place my marriage in the hands of God. I no longer had the strength to fight. This battle with Camden couldn't be won by someone who was weary. I was reminded of Yolanda Adams singing, "The battle is not yours. It's the Lord's."

Instead of focusing on the problems in my marriage, I called Leigh, Dominique, and Nicole and invited them over for a girls' night. It had been a while since I hung out with them, and if ever I needed friends, the time was now. Each of them readily accepted. We decided that the menu for the evening would be fried party wings, pasta salad, string beans, and cheesecake for dessert. Nicole agreed to bring the ingredients for daiquiris. I should have known she would try to get us all drunk.

Camden coming home during our festivities was the furthest thing from my mind, because in recent weeks, he never walked through the door before midnight. By that time we'd be full, tipsy, sleepy, and gossiped out.

At seven o'clock sharp, the doorbell rang. I answered the door.

"Party over here! Party over here!" Nicole sang.

"Girl, you crazy." I laughed. "Come on in here and stop making all that noise on my front porch." I could tell immediately that being with my friends would lift my spirits. Leigh and Dominique followed Nicole into the house.

"Stormy, is the chicken ready yet, because I'm hungry," Leigh blurted.

"Yes, Leigh, the food is ready. I was just about to put everything on the dining room table."

"Do you need any help?" Dominique asked.

Can you help me put my marriage back on track? I wanted to ask, but didn't.

"No. Y'all just sit down and make yourselves at home."

After putting the food on the table, I called them into the dining room to eat. It felt good cooking a meal for friends. Camden was rarely home anymore, so I was left to cook for myself and eat alone, or else I ended up popping in a microwavable meal or ordering takeout food.

During dinner I became reacquainted with my friends. I listened as Nicole bragged about how well her relationship with Jared was going.

Damn, I wish I could say the same about Camden and me. I laughed as she spoke about his freaky bedroom behavior and how she was afraid of him. *What! Nicole was spooked by a man's bedroom actions? Shocking!* I thought.

Leigh filled me in on the happenings at her job and how she was subtly flirting with a good-looking coworker. I told her to be careful before she was slapped with a sexual harassment lawsuit.

Dominique informed me of the drama she recently experienced with one of her second grade students. She explained that he was misbehaving in class and when she scolded him, he called her a black bitch, kicked her in the shin, and ran out of the classroom. She was really upset by the whole ordeal, but felt better knowing that the child was up for expulsion.

Throughout the evening, I put up a good front. I never let on that inside I was full of anguish, at least not until Dominique asked why Camden wasn't home. I wanted to lie and say he was at work, but when I glanced at the clock hanging from the wall, it was well past Camden's quitting time, so I told the truth.

"I don't know," I answered softly with my head lowered in shame.

"You don't know?" Dominique echoed.

There's no turning back now. They know something's going on. I thought.

"No, I don't know." I looked over at Nicole, who was frowning.

"Why don't you know where your husband is, Stormy?"

"We haven't been getting along lately. So when he leaves out the door, he doesn't tell me where he's going, and I don't ask."

"Oh, Stormy," Leigh sighed. "Things aren't getting any better?"

"Actually, they're worse. We've only made love twice within the last month and he doesn't come home until the early morning hours. We rarely talk when he's here, and some nights he sleeps in the spare bedroom."

Nicole was the first to show anger.

"What the hell is wrong with Camden? What have you ever done to him? If anyone should be upset, it should be you. Mr. Married Man has some nerve staying out all night without at least having the decency to tell you where he is!"

"You don't know where he spends his nights?" Dominique asked.

"Probably with Malik," I said sarcastically.

"Malik? What does his trifling ass have to do with this? Camden's seeing him again?" Nicole asked, ready to pull out her boxing gloves.

I explained the events of the past few weeks. I told them about the twenty-seven calls that appeared on our cell phone bill, the secret meetings with Malik that Camden admitted to, and Camden's late hours. When I finished, they all sat in amazement. I was feeling pretty low. I had finally told them how unhappy I was in my marriage, and that wasn't an easy thing to admit.

As always, they gave me their full support. Dominique was so upset, she cried. Leigh sat dumbfounded and Nicole was livid. Of course, Nicole was ready to kick Camden's and Malik's asses, but we successfully calmed her down. A butt whipping wouldn't solve anything.

For a moment the room fell silent. No one knew what to say. I placed my head on the dining room table. I thought about how my life and my marriage were a mess. As I cried, I felt a sharp pain in my stomach. This mess with Camden was literally making me sick. Finally someone spoke.

"What are you going to do about his triflin', sneaky behavior? You can't allow Camden to treat you this way," Dominique voiced.

In between my stomach pains, I found the strength to speak.

"Earlier today I decided to leave it in God's hands. I don't have the strength to keep fighting with Camden. Prayerfully, he'll come around."

"And how long are you supposed to wait for him to come around?" Nicole asked.

Good question.

"I haven't thought that far ahead. We've only been married a short time, and I think—"

I couldn't finish my sentence. I felt as if I was about to vomit. I got up and ran to the bathroom. I made it in the nick of time before all my food came up. I was on my knees for at least ten minutes regurgitating. Once I was finished barfing, I continued to experience excruciating pain in my abdomen. *What is wrong with me? It must have been something I ate.*

When I returned to the girls, they looked at me as if they'd seen a ghost.

"Are you all right?" Leigh asked.

"I don't know. It must have been something I ate. I'm feeling nauseous and my stomach hurts."

"Well, we all ate the same thing and we're all fine," Nicole chimed in.

"Then I don't know what it could be."

"Are you pregnant?" Leigh inquired.

"Please! Camden and I are barely speaking, let alone having sex. I couldn't be pregnant."

"Then I think you need to make a doctor's appointment to find out what's going on," Leigh suggested.

"I agree. You don't look well," Dominique added.

"I think you're right. I will make an appointment to see my doctor first thing in the morning."

Ring. Ring. I grabbed the cordless phone to look at the caller ID. I had no idea who was calling because the ID read unavailable. I answered anyway.

"Hello?" No one spoke. "Hello?" Still no response. "Helloooooo?" No one answered, so I pressed the off button. "That's the third time that's happened this week. I need to stop answering unidentified calls."

"It's probably telemarketers. They can be pesky devils all hours of the day," Leigh commented.

I didn't know who it was, but I wasn't going to spend a lot of time trying to figure it out. I had bigger problems.

"Well, we better get going. You need to lie down and get some rest," Dominique said.

As they prepared to leave, I told them that I would be sure to see my physician in the morning. We shared a group hug and they left.

As I cleaned the kitchen, I began to wonder if I was pregnant, but I quickly dismissed that thought.

"I'm sure that's not the case," I said to myself. "Hell, I hope it's not the case. Camden and I aren't in the position to become parents. The last thing we need to do is bring a child into this unstable marriage."

One week after visiting my doctor, his office manager called and asked if I could come in for my test results. As I drove to the office, I prayed.

Please, Lord, let me be OK. All week, I had prayed the same prayer.

I was a little edgy as I sat in the waiting room of the doctor's office. With the symptoms I was experiencing, the doctor thought it was best to do a comprehensive examination, including a Pap smear and samples of urine and blood. I confirmed that I had been having regular menstrual cycles, but he wanted to do a pregnancy test anyway. The results were negative. That was a relief, but something was still wrong. I knew it.

Now I sat waiting for my results with sweaty palms.

"Mrs. Brooks," the nurse called. "The doctor will see you now."

"Hello, Stormy," Dr. McKenzie said as he entered his office.

Hearing his voice made me fearful. Something wasn't right.

"Hi, doctor," I said nervously.

I watched as Dr. McKenzie sat at his desk, thumbing through my file.

What is he looking for? Doesn't he already know the results? Finally he spoke.

"Stormy, last week when you were here you complained of nausea, vomiting, and abdominal pain. Initially, I thought you may have been pregnant, but as you know, the test was negative."

Thank you, God. I praised him inwardly for that. He continued.

"Your Pap smear came back fine, but your blood test revealed that you have Hepatitis A."

"What? Hepatitis A? What is that?" I demanded.

"Hepatitis A is a contagious liver infection caused by the Hepatitis A virus."

I was listening, but I didn't comprehend what he was saying.

"How do you get Hepatitis A?"

"There are a few ways to contract the infection. Hepatitis A is found in the feces of a person who has the virus, so you may contract it by traveling to countries where Hepatitis A is common, eating raw foods, or working with children who are infected. The most common method of transmission is by men having sex with other men."

"I'm confused. I've heard of Hepatitis C, but I'm not familiar with Hepatitis A. What's the difference?"

"Well, both are liver infections, but Hepatitis C is more severe. It can lead to cirrhosis of the liver or liver cancer. Hepatitis C is also usually contracted by coming in contact with blood and bodily fluids, whereas the A virus is commonly spread by feces. That's why Hepatitis A is common amongst homosexual men."

I couldn't believe my ears. *Did he just say homosexual men?* I had to hear this explained to me again. My mind was clouded and I just couldn't grasp what the doctor was telling me.

"How can two men having sex transmit the disease?" I asked.

"It can be passed in the stool of an infected person or spread by hand-to-mouth contact with the stool of the infected person. Why? Do you think that may be how you contracted this—by having sex with a man who may have been with another man?"

I was too embarrassed to tell him the truth.

"I don't know, doctor. I do work with children, so I could have gotten the disease from one of my students."

"I'm surprised your school district didn't give you a vaccination. Working with children can be risky, especially not knowing their backgrounds."

I knew that I hadn't gotten Hepatitis A from my students. *I got this shit from Camden. There is no doubt in my mind.*

"So, doctor, how can I be treated?"

"Unfortunately, there is no treatment for the infection. People usually recover on their own in two to three weeks. However, I can give you something to treat the nausea and the pain you've been experiencing."

"Thanks, doctor. I'd like that."

As Dr. McKenzie wrote on his prescription pad, I could feel rage growing within me. I planned to kill Camden when I got home. How could he have been so careless? Why would he put me at risk like this? How could my husband do this to me? *He's a selfish bastard.*

Dr. McKenzie gave me prescriptions for nausea and abdominal pain. I stopped at the drugstore to get them filled immediately.

When I walked into our home, Camden was sitting in the

living room flipping through a magazine. I thought of beating him with a baseball bat the moment I saw him. He needed to feel the pain that I was feeling. He turned around to look at me and spoke.

"Hi, Storm. Your mother just called. She wants you to call her when you get a chance."

As he spoke, his words sounded as if he was speaking a different language. I was in such a frenzy that I could not understand the words he'd just uttered. As he continued reading his magazine, I called his name. When he turned and looked in my direction again, I yelled at him.

"You dirty dick son of a bitch! How could you be so cruel?"

"What are you bitchin' about now?" he hissed angrily. This bastard must have lost his mind.

"Bitchin'? Bitchin'? You're lucky all I'm doing is bitchin', because I have a mind to bust your fuckin' head wide open!"

I think that I caught his attention with that comment. He even appeared shocked. Before he could speak, I yelled again.

"Do you know where I'm coming from?" He didn't answer. He just stared at me.

"I just came from Dr. McKenzie's office. And do you know what he told me?"

Still he said nothing.

"He told me that I have Hepatitis A!"

"What do you mean you have Hepatitis A?"

"Just what the hell I said! I have Hepatitis A and I got it from you, you nasty ass banger!"

Camden looked as if he was going to reply, but I didn't give him the chance. I walked up to him, got in his face, and screamed.

"Because of your careless, gay behavior, you've given me a fuckin' liver infection."

He had the nerve to look puzzled.

"You heard me right! Hepatitis A is commonly transmitted to women who sleep with men who have anal sex with men! It's passed through the stool of an infected person."

Camden stepped back and continued to look puzzled.

"Stormy, I don't have Hepatitis A."

"Well then you need to go get your ass checked, because I have it, and I got it from you! I guess during one of your faggot sexcapades you contracted the infection and passed it on to me. You know, the gift that keeps on giving!"

"Honestly, I feel fine. I—I—I don't have Hepatitis A."

Smack! I smacked him across the face.

"I'm sick of you lyin' to me. You cheated on me and didn't have the decency to protect yourself. Now you're unaware that you're walking around with a dirty dick!"

Smack! I slapped him again, but this time, he put his arms around my throat and pushed me into the wall.

"Don't you ever put your hands on me again!" he hollered.

"Fuck you! Get your hands off me!" I violently pushed him in the chest.

Camden turned and walked toward the sofa. As he sat down, he spoke calmly.

"You've got it wrong. I haven't cheated on you, and I don't have Hepatitis A."

I was tired of hearing his lies. Listening to him lie repeatedly fueled my rage. I picked up the closest object to me—a frame holding our wedding picture—and threw it at Camden's head.

"You fucking liar!"

I couldn't take anymore. I ran upstairs and locked myself in the bedroom. Moments later, I heard Camden yell.

"I don't have to stay here and take this shit. Fuck you, Stormy!" Then I heard the door slam.

"Peace out, asshole," I spoke aloud. This was one time I was glad Camden left the house. I couldn't bear hearing any more of his lies. My insides were burning with fury and I didn't know what I was capable of doing.

I needed to talk to someone. I needed someone to help calm me. But who? Then I realized that at that very moment, I needed my mother.

Chapter 29

Malik

Days and nights seem long when you're separated from the one you love. I was miserable without Camden. But after my conversation with Reverend Brooks, I decided to let Camden go. In my mind, I knew it was the right thing to do, but my heart wasn't in agreement.

Camden called several times, and each time I ignored his telephone calls. In his messages, he begged me to return his calls, but I never did. I knew I owed him an explanation, but I couldn't face him. So, I chose to avoid him.

I was glad the spring semester had come to an end. I hadn't been focused in months. My grades had even dropped. I planned to spend the summer getting my life in order. It was time to make some changes for the better. Being gay and committing adultery was against God's law, and I knew one day I'd suffer some serious consequences for my actions.

As I drove around aimlessly, attempting to clear my head, my cell phone rang. I glanced at the phone and saw it was

Camden. I immediately sent his call to voicemail as I had done many times before. A few seconds later, my phone chimed, indicating that I had a message. I pulled into Exxon to get some gas and checked my message.

"Malik, this is Camden. I don't know where you've been the past few days, but I need you to return my call. It is urgent that I speak with you. Something has happened and I need to talk to you ASAP!"

I closed my cell phone and lay my head against the hood as the gas pumped. *What could be so urgent? What could have happened?* Usually Camden's messages were short and sweet, telling me to call him or that he missed me. This time there was something different in his voice. My curiosity got the best of me, so I returned his call.

"Camden, it's me, Malik. What's up?"

Camden was full of questions.

"Where the hell have you been? I've been calling you for days. Why haven't you returned my calls?"

"I've been busy. What's so urgent?" I asked, trying to get to the point.

"Malik, things are fucked up. Stormy came home yesterday from a doctor's appointment pissed. She was told that she has Hepatitis A."

So what are you calling me for? Why should I care?

"Hepatitis A? How did she get that?"

"She claims she got it from me. I told her that I'm not having any symptoms, but she doesn't believe me. She said it was transmitted from me having sex with another man and then having sex with her. It's passed through stool."

I sat dumbfounded as he continued talking.

"Like I said before, I don't have any symptoms. Do you?" he asked hesitantly.

"What are the symptoms?" I asked, even though I knew I was fine.

"I only know some of the symptoms: abdominal pain, fatigue, loss of appetite, nausea, vomiting, diarrhea, and fever. Have you had any of those problems?" Camden asked.

"Not really. I mean, I've been a little tired lately, but I'm not sure that's because of Hepatitis A. What about you?" I asked.

"The loss of appetite may be my only area, but I'm like you. I don't think it's related to the virus. I just haven't been hungry. I don't know. I'm worried. I'm sure Stormy hasn't slept with anyone else, so if she has this infection, I must've passed it on to her."

"How can you be so sure she hasn't had sex with anybody else?"

"I just know. What I'm not sure about . . . is you. Have you had sex with anyone recently, within the last few months, other than me?"

I wanted to lie. *Does he really need to know my sexual resume?* But since I knew he was really upset about this, I decided to tell the truth.

"Yes, I have."

"What? Why didn't you tell me? Who did you sleep with, Malik?" Camden screamed into the phone.

"Whoa! You need to calm down!" I yelled back.

"What do you mean calm down? You were sleeping with someone else behind my back?"

Camden must be crazy. Didn't he just get married?

"First of all, I didn't do anything behind your back. While you were off getting married, I moved on with my life. I met this guy and we kicked it."

"It seems like you did more than kick it. I can't believe you had sex with some other dude."

"I don't know why you're so shocked. What was I supposed to do, sit around and wait for you? You chose Stormy, so I moved on with my life," I said bluntly. He must have taken a moment to comprehend what I said, because he didn't speak. "Hello? Are you still there?"

"Yeah, I'm here. Did you have unprotected sex with—what's his name?" Camden asked.

Why did he need to know his name?

"Beau," I whispered.

"Did you have unprotected sex with Beau?" he asked with a sad voice.

"Most of the time we used condoms, but there was one night when we didn't."

"We both need to go to the clinic. We could very well have Hepatitis A." Camden seemed panicked.

"When are you going? I can probably get an appointment today with my doctor," I said.

"I don't know. It'll be soon, probably tomorrow."

"Well, I need to call my doctor now. I'm going today. I need to know if I have this infection."

"I'll try to make an appointment as well."

I was starting to feel guilty.

"Before I go, I'd like to apologize. I hope you're all right."

"Yeah, right," he slurred, and hung up in my ear. He didn't even say good-bye.

After Camden ended our conversation, I called my doctor to make an appointment for noon. I sighed and shook my head. My life was spinning out of control. My conversation with Camden confirmed my earlier feelings. Things really needed to change and fast.

Waiting five days for the test results got on my last nerve. Each passing day, I felt changes within my body. My urine was a dark, cola color, and my stomach cramped, but I didn't know if it was nerves or if these were truly symptoms. Maybe I was worried for nothing.

On the fifth day, my doctor called, ending the suspense. He delivered the bad news. I had indeed contracted Hepatitis A. I was taken aback by the confirmation, and even more devastated that I had transmitted the infection to Camden. I had to call him to break the news.

I waited patiently for him to answer, and when he did, my tongue felt as if it couldn't move.

"Hello?" he repeated.

"Camden, it's me. I got my results today and I do have Hepatitis A." I sat quietly, waiting for him to explode.

"I got my results today, and I have it, too. I guess I did give it to Stormy."

"I'm sorry. I never meant to hurt you."

"Whatever," he said sarcastically.

"I didn't mean to do this to you. If I had known—"

Camden interrupted me.

"Save the excuses. I've got to go," he said.

He didn't give me a chance to respond before he hung up. I felt as if I was on the bottom of someone's shoe. How could I have been so careless? I should have protected myself. Now, because of my unsafe sexual practices, I'd infected other people.

Camden's voice said it all. He was cold and distant. He was probably never going to speak to me again. Although Camden not speaking to me would be great considering that I was trying to end the relationship, I didn't want things to end on such a bad note. I wanted things to be amicable.

"I won't let it end like this," I spoke aloud. "Not with Camden angry with me."

I decided to give Camden a few days to regroup and then I would give him a call. Until then, I would suffer in silence as both the Hepatitis A virus and guilt burrowed deeper inside my body.

Chapter 30

Stormy

Initially after I was diagnosed with Hepatitis A, I wanted to reach out to my mother and my friends, to cry on their shoulders. But I couldn't. I was too ashamed to tell anybody. As usual, I put up a front and pretended that everything was OK. But it wasn't. I waited a week for Camden to say something, to confirm that he had given me the virus, to apologize, anything. He did nothing. Finally I couldn't hold it in any longer. I could no longer hide what I was dealing with, so I called my mother.

"Hey, Mommy. Thanks for coming over," I said as tears welled in my eyes.

"Your voice sounded shaky on the telephone, Stormy, so I rushed right over. You don't look good. Are you sick?" Mommy asked, concerned. I couldn't hold my tears any longer.

"Mommy, everything is wrong! I'm so unhappy." I fell into her arms and wailed.

"Oh God, Stormy. Let's go sit down so you can tell me what's going on."

We walked over to the couch and sat down. I rested my head on my mother's shoulders. I couldn't speak at first. All I could do was cry, causing my mother to become more alarmed. She must have sensed I was carrying a heavy load because she immediately started praying aloud.

As she rocked me in her arms, she talked to God.

"Please help my daughter, Lord. At this very moment she needs you. Please wrap your arms around her and embrace her. Lord, you have all power in your hands and I know you'll fix whatever my daughter is enduring. In Jesus' name I pray. Amen."

I hoped God heard her prayer because I needed Him now more than ever. I knew that He was the only one who could help me during this dreadful time. After she finished, I lifted my head, wiped my eyes, and looked at her.

"Mommy, I should have never married Camden," I blurted.

"Why do you say that?" she questioned, looking confused.

I took a deep breath because I was about to tell my mother about the hell I'd been going through since I had married Camden.

"He's still gay!"

"What makes you think that?"

"I found out that he has been secretly calling and seeing Malik. When our cell phone bill came last month, Malik's number was listed twenty-seven times and the calls were from all hours of the day and night. Not to mention, he stays out all night and comes home in the early morning hours."

"My God, Stormy. Why haven't you talked to me before now?"

"I thought I could handle it on my own. I thought things

would get better, but they haven't. They're actually getting worse."

"Have you tried to talk to Camden about this?"

"I have, but all we do is argue and then he leaves and doesn't come home until two, three, four o'clock in the morning. He even sleeps in the spare bedroom most nights." She leaned over to hug me.

"Baby girl, I had no idea you were going through this. I'm so sorry."

"Mommy, there's more," I said as I lowered my head with my eyes glued to the floor.

"What you've told me is bad enough. What else could there be?"

"I contracted Hepatitis A from Camden."

"What?" My mother was shocked.

"Yes, Ma. I was having abdominal pain and vomiting. My friends thought I might've been pregnant, so I made an appointment with Dr. McKenzie and explained my symptoms. He did a full exam and a Pap smear and took urine and blood samples. A week later he informed me that my blood test came back positive for Hepatitis A."

"I don't know much about Hepatitis A. Is it curable?" she asked with a puzzled look on her face.

"It is. There is no medication for it. It has to run its course throughout my body. However, Dr. McKenzie gave me medicine for the symptoms. I have a follow-up appointment next week to determine if it's gone."

"Well thank God it's not terminal or something you'll have for the rest of your life. You know the AIDS epidemic has increased considerably among women of color, especially African American women. I just recently heard on the news about a study done in 2004 that reported, women of color accounted for 80 percent of AIDS cases. And African American women made up 64 percent of those cases. You've got to be careful, Stormy. Camden's playing a dangerous game. Like I said, I'm glad it's not something more serious, but I wouldn't continue to play Russian roulette with my life if I were you."

"I know, Mommy. I won't. I'm not trying to be a statistic," I agreed.

There were a few moments of silence. It seemed as if my mother was having trouble digesting all I had told her. I knew this would be hard for her to hear, but I needed to tell her. My mother finally spoke.

"Have you told Camden?"

"Yes, I've told him, but he denies having it. I know I got it from him."

"How can you be so sure? Is it only transmitted through sexual intercourse?"

"Nope! It's carried in feces, and transmitted several ways, but the most common is by someone preparing food without washing his or her hands after going to the bathroom, or from men having sex with men."

"Oh, God, help me!" my mother moaned. "Do you mean to tell me that Camden was having unprotected sex with Malik or some other man, and then brought some nasty disease home to you?" She was livid. She stood up and continued. "I should call your brothers right now and have them kick his—"

"Mommy!" I cut her off before she could curse. In all my years on earth, I'd only heard my mother curse twice. Although Reverend Brooks had said many times from the pulpit that "saints curse," she never did. She lived by the saying that people who cursed lacked vocabulary and possessed small minds. I guess I wasn't a chip off the old block because I surely had a potty mouth.

"I know you ain't about to cuss. God wouldn't be pleased," I teased.

She chuckled. I guess we both needed something to lighten the moment.

"I know God wouldn't be pleased, but I'm angry. I'm damned angry. How dare Camden put my baby's health at risk! If he wants to go around living that life, that's fine, but not at my baby's expense."

"Mommy, I don't know what to do. Do you have any advice for me?"

My mother began to rub her hands together as she paced the floor. She appeared to be deep in thought. It seemed like it took forever for her to answer my question.

"This is hard for me, Stormy. The Christian side of me wants to tell you to do everything you can to make your marriage work. The Christian side of me wants to tell you to seek God about this. But the worldly side of me wants to tell you to pack your bags and come home with your father and me. The worldly side of me wants to call your brothers and let them deal with him."

I like the latter option.

"Marriage is tough. It's like a full time job, but you've got to work at it. Your father and I have had our trials, but we overcame them. We sought God and He answered our prayers. I think you ought to do the same. Before you walk away from this marriage, I want you to do everything possible to make it work."

"But I can't do it alone. Camden has to work with me."

"You're right, baby. You have to fight for your husband. Not physically, but through the power of prayer. You know when prayers go up, blessings come down. It's going to be difficult to pray for him when he's treating you like dirt, but you must believe me when I say, God hears you. He may not come when you want him to, but He'll be right on time."

"I don't know, Mommy. I don't know if I can do it. Sometimes I'm so hurt and angry that I can't even pray for Camden. If anything, my heart tells me to pray that God removes him from my life."

"Be careful what you wish for, because you just might get it. Don't ask God to remove Camden because He just might do that, but not in the way you think," she warned.

"So where do I begin?"

"You start by getting on your knees and asking God to intervene in your marriage. Then you start by talking to your husband—and I do mean talk. No arguing. You have to let him know how his behavior is affecting you. Let him know how he's hurting you."

Camden could care less about how he's hurting me. If he did, he wouldn't do the things he's doing.

"Then ask Camden to go to counseling with you. Hopefully, he'll agree. If not, then you just keep praying. Never cease to pray. Pray all night and day. Also, never stop being a wife. Continue to cook, clean, and hold your tongue. If God sees you doing the right thing by your husband, you'll be rewarded. Once you've done all you can and Camden doesn't change, God will see fit to bring you out of this situation. Again, it's not going to happen as fast as you'd like, but just be patient, sweetie. It'll happen."

"Thanks, Mommy. You made me feel a little better."

"I'm glad to hear that. Now, I've got to get going. I need to go home and be a wife myself." She snickered.

"Mom, please don't tell Daddy, Trey, or Jordan. Not yet. I want to see if I can work things out with Camden first. If things don't get better, then we can tell them what's going on."

"I won't say anything. I'll keep this between the two of us. But you make sure you keep me informed."

I walked her to the door and gave her a hug.

"I will. I love you, Mommy." She kissed me on my cheek.

"You're in the midst of a storm, but brighter days are ahead. Remember what I told you: Seek the Lord and remember to PUSH!"

"Push? What's push?"

"Pray Until Something Happens," she said as she smiled

I hugged her again and she left. I sat on the couch and began to reflect upon my mother's words. Knowing God the way I did, I should have known to seek Him first. I'd seen God make the worst situation better, so why wouldn't He do the same for me? I got on my knees, followed my mother's instructions, and prayed.

Spending nights alone was getting old. I had the urge to go out to enjoy myself. I called Leigh and asked her to meet me for dinner at the Cheesecake Factory in the Inner Harbor. She agreed. As I sat at the table waiting for her to arrive, I wondered if I should tell her everything that was going on.

"Sorry I'm late," Leigh said, sitting down breathlessly.

"No problem. I ordered a drink while I waited."

"Have you decided what you're eating?"

"I don't have much of an appetite, so I think I'll just get a chicken Caesar salad."

"You go ahead and eat healthy. I plan to eat like a pig tonight," Leigh joked.

Once the waitress took our order, Leigh dived right into questioning me about Camden.

"So, how are things going with you and Camden?"

"The same," I said, ashamed.

"I'm sorry to hear that. I wish I could give Camden a piece of my mind."

"No need. It'll be like talking to a brick wall," I said sarcastically.

"I guess you're right. How did your doctor's appointment go? I hope you didn't find out you're pregnant and haven't told me."

"No, I'm not pregnant."

"What did the doctor say was wrong?"

"I have Hepatitis A and Camden gave it to me," I whispered, embarrassed.

"What? You have what?" Leigh yelled.

"Shhhhhh. We're in a restaurant."

"So fuckin' what? That bastard gave you Hepatitis?" Leigh asked in a much lower voice.

"Yes, but he denies it. He says I didn't get it from him." Leigh frowned and pursed her lips.

"Who the hell does he think believes that shit?"

"Not me. He probably got it from Malik."

"Is he still talking to Malik?" Leigh asked.

"He claimed he was going to stop, but I'm sure he hasn't. We no longer have joint cell phone accounts because he claimed he was getting strange, prank telephone calls and needed a new cell number. So I have no way of knowing if they are still talking. But who are we fooling? You and I both know that they are."

We stopped talking abruptly as the waitress placed our food on the table. We waited until she left to continue our conversation.

"When we finish dinner, I'm going to call Malik and ask him myself."

"Do you think he will tell you the truth?"

"He did before. He might do it again."

After dinner, we left the restaurant. Since it was a nice evening, we decided to walk around the harbor. While we walked, Leigh called Malik.

I listened as she talked. During their conversation, she was livid. I didn't know all he was saying on the other end, but she wasn't happy. My palms were sweaty as I wondered what news she would have for me. Was Malik on the other end spilling his guts, telling Leigh all the details about his and Camden's affair? Was I about to have my worst fears confirmed—again?

I snapped out of my daze when I heard Leigh tell Malik she'd call him tomorrow. She hung up the phone and looked at me with anger in her eyes.

Oh shit! It must be bad.

"What did he say?" I asked hesitantly.

"That boy didn't tell me nothing. I tried to get it out of him, but he denied talking to Camden, seeing him, or having sex with him."

"I knew he wouldn't admit it."

"No, he didn't admit it, but I could tell in his voice that he was hiding something. There is more going on and I'm on a mission to find out."

"What are you going to do?"

She looked at me strangely. I could see the wheels spinning in her head.

"What are you doing to do?" I repeated.

"I'm going to conduct my own investigation," Leigh stated.

How the hell is she going to do that? She's an accountant, not a private investigator.

"How?" I asked.

"Stormy, there are many ways to keep track of people these days. I'm just going to pull out some of my old equipment and keep track of those sneaky devils."

I was still confused. I still had no idea what she was talking about, so I kept asking questions.

"What equipment do you have?"

"I have some things at my apartment that I had to use when I was dating that dog, Kevin."

"Really?"

"Remember I got the feeling that he was cheating on me with his son's mother?"

"Yeah."

"Well, I ordered some equipment to keep track of him. That was how I found out that he was not only cheating with his baby's mama, but messin' with her sister, too."

I laughed because I remembered the night Leigh found out. All hell broke loose. It damn near took a whole army to keep her from killing Kevin.

"Girl, you've been keeping secrets. I thought you followed him and that's how you found out."

"Naw! I used my PI equipment to find him," she claimed.

"So, what kind of equipment do you have?"

"I don't want to get into that right here. This is some top secret intelligence. Nobody knows I have it," she joked.

Damn, was my friend in the CIA or something? She was definitely holding out on a lot.

"How about this? The school year is ending next week for you and Dominique, right?" Leigh asked.

"Yes, and I can't wait."

"Let me talk to Nicole to see if she can get off for the weekend, and let's plan to go away."

"Where?"

"Virginia Beach?"

"Virginia Beach sounds good."

"Great! Then we'll plan to go for the weekend after school lets out for the summer. When we go away, I'll tell you about my plan and my private investigation tools."

"I can't wait! Girl, you've got me curious."

"I'll start making the trip arrangements tomorrow. Get ready to pack your bags because we've got some planning to do."

"Just let me know when and I'm there."

Chapter 31

Camden

The summer had come in with lots of drama. I was still fuming about having Hepatitis A and passing it on to Stormy. How could Malik have been so reckless? How could I have been so careless? I didn't necessarily regret having sex with Malik, but I did regret not practicing safe sex. I'd seen commercial after commercial which constantly reminded people about the dangers of having unprotected intercourse. I should have known better. I wasn't a fifteen-year-old child. I was a twenty-six-year-old man. There was no excuse for my mindless behavior. Now I had put my and Stormy's health in jeopardy. I thanked God the diagnosis wasn't something more serious like AIDS. Thank goodness I was spared this time, and because of that fact, I vowed never to make the mistake of having unprotected sex again.

Over the last week I had been consumed with guilt for what I had done to Stormy, so I was on my best behavior. Every day I went to work and came straight home. There were no late nights out. I cooked fabulous gourmet dinners the entire week and I did all the household chores. Verbally, I never confessed to having Hepatitis A or transmitting it to Stormy. I couldn't. I wanted to apologize to her, but I just couldn't do that either. Therefore, I allowed my actions to apologize for me.

Stormy was still angry at first, but as the week progressed, she seemed to lighten up. She started responding to me when I attempted to make small talk with her. We even ate dinner together and shared a laugh. It seemed as if things were looking up.

By midweek, Stormy informed me that she and her girl-friends were going away to Virginia Beach. She explained that she needed to get away for a while. Although I was envious that she wanted to be with her friends and not me, I agreed that she needed time away. Deep down, I knew she wanted to get away from me, which was understandable.

One day that week Stormy ran out to get some things for her trip, so I went down to the family room to lounge around. My thoughts wandered to Malik. I hadn't heard from him since the revelation that we both had Hepatitis A. I was angry with him and for good reason, but I held some responsibility in the matter as well. I decided to give him a call to apologize for the way I acted toward him, and to make amends. Thanks to the annoyance of an anonymous caller, I had finally gotten a new cell phone number. In hindsight, it was the best thing that could have happened because now I could talk to Malik as much as I wanted without having my cell bill scrutinized. But I still had to be careful talking to Malik while I was at home so Stormy wouldn't happen to overhear my conversations.

"What's up?" Malik asked when he answered the phone.

"You," I said slyly.

"Oh?" He seemed surprised.

"Yes. I want to apologize to you for being distant. I was upset with you for sleeping with that dude and about the . . .

you know. Anyway, I realize that it's selfish of me to put all the blame on you, or expect you not to have a life. I hope you can forgive me."

"I do forgive you. I've been worried all week wondering if you were ever going to speak to me again."

"Come on. How could I not ever speak to you again? You're my heart!"

Malik laughed.

"What's so funny?"

"Your father wouldn't like to hear you say that."

"My father? What does my father have to do with this?"

"He called me after Stormy showed him the cell phone bill. He told me never talk to you again or I'd have to deal with him."

"What's that supposed to mean?"

"He mentioned something about the financial support he, your mother, and the church members give me toward school. I think he was alluding to not helping me out with school anymore if I kept talking to you."

"Wow! I had no idea he called and threatened you with your college education. He's off the hook. So are you cutting off communication with me?"

"Honestly, I was. It wasn't until everything happened last week that I decided I had to talk to you one last time to make sure you didn't hate me."

"I don't hate you. I could never hate you."

"I'm glad to hear that."

I then realized that he never answered my question. I asked again.

"So, are you still cutting me off?"

"Not right now. At some point I'll have to because I can't deal with all this drama. And speaking of drama, how's Stormy doing?"

"Things are better. She doesn't appear to hate me like she did last week." I chuckled. "She and her girlfriends are going away Friday to Virginia Beach. She said she needs some time away."

"What are you going to be doin' while she's away?"

"Making love to you," I said seductively.

"Making love to me? You still want to do that after everything that has happened?" He had a point.

"Yes, I do, but we'll have to be more careful now. We can't have unprotected sex anymore. So, go buy some condoms. Lots of condoms. Extra, extra large," I joked.

"I'm always fully stocked," Malik purred. "So, what day are we going to meet at the motel in Columbia?"

A brilliant thought immediately popped into my head. Why pay money for a motel room when I'd have the house to myself for the weekend?

"We're going to be together the entire weekend, but not in Columbia."

"What? Where are we going to be?" Malik asked, confused.

"Here."

"There? Are you crazy? I must not have heard you correctly. Please hold while I wash the wax out of my ear." There was a pause and then he continued. "Camden, your ass is crazy! You want me to spend the weekend at your house, the house you share with your wife? What have you been smokin'?"

"I haven't been smokin' anything. Why spend money if we don't have to?"

"I don't know, Camden. Coming to your house is risky."

"Don't worry about it. Stormy is going to another state and no one comes to visit without calling first. We'll be fine. So, what do you say?"

"All right. I'll do it this time, but I'm not staying in your house all weekend. I'll come over to visit, but I'm sleeping at my own house."

I stopped talking abruptly when I thought I heard the

front door opening. I took the phone away from my ear and sat still and silent. I didn't hear anything, so I continued with the conversation.

"Cool. Well, I'll call you on Friday to confirm everything. I'll also let you know a good place to park your car. We've got to keep your car out of sight."

"Of course."

"Well, I'll holla at you later.

"All right, I'm out."

"Peace."

When I ended the call with Malik, my conscience, or what there was left of it, began to bother me. I wondered if there was any good inside me. Why couldn't I do the right thing? I was so confused, and it was a constant struggle trying to do the right thing. I was a married man and I had just made plans to spend the weekend with my gay lover in the home I shared with my wife while she recovered from a liver infection that I gave her. What the hell was wrong with me? After contemplating the answer for a few minutes, I finally realized what the problem was. I could sum it up in four words: my flesh was weak!

Chapter 32

Stormy

The biggest perks in the teaching profession were June, July, and August. I was officially on a much needed summer vacation. Because of all the turmoil with Camden, I didn't have a really good end of the school year. I planned to take the summer to regroup, get focused, and hopefully start off the next school year on a better note.

Once Leigh was able to confirm that Nicole could get off from work for the weekend, she scheduled our trip for the third weekend in June. It came in a flash. We were excited about our girls' weekend, especially me, because I was dying to find out what Leigh had up her sleeve.

"I could really get used to this," I said while lying on the beach, taking in the sun's rays.

"Me too," Dominique replied. "This is a great way to start summer vacation."

"I know that's right!"

It was now Saturday and the four of us lay on the beach.

We had been dying to get to the beach ever since we checked into our adjoining hotel rooms last night and realized we were right on the oceanfront. When Leigh stepped onto the balcony she screamed in amazement at the beautiful shoreline. We figured it was too late to go to the beach, but vowed to go first thing the next morning. Instead we ate a delicious seafood dinner at the hotel restaurant and made our way to The Beach Club where we saw Lloyd Banks and G-Unit perform. We had a blast. We even got a little tipsy. Well, Leigh, Dominique, and I were tipsy; Nicole was drunk.

As promised, first thing the next morning we ate breakfast, put on our swimsuits, and sashayed down to the beach. None of us were planning to swim because we didn't want to mess up our hair, so we decided to lie on the beach and look cute. Dominique and Leigh were looking especially fly because they were single women on the prowl.

"I have a headache and the sun is hurting my eyes," Nicole complained after about an hour of basking in the sun.

I chuckled at her words because nobody told her to get drunk last night.

"Wonder why," I said sarcastically.

"Forget you, Stormy! I see what kind of friend you are," Nicole teased.

"I'm sorry. I couldn't resist. Why don't you go back to the hotel room? We won't be out here much longer."

"I think I should. I'll stretch out across the bed until y'all return." Nicole got up and began to walk toward the hotel.

"I'm kind of ready to go, too. No one out here is catching my eye," Leigh said.

"OK!" Dominique agreed. "Let's get lunch. I'm hungry."

We gathered our things and headed to our hotel room.

"Hey! Since we're going out later tonight, let's stay in and order room service," Leigh suggested as we made our way back to the room. "We can rest up for tonight. Besides, we need to have a group meeting."

"A group meeting?" I asked, confused.

"Yeah, a group meeting," Leigh repeated as she winked her eye at me.

At first I had no idea what she was talking about, but then it hit me. She wanted to talk about the private investigation equipment.

"OK. We can do that now," I said enthusiastically.

When we walked into the room, Nicole was talking on the telephone. It must've been Jared because she was smiling from ear to ear and talking like a schoolgirl. I walked over and teased her by mimicking her words. After five minutes, she grew tired of me and ended her telephone conversation.

"You get on my nerves, Stormy." She laughed.

"So what! We're going to order room service and we need the telephone."

"Oh good, I'm hungry. Let's order now."

We ordered our food from room service and chatted while we waited. We didn't want to begin the meeting and risk having our conversation interrupted when our food arrived.

"So what's Jared up to?" Dominique asked.

"Missing me," Nicole bragged.

"Oh God! Why did I ask?"

We all laughed and then got quiet when we heard the knock at the door.

Good, our food is finally here. Now we can get down to business. I'm anxious to know what Leigh has up her sleeve, I thought.

Nicole, Dominique, and I dove right into our chicken fingers and French fries. Leigh, however, reached under her bed and pulled out a black bag. She walked back over to where we were sitting and began removing the contents of the bag.

"Leigh, are you going to do this now? I'm eating and I want to be focused on what you're saying," I said.

"OK, I'll wait, but hurry up." Leigh sat down and began eating.

We ate in silence. I guess we were all hungrier than we realized. As Nicole took her last bite, she got up to inspect the equipment Leigh had removed from the bag.

"What the hell is this? This looks like some Inspector Gadget stuff."

"It is. Just call me Mrs. Gadget," Leigh said slyly. She then got up and rapped Nicole on the hand for touching her things. "Don't touch. I don't want you to mess up my equipment."

I was amazed by the contraptions Leigh had on display. Nevertheless, I was ready to be schooled on how I could get the goods on that trifling skunk of a man I was married to. I know Mommy told me to let go and let God, but I was impatient. God wasn't working fast enough for me. I needed a Plan B.

"So, what do you have to show me?" I asked eagerly.

"As we all know, Stormy has been having some trust issues with Camden. She suspects he's cheating, but has no proof. So I have some investigative tools that could help Stormy find the answers she's looking for, or that could ultimately prove Camden's innocence."

"Isn't that illegal?" Dominique questioned.

"Nope, it's all legal."

I wanted Leigh to continue, so I butted in.

"Can you please get on with your presentation?"

"Will do." Leigh held up a black book. "This here, my friends, is a book with a hidden camera. All you do is put this on your bookcase, nightstand, kitchen table, wherever, and it will videotape your subject. Simply attach the wireless receiver into your VCR and begin recording."

"Get the fuck out of here," Nicole yelled and laughed at

the same time. She took the book from Leigh's hands and inspected it. "I can't believe there's a camera in here."

"Well, there is. Now let me finish." Leigh picked up a clock and a smoke detector. "Now, girls, to you this may be a regular wall clock and a smoke detector. But, they are more than that. There is a hidden spy camera installed in both. You can place these anywhere in your home and they will act as a surveillance system. Just like the hidden camera book, you plug the receiver into your VCR."

I looked at Leigh as if I hadn't known her for years. I couldn't believe she had these things and had never told me about them. I made a mental note to ask her about that later. I continued to listen to her presentation.

"Ladies, this here is a pen recorder. It looks and functions as a real ballpoint pen, but this is really a digital recorder. You can record up to eight hours of conversation. It's voice activated so it won't come on until it hears a voice and will turn off when conversation stops. This even comes with earphones or you can attach it to your computer and listen through the speakers."

"This one confuses me," I said. "How would I listen to the recorded conversation if Camden has the pen?"

"In your case, it may work better if you left it in his car. Then you could find out if Malik or anybody else is riding in the car with him," Leigh answered. "The bad thing about this is that you'd have to get in and out of his car or wherever you chose to put it. That might be risky."

"Yeah, you may not want to use that one," Dominique added.

"I like it. She'll be able to record him as he talks on his cell phone while he's in the car," Nicole said.

When Nicole said cell phone, Leigh's face lit up like a Christmas tree.

"Why are you smiling so hard?" I asked.

"I've got something for telephone calls, both land line and cell phones." Leigh pulled out a card that resembled a credit card. She then handed it to me.

"That there is a call recorder card. This is one of my favorites. This will allow you to record all of Camden's home and cell phone conversations without any additional devices. You can also record both sides of the conversations."

I looked at Leigh, confused again.

"How?" I asked.

"On the back of the card is an access number that you call to set up everything. There are prompts to walk you through the setup. After recording the conversations, you can call the same access number and retrieve all recordings. You can also have the recordings sent to you via e-mail. It's totally up to you."

I was dazed. I had no idea such equipment existed. I started to wonder if this was the right thing to do. Besides, I didn't know how to work any of this stuff. I'd be sure to mess it up.

"OK, girls," Leigh continued, "just two more things to show you. This is a global positioning system, GPS for short."

"I've seen police officers use those on television," Dominique blurted.

"You're right, Dominique, but they can also be used by individuals." Leigh then turned her attention back to me. "Stormy, this can be placed inside or under Camden's car. With this device, you can track his whereabouts with real time data. You can monitor where his car has been down to the nearest address, the speed it traveled, and the start and stop times. You can access this data by going to a specific web site."

"Well, damn." Nicole laughed. "I think I've seen and heard it all now."

"Nope. Not just yet. There's one more thing I'd like to show y'all." Leigh went into the bag again and pulled out a box. She held it up. "This is another favorite. This tool is a sperm detection kit."

"What the hell is that?" I yelled and frowned at the same time.

"This kit will allow you to check for dried sperm left in Camden's underwear after sex."

"Oh, God, I thought I heard it all, but I guess I didn't," Nicole said, acting as if she was going to faint.

"On one of those nights that Mr. Camden comes home at two o'clock in the morning, and you think he might have had sex, pull out this kit and it will only take five minutes to identify sperm stains," Leigh explained. "Of course, you'll have to wait until he takes off his underwear to do your inspection."

"But what if the stains are in his underwear because he was masturbating?" Nicole joked.

"That's up to Stormy to decipher. But she has the right to know if and when her man masturbates," Leigh continued with the jokes.

They broke out into laughter. I couldn't help but laugh too.

Once the laughter ceased, I looked at Leigh and shook my head. She truly was Mrs. Gadget.

"So, Leigh, why do you have all this stuff?" I asked.

"When I was dating Kevin, he made me suspicious of his every move, so I started buying things to spy on him. That's how I found out about him cheating. After we broke up, I think I became fascinated with all the investigative stuff out there. So I've been purchasing things just for fun, and just in case I may need them in the future. In a nutshell, it's become a hobby for me."

"Where did you get these spy tools?" Dominique queried.

"I order off the Internet. Most of it came from the same web site, but I ordered the GPS device from trackmaster-GPS.com."

"Why didn't you tell us about it?"

"I thought y'all would think I was crazy."

"Why would we think that? We all have some type of fetish. Yours just happens to be spy equipment. I think we should take a trip to Washington D.C. to the Spy Museum," Nicole teased.

"Well, enough about me. Stormy, is there anything here that you want to take home to use for Camden?"

The room fell silent. All eyes were on me.

"I don't know. This doesn't seem like a good idea. The Bible says, 'Seek and you shall find.' I might stumble across some things that may cause me to have a heart attack. I think I should just leave Camden in the hands of the Lord. I'm sure in time He'll reveal Camden's indiscretions."

"Girl, please! You better set his ass up. Leigh brought all this stuff here for you. The least you could do is take something home," Nicole interjected.

"I'd use the book with the hidden camera," Dominique added.

"Naw! I like that credit card thingy. That way she'll know if he's talking to Malik or some other man," Nicole blurted.

"Personally, I like the GPS. That way she'll know where he is at all times," Leigh said.

I thought long and hard. I really didn't want any of it. Something about spying felt wrong. But what Camden was doing to me was wrong as well.

"OK! I don't want any of this mess, but I'll take the smoke alarm with the hidden camera."

Gasps filled the room.

"The smoke alarm?" Nicole questioned. "Why that?"

"That way I can record any activity going on in my house when I'm not home."

"Stormy, you're not thinking. He's not going to do anything in the house. He'd be crazy to cheat in the home he shares with you."

"I agree with Nicole. You don't need home surveillance. You need to know what he's doing when he's out!" Dominique chimed in.

Damn! They are really pressuring me.

"Look! I don't want any of this, but since y'all are pressuring me, I'm taking the smoke alarm and the call recorder card and that's it."

"Well excuse us," Nicole said sarcastically.

I didn't want to appear ungrateful because I knew Leigh only wanted to help, but I didn't feel comfortable using these tools to investigate Camden. I agreed to take the smoke alarm, but I doubted I'd ever use it.

"Thanks, Leigh. I know you are only looking out for my best interests. I'll take those two items for now, and if I need anything else, I know who I can turn to."

"No problem, Stormy. I understand."

Leigh started putting her spy tools into her bag. We all decided to take naps to rest up for the Beach Music Night Cruise.

As I laid my head on my pillow, sadness came over me. It was a shame that Camden's sneaky deeds had me on the verge of putting him under surveillance. Married life was not supposed to be like this! I hated not trusting my husband. I hated not having a whole marriage. I hated having to contemplate investigating my husband. I hated it all!

I closed my eyes and tried to focus on the fun my friends and I were going to have during our last night in Virginia Beach. With ease, my mind wandered back to Camden and how he had seemed to make a change for the better before I left to come to Virginia. He was cooking great dinners, cleaning the house, and coming home right after work. It kind of felt like it did when we first got married and the vibes were good.

As thoughts of Camden weighed heavily upon me, I began to pray silently.

Lord, before I left for my mini-vacation, Camden seemed to be on the right path. I'm asking that you continue to guide his footsteps. I pray that he is working toward being the husband you intended him to be. I thank you for answering my prayers. In Jesus' name, Amen.

Chapter 33

Malik

"What do you think Stormy would do if she knew I was up in her bed?" I joked.

"She'd kill both of us," Camden replied.

I had gone back on my word and stayed the night with Camden. I had every intention of returning home, but after the out of control sex session, I didn't have the energy to leave. So as I lay in Camden and Stormy's bed, my thoughts turned to her skinny behind. I continued to joke.

"Yeah, she'd cut us up into little pieces and put us in the garbage disposal. No one would ever be able to identify our bodies."

Camden must have been tired of talking about Stormy, so he quickly changed the subject.

"So, what are your plans for the summer since school is out?"

I hadn't put much thought into this summer. Usually I worked for UPS, but this year I had not applied for a summer job. I guess my mind was distracted with other things and I mistakenly let a good summer job fall through the cracks.

"I gotta start looking for a summer job."

"You're not working at UPS?"

"Nope. I forgot to apply this year."

"Well, if you need help getting a job, let me—"

Ring! Ring! Camden was interrupted by his cell phone.

"Shit! It's that damn unavailable number again. I'm sick of dealing with this annoying shit."

"Are you going to answer it?"

"Naw. Why waste the time? They won't say anything anyway."

"But you've got a new cell phone now."

"I know. For the first couple weeks, things were fine—no unexplained calls—but now they've started again."

Camden looked agitated. These calls were bothering him more than he let on. I decided to ask more questions, hoping he would open up a little more about the situation.

"Has the person ever left a message on your voicemail?"

"Never. I wish they would leave a message. At least then I'd know who the hell it was and the reason for these calls."

"You seem to be really upset. Do you have any idea who it could be?"

Camden sat up in the bed with his head against the headboard. He seemed to be searching his mind, trying to identify anyone who could be behind these telephone calls.

"No, I don't have any idea. I'm not sure if the person knows just me, or both Stormy and me. "

"Why do you say that?"

"Because the person is calling our home number, too."

"Damn! Then it could be anybody. Maybe you need to get your home number changed and a new cell phone."

"I'll consider the home phone, but not the cell phone. I can't. I just gave Stormy a one-hundred-seventy-five-dollar cancellation fee for the phone I had on our joint account.

Then I had to pay more money when I signed on with a new cellular dealer, as well as money for a new phone. I can't afford to do that again. Not right now, anyway."

"Maybe you could contact—" Just as I was about to give Camden another suggestion, his cell phone rang again. It must have been the mysterious caller again because Camden answered the phone screaming.

"Who the fuck is this?"

The caller must have been talking to him because Camden wasn't saying a word. Actually his face looked as if he'd seen a ghost. I strained my ears to listen to what the caller was saying, but the words were inaudible. One thing was for sure, I knew it was a male voice.

"How did you get this number?" Camden asked the caller.

Since I couldn't hear what the caller was saying, I listened attentively to Camden.

"What the fuck do you want from me? We have nothing to talk about." Camden got out of the bed and paced the floor. "I don't give a fuck who you are! I don't owe you shit!"

Camden was so irate that the veins in his neck and forehead were popping out.

"Like I told you before, what's done is done. Get over it! Now, listen to my words carefully." He spoke slowly and lowered his voice. "Let this be the last time you ever call me. If you ring my phone again, I will notify the police. Do you understand?"

Oh shit! This must be serious.

I could hear the caller laughing on the phone. This made Camden even more upset.

"I'm glad you think my words are funny! But we'll see who has the last laugh, motherfucker." *Bam!* Camden threw his cell phone to the floor.

I was too afraid to speak. I watched as Camden continued to rapidly walk back and forth across the floor, mumbling to himself. He was so enraged and shaken by the phone call that I thought he'd forgotten I was even in the room.

After a couple minutes of watching Camden, I got the nerve to speak.

"Cam, what's wrong?" I asked in almost a whisper. He didn't respond. I spoke again, louder this time. "Yo, Cam, what's wrong? Who was that on the phone?"

Camden finally came out of his trance.

"Nothing, Malik. Nothing for you to worry about."

"I beg to differ. You're walking around here as if you are about to kill somebody and you say it's nothing for me to worry about. Oh, there is indeed something for me to be worried about. I'm concerned, Camden. Now start talking!"

"Malik, just calm down. The person who called me doesn't have anything to do with you. It's someone I'm beefin' with at work and he called to start the shit up again."

"I don't believe you," I said bluntly.

"It's the truth, Malik. I got into it with this dude at my job the other day and he doesn't want to let it go."

I could tell he was lying. There was more to that telephone call than some guy mad about a situation that occurred at work. I wanted to know more.

"What did you argue about?"

"I don't want to get into it right now. Let's just go to bed. We don't have long. Stormy comes back tomorrow, so we need to enjoy the rest of our time together."

I wasn't too happy about him avoiding my questions, but I let it go. At some point, I would make him open up to me.

The rest of our evening was pretty uneventful. Camden and I watched the movie, *Ray*. He tried to act as if he was really enjoying the movie by singing along on a few of Ray Charles's songs to show that he was really into it, but I knew better. I had been studying his actions since the heated phone conversation ended, and I could tell he was still distracted. His mannerisms told me more than he realized. There was a lot more to that phone call than he wanted to let on.

Once the movie ended, we both fell asleep. I was later awakened by Camden moaning in his sleep. It looked like he was having a bad dream. I watched to see if he would open his eyes, but he didn't. This same behavior continued for most of the night, so much so that I couldn't get any rest. After a couple of hours, I gave up on sleeping.

As I watched Camden struggle with sleeping, I wondered who that male voice belonged to on the telephone, and what he had said to make Camden so upset. I wondered why Camden wouldn't open up and tell me the truth about the call and the caller. My gut was telling me something was wrong. I couldn't quite put my finger on it, but something was seriously wrong. I felt helpless being in the dark. There was nothing I could do with the little information Camden had given me.

As I replayed that night's events in my mind, I wondered if Camden was going to be all right. With all my heart, I hoped he was, but my intuition told me that he hadn't heard the last of his mystery caller.

Chapter 34

Stormy

When I returned home from Virginia Beach, I was greeted by an empty house. Camden was nowhere to be found. Immediately, Satan placed negative thoughts in my mind about Camden's whereabouts. I attempted to ignore them by unpacking my clothes and singing a few of my favorite gospel hymns.

While unpacking, I laughed as I pulled out the smoke alarm with the hidden camera and the call recorder card. I sat on the side of the bed and contemplated if I should use either of these spy devices.

Camden would never do anything in our house. He's done some trifling things, but to bring someone to our home would be low even for him. Using this smoke alarm would be a waste of time. I quickly dismissed the thought of using the spy tools. There was no need to, because I felt confident that nothing would be revealed—not in our home anyway. I hid the smoke alarm in the basement and the call recorder card in my wallet, along with my other credit cards, and then I finished unpacking my clothes.

An hour after being home, Camden walked through the door. I greeted him pleasantly.

"Hey, Camden. How are you?"

"I'm good. Welcome back. Did you have a good weekend?" he asked in a monotone voice.

"Yeah, we had a great time. Virginia Beach is beautiful."

"I'm glad you enjoyed yourself," he said nonchalantly.

Something about him seemed different. He appeared to be almost in a daze.

"Camden, are you all right?" I asked with genuine concern. He didn't answer me, so I walked over to him, placed my hand on his shoulder, and asked again. "Camden, are you all right?"

"Oh, yeah, I'm fine. I just have a lot on my mind."

"Anything you want to talk about?"

"Naw! I'm gonna go in the family room to watch a little television and rest before I go to work tonight. I'll be working the late shift at the hotel. I switched hours with another coworker who needed to work the day shift. He had something to do tonight."

"OK. Well, go relax, get some rest."

Something was wrong with him. I knew it. Even when we were at each other's throats, he didn't look this distraught. Something must have happened while I was gone. I could only imagine what he had gotten into this past weekend. But whatever it was, I'd probably never know, so I chose not to sit up and worry about him or his issues.

Shortly after Camden left for work that night, Dominique called to ask if I wanted to hang out with the girls downtown. I declined because I was still exhausted from the trip. I had no idea where they got the energy to go out after partying all weekend. But then again, most of my energy was drained from worrying about Camden, which barely left any energy for fun. Nicole, Leigh, and Dominique weren't faced with the same issues, so their fuel wasn't spent.

I planned to curl up in bed with a good book and get a good night's sleep.

Ring! Ring! The phone rang at one-fifteen in the morning. *Someone must be crazy to call me at this ungodly hour.* I ignored the phone and went back to sleep.

A few minutes later the phone rang again.

"Damn! Who keeps calling me?" I reached over, grabbed the phone, and looked at the caller ID. It was Leigh's cell phone. "Hello," I said groggily.

"Stormy, I'm sorry to wake you up, but it's important," she declared.

I immediately sat up in the bed. The sound of her voice made me uneasy. A million thoughts went through my head.

"What's wrong?" I asked nervously.

"Where is Camden?" she demanded.

"He's at work. Why?"

"Are you sure about that?"

"That's what he told me earlier. When he left home he had on his work clothes."

"Well, why is his car parked in the parking lot at Club Buns?"

"Club Buns? What in the world is Club Buns?"

"It's a gay club downtown. Nicole, Dominique, and I were leaving a club not too far from here, but we cut through Club Buns's parking lot to get to Nicole's car. As we were walking, Nicole spotted an Acura TL that she thinks is Camden's car."

"Are you sure it's his car?" I asked, hoping that they were mistaken about it being Camden's car.

Leigh confirmed that it was indeed Camden's car when

she told me the personalized license plate read CXB— Camden's initials. What was Camden's car doing in the parking lot of a gay club when he told me he was working? *Has he lied to me again?* I needed to get to the bottom of this right away.

"Leigh, where are you exactly? I'm on my way to meet y'all."

Leigh gave me directions and told me that they would wait for me to get there.

"You wouldn't need directions if you would have used the GPS device I offered you," she said before she hung up. "Then you'd know exactly where to find your husband."

"Now is not the time, Leigh! I'm already upset enough as it is. I'm on my way. Don't move!" I hung up on her and jumped out of bed. I quickly threw on the clothes I was wearing earlier.

While I was speeding through the streets of Baltimore, my heart was beating faster than a thoroughbred horse racing around a track. I was going to put my size seven tennis shoe in Camden's ass when I saw him. He had no right lying to me. For this, he would pay.

When I arrived at the club's parking lot, I saw Nicole, Leigh, and Dominique talking to a couple of guys. As I approached, Leigh saw me and asked the guys if they could give us a moment of privacy.

"So, where's the car?" I asked.

Dominique pointed in the direction of the car and I walked toward it. It was definitely Camden's car. Then I looked up at the brick building that sat directly in front of me. There was a huge sign with bright red, blinking letters that read CLUB BUNS. The U in Club and Buns had a small indentation in the center of the bottom curve. I looked back at the car and thoughts of vandalism entered my mind.

"I should fuck his car up for lying to me and for being in a gay club!" I screamed.

"No, Stormy, don't do it," Dominique responded. "He's not worth it. Just go home and deal with him when he gets in."

"Oh, hell no! I didn't come all the way down here for nothing! I'm gonna wait for him to walk his happy ass out the club and I'm gonna punch him right in his face!"

"Please don't do that. There's always heavy police presence when clubs let out. If you hit him, you might get arrested. Let's just go. Deal with him in private," Dominique begged.

"I want to embarrass that motherfucker in front of all his faggot ass friends!"

"I want you to dig in his shit, too, but not out here," Nicole chimed in. "You don't need everybody up in your business. You came here, saw his car, and now you have proof he lied about being at work. I say pop him as soon as he steps foot in the front door. Don't do it here."

I let the pleas of my friends sink in. Although I was angry, I didn't want to make a spectacle of myself in public and risk getting arrested. I agreed to go home and wait for him to walk through the door. I planned to greet Camden with a blow to the face with the toaster we got for a wedding present. I was going to knock him the fuck out!

The girls insisted on following me home to make sure I arrived safely. They knew I was upset and didn't want me to drive erratically. Leigh rode in my car with me, looking at me with love and concern.

Once at home, I thanked them and told them I'd check in with them later. When I entered the house, I walked directly to the kitchen. I forcefully unplugged the toaster, removed it from the counter, and walked to the living room. I turned the sofa to face the front door and turned off all the lights. I didn't even want him to see me when he walked in the door. I just wanted him to feel this toaster going upside his head.

I waited and waited. Still no Camden. The more I waited, the angrier I got. I had so many thoughts running through my head that I actually thought I felt my head spin around on my shoulders. I even thought I heard a voice speak to me. It must have been my inner self.

The voice told me to pull an Angela Bassett from the movie *Waiting to Exhale*. The voice told me to go upstairs, pack all of Camden's belongings, ride back to Club Buns's parking lot, place Camden's things on top of the car, and set his shit on fire. I was close to following those instructions until I remembered that I would go to jail for certain. Since going to jail was not an option, I decided against the clothes/car/fire course of action.

I looked at the clock. It was five-thirty in the morning. My rage increased. I couldn't take waiting any longer. I had to do something. I decided to move to plan B because the sun would begin to rise at any minute and the living room wouldn't be dark anymore.

I wanted to cry, but I couldn't. I was too irate for tears to form in my eyes. Besides, I was sick of wasting my tears on Camden. I was totally cried out, and I was sick of the lies. Seeing Camden's car in the parking lot of a gay club confirmed that he was, without a doubt, still gay.

"I'm married to a fucking faggot!" I screamed as I headed toward the stairs. It was now time for plan B.

I opened the hall closet door and pulled out a bag of tricks that I picked up from "Pranks R Us"—a prank shop next to the pharmacy where I obtained my prescriptions after I found out Camden had given me Hepatitis A. I purchased the items because I had planned to get revenge on Camden for giving me an infection, but decided against it. I just tucked the stuff away in the closet, hoping never to use them. But Camden had lied to me for the last time. It was now time for him to feel my wrath. I was fully aware that the Bible said, "Vengeance is mine, thus said the Lord," but

I had to do this myself. This time my increased blood pressure and my rapid heartbeat wouldn't allow me to wait on God.

Once I retrieved my bag of goodies from the hall closet, I rushed into our bedroom and snatched open the closet door. I pulled out the right shoe of each pair of Camden's shoes. I squeezed Super Glue into each. Then I went into his top dresser drawer, pulled out his underwear, and sprinkled itching powder into the crotch of each pair. Once I finished, I folded them neatly and placed them back in the drawer. My next task consisted of emptying his lotion bottle and replacing it with Lysol Toilet Bowl Cleaner. My final task led me back to the closet. I pulled out Camden's clothes and began vigorously cutting them to pieces—shirt after shirt, trouser after trouser.

As rage continued to consume me, I spoke aloud to God.

"I know you're not pleased with my behavior, but I'm sick and tired of him. I hate him, God! I hate him! He's a liar! He's a no good husband! He's a faggot! And . . . and . . . I hate—"

I never finished my talk with God because as I was about to grab another article of clothing, I turned to see Camden standing in the doorway. His face was enraged as he saw what I was doing to his clothes.

So what? I'm enraged too. I hate his gerbil ass.

With our combined anger, I knew there was about to be a bitter explosion. Somebody needed to call 911, because it was about to be on!

Chapter 35

Camden

"What the fuck are you doing?" I screamed, rushing toward Stormy.

"What the fuck does it look like I'm doing? I'm cuttin' up your shit." I snatched my shirt away.

"Are you crazy?" I yelled. "Why are you cutting up my shirts?"

"Because you're a goddamn liar! I'm sick of your lies. I'm sick of you coming home all hours of the night. I'm sick of you continuing to live a gay lifestyle, and most of all, I'm sick of you!"

"What did I lie about to warrant my clothes being cut into pieces?"

She got up in my face with the look of death in her eyes.

"You lied about going to work tonight," she answered icily, then walked away.

"What do you mean? I did work, but I got off early."

"So, why are you just getting home at six o'clock in the morning? Were you out fucking somebody from Club Buns?"

I didn't respond. I knew I was busted, so there was no need for a response.

"That's right. I saw your car in the parking lot of that gay club tonight! Are you gonna deny that?"

"My coworkers and I went there for a drink. I wasn't meeting anyone there. And for your information, straight people go to that club, too."

"What-the-fuck-ever! I don't care if straight people do go to that club; you shouldn't have been there. Your ass should have been home! So tell your lies to someone who will believe them, because I don't!"

"Like I told you, my coworkers and I went there for a drink. But I don't have to explain shit to you, especially since you won't believe it anyway."

Stormy looked at me with complete loathing, like I was a roach.

"What the hell do you mean you don't have to explain shit to me? I'm your wife, and I'm due an explanation from my so-called husband who lied about going to work, partied in a gay club, and came home at six in the morning. How dare you say you don't owe me an explanation?" *Bam!*

I can't believe this bitch just punched me in my eye. She hit me so hard, I instantly felt my eye swell. *Now I'm going to have to light into her ass.* I lunged toward her and knocked her on the bed. I then straddled her.

"I told you not to put your fuckin' hands on me again," I yelled. "I should fuck you up for hitting me in my face!"

"Get the fuck off me!" she screamed and struggled with me simultaneously. I didn't budge. "I said get the fuck off me!" Still, I didn't move. I was contemplating if I should knock her teeth down her throat or wrap my hands around her neck to strangle her.

"Are you fucking deaf? You better get off me now or I'll have Trey, Jordan, and Dante kick your ass."

"Fuck you, fuck your punk ass brothers, and especially fuck your cousin! I'll get up when I'm good and ready."

Stormy continued to struggle, but I forcibly held her down on the bed. While straining to free herself, she yelled.

"You're hurting me, and you just made me break my damn nail. Get the fuck off me now!"

"I don't give a shit about your nail. I'll break all them bitches off if you keep fuckin' with me."

Then Stormy did the unthinkable. She spit in my face. I jumped from the shock of having her nasty, slimy saliva running down my face. This allowed Stormy to get her legs free to kick my groin. I doubled over in pain.

Oh my God, she just kicked me in my balls.

"God, bitch! You kicked me in my balls!" I hissed while writhing on the floor.

"Bitch? Bitch? So I'm a bitch now? No, you're the bitch. You're a faggot ass bitch at that! I told you to get off me and you didn't, so that's right, I kicked you in your shit!"

Stormy quickly turned to the dresser and picked up the alarm clock. She threw it as if she were a major league pitcher. I tried to duck, but the clock hit me squarely in my right temple and bounced with a thud against the wall. I was in excruciating pain.

"I told you not to keep playing with my heart, Camden, but you wanted to keep fucking over me!" Stormy yelled after the clock landed against my face. "The shit stops today. I want you to get the fuck out!"

I lay still on the bed, moaning and holding my aching testicles. I was in too much agony to respond to her demand to leave. I needed more time to get myself together.

"Did you hear me? I said I want you out! Go shack up with your boyfriend, Malik, or some other dude that you bump dicks and asses with."

Damn, that comment stung coming from her, but it gave

me the boost I needed to fire back. I slowly sat up on the bed.

"Kiss my ass, Stormy!" I retorted. "Coming home to a sorry wife like you every day would make any motherfucker want to fuck a man!"

"Oh, please, I'm more woman than you can handle. That's why you like to find weak little boys like Malik who make you feel like a man. But I've got news for you, Camden, you ain't shit! You're a punk ass little boy."

I was fuming and I wanted to hurt Stormy for kicking me in my groin, but instead I walked to the closet. I yanked my suitcase out and started packing. While throwing my clothing into the suitcase, I yelled at Stormy.

"I really should fuck you up! I've never had the urge to hit a bitch before, but today may be your lucky day. Keep running your mouth and I'm going to ram my fist down your throat."

"Do it and it will be the last time you ever make a fist again," Stormy dared as she reached under the bed and pulled out a baseball bat.

Where the hell did she get that from?

"Oh, so you play major league baseball now?" I teased. "Is that what you used to break out my car window, you bitch?"

"I didn't break out your car window, but I'm glad you informed me that it's broken. That gives me great pleasure. Serves you right for being someplace you shouldn't have been."

"Stop fuckin' lyin'. I know you and your friends were in the parking lot tonight. Jared told me when he picked me up."

"I wish I could take credit for the broken window, but I can't. I have no sympathy for you. Had your car been parked at home, then maybe your car window would be intact."

"And what about the damn crickets?" I asked while still packing.

"Crickets? What crickets?" she asked with a confused facial expression.

"Don't play dumb! You know damn well you broke out my car window and put a bunch of crickets in my car. There are so many that I don't think I'll ever be able to get them all out. That's why I called Jared to pick me up." She burst into laughter.

"Crickets? Crickets? Someone broke out your car window and put crickets in your car? Why didn't I think of that? I was only planning to flatten your tires and put a brick through your windshield, but crickets are much better."

"The shit ain't funny, Stormy. I know you did it and I should bust your ass for it."

"Yeah, yeah, yeah! You just made my night, or should I say morning. The only thing left to do to make this morning perfect is for you to walk your ass out the door."

I glared at her with the thought of smothering her with one of the bed pillows. But she was still holding the bat. She continued to taunt me with laughter and it pissed me off even more.

"Hurry up because I'm tired of looking at your face," she exclaimed when I rolled my eyes at her. "The sight of you is making me sick."

"My name is on this house. So technically, you can't put me out. I'm leaving because I don't want to see your face either. The sight of it makes me want a man," I retorted and then managed to laugh.

"Fuck you, Camden! Get the fuck out now!"

After my suitcase was packed, I headed for the bedroom door. Before leaving, I turned to Stormy.

"I'm leaving for a little while, but I'll be back," I declared. "This is my house, too, and you can't put me out."

"Well when you come back, there will be crickets waiting for you on your side of the bed," she joked.

I didn't even respond. I just wanted to get out of her presence as fast as I could before I did something I'd regret.

I checked into the hotel where I worked and planned to stay there for a few days. Stormy and I both needed time to cool down before I returned home. But I would be going back home. Neither she nor anybody else would put me out of my home.

As I lay down on the bed, I wondered why my life was spinning out of control. I put an icepack on my swollen, black eye—thanks to Stormy's punch. I rubbed my aching temple, which was contributing to my headache—thanks to that fucking alarm clock. Then I rubbed between my legs because my balls were still sore—compliments of Stormy's kick.

I closed my eyes to make all the pain go away and my cell phone rang.

Why is someone calling me this early? I'm not in the mood to talk to anyone. They'll have to leave a message. After the night/morning I had, all I had the strength to do was sleep.

I must have slept the entire day away. When I looked at my watch, it was just after three in the afternoon. I was thankful that I didn't have to work that day, because I was in no shape to do anything except lie in the bed.

My phone chimed to indicate that I had a message. *It must be whoever called earlier this morning.* I reached for my phone and it rang just as I picked it up.

"Yeah," I said nastily.

"So, did you like the little surprise I left in your car?"

"Who is this?"

"You know damn well who I am. I told you a couple of days ago that I'm going to be your worst nightmare. I'm planning to make your life miserable."

"What do you want from me, Terry? What happened between the two of us in New York is long over. Why can't you accept that?"

"Because you're one arrogant motherfucker. You tried to play me and now it's time for payback."

"I played you? We had a relationship, I ended it, and that's that. Why can't you get over it and move on with your life?"

"Because I can't! So since I can't, you'll now have to deal with me. The phone calls and the crickets are just the beginning. There's more coming your way."

"Fuck you, Terry! I'm going to the police. I won't deal with your threats any longer." Terry laughed.

"Do as you see fit, and I will do the same. Watch your back because when you least expect it, I may be standing right behind you." He hung up. I screamed and started pounding on the walls.

"Why won't Terry leave me alone? Why? What am I going to do?"

For the first time in a long time, I got on my knees and prayed, because only God could help me out of this mess.

Chapter 36

Malik

The day after Camden's fight with Stormy, he called and asked if I could meet him at his hotel room. Because he sounded awful, I immediately left out to meet him. When I arrived at the hotel, I discretely got on the elevator and made my way to the fourth floor. Camden was staying in room 427. As soon as he opened the door, I knew that something was wrong. He looked as if the world was on his shoulders, not to mention his swollen eye.

As soon as the door closed behind me, I asked him what was wrong. Initially, I thought he had an altercation with the so-called coworker that called his cell phone the weekend I stayed at his house. But I was wrong. I was in awe when he filled me in on all the sordid details of the argument he had with Stormy. I was floored when he said she put him out, and even more shocked when he told me about the crickets in his car. He was pissed that he was still finding crickets even after having his car detailed. I asked him why Stormy would go so far as to put crickets in his car and he informed me that she had not. When I asked him who did, he wouldn't answer. His non-response made me realize that whoever had been calling him was the person responsible for the cricket infestation. Since he didn't want to get into it, I left it alone. But this only made me worry about him more. I was really beginning to fear for his safely.

Unfortunately, two weeks after the big blowup, Camden went home. It seemed as if he and Stormy were able to work out their differences somewhat. I tried to talk him out of going back—for selfish reasons, of course—but he dismissed my pleas. He explained that he was tired of paying for a hotel room even though he was receiving the employee discount rate. I wasn't happy with his decision because I enjoyed spending lazy time with him as lovers without having to make that drive all the way to Columbia.

Thinking back on the past two weeks made me realize I hadn't talked to Camden all day. I needed to check on him to make sure he was all right. I dialed his cell phone number and he answered on the first ring.

"Hey, Cam. How are you?"

"I'm OK," he responded flatly.

"Are you sure?"

Yeah, I'm sure . . . well, there is one problem."

Oh no, something else has happened. My heart started beating faster.

"What happened now?"

"Nothing really. I'm just horny and my thang's gettin' hard just talking to you."

I laughed at his reply. I was relieved that his problem was of a sexual nature. Perhaps I could help.

"So, how can I help you with that?" I teased.

"You can come over here and make it go down."

Was he crazy? I wasn't sure I'd feel comfortable going to his house with all the drama going on in his life.

"Where is Stormy?"

"She's at a woman's retreat for the weekend with my mother. She won't be back until tomorrow."

"I don't know, Cam. Stormy just let you back up in the house after that big fight. Remember? I think we ought to chill with me coming over to your house."

"Why? I'm holding things down here. You see I ain't staying up in that hotel anymore."

"That's because Stormy's weak, and for whatever reason, she loves you."

"She knew she was wrong. I had proof that I had gone to work that day. When I threw a copy of my time sheet in her face, all she could do was eat crow. I had her eating out the palms of my hands after that."

"So, what was your explanation for being at Club Buns? I don't even hang out there. I'm kind of suspicious of that myself."

"I was just chillin' with my coworkers. I named a few who could confirm my story. But what she didn't know was that they are in the life, too. Needless to say, she was all apologetic and begged me to come home."

"She's crazy. There's no way you gonna tell me you were at that club and not getting into anything. I know you, Cam. I know you was up to no good. You may be able to pull the wool over Stormy's eyes, but not me. Let me find out you messin' with one of those supposed coworkers, and it's on. Believe that! I can deal with you being married to Stormy, but another dude—naw, that ain't happenin'."

"Look, I've explained all that to Stormy, and I don't want to rehash it again with you. Dealing with Stormy is enough. You're supposed to be my release. I don't wanna hear it from you, too. So, are you coming over or what?" Camden asked, getting agitated.

"Are you sure it's safe?"

"I'm sure."

"OK, I'll be right over."

"Good. Don't forget to park your car one block away, out of sight."

"I won't forget. I'll see you shortly."

When I saw Camden's luscious, naked body at the door, all I could do was smile. I knew from the moment I walked in the door that this was going to be a session for the record books.

"Come on in and go straight to the bedroom. Once you get there, take your clothes off immediately," Camden commanded.

"Yes, sir," I saluted. "I'm on my way."

When I reached Camden and Stormy's bedroom, I immediately did as I was told. I stripped down to my birthday suit and Camden was right there to greet me as my boxer shorts hit the floor. He forcibly pushed me back on the bed and began kissing my neck. He then slowly moved down my body inch by inch. On his way down, he kissed my chest, then my stomach, and finally he landed on my rising manhood. This was bliss. Camden was giving me the best blow job ever! My eyes rolled to the back of my head and my toes curled. I was feeling delicious tension all over.

"I'm about to cum," I whispered. Camden ignored me and continued to perform even more vigorously.

"I'm . . . I'm . . . I'm about to—"

Ding dong! Ding dong! Ding dong!

Camden stopped abruptly, causing my orgasm to subside. He looked at me and I looked at him. We stared at each other in silence. Frozen, we didn't know what to do. Who the hell was at the door?

"Who is that?" I asked nervously.

"I don't know," Camden whispered.

Ding dong! Ding dong! Ding dong!

"Let me check to see who it is. Get your things and get in the closet."

Without hesitation, I gathered my clothes and shoes and hopped into the closet. I was scared as shit. I knew I shouldn't have brought my black ass over here. Fuck! Now I felt like R. Kelly, trapped in the closet minus the Beretta.

Chapter 37

Camden

After I damned near tossed Malik in the closet, I quickly closed the door behind him and demanded that he not say a word. I swiftly threw on a pair of sweat pants and a T-shirt, ran downstairs, and looked through the peephole.

Shit, it's my father! I slowly opened the door and nervously greeted him.

"Hi, Dad. What brings you over?"

"May I come in, or do I have to stand on this porch to talk to you?" he asked with one eyebrow cocked.

I stood to the side and allowed my father to enter.

Malik, you better not make a sound.

"Camden, I came over here to talk to you about your marriage."

Here we go again with the same old, tired speech!

"What's this I hear about you and Stormy having a fight and you staying at a hotel?"

"We did have a fight, Dad, but that was two weeks ago. Things are fine now. As you can see, I'm back home."

"Son, I don't think I believe that," he said frankly.

"Why don't you believe me, Dad?"

"Where should I begin? Let's see . . . first, you don't have a good track record for telling the truth. Second, rumors are starting to float around the church again about you seeing Malik."

"Oh, God. Who's starting that rumor again? Church-folk just want to keep something going. They heard one rumor previously about Malik and me and now they won't let it go. You can't get suckered into believing that mess, Dad."

I was laying it on thick, hoping my father wouldn't see right through me.

"Camden, one of the deacons at the church found out about you staying at that hotel. See, what you don't know is that he has a son who works with you and he told him that you'd been staying there."

"Who's the deacon and who is his son?"

"I won't divulge that information. But I will tell you that his son also saw Malik coming in and out of the hotel frequently during your stay. Is that a coincidence?"

My father gave me a look as if he already knew the truth, but I wasn't about to confess to anything.

"I don't know what you're talking about. Malik wasn't coming to see me at the hotel."

"Camden, if you think I believe that, you're crazy. But let me continue with my list of reasons for why I know things aren't right in your marriage. I notice that you and Stormy don't sit together in church anymore. The two of you had your favorite spot in the middle aisle on the third row every Sunday morning. But now Stormy sits there alone. That speaks volumes to me. Also, I've noticed that Stormy often comes to church with a heavy heart. Her face shows her pain and she cries throughout the entire church service. I've known Stormy a long time, and I don't recall her demeanor being so sad until she married you."

"Aw, Dad, Stormy's emotional. She cries when she watches Oprah."

"It's not the same, son, and you know it. I'm not going to stay long, but I do want to tell you this: You better get yourself together and get right with God before you begin to suffer the consequences of your actions."

"Come on, Dad, you're being hard on me for no reason. Married couples have problems. I'm sure you and Mom have had your share. Stormy and I went through a rough patch and now it's over. I really don't need a sermonette on how I need to get myself together. For all you know, it could be Stormy that's causing the problems in our marriage. Have you ever thought about that?"

"Don't you dare sit there and disrespect me, boy! I'm your father and you will show me some respect. Now, you will listen to my 'sermonette,' and you better take heed, because if you don't, God will take you out! You keep playing with this woman's life and I promise you, you will reap what you sow."

As he spoke, his words fell on deaf ears. I already knew I was a sinner, an adulterer, an abomination, and that I was going to suffer the consequences for my actions. Being raised in the church, I hadn't forgotten the word of God. I knew the word just as good as my father did. My problem was that I was too weak to apply God's word to my life. I was struggling to fight the demons inside me. I was confused about my sexuality, about being married, about everything. I was at war within myself about my feelings toward men. I was battling myself daily about the hurt I'd caused Stormy. Unfortunately, in the end, Satan always seemed to win over God, because I was too fragile to fight this battle alone.

It surprised me that my father, the holy one who helped save souls daily, could look in my face and not see the anguish I endured. He only wanted to berate me in order for me to get my life together to save his reputation. How was it that he could help others in need, but couldn't seem to help his only son who clearly was struggling in his walk with God? For that, I was resentful, and that was why his words went in one ear and flew out the other.

"You also need to understand that your behavior isn't just affecting Stormy. Your mother and I have to deal with it, too. It's not fair to us. We're constantly defending your unrighteous ways to others, knowing deep down you're just as trifling as everyone says you are. I realize now that marrying you and Stormy was the worst thing I've done in all my years as a pastor. Now I may suffer a few consequences myself for marrying the two of you and believing that you'd change. But I can tell you this: If the backlash from your behavior affects me, your mother, or my church in a negative manner ever again, you're gonna pay, and I mean it. Now be a real man and get your house in order." He stood to leave.

Good, he's been here way too long.

"I'm leaving now, son, but consider yourself officially warned," he bellowed on his way out the door.

"Good seeing you, too, Dad," I said sarcastically and then slammed the door behind him. I knew what my father said was true. I was a train wreck waiting to happen. I needed God's help on this because I couldn't do it all by myself. I knew I was living a foul life and needed to change because nothing good could possibly come from the way I'd been treating Stormy.

I stood in the window and watched as my father pulled off. After his car was out of sight, I ran upstairs to get Malik out of the closet.

"You can come out now. The coast is clear."

"Man, I almost peed on myself when I heard your father's voice." Malik looked flustered.

"Yeah, I almost did the same when I saw it was him at the door."

"So what did he want?"

"To chastise me about my marriage, to call me out about my lifestyle, and to remind me that I'm going to feel God's wrath for my despicable behavior."

Once my father made his unannounced appearance at my house, the mood between Malik and me was shot to hell. I was too angry and guilty to have sex, and Malik was too afraid.

"Well, I think it's time for me to leave," Malik said, looking uncomfortable.

"I agree. We'll do this again another time."

"Please! I'm never coming back over here. If we want to see each other, we'll have to get a room. Your house is definitely not the place."

"Yeah, yeah, yeah! You say that now. We'll see."

"You can think I'm joking if you want, but I'm serious."

Malik followed me down the stairs, continuing his rant about never coming to my house again. When we reached the front door, I stopped Malik from exiting.

"Let me check outside first before you leave. I want to make sure no one sees you."

"That's a good idea."

I looked up and down the street and didn't see anyone. I told Malik it was cool for him to leave, and I gave him a quick peck on the lips.

"Call me when you get home," I said.

"I will."

As he left, I noticed a car slowly driving down the street toward my house. The speed limit for our neighborhood was relatively slow, but not as slow as this car was going. I was startled at first because I didn't want anyone to see Malik leaving my house. Then as the car approached, I noticed the car wasn't familiar. I sighed in relief. Malik must have seen the car as well because he began to walk briskly toward his car. When the sedan reached the front of my house, I looked at the driver and my heart stopped.

"Shit, that looks like Terry," I said, running inside the house and closing the door. I leaned against the door and replayed the picture of the driver's face. It looked a lot like Terry, but it couldn't be.

The thought of Terry caused me to break out in a sweat. I went into the kitchen and grabbed a beer. As I took a big gulp, I tried to rationalize that the driver wasn't Terry, that my eyes were playing tricks on me. But I knew they weren't. If Terry was capable of obtaining my house and cell phone numbers, then it would be just as easy to find out where I lived.

I sat at the kitchen table disconcerted, tossing back one beer after the other.

"Fuck!" I yelled, slamming my fist on the wooden table. "How am I ever gonna get myself out of this mess?"

Chapter 38

Stormy

After Camden came with proof that he had been working the night his car was at Club Buns, it didn't change the fact that he was still at a gay club. I allowed him to move back home because it was his home, too, and by law I had no right to put him out. But just because he returned home, didn't mean I was falling into his arms again. I realized that I deserved much better than I had received in this marriage. I had forgiven Camden time after time for his indiscretions because the Bible said in Ephesians, chapter four, verse thirty-two: "Be kind to one another, tenderhearted, forgiving one another, even as God in Christ forgave you." And in Colossians, chapter three, verse thirteen: "Bearing with one another, and forgiving one another, if anyone has a complaint against another; even as Christ forgave you, so you also must do." I tried being a good Christian by following God's word, but forgiving Camden repeatedly had only made me his doormat.

I was done being a sucker. I had just about as much as a

person could take. The bullshit stopped now. It was time to get even. I really didn't want to give up on my marriage, but I was tired of being a fool, so I decided to dust off the smoke alarm spy tool stored in the basement and activate it to begin recording. The call recorder card had also been activated to record all home telephone calls and for Camden's cell phone. Oh yeah, Stormy Adair Knight-Brooks was preparing to do battle.

Yes, the use of the spy tools was wrong, but Camden's emotional abuse during this marriage was wrong as well. Besides, in the Bible Moses sent men to spy on the land of Canaan. If Moses could do it, so could I.

Mama Sheryl must have sensed my newfound attitude toward my marriage during the women's retreat because she had some of the female church members pray on my behalf the entire weekend. The intercessory prayer was uplifting, especially when you didn't have the strength to pray for yourself or your situation. I could feel myself getting stronger and gaining more energy.

After the retreat, Mama Sheryl dropped me off at home. She asked if she could come in and pray over our home. Without hesitation, I agreed. As soon as she entered, she said she could feel Satan's presence in our home. *Not too far-fetched with Camden residing here*, I thought. Before I knew it, she was walking through the house asking God to bless our home and its occupants. She continuously prayed as she walked from room to room. When she reached our bedroom, she fell to her knees. Her prayer seemed to be more rapid and assertive than ever, and this is where she prayed the longest. I don't know what she felt to bring her to her knees in our bedroom, but I hoped that whatever she felt when she entered would be gone after she got done praying.

Once she finished, I hugged and thanked her. She told me to keep in touch and I promised that I would.

I was surprised to see that Camden left a note stating that

he would be at work when I returned. He wanted me to call him as soon as I got in. I called and we spoke briefly. He ended the call by telling me he would see me as soon as his shift was over. I wanted to believe him, but I refused to hold my breath.

Before leaving for the retreat, my mother scolded me for asking Camden to leave. I listened to an hour-long lecture on how my actions were against God's word. She even proved her point by quoting scripture after scripture. After she was done reading me, I felt as small as an ant. I thought about all the things I did to Camden's lotion, underwear, and clothes. I didn't disclose that to her, but inwardly I felt bad.

When Camden first returned home from his stay at the hotel, we discussed in great detail all that occurred and agreed that we both made mistakes. He promised to work harder at being a better husband, but I didn't believe a word he said. Something within the depths of my soul wouldn't allow me to trust him—not this time.

I thought I'd die of laughter when he kept complaining that his crotch was itching and he didn't know why. If only he knew I was the person responsible for his itch, he might've gone back to the hotel.

Camden had no idea that I no longer loved him with my whole heart. With each unkind word and despicable act he had successfully cut out chunks of my heart. Although things appeared to be better between us since he returned home, I was doubtful they'd remain that way. All I could do from that point was hope for the best and prepare for the worst.

After unpacking my clothes from the women's retreat, I turned on the television and began flipping through the channels. Nothing interesting caught my eye, so I decided to read the book I got from the retreat, *The Power of a Praying Wife*.

Unfortunately, I didn't get through five pages of the book before the phone rang. I reached over to grab the cordless from the nightstand.

"Hello," I said, annoyed.

"You don't know me, but I have something important to tell you," the caller announced.

"Who is this?" I asked, confused. The caller's voice sounded muffled.

"Don't worry about who I am. The information I have to tell you is more important."

"Malik, is this you playing games?"

"This is not Malik."

"Well, who the hell is this?"

"Like I said, it doesn't matter. All you need to know is that your husband had his young lover in your house yesterday."

Was I hearing this caller correctly? Did he say Camden had someone in our house this weekend?

"What did you say?" I asked as if I didn't hear him correctly.

"Your husband's little boy toy was in your house yesterday," the caller repeated.

"Who is this? Stop playing games with me!"

"I will not reveal my identity. Just know that I have my eyes on your husband." Then I heard the dial tone.

I clicked off the phone and checked the caller ID. The screen read unavailable again.

I was a nervous wreck. I began walking around the room trying to figure out what I should do. Something in the caller's voice frightened me. Was the house being watched? Was Camden being watched? I no longer felt comfortable being in the house alone. I had to call someone, but who?

"Hello, Trey?" I asked frantically.

"Hey, sis. What's going on?"

"Hold on, Trey. I need to click over and call Jordan."

"Stormy, what's wrong? You sound upset."

"Just hold on. I'll tell you in a minute."

I clicked over to call Jordan. When he answered, I clicked him into a three-way conversation.

"What's up, siblings?" Jordan asked cheerfully.

"Listen, I need the two of you to meet me at Mommy and Daddy's house! Something has happened and I need to get out of here ASAP," I said rapidly.

"What's wrong, Stormy? Are you in any danger?" Jordan asked.

"I don't know. I just need you to meet me. I'm packing some things and then I'm leaving."

"I'll call Mommy and Daddy to let them know we're coming over. Then I'll leave out immediately," Trey said.

"You do that, Trey. I'm gonna stay on the phone with Stormy while she packs. When I know she's out of the house safely, I'll be right over."

"Cool. I'm gone." Trey hung up.

I was glad Jordan talked to me as I hurried to pack the same bag I had just unpacked a couple hours earlier. He continuously asked me what was wrong, but I didn't want to get into it over the phone because I knew it would slow me down.

"Stormy, if this has anything to do with Camden, I'm going to put my foot in his ass!"

"Not now, Jordan. I'm finished packing and I'm on my way out the door. Hurry up and get to Mom and Dad's."

"I'm on my way."

Usually the drive to my parents' house took twenty minutes, but I managed to get there in ten. I was scared and I needed the comfort of my family. As I approached the front door, my father opened it. He must've been looking out for my car.

"Stormy, Trey called and said you sounded hysterical on the phone. What's going on, baby?"

I couldn't answer. I felt like a zombie, like I was in a trance. Everything seemed surreal. My mother and Trey came running to the door as they heard my father talking to me.

"Drake, bring her in here," my mother ordered.

My father followed her instructions and walked me into the living room. No one said a word. They knew my heart was heavy and they patiently waited for me to regain my composure so I could explain what was going on. Then I heard my father speak.

"Jordan, I'm glad you're here. Something is wrong with your sister."

"I know. She called me and told me to meet her over here," Jordan replied.

"Stormy, baby, we're all worried about you. You've got to tell us what's going on," my father stated.

I looked up at my mother, who had a combination of hurt and worry in her eyes. "Mommy, can you tell them, please? I can't do it right now."

"Tell them what?" she asked.

"Tell them everything, Mom. It's time they know."

"Know what?" my father asked. "Have you two been keeping something from us?"

"Drake, Stormy has been confiding in me about some things she's been going through with Camden. She didn't want you all to know because she didn't want to upset you."

"Well, what is it?" my father demanded.

As my mother began telling my father and brothers about the turmoil I had been experiencing in my marriage, I sat holding my head. She related all of the ugly and hurtful incidents including the cell phone bill where Malik's telephone number appeared, Camden admitting to seeing Malik, Camden staying out all hours of the night, my contracting Hepatitis A, Camden's car being in the parking lot of Club Buns, and she ended with the fight we had and Camden staying at a hotel for two weeks. As she spoke, I started having flashbacks of the day I sat in my parents' house and announced to my family that the wedding was on again and how they were against it. I thought about how they put their feelings for Camden aside because they loved me. I felt like shit. I had been warned time and time again, but never listened. Now I had to admit that they were right about Camden all along.

When my mother finished with all she knew, I filled them in on the telephone call I received earlier informing me that Camden had someone in my house, probably Malik. I told them the caller frightened me by knowing things about Camden and me, especially where we lived. I told them I was afraid to go home.

"I'm going to kill Camden," Jordan calmly pronounced.

"Well, let's go. We can do it together. Let's call Dante," Trey added.

"Trey! Jordan! You will do no such a thing," my father commanded. "Camden will pay for what he's done to your sister, but not at your hands. You let the Lord handle that. I promise you, he'll get what's coming to him."

Trey and Jordan looked at each other as if they were speaking with their eyes. A few seconds later, Trey turned to my father.

"Dad, you know we love you, but you can't talk us out of this," Trey said. "Camden can't keep disrespecting our sister the way he has. It's time he learned a hard, cold lesson, and today we're gonna be his teachers." He paused, looked at Jordan, and then back at my father. "We're out of here. We'll call you later."

"No! Jordan! Trey! Don't do it. Please don't hurt that boy," Mommy begged, but to no avail. We heard Trey's car as they drove away.

"Oh, Mommy, I have caused such a mess!"

"Your brothers are upset right now, which they have every right to be, but they're smart men. They won't get into any trouble. They'll probably just scare Camden," my mother said, trying to comfort me.

"Well, I'm not going to sit back and do nothing either," my father declared.

I watched as he walked over to the telephone and began dialing.

"Who are you calling, Drake?" my mother questioned. He didn't answer. We just sat there waiting for him to speak to whomever he was calling.

"Praise the Lord, first lady. This is Brother Knight. Is Reverend Brooks available?"

My mother and I looked at each other with the same thought: *why is he calling Camden's father?*

"Hello, Reverend. I apologize for calling you at home at this hour, but we have a situation going on here and I'd like to talk to you about it." My father paused as Reverend Brooks spoke to him. Then he continued. "I really don't want to get into it over the telephone. I'd like to meet with you tomorrow at the church. What time is good for you? Five o'clock? Great. I'll see you then."

When my father hung up with Reverend Brooks, he pulled out the church directory, flipped through a couple of pages, and then dialed another number.

"Dad, who are you calling now?" I asked, but was ignored. My mother and I listened attentively as he completed the call.

"May I speak with Sister Blackwell, please? This is Brother Knight calling from True Gospel."

My mother and I looked at each other again with the same thought running through both our minds. *Why is he calling Sister Blackwell, Malik's grandmother?* Again, we listened to his conversation.

"Hello, Sister Blackwell. How are you this evening?"

He paused to allow her to reply and then he spoke again.

"Good. I'm glad to hear that. I'm calling you because I would like to know if you could meet Reverend Brooks and me at the church tomorrow evening at five o'clock. Our family is dealing with a crisis and someone close to you is directly involved. I'd rather not get into the details over the telephone, but I really need to meet with you tomorrow to discuss this. Will you be able to make it?" He paused again and then said, "Good! Then I'll see you tomorrow at five. Have a good night."

"Why are you meeting with both Reverend Brooks and Sister Blackwell?" my mother asked when my father hung up the phone.

"I'm tired of Stormy suffering because of Camden and Malik's scandalous actions. It's time to get to the bottom of this once and for all. Tomorrow I plan to give everybody a piece of my mind, and I want the two of you to be there as well."

"OK, Daddy. I'll be there," I agreed.

"Oh, you don't have to tell me. I'm going to be there anyway. Something tells me you may lose your religion tomorrow and I need to ensure that you don't say anything inappropriate in the house of the Lord, or to Reverend Brooks." My mother laughed.

"Yeah, well don't count on it." My father laughed as well.

I just sat and looked at the two of them. I hated that I was putting my family through this. This was all my fault. If I had never married Camden, then my brothers and cousin wouldn't be in the streets trying to track down my husband, and my father wouldn't be preparing to give our pastor a piece of his mind. I felt horrible for doing this to all of them.

My parents and I persistently called Trey, Jordan, and Dante on their cell phones, but we were unsuccessful in reaching them. As a family, we prayed for their safety and hoped they wouldn't do anything dangerous.

Later, I retired to my old bedroom. I called Dominique, Nicole, and Leigh to fill them in about the mysterious telephone call and told them I'd be staying with my parents for a few days. I ended the call by telling them that I'd stay in touch.

I sat with my head in my hands and thought how things had gotten totally out of control and there was nothing I could do to stop it. I also had a feeling in my gut that at tomorrow's meeting, all hell was going to break loose.

Chapter 39

Malik

My eyes watered as I watched Uncle Sonny in his usual inebriated state. He was dancing around the living room mimicking the moves of The Temptations. He held up his Colt 45 forty-ounce bottle as a microphone and sang "My Girl." His speech was slurred, as he sang.

"I . . . guess . . . you . . . say . . . what can make me feel this way . . . My girl, my girl, my girl. I'm talkin' 'bout my girl. My girl!" He spun around a little too hard on the last "my girl" and lost his balance. When he hit the floor, I doubled over in laughter.

"You all right, unc?" I asked.

"Ain't shit funny, Malik," he muttered while rubbing his buttocks. "I think I broke my butt bone."

Watching him lay immobilized only added to this humorous situation, especially when I saw him take a swig of his beer. He may have hurt his butt bone, but he made sure not to spill his drink. Moments later, he was back up again, trying to get his groove on. Thankfully, the telephone rang, which took my attention from Ned the Wino's horrible imitation of The Temptations.

"Hello," I answered.

"Why the hell were you in Stormy's house with Camden?" Leigh yelled.

"What are you talking about, Leigh? I've never been in their house," I lied

"Don't lie to me, Malik! I know you've been in their house."

How in the hell does she know I'd been to Camden's house? No matter how she knows, I'm going to keep denying it.

"Honestly, Leigh, I don't know what you're talking about. I have never been in their house."

"I know you're lying to me, Malik, but that's cool because all your secrets are about to come out."

"What do you mean all my secrets are about to come out?"

"Where is Sister Blackwell?" she asked.

"She left a few minutes ago on her way to the church. She said something about having a meeting."

"Well, Malik, Mr. Knight has requested a meeting with Reverend Brooks, Stormy, and guess who else?"

"Who?" I asked nervously.

"Your grandmother," she emphasized.

"Why does he want to meet with my grandmother?" I asked angrily.

"Let me put it to you this way. Stormy got a call saying you'd been in their house. She was so upset after receiving the phone call that she went to her parents' house. When she informed her parents that the caller said you were in the house with Camden, her father was pissed. So he called Reverend Brooks and yo' grandma and asked to meet with them today. They are probably meeting as we speak."

"Oh, shit, Leigh! Why didn't you tell me this before now? I could've stopped my grandmother from going."

"I was mad at you for being up in their house. Although you won't admit it, I know it's true. You can deny it until you're blue in the face, but it's all coming out right now," she said sarcastically.

Damn! The day I hoped would never arrive was finally upon me. I didn't know how in depth that meeting would be, but I had a feeling my grandmother would leave with a wealth of information about my sexuality and my relationship with Camden.

"Leigh, I've got to go. I'll talk to you later."

I hung up without giving her a chance to respond. I was frantic. Why did my grandmother have to be involved in that damn meeting? And why didn't Camden tell me about this? I needed to call him and find out what the hell was going on.

I dialed Camden's cell phone and the call went straight to voicemail. I left a message.

"Camden, this is Malik. Some shit is going down at the church. I need you to call me right away!" I then dialed Camden's work number and was told he wasn't in. Where could he be?

I paced the floor. I paced and worried so much that I broke out in a sweat. I wondered if I should go to the church and intervene in the meeting. Hell, they were probably talking about me, so I should have been included.

Ring! Allowing the phone to only ring once, I grabbed it in haste.

"Hello, Camden!"

"No! This is not Camden, little boy! This is your worst fucking nightmare," the caller said.

"Who the fuck is this?"

"Don't worry about who I am. All you need to know is that you better stay away from Camden or else you'll pay with your life!"

"Whoa, you need to slow your roll. No need to be threatening anyone's life here."

"Yeah, well, consider yourself warned. Camden is my man and you better back the hell off or you'll regret it!" The caller hung up in my ear.

What in the hell was going on? First I found out that there was a meeting at the church involving my grandmother, then I get a phone call from some strange person threatening me. This was all too much to take. Truth be told, I was scared shitless.

I wondered if the caller was one of Stormy's brothers or cousins, but I quickly dismissed the thought when I remembered how the caller referred to Camden as "my man."

"Fuck!" I yelled in frustration. I needed to talk to Camden and he was nowhere to be found.

An hour later I called Camden's cell phone again. This time he answered.

"Where the fuck have you been? Did you get my message?" I screamed in his ear.

"I'm at home. I got your message, but couldn't call," Camden said, moaning.

"What's wrong with you?"

"I had a run-in with Stormy's brothers and her cousin, Dante, last night. They came to my job and were waiting for me when I got off."

"Damn, what happened?"

"I don't remember a lot, but I do recall them saying something about you being in our house and some other stuff that Stormy must've told them."

"Are you hurt badly?"

"Yeah, they fucked me up, but I'll live."

"Why didn't you call the police? You shouldn't let them get away with beatin' you up."

"Naw! I'ma let it go."

"Well, did you know about the meeting that's going on at the church?" I questioned.

"No. What meeting?" Camden asked.

"The meeting with Stormy, her parents, my grandmother, and your father!"

"Oh shit! Are they meeting now?" Camden asked, no longer sounding as if he was in pain.

"I don't know what time they were supposed to meet, but my grandmother left a while ago."

"This could get ugly. I need to go find out what's going on. I'll call you back."

"Wait! Before you go, you need to know that I got a phone call from someone saying that I better stay away from you or I'd pay with my life. What the fuck is that all about, Camden? Is this the same person that's been calling you?"

"Yeah, Malik. That was crazy Terry. He's the one who saw you leaving my house and told Stormy. I can't get into details with you now because I've got to get to the church. I'll call you when I find out what's going on."

"Yeah, well, you better call. This conversation is not over. I need to know what else this Terry person knows about me and why my life is being threatened."

"I will."

"Good-bye!"

Now I played the waiting game. I wasn't sure if I would hear from my grandmother or Camden first, but either way, I knew it wouldn't be good.

Chapter 40

Stormy

I couldn't sleep after receiving the phone call from that mystery man. Although I felt safe at my parents' house, I was still a bit unnerved about the call. Then I was uneasy about the meeting my father had arranged. I was walking on eggshells trying to figure out what he was going to say to Reverend Brooks and Sister Blackwell. Something in his tone led me to believe he was out for blood—Camden's blood.

I attempted to reach Trey, Jordan, and Dante several times that night, but had no success. I still had no idea if they had met up with Camden. I could only hope that they hadn't, because Camden would've surely wound up in the intensive care unit. Even though he would have deserved every lick that landed on his body, I still didn't want him hurt.

As Reverend Brooks invited Mommy, Daddy, Sister Blackwell, and me into his office, I whispered, "Father, I stretch my hands to thee."

We all spoke to Mama Sheryl, who was sitting in a chair next to Reverend Brooks' desk. I could tell she knew something wasn't right, because she wasn't her normal, bubbly self. After we filed in, we sat down. The room was full of tension, so Reverend Brooks suggested we pray.

"Before this meeting begins, I'd like to have a word of prayer. Let us bow our heads." He took a deep breath and commenced to pray. "Dear God our Father in heaven, we come to you with thanksgiving and praise for your many blessings. Lord, I ask that you bless each family represented in my office today. I ask that you ease the tension, Lord, for we know there is not a problem that you cannot solve. Remind us that we are all brothers and sisters in Christ and we should treat each other with love and respect. Finally, I pray that the outcome of this meeting be pleasing in your sight. In Jesus' precious name, we pray. Amen."

"Amen," we all said in unison.

"Now what brings us all together on this blessed day?" Reverend Brooks asked with a nervous smile. I could tell in his face that he had a strong suspicion what this meeting was about. Daddy spoke first.

"Reverend Brooks, my wife and I are here because we need to talk to you about your son."

"Oh?" he said.

"Yes! This marriage was a big mistake. Your son has not changed one bit. He's still gay and he's still—" Daddy abruptly stopped and turned to Sister Blackwell, then continued. "He's still seeing your grandson, Malik."

"My grandson? What do you mean seeing my grandson?" Sister Blackwell asked with a puzzled expression.

Lord, please bless and protect Sister Blackwell because she might have a heart attack after Daddy drops this awful news on her.

"Sister Blackwell, Camden and Malik are both gay," Daddy announced. "They've been having a gay relationship for years. It was supposed to be over once they were outed a year ago, but now it's come to my attention that they are still involved."

Sister Blackwell's eyes were as big as tennis balls.

"I don't believe what I'm hearing! I have asked Malik repeatedly if the rumors I heard were true, and he looked me dead in my face and lied. Although in the back of my mind I knew he wasn't telling me the truth, I chose to believe him and let it go. Did you know about this, Reverend?"

"Unfortunately, I did, Sister. I found out sometime last year. I scolded both of them for their behavior. I told them to end it immediately. After I met with them both, Camden changed his life and chose not to live a gay lifestyle any longer. I thought Malik had done the same."

"Well, you thought wrong, Reverend," Daddy blurted.

"Drake! Take it easy. You can't disrespect the man of God," Mommy cooed.

"That's OK. I know he's upset. I'm upset by this whole situation, too."

"You have no idea how upset I am, but I'll fill you in. First, I'm upset to find out that my daughter has been living in hell since she married your son. Do you know all the things he's done?" My father's voice was elevated. I could see his pressure rising with each word he spoke. I knew it wouldn't be long before he erupted.

"I'm aware of some things. I've been hearing through the grapevine that Camden's been seeing Malik again. I've also heard about him being at a gay club."

"Well, do you know he gave my daughter Hepatitis A?"

Reverend Brooks was flat-out stunned. His mouth flew open.

"I knew nothing about anybody having Hepatitis A."

"That's right. Your son cheated on his wife with another man, contracted a liver infection, and passed it to my daughter."

"My Lord! I had no—"

"Let me finish. Not only that, he's been staying out all hours of the night and he's even had a physical altercation with my daughter. Now, to top it off, she received a telephone call last night from some strange man telling her Malik had been in her house."

"Oh my God!" Sister Blackwell exclaimed.

"That's right. Your son," Daddy said, pointing to Reverend Brooks, "and your grandson," he said, pointing to Sister Blackwell, "are having sex in my daughter's house!"

Sister Blackwell turned to me with tears in her eyes.

"Stormy, baby, I'm so sorry. I don't know what's gotten into Malik, but I surely don't approve of his behavior. I regret that he and Camden have been putting you through all this turmoil."

"No need to apologize—" I started to say, but was abruptly interrupted by Camden storming into the office. He looked like an unholy mess. The right side of his face was swollen, both of his eyes were blackened, and he had a fat upper lip.

"What's going on here?" Camden asked.

"Well, well, well, look what Satan dragged in from hell," Daddy commented.

"Stop it, Drake!" Mommy demanded.

Mama Sheryl took one look at Camden and ran to him.

"Camden, what happened to you?" she asked.

"I'll talk to you about it later, Ma. I want to know what's going on in here."

"Camden, the Knights called this meeting because Stormy received a telephone call from a strange man stating that Malik had been in your house. Is that true, son?"

Camden didn't answer. He dropped his head.

"Answer me, son!" Reverend Brooks commanded with an edge to his voice.

Camden looked at me, then his eyes shifted to my parents, and then to Sister Blackwell. After what seemed like an eternity, he responded.

"No, Malik has not been in our home. I would never do a thing like that."

Daddy stood up and pointed at Camden.

"You're a liar!" he yelled.

"Brother Knight, please calm down," Reverend Brooks ordered.

"Calm down? Calm down? Don't tell me to calm down! Your son has successfully screwed up my daughter's life with his . . . his . . . his lifestyle. He has repeatedly stepped on her like an insect. He has no respect for her or the sanctity of their Christian marriage. How dare you tell me to calm down? If anything, you should be lucky I'm this calm."

"Daddy, please sit down. You're scaring me," I said while tugging on his shirt.

He totally ignored me as he continued to stare at our pastor.

"I blame you as well for this! You knew damn well when you married them that Camden was still gay. You deceived Stormy into believing that Camden was delivered from homosexuality!"

"That's not true! I watched as Camden made a complete turnaround. He was a changed man when I married them," Reverend Brooks retorted.

"I now see where Camden gets his lying ways from. The apple doesn't fall far from the tree. Both of you are liars!"

"Drake, please!" my mother pleaded.

"Victoria, let me be! I'm speaking God's own truth." He turned to Sister Blackwell. "I advise you to tell your grandson to stay out of my daughter's house. If I hear he's been in there again, I will deal with him."

"Brother Knight, I'm going home to deal with Malik right now. If you all don't need me any longer, I've gotta go," she said, rising briskly from her chair. I think Sister

Blackwell had heard enough and was downright scared at how my father was acting.

"You're no longer needed. I felt it was time you know about your grandson and how his and Camden's behaviors have affected my daughter. Please don't forget to give him my message."

"I'll deal with Malik, Brother Knight. No need for you to say or do anything to him. Moreover, Stormy, I'm so sorry you've gone through this. I'm going home now to have a talk with my grandson. I'm sure you won't have any more problems after I'm through with him."

"Again, you don't have to apologize. None of this is your fault," I said while hugging her.

Once Sister Blackwell left, Daddy turned his wrath toward Camden again.

"And you," he said as he glared at Camden, "you worm! You have no idea how much I loathe you. What you've done to my daughter is unforgivable. You put her health at risk and you've treated her like pure garbage. I won't allow you to do it anymore. Your abuse stops now!"

"Brother Brooks," Mama Sheryl intervened, "I think we need to handle this in a Christian-like manner. We are in the house of the Lord and we should conduct the rest of this meeting respectfully. I know you're upset, but can you please refrain from insulting my son any further?"

"No, Ma, he's right. I deserve every bit of it. I have treated Stormy wrong and I deserve to be punished," Camden admitted with tears rolling down his cheeks. He walked over toward my chair, got down on his knees, and said, "Stormy, I'm so sorry. I have lied to you, cheated on you, and disrespected you. I'm not worthy of your love. If you want to leave me, I'll understand, but I want to work this out. Please forgive me for how I hurt you. Please don't leave me, Stormy. I need you . . . I need you."

Did I just hear what I think I heard? Did Camden finally

admit he was wrong? Wasn't acceptance the first step toward recovery? Maybe that beat-down he received had
knocked some sense into him.

"I love you, Stormy," Camden bawled. "No one has
treated me as good as you do. I want to change, not only for
me, but for you, too."

I looked at Daddy, whose facial expression said, *Negro,
please!* Mommy was dabbing her eyes with a tissue, and
Sheryl looked as if her heart was breaking for Camden. As
crazy as it may seem, my heart was breaking for him, too. I
didn't know if it was his heartfelt words or the fact that he
looked so bruised, battered, and pitiful.

"Stormy, please don't leave me!" Camden shouted while
continuing to sob. "I'm going to change! I promise I'm
going to change! I can't make it without you. I need you in
my life. I need you to help me walk the right path. Please,
Stormy, please help me."

"You need God, son! God has to be your strength to
change. Stormy can't do it alone," Reverend Brooks stated.

"So you're buying this act?" Daddy snickered. "Please!
Can't you see he's just trying to cover up being outed with
tears and pleas for forgiveness?"

"I don't know, Drake. He seems sincere to me," Mommy
chimed in.

"He seems sincere to me, too," Mama Sheryl agreed.

"Well I don't buy it! He admitted that he's gay, but still
wants to be with my daughter. Why would she want to be
married to a gay man? Furthermore, why should Stormy
believe he'll change? His words mean nothing. It's his actions that account for something." Camden looked up at
Daddy.

"I am sincere. This is not a joke. I want to change, but I
don't think I'll have the strength to do it without Stormy."
Camden then looked at me and fell to his knees. "Will you
stick by me? Please, baby, I promise I'll change. I promise!"

Reverend Brooks's office grew silent. All eyes were on me. I was torn. Why should I believe him this time? I looked about the room, searching for an answer, but no one said anything.

"Well, Stormy, what is it going to be? Are you going to work things out with Camden or not?" Daddy asked. I looked down at Camden.

"Will you go to counseling with me?" I asked.

"Yes, baby!" Camden eagerly answered. "I will do anything you want. I promise."

"Stormy, please don't tell me you're falling for this act?" Daddy lamented.

"Daddy, when I took my vows, I agreed to stay for better or for worse. It takes a strong person to stay when things are going good in a marriage, but it takes an even stronger person to stay when the marriage is at its worst. I want to help Camden get through this. He asked for my help and I want to be there for him."

Daddy was none too pleased. He looked at Camden.

"One more chance, Camden! One more chance. If you mess up again, you will be dealt with. Do you understand?"

"Yes, sir. I'm gonna change. I give you my word."

"Save it! I don't believe you. I'm just warning you!" Then my father turned to Reverend Brooks. "Under the circumstances, my wife and I can no longer be members of True Gospel. I can't continue to sit under your leadership feeling about you the way I do. Expect our resignation letters by the end of the week."

"Brother Knight, don't you think this is a bit rash? You and Sister Knight have been members for many decades now. Please don't leave like this."

"You can't talk me out of leaving. We are done with True Gospel and that's the end of this discussion." Daddy grabbed my mother by the hand and told her it was time to go. With that being said, we all prepared to leave. As I left, I turned to Camden and mouthed, *I'll see you at home.* He nodded.

Before Daddy got completely out the office door, he turned to say one last thing.

"When the two of you seek counseling, make sure it's not with Reverend Brooks. I don't trust him to lead you two in the right direction. You'll be better off talking to a stranger. And don't forget, you've got one more chance, Camden! One more chance!"

Chapter 41

Malik

It was a little after eight in the evening when Grandma returned from church. *Bam!* I could tell she was livid when I heard the door slam.

"Malik! Malik!" she yelled from downstairs.

"Yes, Grandma?"

"Come down here. I need to talk to you—now!"

I rolled off my bed. I slowly walked down the stairs, one by one. I felt as if I was next in line to see God on Judgment Day to determine if he was going to allow me to enter into the pearly gates of heaven or be dammed to hell. When I reached the living room, I looked at Grandma and I could see the pain in her eyes.

"Yes, Grandma? You need to talk to me?"

"Yes, I do, Malik. Have a seat."

I sat down on the sofa end farthest away from her and tried to focus on something in the room other than her. I was so ashamed that I couldn't even look at the woman who raised me.

"Do you know where I'm coming from?" she asked.

"Yes, you told me you had a meeting at church."

"Do you know who I met with?"

"No," I lied.

"Well, let me tell you. I just had the unfortunate pleasure of meeting with Reverend and First Lady Brooks, Brother and Sister Knight, and Stormy."

"Oh, really?" I asked, playing dumb.

"Yes, really! And do you know what I learned in that meeting, Malik?"

"No, ma'am, I don't."

"Hmmm, where shall I begin? I'll start at the beginning. The meeting began with a confirmation that you're without a doubt gay." She paused and stared at me.

I showed no expression after her statement.

"So, did you lie to me before when I asked you? Is it true what they told me about you? And this time tell the truth."

"It's true," I whispered with my head lowered.

"What? Speak up! I can't hear you."

"It's true," I repeated with a little more bass in my voice.

"My God! I was hoping that it was all a lie."

"No, Grandma, it's true. I'm sorry I lied to you before. And I'm sorry you had to hear it from Brother Knight. I should have told you myself a long time ago."

"You're darn right you should have. Do you know how it made me feel to know that everybody in the church knew what was going on with my grandson and I didn't? Yeah, I heard the rumors, but wanting to trust in my grandson, the child I raised, I believed you. Then to have the truth come out in a meeting with everybody else around, I felt like a fool."

I felt tears in the back of my eyes.

"I'm sorry, Grandma."

"You should be! However, you being gay is not all I was told. I was also told that you've been sleepin' with Camden. Is that also true?"

I wanted to lie, but I couldn't. Not to my grandmother. Not to the woman who took me in when my own mother and father didn't want me.

"Yes, I've been messing around with Camden." My answer infuriated her.

"Malik, have you lost your natural mind?" she yelled. "Why are you messing around with a married man?"

"He wasn't married when I started messing with him."

"Does that make it right? And how long has this been going on?"

"I have been confused about my sexuality for years, but it wasn't until high school that I realized that I was in fact gay."

"So, when did you start having sex with Camden?"

"Do you remember when I started messing up in high school and you took me to Reverend Brooks's office so he could talk to me?"

"Yeah."

"At that meeting, he suggested that Camden become my mentor. At first Camden was like a big brother to me. Nevertheless, as time passed, I began to feel close enough to him to open up about my feelings toward men. Surprisingly, he admitted to me that he was bisexual. It was his revelation that started our relationship."

"How dare he? He was supposed to help keep you focused on your school books, not have sex with you," she angrily spat.

"Don't blame Camden. It's my fault as well. I was old enough to know what I was doing," I said, defending Camden.

"I totally agree with you. I guess the better question is: are you old enough to know that sleeping with a married man is wrong and a sin?"

I was embarrassed to be having this conversation with my

grandmother. If I could have crawled under a rock, I would have at that very moment.

"Yes, I know it's wrong."

"Then why in God's name are you sleeping with that woman's husband and in her house? Your grandfather and I raised you better than that, Malik. I'm sure your grandfather, God rest his soul, is doing somersaults in his grave knowing that his grandson is having a gay relationship with a married man."

Damn, why did she have to bring Granddad into this? I already felt like shit and I didn't need the added guilt.

"I know it's wrong and I plan to stop. It's just hard . . . um . . . it's just hard letting go."

"Well, you better get it together soon because Stormy's father is out for blood. He's angry with our pastor, angry with you, and he looked like he was about to kill Camden."

"Camden was there?" I asked, surprised.

"Yeah, he came in looking like he had been in a fight. From the way he looked, I think he lost."

Although Camden had told me he had been in a fight with Stormy's brothers and Dante, I didn't know it was that bad. He must have gotten a serious beat-down.

"So, what did Brother Knight say to him?"

"I didn't stay long enough to hear what was said to Camden. Once they told me that you were gay and sleeping with *our* pastor's son, I really didn't want to hear anymore. I gave Stormy a hug and apologized for your behavior."

Why are you apologizing for me? And to Stormy of all people?

A few moments passed before she spoke again.

"Malik, I didn't appreciate being blindsided today by Brother Knight. Why didn't you tell me before now?"

"I didn't think you'd understand. I didn't know how you'd handle me being . . . um . . . you know." I couldn't bring myself to say the word "gay" to my grandmother.

"Let me tell you something, and you better listen good. You are my grandson. Hell, you're like my son since I raised you. I love you no matter what lifestyle you choose. No, I don't like that you've chosen to live a homosexual lifestyle, but I love you nonetheless. Yes, you're living in sin, but who isn't? Nobody is perfect and if you ask God to forgive you for your sins, he will. Although I don't like the sin, I don't hate the sinner."

She is handling this much better than I thought she ever would. Makes me wish I had told her a long time ago.

"Now, this adulterous relationship you are having with Camden is another story." She must have noticed that my eyes were glued to the floor because she firmly ordered, "Look at me when I talk to you. This so-called relationship you have with Camden is over! You will not continue to mess around with *Stormy's husband*. And I stress *Stormy's husband* because I'm a woman, and I know what it feels like to deal with infidelity in a marriage."

My eyes widened. Was she saying my grandfather had cheated on her?

"That's right. You heard me. I loved your grandfather dearly, but he was out in those streets in the beginning of our marriage. You don't know the many nights I sat up worried about my husband being with another woman. I stressed so much that my hair started falling out and I dropped fifteen pounds that I wasn't even trying to lose. Dealing with your grandfather's infidelity was tough, but I stayed on my knees in prayer. Thankfully, God answered my prayers because your grandfather got himself together and we lived the rest of his days on earth as a happily married couple. When I looked into Stormy's eyes today, I saw myself. My heart went out to her because I have felt the pain she's feeling today. The difference is, my husband was with another woman, and her husband is with a man. There's no way she can compete with another man. Therefore, unless Camden gets himself together, she's going to lose him for good. There isn't anything she can do to please him if it's not in his heart to be with a woman." Grandma walked over to where I was sitting and put her arms around me. "I'm going to end my little lecture by telling you this— Camden is not your man. He has a wife. Nothing good can come from messing around with a married man! You will leave Camden alone starting today, or I promise, you'll feel the wrath of God, and it won't be pretty."

I couldn't hold back my tears any longer. I put my face in my hands and sobbed like a baby.

"Come here, baby. Give your grandma a hug," she said, holding me in her arms. "You wipe those tears away. You've made some mistakes, but it's never too late to fix them. Now hold your head up high and remember God loves you, and so do I."

She smiled at me, kissed me on my cheek, and then went upstairs.

I sat on the couch taking in all Grandma had said. She was right. Camden wasn't my man. He belonged to Stormy. If he loved me, he would not have chosen to marry her. I hadn't gained anything by messing around with him all these years, except for heartache and grief. It was time I sat back, reevaluated my life once again, and made some serious changes before God intervened and made them for me.

Chapter 42

Camden

It was a little after midnight. The ride from downtown all the way out to Randallstown was a long one, so I popped in my John Legend *Get Lifted* CD and thought about Stormy, our marriage, and our future.

The month of August had bought about significant changes in my life. After what I endured the previous month with getting my ass kicked by Stormy's family, and the meeting from hell with our parents, I welcomed the changes. I was grateful when Stormy agreed to give me another chance. I knew I didn't deserve it after all the heartache I had caused, but Stormy didn't see it that way. She was determined to honor our marriage vows. I had no idea why she continued to put up with me, but I was sure glad she did.

Stormy and I started marriage counseling. It seemed to be helping. The counselor was teaching me how to be a husband, which I didn't think I ever really knew how to be.

I had to admit, though, thus far counseling hadn't taken away my sexual desire for men, but it had helped me not to act upon those desires.

Of course, I thought about Malik constantly and sometimes had the urge to call him, but I didn't. Since the meeting, I hadn't heard from him. I could only assume that his grandmother must have told him not to contact or see me anymore. I had also heard through the grapevine that he might be leaving Baltimore. I wasn't sure where he was planning to go, but I was certain it was a move designed to get away from me. The thought of Malik leaving bothered me, especially since there was nothing I could do to stop him. Since I was in the process of working on my marriage and changing my life for the better, I had to let him go. It hurt, but it was for the best.

During the past month, I found myself feeling depressed as I thought about my actions and the hurt I'd caused Stormy, Malik, and my parents. I'd been a selfish bastard and all this treachery was destroying my spirit. I was now taking time to ask the Lord to help remove the mask I'd been wearing, and to give me the strength to be a better husband, son, and person overall. I hoped those close to me could be patient with me because God had his work cut out for Him, trying to shape and mold me.

Bam! I jumped as I sat at a red light on Liberty Road. Someone had just rear-ended my car. The impact caused my head to lunge forward, and then violently backward, which caused my head to hit the headrest with great force. I sat stunned for a moment, trying to regroup. I looked in my rearview mirror and saw a car behind me. Since I was in a daze, I waited for the driver to approach me. *Bam!*

"Fuck!" I yelled. I was hit from behind again. I didn't know if it was the same car twice, or if there was a multiple car collision. I grabbed my throbbing head and attempted to get out of the car to assess the situation. As I opened the car door, I heard the tires screech from the car behind me, and then I was blinded by bright headlights speeding toward me. I quickly hopped back in the car and closed the door. The driver of the car pulled up beside me and rolled down the tinted passenger side window. It was Terry.

"I see you still riding around in the Acura TL I bought you," he said with a sinister laugh.

I was on Liberty Road after midnight on a weekday and there was almost no traffic. I was scared to death.

"Leave me alone, Terry! I'm calling the police."

"Call 'em. They won't stop me. Nobody can. Do you think you can drive around in the car I bought you and not be with me? Are you crazy? Do you think you can use me and still benefit from my kindness? You must have lost your fuckin' mind."

"No, you're the one that's crazy," I said, reaching for my cell phone on the passenger seat. Once I retrieved it, I dialed 911. I put the phone to my ear and looked Terry directly in the eyes as I spoke to the 911 operator. "Hello. I need the police. My name is Camden Brooks and I've just been rear-ended by the man that's been stalking me. I am on Liberty Road."

Terry seemed unfazed when he heard me speaking with the police. I knew then, without a doubt, that this dude had lost his everlasting mind. It was imperative that I took precautions to protect myself and Stormy.

"OK. Thank you, ma'am. I'll be here," I said as I hung up with the operator. "The police are on their way, Terry, so you better leave me alone. Go on about your business, man. What's done is done. It's been over between you and me for the longest. How can you still be upset over a breakup that took place many moons ago? Don't you think it's about time to move on? Find another lover?" I was trying to reason with him, but wasn't successful.

"Save it, Camden! I don't wanna hear it. You ruined all my chances of loving anyone ever again. You scarred me and since I can't ever be happy, neither will you."

I attempted to keep Terry talking until the police arrived, but as soon as he heard the sirens, he fled.

"It's not over, Camden," he yelled as he sped off. "I won't be satisfied until you're six feet under." Then he disappeared down a dark side street.

When the police came, I told them everything that had been going on with Terry. I gave them his full name, physical description, last known address, last known telephone number, and description of his car. The police instructed me to file a restraining order against him immediately. Jared suggested I do the same thing a while ago, but I hadn't because I didn't think Terry would follow through on his threats. I kind of thought he was blowing hot air. But after tonight's episode, I wasn't so sure.

Since I was running late, I called Stormy to let her know I was on my way home.

"Hi, babe."

"Camden? Where are you?" she asked, half asleep.

"Don't be alarmed, but I was in a car accident. I'm fine now, but I just wanted you to know why I'm late coming home."

"Oh my God. Are you hurt?" she asked in a panic.

"My neck and head are a little sore, but I'll be fine. I was rear-ended twice, but I can still drive the car."

"Twice? How did somebody ram into you twice?"

"I'll tell you about it when I get home. I just didn't want you to worry about me. I'm almost there."

"I'll wait up for you. Be careful," Stormy said before disconnecting the call.

I found myself putting on this tough guy role whenever I talked to anyone about Terry, but honestly, I was a little shaken by his boldness. He really wanted to hurt me, or even worse, kill me. If I never believed it before, I certainly believed it now. Terry's intimidations were no longer threats. They were promises he had vowed to keep. I just hoped I could pursue legal action before it was too late.

Chapter 43

Stormy

After four months of a rollercoaster ride of a marriage, things seemed to have finally changed for the better—again. We took my father's advice and didn't go to Reverend Brooks for counseling. We found a Christian-based counseling center not too far from our house. Our sessions had been going well thus far. When we first started counseling, I spilled my guts to the psychologist.

The first words that flew out of my mouth were: "All I ever wanted was a God-fearing man to love me without having to deal with a bunch of lies and deception. I thought I had found that in Camden, but after only a short time of being married, I discovered he didn't fear God, didn't love me, was a pathological liar, and was huge on deception. But should I have been the least bit surprised since the skeletons were flying out his closet before we got married? I entered into this marriage with Camden because I honestly thought he'd changed—at least that's what he and his father, Reverend Brooks, led me to believe. But after that explosive meeting last month with our families, I learned they were both wrong."

Camden almost had a heart attack after I revealed such intimate details about our marriage. I didn't care. I wanted my marriage to work, and if I had to give in-depth information, that was what I planned to do. Camden eventually adjusted to counseling well, after he realized it wasn't going to be a bashing session. I actually thought he had grown spiritually and as a spouse since we'd been going. I welcomed the positive changes I'd seen in Camden and in our marriage. Things were slowly but surely improving. I prayed daily that we would continue down this path.

After I returned home from the Women's Retreat and Mama Sheryl prayed as if she was trying to rid our house of demons, something in my gut told me things weren't right. At that time, I activated the spy tools. But just a few days ago, I'd considered dismantling them since I'd found nothing incriminating. My decision wasn't final yet, though. I was still deliberating.

Today was my twenty-eighth birthday. I was anxious because Camden had been hinting that he had something special planned. This was going to be a big change from last year's birthday, because I was too busy to celebrate then. All I wanted to do was plan the most spectacular wedding day ever, so I skipped celebrating my birthday. However, this year was going to be different. I could feel it.

As I was getting dressed, Camden entered the bedroom with a small gift in his hand.

"Happy Birthday again, sweetheart. This is for you." He handed me a black velvet box. When I opened it, there was a small card that read: A HEART FULL OF DIAMONDS. When I removed the card, I saw a beautiful, heart-shaped pendant, encrusted with small diamonds and set in gold, attached to a gold necklace.

"Oh, Camden, this is gorgeous."

"Do you like it?" he asked.

"I love it," I replied, hugging him.

"Good! I'm glad you like it. Turn around so I can put it on you."

"This will go great with my dress," I said as I turned my back to him.

"Well, hurry up and get dressed. We don't want to be late."

"And where is it we're going again?" I asked, trying to pry some information out of him.

"You'll see when you get there," he said slyly.

When Camden pulled up in front of Ruth's Chris restaurant, I almost fainted.

"Camden, are we going in there?" I pointed to the restaurant.

"Yes, we are."

"But . . . but . . . Camden, this place is so expensive."

He placed his index finger over my lips.

"Shhhhhh, this is your day. Money is not an issue."

I reached over and kissed him passionately.

"Thank you, Camden. This is wonderful."

"Don't thank me yet. You haven't even had dinner."

Once the valet took Camden's car keys, we entered the restaurant. Camden announced our reservations to the host and he led us to our table.

"Surprise!" everyone yelled when I approached the table. My eyes widened, my jaw dropped, and I thought I felt my heart stop. I was flabbergasted. Here I thought Camden and I were dining alone, but my parents, Dominique, Leigh, Nicole, Jared, Hassan, and his girlfriend, Cymone, were all there.

"Camden, did you plan this?" I asked while my hands still cupped my mouth in amazement. How could all the people close to me know about this birthday celebration and not one of them had slipped up and said a word.

"Yes, I did, baby," he replied, pulling out my chair for me to sit down.

"Oh, this is way too much. Thank you, baby, and thank you all for coming. I'm so happy to celebrate my birthday with all of you."

"And we're happy to be here, Stormy," my father said.

"Ditto," Hassan added.

Dinner was superb! I couldn't remember the last time I had such an exquisitely good New York strip steak. The luxurious atmosphere was great as well. My parents and friends were not fond of Camden, but they seemed to set their resentment aside to help make my birthday dinner a pleasant experience. The dinner conversation was cordial. There were no evil stares, no whispers, no nothing. For that, I was extremely appreciative. When the waiter brought the check, he gave it to Camden, who paid for everyone.

Damn! He's going all out. The bill has to be close to five hundred dollars. Oh well, it wasn't my money, so I won't complain.

After dinner, Camden had tickets for everyone to see Tyler Perry's stage play, *Madea Goes to Jail.* I laughed during the whole play because Madea was off-the-hook funny. Her character was portrayed so well that I forgot it was actually Tyler playing the part.

Once the play was over, everyone wished me happy birthday again and said their good-byes. Camden asked if there was anything else I wanted to do, but I declined. After the wonderful evening I had, the only thing I wanted to do was seal the evening by making love to my husband. Despite all of our turmoil, I still had needs and I felt myself getting moist just thinking about cementing our new understanding with a memorable night of making love.

When we arrived home, Camden opened the front door and told me to enter. I walked into what looked like a florist's shop. Red, pink, yellow, and white roses filled the living room.

Then I looked on the floor and saw a path of red rose petals. I was stunned.

"Camden, who did all of this?"

"My mother. I asked if she could come over to decorate the house while we were out."

"Camden, this is so nice. I haven't been in such high spirits in a long time."

"Well, you deserve all of this and more. Oh, and before I forget, my mother said she left a gift for you on the dining room table. I know you're anxious to open it, but I'm anxious to see where these red rose petals lead us."

"No, I wanna open my gift first. You know I like presents."

"Hurry up, girl." Camden sucked his teeth and waited impatiently as I tore into the bright red gift bag.

First I opened the birthday card enclosed in the bag from Reverend Brooks and Mama Sheryl. Then I pulled the tissue paper from the bag to reveal a pair of fourteen-karat gold and peridot earrings, which was my birthstone, and a gift certificate to a day spa, which was redeemable for an hour long Swedish massage, a facial, a pedicure, a manicure, and lunch. The final gift in the bag was a book by T.D. Jakes's wife, Serita Ann Jakes, titled, *The Princess Within: Restoring the Soul of a Woman.*

"This was very thoughtful of them, Camden. I've got to call to say thanks."

"Not right now," Camden said, pushing me out of the dining room toward the stairs. "I told you I want to see where those rose petals lead us."

We began to follow the path, which started at the front door, ran through the living room, and led to the stairs. As we climbed the stairs there were petals on each step. At the top of the stairs, the path continued, stopping at our bedroom door. It was closed.

Camden opened the door and a fruity scent drifted up our nostrils. When we entered, there were lighted, scented candles surrounding our bed. Twelve long-stemmed, coral roses lay on the bed with a card attached. I walked over to the roses and picked up the card. It read: CORAL ROSES CONVEY DESIRE. IF YOU'LL HAVE ME, I WANT TO SHOW YOU HOW MUCH I DESIRE YOU.

This was all too much.

"So, Mrs. Brooks, can I show you how much I desire you?"

"Yes!" I said without hesitation.

Camden and I made mad, passionate love. It felt as if both our bodies needed what the other was giving. Feeling him inside me was pure bliss. I was taken aback when he willingly used a condom. It saddened me a little that I couldn't make love to my husband without protection. But after contracting Hepatitis A, I didn't want to risk getting any other sexually transmitted disease. I might have been horny, but I wasn't foolish enough to put my life in jeopardy. Nevertheless, the sadness subsided due to Camden's tender whispers of "I love you." The intimate bond of love that Camden and I shared on my twenty-eighth birthday confirmed that I indeed had my husband back.

Exhaustion wasn't the word I felt after climaxing several times. Camden went all out to please me once again. I thought after having his car slammed into twice by that maniac, Terry, the previous night, Camden would not have been able to perform, but he fooled me. As I lay in his arms, I felt rejuvenated, like a whole woman again. This was a feeling I spent weeks longing for and it felt just right.

"Thank you, Camden, for making my birthday so special."

"No need to thank me. I told you earlier, you are deserving of everything and more."

"Oh? So, what *more* can you give me?" I asked, massaging his manhood.

"You don't want to go there, Stormy. I might put it on you so hard that you won't be able to return to school next week. You'll be teaching on crutches," he teased.

"Please don't say the S word. I'm not ready to go back to work. I hate that my summer vacation is already over. If only I could get one more month."

"No can do! You've been off since June. That's way too long. Who else gets three months of vacation? It's time for you to go back."

"Don't hate!" I said as I playfully hit him.

Just then the phone rang. Camden picked up the cordless telephone and showed me the caller ID. It read unavailable. Camden replaced the phone on its base without answering it. He turned to me and sighed. I looked at him and grimaced. I hated the fact that Terry wouldn't leave us alone. It was already tough enough to learn about Camden's relationship with Terry during our counseling sessions, but with continued therapy and much prayer, I tried not to let it consume me. I was still a little apprehensive about Terry's threats toward Camden, but he assured me that he had taken precautions to protect us. And although I didn't appreciate the intrusion of the unwanted caller, I wasn't going to let it spoil our evening.

It became apparent that we were thinking the same thing because as soon as the telephone stopped ringing, we said in unison, "Tomorrow we get our number changed." We laughed. Shortly thereafter, we were fast asleep.

Chapter 44

Malik

The fall was upon us, and with a new season came change. I was leaving Baltimore in two days. As I packed my clothes, I had mixed feelings about departing, but it was for the best. Grandma and I had many late night talks about my life and the direction I was going since the infamous meeting at the church. Fortunately, she showed me I was on the wrong path. Although she didn't agree with my lifestyle, she was adamant about me cutting things off with Camden. So I did.

Even though I wasn't physically involved with Camden anymore, emotionally he was still a part of me. I didn't think there was anything in the world that could ever change that. As unnatural or perplexing as it may have seemed, I loved him. He was always in my thoughts and I desired to have him every waking moment, but it was no longer worth it to me.

Therefore, in an attempt to regain control of my life and

get away from all the madness, I went to an Air Force recruiting station. It didn't take long for them to sell me on joining. The fact that I was going to travel and see different parts of the world, as well as having my college education expenses paid in full, kind of sealed the deal for me. I enlisted in the United States Air Force and was packing to leave for Lackland Air Force Base in San Antonio, Texas, for basic training in forty-eight hours. I felt like this was the only way I could successfully get away from Camden, no matter how much I didn't want to leave him.

It was going to be hard leaving Camden, but it was for the best. Our relationship had caused me nothing but grief, and now it was time to move on.

Ring! Ring! The ringing of the phone interrupted my thoughts.

"Hello?"

"Hey, baby boy," Leigh said.

"Hi, Leigh. How are you?"

"I'm fine. Are you finished packing yet?"

"No, but I'll be finished soon. Why?"

"Because I want to take you out to Red Lobster for dinner before you leave. I'm gonna miss you and I want to spend a few hours with you before you roll out."

"Aw, thanks, Leigh. I'll be glad to go out with you. When do you want to go?"

"How about tomorrow, the day before you leave?"

"Great! I can't wait."

Just then my phone beeped, indicating another call. I took the cordless phone away from my ear to look at the caller ID. It was Camden. I was perplexed. Should I talk to him? Or shouldn't I?

"Leigh, I'll call you back. I have another call," I said, giving in to my urge to speak to Camden.

"OK! Bye."

I clicked to the other line.

"Hello," I said, unenthused, although I really was quite excited.

"Hey, stranger. How are you?" Camden asked.

"I'm good. And you?"

"I'm taking things one day at a time."

I wasn't in the mood for small talk. Talking to him was already making me hot and bothered, so I wanted him to get to the purpose of his call.

"So, why are you callin'?"

"Damn! You're curt today, aren't you?"

"It's not that I'm tryin' to be rude, but I'm in the middle of doing somethin'."

"OK, since you're rushin' me, I'll get to the point. I heard that you were leaving town. Is that true?"

"Yeah. How do you know?"

"My mother alluded to it a couple days ago. I guess she heard it from somebody at church." Camden sighed. "Where are you going?"

"I'm going to Lackland Air Force Base in San Antonio, Texas."

"Air force base?" He laughed.

"Yup, I've enlisted in the United States Air Force."

"The air force? Why do you want to go into the military?"

Do I really owe him an explanation? No. But of course, I gave him one anyway.

"I need to get away, Camden."

"You're leaving because of me, aren't you?"

"Yes and no. Yes, I'm tired of dealing with the drama associated with being in love with a gay, married man. I'm also fed up with the telephone calls I'm getting from your stalker. My grandmother was heartbroken when she found out I was gay and having a relationship with the pastor's son. Look, Camden, the list goes on and on. I can give you plenty of reasons why I'm leaving, but let's just say I'm doing it to better myself."

"I guess I've scarred you, huh?"

"I'm strong. I've been through worse. Remember, I'm the child who doesn't have a mother or a father. Nothing you've done can compare to that. I don't like my life right now. I'm unhappy and changes need to be made. So I made the decision to go away."

There was an awkward pause. I thought Camden hung up until I heard him shout in my ear.

"Malik, you can't go!"

"What do you mean I can't go?"

"Just that! You can't go. What am I going to do without you? You're the only one who understands what I'm feeling." His voice turned low and husky. "You're the only one who can satisfy me sexually."

"What about your wife?" I asked sarcastically.

"Stormy's a great person. I love her dearly, but my need for you outweighs my love for her. I've been trying to fight it for weeks now. We've been going to counseling and really trying to work on our marriage, but there's something that keeps me coming back to you."

"Well, whatever it is, it didn't stop you from marrying Stormy, knowing that I was in love with you."

"I fucked up, Malik. Big time. I know I did. If I could do it all over again, I would have never married Stormy."

"Too late now."

"No, it's not! If you promise not to leave me, I'll divorce Stormy and be with you."

I laughed hard because he had jokes.

"Camden, please. I'm not putting my life on hold for you. You're not divorcing Stormy, and we both know it."

"I swear on the Bible I will divorce her if you stay. Give me one more chance. I'm begging you, Malik. Please don't leave me," he whimpered.

Camden's pleas were getting to me, but I had to stay strong. I had to stand my ground. Besides, I had to look out for myself first.

"I can't stay, Camden. I love you and really wish things could have been different, but I've already signed up to go."

"Well, can you at least come see me one more time before you go? Let's have one last good time together before you become a military man."

Why was he doing this? He knew I was weak. And he knew I'd give in.

"Camden, I wouldn't mind seeing you one last time before I leave. However, you must know it's not because I want to continue a relationship with you. It's only because I do love you and would like to be with you one last time."

"So, you'll meet me?"

"Yes, for the last time."

"Great! That makes me feel somewhat better."

"Do you want to meet in Columbia like we used to do before?"

"No, I can't. I don't have the money for the motel right now. I'm broke from Stormy's birthday last month."

"So, where do you want to meet?"

"Come here," he announced.

Is this dude crazy? Doesn't he remember what happened the last time I was in his house?

"Camden, you must be smokin' dope, man. The last time I was at your house, your father stopped by unexpectedly and I had to hide in the closet until he left. Then on my way out, your crazy ass stalker rode by, saw me leaving, and told Stormy. Am I refreshing your memory, or do I need to remind you of the beat-down you got from Trey, Dante, and Jordan when they heard I was in your house?"

"Man, fuck Trey, Jordan, Dante, Terry, and my father! If anybody comes here today, I won't answer the door. And this time you'll leave out the back door instead of the front."

"Where is Stormy?" I asked, not believing that I was considering going to his house.

"She's at work. She doesn't get off until three o'clock. It's a little after ten now. If you come now, we can do our thing, say our good-byes, and you can be on your way. So, what's it going to be?"

I didn't answer. I wanted to see Camden one last time, but not at his house.

"Hello? Malik?"

"I'm here," I whispered.

"I love you, Malik. It hurts to know you're going away and that I may never see you again. I'm going to be lost without you and I need to see you, feel you, smell you, taste you, and make love to you one last time. Please say you'll come."

"I'll leave out in thirty minutes. I'm coming through the back way, so be on the lookout."

"I will," he said gleefully.

"And, Camden, if anyone comes, don't answer the fucking door. I'm not for the closet shit today."

"See you soon," he said and laughed, and then he hung up.

Wow! It seemed like my late night talks with Grandma had just went straight down the toilet. Oh, how she would kill me if she knew what I had just planned.

Although I didn't feel right about going over to Camden and Stormy's house again, I couldn't decline Camden's offer for a final lovemaking session. I loved him so much and couldn't imagine leaving without saying good-bye. Not to mention, I wanted to see his sexy smile and get some of his good loving before I left. No telling when I would get that opportunity again.

I struggled with myself the entire time I was getting dressed. Should I go or shouldn't I go? Is this a good or bad idea? After about fifteen minutes of going back and forth, I finally decided to see Camden. What harm could there be in going to see the man I loved one last time?

Chapter 45

Stormy

Life was good. Things were going well between Camden and me. The first month of the new school year was off to a wonderful start as well. I had been praying for things in my life to change for the better and they had—considerably.

"Thank you, Lord," I whispered aloud.

While my students were completing an independent assignment, I logged on to my computer to check my e-mail. My account showed ten new messages. I scrolled down my inbox, reading the names of those who had sent messages. I came across a message from call recorder. I clicked on the message and it read: a new recording from 410-555-6798 has been downloaded. *Hmmm*, I thought as I realized a call was recorded from my home telephone number. Then I realized I had never deactivated the card. My first reaction was to delete the e-mail because things were going so well between Camden and me. There really was no need to spy on his telephone calls. But then curiosity sank in. My nosiness and my need to confirm that Camden was truly on the up and up wouldn't allow me to delete the message.

I waited until I dismissed my students for lunch to listen to the downloaded recording. It took about two seconds for the message to download. Once it was completed, I clicked on the play button to listen to the conversation through the speakers on my computer. The first words I heard were those of Camden.

"Hey, stranger. How are you?" *Who in the world was he calling stranger?* I wondered as I continued to listen. No sooner had that thought entered my mind, than I got my answer when I heard none other than Malik respond.

"I'm good. And you?" I was totally floored. I couldn't fathom Camden calling Malik from our home telephone after all the hell we'd been through. How dare he!

I squirmed in my chair as I heard my husband tell Malik how he wanted him, how he should have never married me, how he was going to divorce me to be with Malik, and how he begged his boy toy not to leave him to go into the Air Force. However, the ultimate shocker was Camden asking Malik to come over to *my house* to fuck him one last time.

I jumped from my desk, hitting my knee against it.

"Shit!" I yelled as I limped around the classroom to gather my things. There was no way in hell I was staying at work after what I had just heard.

I calmly walked down to the main office and informed the secretary that I wasn't feeling well. I asked her if someone could take over my class for the rest of the day. Thankfully, a very dependable substitute was in the building and agreed to take over my class.

I quickly walked back to my classroom and assembled lesson plans for the rest of the week, because after what I had just listened to, I didn't think I would be coming back to work this week. If anything, I might be in jail after killing both Camden and Malik.

I drove through the streets of Baltimore, doing seventy miles per hour. My adrenaline had completely taken over. I didn't care about red lights, cameras, the police, or pedestrians. I only had my sights set on one thing, and that was the homicide I was about to commit when I arrived at my house. Surprisingly, I wasn't crying. I was angry, I felt my blood pressure rising, but not one tear dropped. After all the turmoil I endured with Camden, I was all cried out. At this point, I just wanted to skin him alive.

After what seemed to be the longest ride ever, I pulled up in front of my house. I didn't see Malik's car, so I must have missed him.

Too bad. Camden's going to have to deal with Hurricane Stormy all by himself. As I parked, I noticed a strange man walking toward the front door. He didn't look familiar, so I assumed he was at the wrong house. Just as he was about to knock on the door, I jumped out of my car.

"Excuse me, sir. May I help you?" I asked.

I must have startled him because he jumped when he heard my voice.

"I'm sorry. I didn't mean to scare you."

He began walking toward me.

"No problem," he said, smiling.

"So, may I help you?"

"Do you live here?"

"Yes, I do." I was extremely anxious. I needed to get in the house to strangle Camden, and this stranger was out here playing twenty questions.

He extended his hand to shake mine.

"I'm here to see Camden Brooks. You must be his beautiful wife, Stormy."

I looked at him suspiciously. *Who the hell are you?* I wanted to ask. But I didn't.

"Yes, I'm Stormy. Who might you be?" I asked instead.

"I'm Terrance Smith. I attended St. John's with Camden. He and I are very good friends."

Terrance Smith? Who is Terrance Smith?

"I'm sorry, Camden's never mentioned your name before."

Terrance went into this long song and dance about how he knew Camden. He gave me the run-down from the day they met up until now. He mentioned knowing Jared and Hassan as well, and explained how he was disappointed that he missed our wedding. He claimed Camden invited him, but he had a death in his family and couldn't attend. Terrance said he hadn't talked to Camden in months and happened to see Camden's cousin, Tyler, in California, who gave him Camden's address. This dude was killing me. I really didn't want to be rude, but I had something important to take care of. I shifted my weight from one foot to the other as I grew impatient with his speech. I really didn't give a damn about his history with Camden. I just wanted to get in the house.

"Do you mind if I come in? I haven't seen Camden in years, and I'd like to get to know his beautiful wife."

Shit! I wasn't in the mood for company. I wanted to fuck Camden up, but now I had to wait to confront him once his reunion with Terrance was over.

"Come on in, Terrance," I said hesitantly. "Camden's car is here, so he's probably in the house."

I put my key in the door and entered the house with Terrance following me. I walked toward the living room and started to call Camden's name. Before I could utter the first syllable in his name, I was stopped dead in my tracks. I blinked my eyes repeatedly because I thought they were playing tricks on me. I was stuck—paralyzed as I stared at the scene before me. I couldn't believe it. Camden was having sex with Malik on my living room floor! They were so into licking, fucking, and sucking that they didn't even see me or the strange man standing behind me.

Finally I mustered up enough strength to speak.

"Camden! What the fuck are you doing?" I screamed. Camden and Malik immediately froze in mid suck, their tongues hanging limp as saliva and semen dribbled out of their spermy mouths. They both looked as if they saw Jesus himself standing before them. Camden jumped up with his manhood standing at full attention.

"Stormy! What are you doing here?" he asked.

At that moment, I must've had an out of body experience, because before I knew it, I charged Camden, ramming into him like a raging bull. I guess the element of surprise caught him off guard, because I knocked him over. With all my might, I violently kicked, punched, and slapped him.

"What the fuck do you mean, what am I doing here? Why the hell are you fucking Malik in my house?" I screamed as I continued to beat the life out of him.

Camden tried to get the upper hand by attempting to re-strain me, but I took that opportunity to claw at his face and kick him. Finally Camden exerted his strength and was able to take control of the situation. He flipped me over on my back and straddled me.

"Get off me, you son of a bitch." I struggled with him, but couldn't release his grip. "Why would you bring Malik to my house to fuck him?" I spat as Camden held my arms down to the floor. Still he didn't answer me. I watched as his chest heaved in and out He looked like a deer caught in headlights.

Just then, Terrance walked up behind Camden.

"Answer her, Camden. Why are you in here fucking that little boy in her house?" When Camden looked up to see Terrance standing before him, his eyes screamed with fear. He recoiled, giving me an opportunity to get off the floor.

"Terry . . . what . . . what are you d-doing here?" Camden stuttered. Terry laughed.

"Now, Camden, darling, you're too smart to ask such a dumb question. You know why I'm here. I told you I was coming for you. I guess you didn't believe me, huh?"

I was standing there trying to figure out what they were talking about. I wanted to interject and finish beating Camden's ass, but I decided to pick myself up off the floor and focus on the man who had introduced himself to me as Terrance.

Terrance was Terry? Terrance was Terry? How did I not connect the two names?

I guess I was so focused on approaching Camden and exposing him for the liar that he was, that I didn't even deduce that the person I invited into my home was Terry, the man who had been stalking Camden.

"And look at you," Terry said, talking to Malik. "You look like one scared little bitch right now, which you should be! I told you weeks ago to stay away from Camden, but you took my warning for a joke."

"Fuck you, Terry!" Camden yelled. "Get out of my house now before I call the police. I have a restraining order against you, so if you stay one more minute, I'll have you arrested."

"If you take one step toward the telephone, it will be the last step you take," Terry said matter-of-factly.

"I'm sick of your threats, Terry. If you're going to do something to me, then do it. I'm not afraid of you." Camden bucked, trying to act like he was tough.

Terry chuckled and then walked toward Camden. I was scared. It crossed my mind that there was more going on around me than catching Camden having sex with Malik, something far more serious. Just the mention of Terry's name sent shockwaves down my spine. I knew I needed to do something, and quickly. I slowly backed out of the living room toward the front door. The three of them were so engrossed in their confrontation that no one noticed me slide out the living room. I slyly pulled my cell phone from my purse and dialed the police.

"911 operator. What's your emergency?" the operator asked.

Before speaking, I peered into the living room to make sure no one could see me on the phone. They didn't. Camden and Malik were consumed with putting their clothes on while Terry continued to spew threats.

"My name is Stormy Brooks," I whispered. "I live at 4202 Winans Road. I think I'm in danger. There's a strange man in my house threatening my husband."

"Ma'am, are you OK?"

"Yes, but I need you to send someone quickly."

"An officer has been dispatched. Do you need me to hold on the line?"

"No, just please send someone fast. I'm scared." I ended the call with 911 and hurriedly dialed Trey. I got his voicemail. I left a message.

"Trey, it's Stormy. I'm at home and I think I'm in danger. Please call Jordan and Dante, and hurry up and get here. I'm terrified." I pressed end on my cell phone and placed it back in my purse. I silently prayed that the police were on their way and that Trey checked his voicemail soon. I hoped he would understand what I said through my whispers. My fear had risen to the levels of soldiers in the middle of a war zone.

I gradually returned to the doorway leading to the living room where angry words were being exchanged between Camden and Terrance. Because of my fear, I didn't want to be in plain sight, so I stood off to the side.

"That's right. I'm the one who sent the letter to your lovely wife telling her not to marry you. I know your slimy

ways, Camden. I knew she'd be sorry if she married you."
He then turned to me. "I tried to tell you not to marry him,
but you didn't heed my warning."

I didn't respond. I continued to stand off to the side, positioning myself to run if need be. I didn't give a damn about
what Terry did to Camden and Malik, but I wanted my life.
So I had an every-person-for-themselves attitude.

Terry appeared to have an awful lot of information to
share with me. He continued to focus his conversation toward me.

"That's right. I've been keeping tabs on your husband for
months, and when I heard he was getting married, I had to
intervene. You see, he did the same thing to me in New
York that he's been doing to you. Camden claims to love
you, but the only person he loves is himself. You should
have heard how he used to profess his love to me and how
he wanted to spend the rest of his life with me."

Camden interrupted.

"I never told you that!"

"Shut the fuck up before I shut you up permanently. I'm
talking to your wife, not you."

Surprisingly, Camden did as he was told, and Terry continued.

"He used me. I did everything possible to please this man
and he did nothing but rip my heart out of my chest. I loved
him and when he did not return my love, I plotted to get
even. Your slick ass husband messed with my mind and my
heart. Now he's got to pay," he said, pointing to Camden.

I continued to listen to Terry rant about how Camden
had hurt him. Although I was petrified, I was genuinely interested in hearing what he had to say. Camden and Malik
remained silent while listening as well.

"I started getting even when we were in New York. I got
him fired from his job and I vandalized his car—the car I
bought—and his apartment. How'd you like the dead rat?"

He laughed as he looked at Camden. Camden did not respond. Terrance turned to me to finish his story. "I was hurt and I tried everything I could to destroy Camden's life. I made it my mission, but then the son of a bitch was nowhere to be found. Months went by and I had no luck locating him. Then I found a way to do a people search on the Internet. It didn't give me a lot of information, but I was able to obtain an address for his parents. Elated with having some information, I left New York on a mission to repay Camden for what he had done to me."

"I didn't do anything to you, man. I wish you would stop sayin' that. You and I had some sex, but then it got old. I moved on. You should do the same."

Did he just say some sex? I shook my head, wondering why I ever married this clown ass dude.

Camden's comment infuriated Terrance because he quickly got in his face and yelled at him.

"You're a fucking liar, Camden Xavier Brooks. You not only enjoyed sucking and fucking me, but you also told me you loved me. Then you walked out on me as if I were a dead cockroach, or should I say cricket? Who do you think you are? You can't treat people like shit. Unlike you, most people have feelings. I guess you get your rocks off by fucking over people's feelings, huh?"

"I do care about people's feelings," Camden responded.

"No, you don't. Look how you've treated your wife in the few weeks you've been married." He turned to me again. "Stormy, you have no idea how slimy your husband really is. He's been fucking his boy toy damn near since the time you returned from your honeymoon. He's been meeting him in Columbia at a hotel three or four times a week. I won't even get into the number of times this little bitch has been in your house while you weren't home, or the number of times he came to see Camden when he left home and stayed in a hotel for a few weeks. This young buck has been a part of your marriage since day one, and Camden knows it."

I stood dumbstruck as Terrance spewed ugly information about Camden. I didn't know a thing about Terrance, but I knew he was speaking the truth. I wanted to say something, but I couldn't. I just stood there frozen as my blood boiled.

I continued to listen to Camden and Terrance argue. My anger intensified. My head was spinning. My belly started cramping. This was all too much for me to hear. I just wanted it to end.

"Stop it!" I yelled. "Just stop it! I can't stomach any more of this. You're makin' me sick. Camden, Malik, and Terry, please get the fuck out of here now! I've already called the police. They're on the way. So y'all better leave now." I pointed to the door.

Terry began walking toward the door to leave. I stared at Camden and Malik, wondering why they weren't following him. When Terry reached the door, he stopped and turned around.

"I can't leave until I complete my mission."

"And just what is your mission?" I asked, impatiently wanting him to leave and to take Camden and Malik with him.

Terry didn't answer. He slowly reached inside his pants and whipped out a handgun. He raised his arms and directed his weapon toward Camden.

"My mission isn't complete until I kill you," Terry announced and fired the gun repeatedly.

I heard gunshots, screams, and then everything turned black.

When I regained consciousness, my vision was blurred and I was groggy. I thought I saw someone in a police uniform walk past me. I didn't recognize the voice of the uniformed woman holding my hand.

"Stormy, I'm an EMT. Are you all right?"

"I think I am. What happened?"

She did not answer me. She just continued to examine me. The paramedics asked me my name, today's date, my birth date, the name of the president of the United States, and a host of other questions. When I answered all the questions correctly, she informed me that my family was outside. They weren't allowed in due to the house being a crime scene, but she assured me that he'd let them know that I was doing all right. They asked if I wanted to go to the hospital, but I told them that I was fine. Then it hit me. Why were the paramedics and the police in my house?

When I sat up, I saw Camden being taken out on a gurney. Terrance was handcuffed, and Malik was being escorted out of the house by the police.

"What happened?" I asked again.

"Your husband's been shot," a police officer answered.

"Shot! He's been shot! Why? What happened?" I screamed.

Another police officer rushed over to me and asked if I needed anything.

"I need for you to tell me what happened here."

"Ma'am, I'm Officer Nicholson. It seems a man named Terrance Smith has been stalking your husband. Your husband recently obtained a restraining order against him because of harassing telephone calls and threats made against his life. I guess today was the day Mr. Smith decided to follow through on his threats."

"What did he do?" I asked, confused.

"Mr. Smith shot your husband multiple times."

"Oh no!" I wailed. "Is he going to be all right? Is he going to live?"

"I can't tell you that, ma'am. He may have a chance since it didn't take long for us to get here. Your 911 call may save his life. I hope that the early response of the paramedics will give your husband a greater chance of survival. He's on his way to the Shock Trauma Center at the University of Maryland Medical Center. I know you want to get to the hospital to be with your husband, but I have a few questions I need to ask you first."

"OK. But can you please make it fast? I need to see my husband."

Officer Nicholson asked me to explain the events that led up to Camden being shot. At first, I had difficulty remembering what occurred. However, as I forced myself to remember, I could vividly hear Terry telling me how Camden had been seeing Malik the entire time we'd been married. I could hear Terry describing Camden secretly meeting Malik at a hotel in Columbia and having him in the house when I wasn't home. I then had a flashback of the cell phone bill with Malik's number, Camden admitting seeing Malik, Camden staying out all night long, contracting Hepatitis A, Camden at a gay club, and the call recorder message I had heard between them earlier. Then the sight of Camden and Malik having sex on the floor in the living room popped into my head. My distress was evident to everyone around me.

"Mrs. Brooks, are you all right? Would you like to finish the questioning later?" Officer Nicholson asked.

I didn't answer. I was panting and rocking from side to side. I couldn't believe the hell I had been going through for the past five months. I was bone weary, but I had to take a stand.

I heard Officer Nicholson tell another detective that he would finish the questioning later. He thought it would be best if I went to the hospital.

"Officer, I will not be going to the hospital," I said.

"Are you sure, ma'am? You don't want to be with your husband?"

"No! Call his parents. I want nothing more to do with

him. This should have been done a long time ago. I'm done! Call his parents because I'm not going to the hospital, not now, not tomorrow, not ever."

The officer gave me his card and told me he would be in touch. There were still some questions they wanted to ask. I gave him Reverend and Mrs. Brooks's telephone numbers. Shortly thereafter, the police and the investigators left.

My parents, my brothers, and Dante stayed with me until I packed an overnight bag. I was planning to stay with my parents that night. However, I wouldn't be staying away from home for just one night. I was leaving behind Camden, the bad memories, my poor judgment, and this house for good.

Chapter 46

Reverend Brooks

For the past few weeks I'd been ashamed to call myself a man of God. I had been grieving over the entire situation with Camden, Stormy, Malik, the Knights, and Sister Blackwell. As a father and pastor, I'd dealt with a wealth of guilt because I had failed them all.

"Theo, are you all right?" Sheryl asked. I was sitting in my study preparing to speak to the congregation.

"I'll be OK as soon as I speak to the congregation during morning service."

"Just let God lead you. He'll give you the right words to say. I'm proud of you, honey. Not many people would have the guts to do what you're about to do."

"Well, I've got to. I owe it to Camden. I was so wrapped up in my image of being a pastor of an affluent congregation that I put my son on the back burner. I was too busy serving the parishioners to take an honest look at my son and see that he was in deep trouble. Today I'm doing this for Camden, my only son."

As the choir returned to their seats, I nervously rose from mine and approached the pulpit.

"Praise the Lord, saints," I said in an elevated voice.

"Praise the Lord," the congregation replied.

"You know, I stand before you this morning burdened because I realized that I've fallen short of the glory of God. The Bible says, 'Lord, be merciful to me, heal my soul for I have sinned against you.' Saints, I'm hear to confess my sins and to ask God for forgiveness."

"Go 'head, pastor," one parishioner yelled from her seat.

"You see, some time ago, rumors began to surface that my son, Camden, was . . . was . . . was living a homosexual lifestyle. When I heard this, I immediately scolded him, threw Bible scriptures at him, and tried to pray homosexuality out of him. I also disowned him for a while, all because I was worried more about my reputation and my good name than I was about my son."

I took a deep breath because the words were becoming harder and harder to say. The members were silent. No one said a word. No amens, no nothing. I couldn't stop now. I had to speak the truth, because the Bible said the truth would set you free. I desperately needed to be free. Confessing my sin was what God placed on my heart to do, and I was going to do it.

"No father should ever put anything before his child, no matter what others may say. I turned my back on my only son when I learned he was gay. And now as he lies in a hospital bed fighting for his life, I realize that I don't care if he is gay. He is still my son."

Still no one said a word. The cold, hard stares made me feel uncomfortable, but I had to do what God told me to do—acknowledge my wrongdoings.

"So, True Gospel, I'm here to tell you that if my son has chosen a different way of life, I will love him no less. Because my son has chosen a lifestyle that goes against the word of God, I will not stop being his father. I will not turn my back on him, I will not disown him, but instead, I will continuously wrap my arms around him and profess my love for him just as God does for all of us. I don't know about you, saints, but I sin daily, and I need God's forgiveness. And if God can forgive me for my indiscretions, then who am I not to forgive my son."

"Amen, pastor!" a parishioner commented.

"As a vow to my Lord and Savior, and to my son, True Gospel, I will not turn my back on those who practice a homosexual lifestyle and I'm asking that you do the same. We don't shun the alcoholic, the substance abuser, the fornicator, the adulterer, or the thief. Instead, we uplift them in our prayers. My job as the shepherd of this house is to teach them the word of God that will lead them to the path of righteousness. But I will not judge people based on their sins. We as a church family will embrace them and love them no less, regardless of their lifestyle. Truth be told, with some of the skeletons in all of our closets, we don't have the right to judge or look down on one another. And remember, God loves and forgives all of us, even though we're sinners."

"Tell it!" another parishioner voiced.

"Are you with me, True Gospel?" I asked from the pulpit. "Are you all in agreement that we will love each other as Christ loves us?"

All over the sanctuary, people began to stand and applaud in agreement. A smile grew on my face. I felt good. I felt God's presence in the building. I felt my burdens immediately being lifted from my shoulders. I was sure this was a sign from God telling me he had forgiven me, too.

In the midst of all the praises, I felt compelled to go to Sister Blackwell. She remained true to me and True Gospel even after the Knights, Stormy, and Malik had all moved on. I walked up to Sister Blackwell as she worshipped and wrapped my arms around her.

"I'm sorry," I whispered in her ear. "Please forgive me." She didn't speak, but she hugged me tightly as she continued to give all praises to God.

As I headed back to the pulpit, I looked over to my wife, Sheryl, who praised God with tears pouring from her eyes.

I love you, I mouthed. She nodded, too caught up in the spirit to speak.

Then I raised my hands in praise.

"Thank you, Jesus!" I shouted.

Epilogue

Four months later

Malik

Enduring a near death experience four months ago without a doubt changed my life. I attribute my life being spared to two things—me being quick on my feet, and the fact that Terry was more focused on killing Camden than me. As soon as I saw the gun and heard the first gunshot, I bolted. Being a previous visitor in Camden and Stormy's home actually had its benefits. It allowed me to remove myself to another room in the house, and out of the line of fire just as Terry began to shoot. Needless to say, I was shaken. I knew at that very moment that God wasn't happy with my actions. He did everything possible to warn me about messing around with Camden. I was alerted repeatedly, but never listened. God even saw to it that Grandma, the person I loved the most on this earth, found out about my deepest, darkest secret. Still, that didn't change me. Her long, heartfelt talks regrettably fell on deaf ears. Damn shame my hormones encouraged me to go see Camden one last time. That one last time could have possibly been the end of my life.

After the dreadful incident, I was escorted to the police station for questioning. I was there an hour and then released. When I returned home, I walked into my bedroom, fell on my knees, and prayed. I thanked the Lord repeatedly for sparing my life. I prayed for Camden and Stormy as well. I even asked God to forgive me for being involved in an adulterous affair. I promised God that I would never get involved with another married man again. As I prayed, my grandmother entered. She got on her knees and talked to God with me. Together we prayed and cried. Grandma knew what had happened at Camden's house, but she never said a word. I think she realized I had learned a tough lesson and didn't need another lecture.

Two days later, I departed Baltimore, headed toward Lackland Air Force Base for basic training. After exchanging hugs and kisses with Grandma and promising to keep in touch, I boarded the bus. I sat in a window seat and looked intently at my surroundings. I knew that it would be a long while before I ever called Baltimore home again. Although I'd miss my grandmother, I was glad to leave and had no plans to ever return.

Camden

After four long months in the rehabilitation center, I was finally released. Thanks to that gun toting fool, I suffered three gunshot wounds to my neck, shoulder, and spine. In my haste to duck away from the barrel of Terry's gun, I turned around. That's when I felt a burning sensation in my lower back—the shot that caused me to become a paraplegic. I woke up a week later after the shooting, only to learn that I was suffering from paralysis from the waist down, with no possibility of ever walking again. I was devastated. Life as I knew it would be no more. My new life now consisted of wheelchair confinement and constant physical therapy.

I guess I could say this was partially my fault because I continually hurt those who loved me—especially Stormy. Because I never wanted to come to grips with my sexuality, I proposed marriage to Stormy twice—hoping to camouflage my lifestyle. I thought I could pull off both a heterosexual and homosexual relationship. Little did I know, I was playing a deadly game. Being the son of affluent parents, I was spoiled, pampered, and always the church pet, so I thought I had a sense of entitlement. I allowed Satan to guide my footsteps and now I was dealing with the ramifications of being self-centered and not being right with the Lord. My father, Jared, Hassan, and others had all said I'd one day suffer the consequences for my sins, but I never believed them. If I could move my legs, I'd kick myself for not listening to their warnings.

During my rehab stay, I never heard from Stormy. She never called or came to visit. My parents, however, never left my bedside. Each day I'd ask them if they'd heard from Stormy, and finally they told me, hesitantly, that they spoke with Stormy briefly. They informed me that she was planning to petition the court for a divorce. My heart sank when I heard the news, but what else could I expect? After all the hurt I'd caused, I should have been elated that all she wanted to do was divorce me.

Hassan came to visit often during my hospital stay, and Tyler called every day from California. But I never heard from Jared. I could only surmise that our friendship was over. I was also informed that my crazed ex-lover, Terry, was in jail awaiting trial for attempted murder.

My last week in the hospital was extremely depressing

because I received a tremendous blow to my heart. My mother walked into my hospital room with an envelope. She handed it to me and I opened it immediately. It was Stormy's petition for divorce. I broke down in tears. At first I wasn't going to sign the papers, but after doing a lot of soul searching, I knew it was for the best. I decided to let Stormy go—to let her be free.

I hadn't heard anything from Malik. I could only imagine him being off in some other state serving our country. I put Malik through a lot as well, and I was glad to know he had moved on with his life. I sincerely hoped he lived a full and happy life.

As I rode in the car with my parents, headed to their home, a teardrop fell from my eye. I couldn't believe that I would never walk again and had to live with my parents because my wife wanted nothing to do with me. Funny how the same place I desperately wanted to get away from was the place I'd call home once again. I felt empty. I felt like no one was in my corner. Fittingly enough, I was truly reaping what I had sown.

Stormy

I'd been working steadily to restore order in my life over these past months. With the help of my father and brothers, I was able to move my things out of the house I had shared with Camden and into my new apartment. Camden's things were packed and sent to his parents' house. I spoke at length with our mortgage company who explained that I couldn't put the house up for sale without Camden's permission, so I chose to wait until he was released from the hospital before making any decisions on the house. But one thing was for sure, either we sold the house, or Camden could keep it, but solely in his name. I wanted no part of the home where

Camden repeatedly disrespected and cheated on me with Malik. Suspecting that he'd probably had sex in the bed we shared, I gave it away to Goodwill and purchased another one. I didn't want any reminders of my life with Camden in my new residence.

I sought the advice of a divorce attorney. Initially I thought I could file for an annulment since Camden and I were married less than one year. Unfortunately, Camden's deception was not grounds for nullification in the state of Maryland. Therefore, I wound up filing for a divorce. Since my ground for seeking a divorce was adultery, I did not have to wait the lengthy separation period before filing. For that, I was thankful.

I'd be lying if I said the past four months had been easy. Actually, they were just the opposite, but I'd thrown myself into my job, family, friends, and God. As always, Leigh, Dominique, and Nicole were there to console me on my depressed days. The entire process would have been hell to get through without them. Nicole and Jared had actually become a lot closer. She informed me that Jared had kept his distance from Camden. He still considered him a friend, but from afar.

My parents talked me into attending their new church, which I did. They joined Shiloh Christian Church under the leadership of Reverend Trent Jackson. Shiloh wasn't a mega church like True Gospel. There were far less members and it felt more family oriented. I hadn't officially become a member yet, but I was seriously considering it. Trey and Jordan had visited after several requests from my parents, and they actually liked the services. They'd become regular churchgoers again. Dante even attended from time to time. I was so blessed to be surrounded by my family. They had continued to show their love and support for me without saying, "I told you so." For that, I was truly grateful.

While I sat in Bible study one Tuesday evening, Pastor Jackson's teachings spoke volumes.

"Some women want to be married so badly that they settle for any man—the first man to show them some attention." Pastor Jackson spoke, stinging me with his words. "Don't let a handsome, charming man smile at these women, say hello too nicely, or wink, 'cause then they're ready to walk down the aisle. Women don't take time to get to know a man before they claim to be in love, and want to be his wife and have ten children with him. Some women don't care if he's a thief, a liar, a cheat, a playboy, a convicted sex offender, or even gay. As long as they can say, 'I got a man,' it's all OK."

Pastor Jackson paused and looked out into the congregation. I wondered if he sensed his last statement was all about me. Pastor Jackson wiped his forehead with his handkerchief and continued.

"Come on, ladies, you're smarter than that. You've got to love yourself and let God place the right man in your life. The Bible says, 'He who finds a wife, finds a good thing.' You've got to start acting like the good thing that God intended you to be. Stop trying to seek out your husband. Delight yourself in the Lord and allow yourself to be sought."

Pastor Jackson's statements were so profound. I found myself nodding in agreement. I felt like jumping up and testifying before the church. I wanted other women to hear my testimony, to hear what I had endured when I ignored all the signs given to me. I wanted women to know never to settle, especially if you'd been warned repeatedly about your mate. No woman needs a man to complete them, and a wedding ring doesn't make you whole.

When I married Camden, all I wanted was to be loved. I wanted to be married. I loved the idea of being married, but I had no idea of the consequences that awaited me for entering into a marriage I knew wasn't right in the eyes of

God. I wanted to be loved so badly that I was willing to ignore all the signs. I was ashamed at how I allowed myself to
be easily misled by something as fundamental as Camden's
sexual orientation. I guess my desire for the man was
greater than the truth. I paid a hefty price for not listening
to God when he spoke to me directly through the mouths
of others.

I always believed that when you went through things in
life, there was always a lesson to learn. Now I could say with
certainty that I'd learned a lesson that I would never, ever
forget. However, what doesn't kill you can only make you
stronger. I was a stronger person for all of the drama and
trauma I had gone through.

Thanks be to God that that part of my life was over. I was
now working on surviving the storm and working to better
myself. I was slowly but surely understanding that being
alone didn't necessarily mean you had to be lonely. I was
now free—free from a prison cell surrounded by bars of lies,
deceit, infidelity, and heartbreak. I was now on a mission to
minister my freedom to other women who were bound by
infidelity in their marriages.

I praised God daily for deliverance from my tumultuous
marriage. I praised him for peace. But most of all, I thanked
him for allowing me to go through the storm, only to come
out a new creature. With Camden now a part of my past, I
knew a brighter future was ahead. At some point I knew I'd
learn to trust and love again, but not until I first loved myself. I was on a spiritual journey to recovery and restoration.
And in my walk with God, I hoped to let go of the pain and
somehow find forgiveness.

LOOK FOR

HEAVEN
SENT

A NOVEL BY
DYNAH ZALE

AUTHOR OF DRAMA IN THE CHURCH

COMING AUGUST 2007

Heaven Sent

By Dynah Zale

Instead of heading back downstairs, I decided to see if I could find Reverend Washington. Knocking at a few doors and listening at others, it took several tries before I was successful in finding him. The pastor was laid out on his king size bed still dressed in black slacks and a button down shirt. He was balled up in a fetal position at first, facing the window, probably staring into the sky. He did a quick change of position and turned over in my direction, stretching out his long legs. He fixed his eyes on me, but didn't look startled or surprised by my presence. His stares made my stomach do flips. He looked much better now than he did earlier.

"I'm sorry. I was looking for the bathroom." He seemed incoherent with eyes that gazed straight through me. "Are you alright?" I walked further into his bedroom. "Everyone's worried about you, and you didn't look too good at the cemetery."

He looked numb, and his eyes had no life behind them. *Maybe this wasn't such a good idea*, I thought. Accepting defeat, I turned to walk out. "No," he said. "Don't go." I turned back around. "That perfume you're wearing. My wife wears . . . wore the same fragrance."

"I'm sorry. I didn't mean to—"

"No. It's okay." He beckoned for me to come closer, fixing his attention on my face. "Aren't you the girl from the halfway house? Heaven Stansfield with the green eyes?" Taking a seat on the edge of his bed, I nodded. "I appreciate you attending my wife's funeral. I know you didn't know her, but it was thoughtful of you to come."

"It was a beautiful service."

"Yes, it was. My wife would have loved it. The church was full of purple and white lilies—her favorite flower." He appeared to momentarily go back over the days events.

"Would you like something to eat? I can run down stairs and fix a plate," I offered.

"No, thank you. I'm not hungry. Can we just talk?" he asked.

I shifted my body uncomfortably. I hoped he didn't want to talk about Celeste.

"You're scared I'm going to talk about Celeste." He laughed. "Being a pastor I can read body language pretty well."

Laughing along with him, I was ashamed for being so transparent. "If you want to talk about Celeste that's fine. I'd feel honored that you feel comfortable enough to discuss her with me."

"You are probably the only person I have talked to about Celeste. Up until now, I haven't really been in the mood for a lot of company. Celeste's death happened so suddenly. It was a surprise to all of us." He closed his eyes. "In the delivery room, she had just delivered the baby, and the doctors had taken my son to check his vitals. The nurse handed him back to me. I took him in my arms and held him up so that Celeste could get a look at him. She smiled and reached out then in mid air her hand went limp. Monitors started beeping, one nurse snatched Wesley from me and another escorted me out the room. I tried to ask them what was going on, but no one would answer my questions. That's when the doctor came out to tell me that she had passed on."

I wished he hadn't relived that moment with me. How was I supposed to comfort him over the loss of his wife when all I could think about was how inviting his lips were?

Someone tapped lightly on his bedroom door. Glad for the disturbance I got up to answer the knock. I was disappointed when I opened the door and found Emalee. She stood at the entrance with a tray full of food for her brother. The mean smirk on her face said that she was not pleased to find me with him. "I'm sorry. I don't mean to interrupt," she finally said.

"No, that's okay. Heaven, I would like you to meet my sister."

Emalee put on a phony smile for the sake of her brother. "Its nice meeting you. Hasani, I thought you might be hungry. I brought you something to eat." She placed the food down on the bed and pulled up a chair from the writing desk that sat in the corner of the bedroom.

"I have to go." I excused myself. I wasn't allowing Emalee to run me off, but I felt like I had done what I set out to do. "It was really nice talking with you reverend, and I hope to see you in church."

"Likewise," he replied.

About the Author

Latrese N. Carter was born and raised in Baltimore, Maryland. Her philosophy is inspired by the bible verse from Philippians 4: 13, "I can do all things through Christ who gives me strength." Her arrival on the writing scene is testament to the power of this belief in addressing challenges and overcoming difficulties.

As a girl, Latrese possessed a vivid imagination. She loved writing in a journal, and sharpened her writing skills through her studies. Latrese loves reading and possessed a long-standing desire to write. Through God's grace, she was moved to pursue her dream of becoming a novelist.

After completing her first novel Latrese received many rejection letters, but with the encouragement of family and friends, she pressed on, knowing that all it takes is one "Yes." Maintaining this faith and determination, Latrese was offered a publishing contract by Q-Boro Books.

Latrese is a graduate of University of Maryland Eastern Shore where she received a BS degree in Criminal Justice. She then attended Coppin State University and received a Master's degree in Special Education. Latrese is a Special Education teacher and her favorite subject is English, where she shares her love of writing with her students.

Latrese enjoys reading, writing, Florida vacations, watching reality shows and soap operas. She is a member of African American Sisters in Spirit Book Club, Ebony Readers and Black Writers United. Latrese currently resides in Alexandria, Virginia with her husband, Reginald, and their daughter, Reagan.

Her future plans include writing more novels that explore the complexities of relationships.

http://www.latresencarter.com

LOOK FOR MORE HOT TITLES FROM

Q-BORO
B O O K S

DARK KARMA - JUNE 2007
$14.95
ISBN 1-933967-12-9

What if the criminal was forced to live the horror that they caused? The drug dealer finds himself in the body of the drug addict and he suffers through the withdrawals, living on the street, the beatings, the rapes and the hunger. The thief steals the rent money and becomes the victim that finds herself living on the street and running for her life and the murderer becomes the victim's father and he deals with the death of a son and a grieving mother.

GET MONEY CHICKS - SEPTEMBER 2007
$14.95
ISBN 1-933967-17-X

For Mina, Shanna, and Karen, using what they had to get what they wanted was always an option. Best friends since day one, they always had a thing for the hottest gear, luxurious lifestyles, and the ballers who made it all possible. All of this changes for Mina when a tragedy makes her open her eyes to the way she's living. Peer pressure and loyalty to her girls collide with her own morality, sending Mina into a no-win situation.

AFTER-HOURS GIRLS - AUGUST 2007
$14.95
ISBN 1-933967-16-1

Take part in this tale of two best friends, Lisa and Tosha, as they stalk the nightclubs and after-hours joints of Detroit searching for excitement, money, and temporary companionship. These two divas stand tall until the unforgivable Motown streets catch up to them. One must fall. You, the reader, decide which.

THE LAST CHANCE - OCTOBER 2007
$14.95
ISBN 1-933967-22-6

Running their L.A. casino has been rewarding for Luke Chance and his three brothers. But recently it seems like everyone is trying to get a piece of the pie. An impending hostile takeover of their casino could leave them penniless and possibly dead. That is, until their sister Keilah Chance comes home for a short visit. Keilah is not only beautiful, but she also can be ruthless. Will the Chance family be able to protect their family dynasty?

Traci must find a way to complete her journey out of her first and only failed

LOOK FOR MORE HOT TITLES FROM

NYMPHO - MAY 2007
$14.95
ISBN 1933967102
How will signing up to live a promiscuous double-life destroy everything that's at stake in the lives of two close couples? Take a journey into Leslie's secret world and prepare for a twisted, erotic experience.

FREAK IN THE SHEETS - SEPTEMBER 2007
$14.95
ISBN 1933967196
Librarian Raquelle decides to put her knowledge of sexuality to use and open up a "freak" school, teaching men and women how to please their lovers beyond belief while enjoying themselves in the process. But trouble brews when a surprise pupil shows up and everything Raquelle has worked for comes under fire.

LIAR, LIAR - JUNE 2007
$14.95
ISBN 1933967110

Stormy calls off her wedding to Camden when she learns he's cheating with a male church member. However, after being convinced that Camden has been delivered from his demons, she proceeds with the wedding.

Will Stormy and Camden survive scandal, lies and deceit?

HEAVEN SENT - AUGUST 2007
$14.95
ISBN 1933967188
Eve is a recovering drug addict who has no intentions of staying clean until she meets Reverend Washington, a newly widowed man with three children. Secrets are uncovered that threaten Eve's new life with her new family and has everyone asking if Eve was *Heaven Sent.*

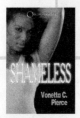
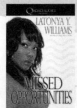

LOOK FOR MORE HOT TITLES FROM

Q-BORO
B O O K S

DOGISM
$6.99
ISBN 0977733505

Lance Thomas is a sexy, young black male who has it all: a high paying blue collar career, a home in Queens, New York, two cars, a son, and a beautiful wife. However, after getting married at a very young age he realizes that he is afflicted with DOGISM, a distorted sexuality that causes men to stray and be unfaithful in their relationships with women.

POISON IVY - NOVEMBER 2006
$14.95
ISBN 0977733521

Ivy Davidson's life has been filled with sorrow. Her father was brutally murdered and she was forced to watch, she faced years of abuse at the hands of those she trusted, and she was forced to live apart from the only source of love that she'd ever known. Now Ivy stands alone at the crossroads of life, staring into the eyes of the man who holds her final choice of life or death in his hands.

HOLY HUSTLER - FEBRUARY 2007
$14.95
ISBN 0977733556

Reverend Ethan Ezekiel Goodlove the Third and his three sons are known for spreading more than just the gospel. The sanctified drama of the Goodloves promises to make us all scream "Hallelujah!"

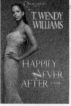

HAPPILY NEVER AFTER - JANUARY 2007
$14.95
ISBN 1933967005

To Family and friends, Dorothy and David Leonard's marriage appears to be one made in heaven. While David is one of Houston's most prominent physicians, Dorothy is a loving and carefree housewife. It seems as if life couldn't be more fabulous for this couple who appear to have it all: wealth, social status, and a loving union. However, looks can be deceiving. What really happens behind closed doors and when the flawless veneer begins to crack?

Novel Dedication

I dedicate my debut novel to my wonderful husband, Reginald C. Carter and my precious daughter, Reagan C. Carter. I love you more than words can say.

Acknowledgments

First giving honor to My Lord and Savior, Jesus Christ.. To You I give all praise and glory! **To my husband**, Reginald C. Carter. Thank you for all your constant love, inspiration and support. I thank God daily for blessing me with you. **To my daughter**, Reagan C. Carter. You are truly a gift from Heaven. Thank you for being patient with Mommy as she took time to write. I love you more than you will ever know! **To my parents**, Derek B. Stewart, Sr. and Mary E. DeLoatch. Thank you for all your support you've given me throughout my life. Thank you for shaping and molding me into the woman I am today. **To my older brother**, Derek B. Stewart, Jr. and my younger brother, Drew E. Stewart. I know it has not easy putting up with your sister, the middle child, but no matter what, you always have my back. Always know that I love you. **To my mother-in-law**, Diana Henderson. Thank you for taking care of Reagan to give me time to write. The free time was appreciated more than you'll ever know. **To my grandmothers**, Delores V. Brown and Florence R. White. **To my cousin**, Shante D. Massenburg. **To James A. Womack, Jr., Nikia Carter, Joyce B. Davis and Michael Barksdale. To my wonderful friends**, Adrianne L. Atwater, Lisa D. Brown, Nikki Burns (thanks for the scenes *wink, wink*), Valerie. D. Carter, and T. L. Price. You're truly my girlfriends, there through thick and thin. **To Lotticia Mack, Amanda Hol-**

loway and A. LaChette. Thanks for being great friends and for reading and critiquing the early version of *Liar, Liar*. To my freelance editor, Judy C. Allen of Marketing Solutions. I truly thank God for you. To Tasha Beckman and the members of African American Sisters in Sprit Book Club (ASiS). I am truly thankful for my agent Portia Cannon for supporting me in my vision. To my fellow authors, Tracy Brown, Candice Dow, Torrian Ferguson, Brenda M. Hampton, Dwayne S. Joseph, Karen E. Quinones Miller, Naiomi Pitre, Trista Russell, and Alisha Yvonne. Thank you for all of your advice and guidance throughout this literary journey. To my Q-Boro Family, Mark Anthony, Candace K. Cottrell. I'm proud to be a part of the Q-Boro family. Special shout outs to some of the "little people" in my life: to my nephew, Darren Meredith; my nieces, Kyila N. Stewart, Kemiya N. Stewart, Kobi N. Stewart, Erica Carter and Nalia Carter, to my cousins, goddaughters, and all the other children who have touched my life in special way. Also, my Team 7-3 Students at Whitman Middle School (2004-2005 school year) and my Pulley Career Center students. Last but not least, I'd like to thank all the readers for your support. Thank you for purchasing the book and spreading the word.

Please visit my website www.latresencarter.com. Thanks again to all of you!

God Bless,
Latrese N. Carter